Meet Me in Milano

A novel by

Mariuccia Milla

For Roberto, and our future in Italy.

A special thanks to my readers: Arturo, Penelope, and Ashley.

And to Oksana.

Italian words and phrases can be found in the Glossary at the end of the story.

Table of Contents

Meet Me in Milano

Mariuccia Milla left New York City and her boyfriend behind at the age of 25 to find a job in the field of design in Milan, Italy. This fictional story shares that same beginning.

While I found this story entertaining, it doesn't wholly transmit the deep appreciation, on an aesthetic level, that the Italian male has for women.
–*Alberto Rossi*

Melinda embarks

It was a hassle getting to JFK. Mel took public transportation to save money. She had two pieces of luggage plus a carry-on that held her slippers, a book, and a toothbrush to get her through the trip. Her personal bag was reserved for her passport, ticket confirmation, and wallet. There was also a letter from Cecil.

He had given it to her at the end of their last meeting at the Szechuan House on Mott Street. He had made her come to Manhattan, not bothering to make the trip to Brooklyn.

Mel decided not to open the letter until after takeoff, to assure that she wouldn't act upon the message it held, whatever it was. She didn't quite trust herself to keep its contents clearly outside of the margins of their story.

Security at JFK was predictably slow. Multiple layers of scrutiny were threaded with conveyors and populated with uniformed personnel. A parade of dull gray bins marched through the black fettuccini curtains, loaded with shoes and phones and Clinique free gift sets. This was her limbo between New York and the rest of the world.

Mel was uncharacteristically calm. Everything was ahead of her: she loved the suspense of not knowing what the future held. It made her feel immensely wealthy in time and possibility. She settled in at the gate with plenty of time to spare.

* * *

Goodbye, she thought, to the morning subway ride into Manhattan with my nose in a book to avoid the overwhelming humanity. Goodbye to the *pain au chocolat* I bought every day at the coffee shop. Goodbye (and good riddance) to the construction workers and their lewd comments. Goodbye to my boss with her charming indecision, and *her* boss who stunk of alcohol after lunch. Goodbye to the ping and swoosh of elevators, and the polished terrazzo floors of lobbies. Goodbye to the Lever and Seagram buildings on Park Avenue, backdropped with a bright blue sky in the spring. Goodbye to the woman with the long white fox coat hailing her driver while a homeless man rummages through the waste container behind her. Goodbye to the Muenster cheese, lettuce, and mustard sandwich on rye, with a bag of chips, from the deli on 53rd and Lex (I will sorely miss you). Goodbye to the vaguely familiar people I kept running into at the gallery openings. Goodbye to the sweaty passenger pressed against me, dampening my blouse as the D-train crawled over the Manhattan Bridge on a hot summer evening. Goodbye to the golden late afternoon light on the Chrysler Building. Goodbye to the guy who adjusted my stirrups at the stables in Prospect Park and then gave me his business card: *call me?* Goodbye to picking up my laundry and finding the mother-of pearl buttons on one of my shirts substituted with plastic ones. Goodbye to walking over the Brooklyn Bridge, marveling at its web of muscular cables. Goodbye to freezing outside of clubs on Saturday nights, and the inhospitable ladies' rooms inside. Goodbye to the thick and rich Sunday Times at brunch. And goodbye–*whack*–to soiling the back of my bedroom slipper with cockroach guts. *Amen,* she thought.

Mel wasn't really, rationally, afraid of flying. She checked to see if Cecil's letter was still tucked behind her passport. She wasn't quite ready to open it. It made her mind wander, just the same, to the time they met.

* * *

Her friend Sandra had called and asked her if she wanted to work at a party being held by her big shot photographer boss. She would check coats for $100 plus tips.

"Sure." Mel had said. The party was held at the height of fashion season, and she was curious, in a purely sociological way, to have a look at the scene. She needed the extra money, too. Mel didn't have anything stylish to wear, so she settled on something close fitting and black. She wanted to disappear into the background.

The party was held in a large loft on West 34th Street, accessed by a clunky freight elevator. The space was spare and dim, and a DJ was setting up at the far end of it. Some folding banquet tables had been arranged in a "U" near the door for the coat-check, with racks on wheels behind them. A ticket roll like a thick LP record sat on the front table. Mel and her three co-checkers got their instructions, and people started streaming in. Sandra would stop over from time to time to point out the celebrities. Mel raised her eyebrows and nodded, trying to avoid distraction from her task.

A young photographer wearing a peacoat approached Mel and introduced himself. He had an English accent. He looked boyish and very British with straight blonde hair like a young Peter O'Toole.

Mel's boyfriend was home in Scarsdale, NY, for the Jewish holiday (to which Mel was specifically NOT invited) and she was feeling resentful enough to flirt.

"Have you ever seen the British series of the Sixties, *The Avengers*?" he asked. "You look like Emma Peele." Mel had never seen *The Avengers*, nor was she up on vintage TV shows.

"It's probably just the light," Mel replied, looking around the room.

The photographer, whose name was Cecil, had likely crashed this party. He hung around a bit, chatting, and then asked if he could call her. Mel couldn't help being flattered. In a moment of indecision she gave him her number at work, concluding that it was totally harmless. *Why should I make assumptions? Isn't it sexist, not to mention conceited, to think that he is trying to hook up? Couldn't she make friends with a guy, innocently?*

Mel pondered her decision during the cab ride home. She was conflicted between guilt and her desire to be open-minded. Maybe they could

3

be friends, and she could meet some more British expats. Isn't that why she was in New York, to expand her horizons and prepare for her European experience?

He probably wouldn't call her anyway.

* * *

During her stay in New York, Mel worked at Higgins, Olson, and Benson, a middling architectural firm that was a vestige of former glory days. Mr. Benson was the only remaining name partner, just along for the ride until his hard-working captains squeezed every possible commission from their long-standing clients. He sat in his office, removed from the real work, puffing on a pipe and guffawing on the phone. He drank martinis at lunch, came back late, and left early.

The office consisted of three rows of six tables, each back-to-back with a desk. Low walls were arranged here and there to break up the space. The decorating budget was entirely focused on the reception area and Mr. Benson's office, both adjacent to the elevator lobby.

The younger members of the firm were all trying to find better positions elsewhere. In the meantime, they tried to look at the bright side. HOB's clients were well heeled, and the junior designers were given a lot of responsibility. Their friends at the big name firms just designed toilet rooms and stairwells, if they were lucky.

Walter was Mel's particular friend at work. He was a muscular, olive skinned, impeccably dressed young architect. Without Walter, Mel would never have seen the inside of the any of the hip clubs, including the legendary ones that were beyond their heyday. The younger staff also included a midwestern college football player named Frank, and a Greek American woman from New Jersey named Alexis, who worked in bookkeeping.

4

Mel and her coworkers stood around the back end of the receptionist's cubicle during their breaks. Leaning on the files, they discussed impossible deadlines, love interests, and the pros and cons of living together before marriage. Walter was considering moving in with his boyfriend. Mel was living with Jonathan. She couldn't afford to do otherwise. Frank was against it.

He said, "You know what they say: *Why buy the cow when the milk is free?*"

Lindsay the receptionist, who rotated her chair to face them, thought this was the funniest thing she'd ever heard, although she privately wasn't sure she understood. With the ding of the elevator, everyone scattered, trying to look busy. For the rest of the day, Lindsay mooed into the phone when she transferred Mel's calls. She was from Queens and only knew cows from the side panel of a milk carton. Frank had a pet cow named Millie, out in the Midwest.

On the Wednesday following their meeting, Cecil called. Mel's elder sister had once told her that guys you met on Saturday would always call on the following Wednesday. That way, they didn't look eager, while still having enough time to secure a date before the weekend.

"Hello Mel? It's Cecil," he said.

Mel was a little off balance, not completely expecting this call to occur. "Oh, hi, Cecil."

"I wondered if we could get together. Are you free some night soon?"

"What do you have in mind?" Her right shoe had fallen off, and she was trying to recover it with her foot.

He mentioned a pub on MacDougal Street. Suggested tonight or tomorrow.

Mel considered. He was not inviting her out on the weekend, which meant it would be a harmless meeting. But what was she going to tell Jonathan?

"Mel?"

"Sorry, I was just looking at my calendar. Thursday would be better."

"Excellent! Seven o'clock, then. Cheers."

"Bye." Mel set her phone down, exhaling. *What am I doing?*

Then she reminded herself that it was unfair to make assumptions. I mean, why the hell couldn't she make friends with him? She wasn't looking for a boyfriend. Just the same, she was angry about Jonathan's trip home without her. His mother thought the old timers would be put off by her presence on Rosh Hashanah. No offense was meant.

Mel had taken offense anyway.

As Mel waited for the elevator, Lindsay called after her, "Remember, girl, why buy the milk...?"

"Right! Sort of...," Mel answered, knitting her brow.

* * *

Thursday after work, Mel walked a few blocks west of home and slid into a booth at the appointed pub. She was wearing her favorite camel hair coat and a magenta beret, looking a bit like a Village throwback to the Sixties. She slipped off her coat and slowly sipped a beer, waiting. She took a furtive look around the room, trying to locate Cecil. People were having dinner, or standing near the bar, each of them a dark, shifting, unintelligible blob. After half an hour, she drained her glass and decided to leave.

She had been stood up.

She should have known then that this was a bad idea.

She went home to get something to eat.

* * *

Jonathan, who had returned from Scarsdale, was in the bathroom developing film. Mel gave a couple of taps on the door.

"Hi, I'm home."

6

"Hey...I'll be out in a minute. I brought back some challah and some other stuff," Jonathan said through the door.

"As long as you left the ram's head behind," Mel answered, peering into the refrigerator.

She needed to pee, but decided to heat up leftovers while she waited. She was not feeling in great demand today.

* * *

Cecil called Mel at work on Friday.

"Where were you last night?" he said.

"I was there, sitting in a booth for half an hour," she replied, annoyed.

There was a pause.

"I wasn't dressed in black," Mel said. "Why didn't you call?"

"Phone was dead. Try again? Do you have any time for lunch?"

"Well," she said, "I don't have a long break and I usually brown-bag it. If you can pick up something, we can meet in the sunken court next to my office building. There are tables with umbrellas."

"Then I will meet you at one umbrella or another," he said, "shortly after noon."

"Okay, bye."

"Cheers."

Yuk, Mel thought, feeling suddenly sick to her stomach. Walter leaned over the low wall between their drawing boards. Mel had told him about last night.

"I am totally going to check him out," he said. "Alexis and I will get some take out."

"Great," Mel replied. "Just what I need...an audience!"

She managed to recompose herself for the morning's work, and then left promptly at noon to pick up her Muenster cheese with lettuce and mustard on rye from the deli across the street.

As she settled into her seat, she saw him coming down the steps, wearing workclothes under his pea coat.

"There you are!" he said.

"So you *can* recognize me in something other than black," Mel said in a congratulatory tone. She glanced up to street level and saw Walter and Athena eating sandwiches on the wall, in sunglasses, and quickly returned her attention to Cecil.

She told him she was planning to go to Italy.

"Italy is lovely," he said.

He told her the story of his travels. It started when he was seventeen, on a school trip to Venice. He saw that people were selling paintings to tourists in St. Mark's square, so he found an old shop with some cheap paintings, and set up in the piazza with an easel. He was able to finance another month there as an "artist." It was hard to leave. He wanted to travel more.

During his first year at Oxford, he responded to an ad for a photographer by a cruise company sailing for the Caribbean, and spent the next two weeks learning photography. That was the start of his career. Once he had gained a credible amount of experience, he came to New York.

Mel thought this was quite brave compared to her deliberate planning. He just dove into things! She was attracted to his pluck, thinking it might be contagious. At the same time, she felt like she was wandering somewhere hazy, and a part of her was calling for Mel to come back. She was intrigued and afraid at the same time.

Just then, a gust of wind whirled into the sunken court, lifting the umbrellas out of their supports, *one, two, five, seven!* The staff scurried through the space trying to recapture them as they bobbed in the air. Mel watched, amazed. She laughed like a child, soaring above her murky thoughts, as a crowd gathered on the sidewalk above them.

Walter caught one of the umbrellas and anonymously returned it to its stand in the middle of their table. Then he gave Mel a "thumbs up."

The other umbrellas were returned to their poles, and nobody was hurt.

It felt like a sign: *Do something crazy: give in to destiny.*

* * *

Mel's flight was boarding, and she drifted back into the present, smiling at the improbable image of green umbrellas dancing in the air. Life was full of spontaneous nudges that were especially meaningful to confused and searching minds.

In the end, she had given in to Cecil's charm, after he convinced her to attend a Bach organ concert at St. Barts Church on Park Avenue. The music and the space were beautiful. They sat in a pew together, silent strangers. Afterwards, they made love at his Chelsea loft. It was furnished with discarded office chairs and filing cabinets he used to store his clothes. The toilet was barely partitioned from the kitchen and you had to wash your hands in the sink over the dirty dishes. Cecil had seemed such a perfect blond-haired, gray-eyed Englishman, one that had stepped out of one of the classic nineteenth-century novels she loved. But somehow the context felt squalid, ruined it.

Afterward, he walked her down the stairs, nothing more than friendly. She looked straight ahead and endured the eternity before her cab arrived. In Victorian novels, you tended to get your just desserts, and now Mel was getting hers, punished for her delusion. She had purged something, but what?

She continued to see Cecil over the next few months. Pounding one nail in after another.

Mel tried to put the memory out of her mind as she fastened her seatbelt. She was flying to Italy on a one-way ticket. Wipe the slate and start again. She closed her eyes and waited for the surge of the engines as the plane accelerated and lifted into the air.

Melinda mails a letter

To be up in the air and propelled toward the unknown was a liberating sensation for Mel. She had sold her belongings from the apartment in Park Slope. It was on Seventh Avenue above a shop, and only a couple of blocks from Prospect Park. Mel had lived there for a year with a friend from college after her story with Jonathan broke down. Cecil was the catalyst, though not the cause. Jonathan couldn't stand up to his mother, who would not recognize Mel as a legitimate partner.

His father *had* liked her, though.

"She worked her way through college, you should be so ambitious," he would say to Jonathan. "I started out collecting other people's junk, you know," he would tell Mel.

Well, so much for that. Maybe Mel needed an excuse at the time, to refocus on Italy. It was way too early in life to get bogged down in a relationship.

Once Mel was free, Cecil needed to defend himself. He pulled other women between them like a smokescreen. She remembered the Asian woman who wrote a porn column and wore vintage clothing. When they visited the Soho apartment she shared with her boyfriend Alan, Lola and Cecil would flirt away while Alan and Mel tried to make small talk, pretending not to see.

Then, Mel and Cecil visited another friend near Water Street, and he was all over a Jamaican woman with dreads who had just returned from a stay in London (and whose affected English was so tight she barely separated her teeth when she spoke).

"I absolutely love a cricket match!" She said, the beads in her hair rattling.

11

That was shortly after Cecil himself had just returned from London. After the evening with Miss Tight Teeth and her entourage, he asked Mel to meet him in Chinatown for dinner. He had some important news.

"I am engaged!" he said, unwrapping his chopsticks. This had occurred during a three-week visit to London. "She's graphic designer. *So* much like you. I told her I had to return to New York to tie up some loose ends at work. She is presently stomping her little foot for my return, but I had to say a proper goodbye to you."

There was a television set in the restaurant. *Jaws* was being aired, and Mel had her eye on the scene where the shark had devoured half of a small boat and the guy abroad was sliding toward to its gaping mouth. She was digesting what she had just heard.

"You know, I have an early start tomorrow, and I have to get back to Park Slope." She pulled out her wallet. "Here's ten bucks for the dumplings."

"Nonsense. Use it for the cab." He slid her an envelope, then assumed a serious expression. "Read this when you are not feeling angry."

Mel tried to numb her feelings and block her thoughts on her way home that night. She knew if she analyzed it, she still wouldn't understand.

* * *

After the "Fasten Seat Belt" light went off, Mel peered down the aisle to check out the line for the toilet. She made her way down and waited her turn and, once inside, pulled the latch and took a deep breath. Well, not too deep because the tiny space smelled of disinfectant and perfumed soap. As usual, the rubber flooring was spattered, and paper towels had fluttered out of the dispenser. Mel unzipped her small bag and took out Cecil's letter. She lifted the toilet lid, and dropped it into the stainless steel bowl. Usually, she put the lid down before flushing because of the horrendous sucking noise of the pneumatic vacuum. This time, however, she wanted to witness Cecil's letter getting sucked into the 200-gallon holding tank with everybody else's shit. She held onto the counter as she pushed the lever.

Whoosh!

"Farewell to thee, O false prince! Parting is such sweet...*well, it is sweet.*"

The ritual complete, Mel went back to her seat to watch a movie.

Jonathan follows

It was still early enough to get a spot by the window at the Starbucks on Broadway. Jonathan often stopped here because it was halfway between his apartment and the studio. They had a big photo shoot this afternoon, so there would be a lot of logistical preparation, as well as general schlepping. He sat on his stool, in his jeans, a sweatshirt, and a wool cap that he pulled up when he came indoors, so it looked like it was perched on his head. He watched the people on the street. The noise of the cabs and the Ubers and the fuck-you's of cyclists were softened just enough by the glass to merge into a hypnotic piece of urban music. Jonathan scanned the pedestrians, looking for an interesting subject. It was a game he played. He liked to choose someone from the stream of people walking by, and imagine their story. The guy in the red scarf, for example: *He looks mildly upset, as if he exchanged some brusque words with his girlfriend this morning. He should probably call her once he gets to work. Maybe he was unhappy that she invited those friends he didn't like for dinner.*

Jonathan continued the story in his mind until the protagonist was out of sight, then he looked for another subject. This meditation gradually extracted all of the inner workings of all of the people out there: their hurt, their worry, their little joys, and hopes; and it became a soft red throbbing of humanity that both connected him to the whole while alienating him from each.

"Jonathan!" the barista called. His Caffè Americano was ready.

He spotted his friend Hare as he snapped the lid onto his drink, and went back to the counter by the window. He cleared his stuff from the smooth wood surface to make room. Jonathan wrapped his hands around the warm cardboard cup, waiting. He did not look outside, not wanting to get drawn into his humanity game again.

Harold was an acquired friend, the son of an acquaintance of his parents' who was also working in New York. He was wearing a coat and tie (because he had a Real Job), topped with a mountaineering jacket to soften the effect.

They grabbed each other's hand the way that guys do, in a grip that had a deeper, more fraternal meaning than the conventional gesture used by businesspeople.

"How's it goin', my man?" Hare said.

"It's going. Mel left a few days ago, but I'm fine."

Hare sighed. "That's gotta be hard." He had been hearing about this for months, and was a bit tired of Jonathan's obsession with Mel.

"It obviously wasn't going to work out."

"It obviously wasn't."

They sipped their coffee in unison.

"Are you still considering Plan B?" Hare asked.

"Yeah, but it's not what you think. I found two really good photographers that are interested in having an American assistant with *New York* experience. They don't pay much, but neither does Jenna. One of them offered me a place to stay."

"Are the Founders willing to subsidize?"

"Mother yes, but dad is on the fence."

"Do they think you're doing this for her?"

"I'm *not* doing this for her. I mean, I just don't want her experience to so drastically diverge from mine."

Hare looked at Jonathan skeptically, raising his eyebrows.

"Milan is objectively a good move. It'll give me a bump here when I get back."

"Likely true," Hare agreed. "And once you get settled, maybe I'll come visit."

"Counting on it!" Jonathan knew he wouldn't.

They both drank, as if sealing the deal.

"Gotta go," said Hare, placing his hand on Jonathan's back. He did it slowly, as if to leave an imprint of concern. He personally wouldn't have wasted so much time on someone who had cheated on him, unless there was some sort of a mutual agreement, or if she came from an important family. Mel was just one of many smart, pretty girls.

* * *

Jonathan's parents were unaware of Mel's departure for Italy, although they knew she had gone to live elsewhere. He was now footing the rent on his own, or rather, with their help, so it was impossible not to know. Jonathan really wanted to be financially independent, but he didn't know what that felt like, and whether he could give up some of the perks his mother never hesitated to give him (and point out to him after the fact). He wondered if his mother was supportive of his plan to work "for few months" in Milan because she believed it would "clear his palette." Maybe she thought he would return home afterward and get a better job or a more suitable girlfriend. A *Jewish* girlfriend. The problem was, all the Jewish women he had met in New York felt the same to him: been there, done that. And when he was dating Becca, who was Rabbi Feldman's niece, mother complained about her lack of ambition. Jonathan wasn't so sure that anyone would meet her criteria. Maybe if he had stood up for Mel she wouldn't have strayed. That was the thing.

He didn't know whether he was in any position to judge Mel for what happened with the English guy. After all, Jonathan had wavered for months when they started dating. Becca wouldn't let go, and she kept calling him when she knew he would be alone with Mel, late at night, early in the morning, asking if they could "talk." Mel always gave him all the cord he wanted. He respected that, even if he wasn't sure it was wisdom or lack of self-esteem that drove her sense of fair play. Becca had always told him what decisions he should make.

The other factor was that Mel was perfect prey for the wrong kind of guy. What would happen to her in Milan, with all those suave Italian men in their Ermenegildo Zegna suits?

Jonathan was roused from his thoughts by a near collision with the scaffolding blocking the sidewalk on West 27th Street, and the noise of construction. The sound of jackhammers in Manhattan was like the return of the swallows to the Mission San Juan Capistrano: the harbinger of spring. He skirted the structure and ducked into the entry to Jenna's studio. Before calling the freight elevator, he looked at his watch and made a call.

"Pierpaolo, this is Jonathan Goodman calling, from New York."

After a flurry of half Italian, half English coming from the other end of the call, Jonathan smiled a smile he had, where only one side of his mouth turned up.

"I think I can get there by the end of the month... I'll let you know the exact date once I get my ticket... No, no, I am not expecting anything fancy, just a place to sleep and keep my stuff. Great. And, *arrivederci*!"

Mel's debut in Milano

Lella Rossi was sitting on her designer sofa with her cousin Alberto, enjoying an after-lunch espresso. The French doors to the balcony were open, and the breeze, though not yet so warm, was welcome. She would have liked to take a little nap, but she was expecting her new guest soon.

"So, what do you know about this American?" Alberto asked.

"She seems very friendly, perhaps a little shy. We only spoke for fifteen minutes. She is going to be here for a month. Her name is Melinda."

"Is she looking for work?"

"Yes, in an architectural studio. She has a list of places she'd like to try. I might have a couple of contacts she can explore as well."

"Maybe you could suggest Giorgio's. I can give him a call if you'd like."

"Let's first see what she's like, before we go out on a limb."

"Agreed. Well, I have to get back to the office. Thanks so much for lunch."

Alberto went on his way. Lella closed the door behind him, feeling a little sleepy. She wasn't sure about this Airbnb thing. It was just that her resolve to be more social abandoned her when she was digesting a meal. And she was behind on the manuscript she was editing for Alberto.

Lella heard the elevator stopping at her floor and waited for the knock. She stood up straight, took a breath, and opened the door. Mel was standing there, boxed in by her two suitcases and her carry-on. Her fresh looking face and bright eyes were so... *American*, making Lella smile. She made way for her and asked her about her trip.

"This is such a charming neighborhood," Mel said, "and so close to the *Metropolitana*. I won't have any trouble getting around."

"Come, I'll show you to your room," Lella said.

She followed Lella to the lower floor, which was accessible by a stairway hidden behind an impressive wall of books in the living room.

"We'll get your bags down here with the lift," Lella suggested. Now, you will probably want to rest, or get cleaned up, so I will let you get comfortable. I would love to have you join me for dinner this evening. Is seven-thirty a good time?"

"Oh, yes, and thank you so much," Mel answered.

After Lella returned upstairs, Mel explored her new digs. It was certainly nicer than she had expected. Her room was simple, with two single beds, an armchair with an ottoman by the window, and a wardrobe along the opposite wall. There was a beautiful, newly done bathroom next door, and two other rooms down the hall. The open stairway was against the wall. The hall was wider before and beyond the stairs, creating two niches. The one across from Mel's room had a large table and a desk chair, and the other had a cook top, a coffee maker and a small refrigerator. Mel found some tea in the cupboard and put on the kettle. She ate a banana from the fruit bowl while she waited for the water to boil.

She knew that she wasn't going to be enjoying this luxury for long. Lella had given her a deal for the month, but it was a stretch just the same. If Mel couldn't find a job, she would just go back home, she guessed...but failure was not an option! She pushed the thought out of her mind.

Lella was a little older than she had expected. She was very chic, with her short silver hair, beautifully tailored slacks, and soft cashmere sweater. Mel was curious about her, but thought it better not to be intrusive. She set her tea on the nightstand, took off her shoes and her watch, and lay down on one of the beds.

Despite all of the thoughts and fears swirling around in her head, she fell into a hard sleep.

19

* * *

When Mel awoke, she reached for her tea and found it was cold. She drank it anyway, dehydrated from the plane. She unpacked a few things and went into the bathroom for a shower.

There were two sinks in the bathroom, and an ample shower enclosed with glass. There was also a bidet. She studied that for a minute, turning on the faucet and imagining in which direction one would sit on it, then entered the shower. The showerhead was on a long flexible hose like a wall-mounted telephone. She later learned it was called a *doccia telefono*. Telephone shower. She pretended she was calling room service, and then washed her hair.

After her shower, Mel retreated to the armchair, wrapped in her robe. Her third-floor window allowed her a detached view of the activity on the street. The shopkeepers were busy serving their customers, or stood in their doorways greeting the passers-by with a smile. The greengrocer was loading a brown paper bag from crates arrayed outside his shop windows, nodding while his animated client perhaps told him a story, discussed the weather, or complained about politicians. Jonathan was really good at inventing stories about people on the street. He seemed to be able to connect to them through the outward expression of their state of mind. This thought made Mel smile.

She pulled a few books from her bag and set them on the side table next to the armchair. Mel thought how wonderful it would be if she could just sit in that spot and read for the entire month, and *then* worry about her life. Just a little break.

She selected a pair of nice trousers and a silk shirt for dinner, not really sure of how she should dress. She put on the earrings Jonathan had given her for her birthday, and made her way upstairs.

There were several other people in the living room, to Mel's surprise. Lella came out of the kitchen with a couple of glasses of wine, set them down, and made introductions.

Mel greeted them one by one in her faltering Italian: Alberto, a cousin; Antonia, a friend, and her husband, Gianmarco; and Lella's own son, Umberto. Mel was shy when she met people, forgetting their names almost immediately. She tried to imprint them in her mind now, tying them to each person's characteristics. Antonia was in her fifties, had shoulder-length hair, and was wearing a dress (she had arrived straight from work); Gianmarco wore chinos and a button-down, perfectly pressed, and soft leather shoes; Umberto looked a little younger than Mel, with light brown, curly hair and a three-day beard, in jeans and a sweater; and Alberto, a finely ripened forty-something man in a perfectly tailored suit.

They stormed Mel with questions: where was she from, what were her plans, did she have a boyfriend, what was her profession, and so on.

Once at the dinner table, as the risotto was being served, Alberto asked Mel what she thought of the current American scene.

"Well," she answered, "I have been feeling like I don't belong. My country is becoming a cultural wasteland."

"Not to mention the moral decrepitude," Umberto broke in.

"We have no right to throw stones in that regard, Umberto," said Lella.

Mel continued, "I mean, I am not speaking from a position of great authority, but this is what motivated me to come to Milan. To understand the culture of beauty, to soften my own rough edges."

Alberto chuckled, amused by her response. "We will make you so round, you'll roll."

"We have a long tradition of aesthetic excellence," Antonia offered.

"Yet consistently undermined and corrupted," Lella added.

21

They all started talking on top of one another, so Mel retreated, turning her head from one to the next as they vied for attention. It wasn't really clear, except in Umberto's case (he was the youngest) that they were expressing their own beliefs. It seemed rather as if they were engaging in some kind of rhetorical sport in which they threw out arguments to elicit a response. She wasn't equipped for that game. But it was fun to watch. They were speaking in English, but when verbally frustrated, reverted to Italian.

When everyone left after dinner, offering all kinds of good wishes to Mel as they said goodbye, she turned to Lella and smiled.

"The *risotto* was delicious. Thank you so much for dinner."

Mel went down the stairs behind the bookshelves to her room, tired though uninterested in sleep. She pulled out her laptop and went through the list of contacts she had assembled, checking which ones had already responded to her initial inquiries. Eventually, she became sleepy and climbed into bed.

Jonathan hits the "Bel Paese"

Jonathan arrived at Malpensa airport exhausted from his trip. The poor woman behind him was traveling with a baby that had started crying, it seemed, every time Jonathan fell asleep. Not that he would have slept long anyway, with that nasty metal armrest poking his thigh, and that blowing air noise. He looked forward to lifting his window shade when they were two-thirds through the trip, so he could see a glimmer of sunrise. It made him feel like he didn't have to try to sleep anymore. As soon as he peeked out the window, the baby's mother tapped on his shoulder.

"Would you mind closing that?" she whispered. "My baby has just fallen asleep."

Oh, well.

Now he had to get his bags and navigate this place. He wished that he had paid more attention to Mel when she recited her Italian on the couch during TV commercials. As it was, his first question to everyone was: *Do you speak English?*

Jonathan found his way to the train for Milan, and afterward took a cab to his hotel. His mother had insisted that he spend the first night on his own to rest up, have a shower, and get a good meal. As long as she was paying for it, whatever! It wasn't a fancy place, just a solid three-star in the center of the city. There was a bar-café on street level with some scrumptious-looking brioches in the window, so Jonathan plopped his bags down by the counter and ordered a cappuccino and a chocolate brioche. Mel had told him that it was uncool to order a cappuccino that late (it was eleven-thirty), but it was first thing in the morning as far as he was concerned.

The bed in the hotel was so welcome! He dove onto it and pushed his running shoes off with his feet as he hugged the pillows. Just these few moments of pure joy at finally being comfortable, that's all he wanted. It even obscured, momentarily, the soft ache in his heart.

He took a short nap and a shower, and then hit the streets in some clean clothes. Jonathan headed down Via Torino, trying to get lost. He carefully observed the people he passed on the sidewalk. Via Torino was well populated though not crowded. The side streets were enticingly crooked–they all called to him. He wandered down the ones that were most mysterious. He saw a beautiful Romanesque church, some Roman walls, and then...the stock exchange. The juxtapositions were crazy. It was as if all of history had been shaken and poured out for him.

That image made him thirsty.

Jonathan emerged from the labyrinth onto Via Torino again, where Via Spadari meets Via Speronari. There was another short block (if you want to call them blocks; none of them were rectangular!) and then the space opened to the Piazza del Duomo. The rather squat Gothic cathedral sat at the far end of of the square, looking like a marble wedding cake. Pigeons took to the air, and some Japanese tourists had managed to get them to perch on their sleeves for pictures. Jonathan had no interest in taking tourist snapshots, although he did have his camera with him. He walked across the piazza and into the *Galleria*, an incredible covered space full of tourist traps, boutiques, bars, and what looked like a couple of high-end restaurants. The roof was made of iron and glass, and the floor was a warm mosaic of marble. Jonathan passed through the Galleria into another, smaller piazza. There was the opera house, *La Scala,* to his left! Leonardo (daVinci, he assumed) looked down at him with his arms folded, from his pedestal in the center of the space. An irreverent pigeon was perched on his stone beret.

Jonathan headed toward the street to the right of *La Scala*. He walked for a bit, feeling the texture of the stone paving underfoot. He eventually came to a place where tables had overtaken the street, and sat down to get a drink. He was in Via Brera, the stone plaque said.

A Negroni seemed like the easiest cocktail to order, given Jonathan's language limitations. He was comfortable in his plastic chair at a table under the awning. A guy walked by, gesticulating while he spoke to someone animatedly on bluetooth. Two women in sunglasses, tight slit skirts, and stilettos passed, carefully picking their way over the stone pavement. A young couple sat on an idling scooter at the corner, talking to friends on the sidewalk.

The waiter arrived with Jonathan's Negroni, on a tray with little pieces of focaccia, a small bowl of chips, and one of tiny pickles. The waiter held up his hand and made a sideways circle with his finger, as if unreeling something, when Jonathan reached for his wallet. He guessed that meant *pay later*.

Negronis have such a beautiful ruby color, especially when held up to the late afternoon light. And the little orange peel is chromatically perfect. A lime would be so dissonant; a lemon, too harsh. Jonathan twirled his drink, listening to the sound of the ice cubes against the glass. He was thoroughly enjoying himself, despite the occasional twinge of regret. It was better to be around people.

A group of girls, obviously American, sat down at the next table, laughing and arranging their shopping bags around their chairs.

"My mom is going to *kill* me when she finds out what I spent on that dress!"

"Just tell her it was marked down from eight hundred fucking Euros!"

There was a barely perceptible moment of silence at the bar-café when everyone heard this young woman uttering the F-word so loudly. The girls giggled and lowered their voices to a whisper.

"You know, when I was at the cash register, I had the most incredible urge to fart."

"Did you?"

"Not until I was on my way out. I let loose near the handbags. I mean, I didn't want to do it in *Via Monte Napoleone*!"

"You're a woman of class!"

They each took their glass of prosecco as their waiter set some olives and pearl onions on the table. Then he hesitated.

"Perhaps I will take the onions back," he said, "in case you are still in the mood."

Jonathan couldn't suppress a smile, and gestured to the waiter to bring his check. He leaned over to the girls, who were alternately laughing and hiding behind their hands.

"A lot of people here understand English, you know," he said.

"Oh my god, are you American?" one of the girls asked him.

Jonathan had already turned away, unwilling to associate himself with them any further.

Mel makes a friend

Mel settled into her armchair after her late afternoon shower, with a fresh cup of tea on the coaster with the raspberry pattern. Today's effort at job hunting went pretty well. She had called five studios, made appointments with four of them, and visited one just after lunch. Now all she had in front of her was self-doubt and fear. She picked up a book in an attempt to evade them. It was unclear to her why she felt the way she did. Most everyone was so friendly and open about meeting her, and in her heart she believed she would succeed.

Lella came down the stairs, knocking on the wall at the landing to announce her approach.

"Melinda? May I come down?" she asked.

"Certainly!" Mel called from her room. She adjusted her robe and tightened the belt, then opened her bedroom door. "Please come in."

Lella took the desk chair from the niche outside of Mel's room and placed it just inside the door.

"So, how did your first day of job hunting go?"

"Well, I met with Antonio Benfatti, and I have three more appointments this week. I'll make some more calls tomorrow morning before I go out."

"I am sure you will do fine. Everyone likes having Americans in their studio."

"Do they?" Mel asked. "I would think the Italian designers are so much more creative and in tune with the culture."

Lella laughed, "Well, there is truth to that, but you must consider two things: One, you will work harder. Two, you will cost less. If they hire an Italian they will have to pay the *contributi* to the government."

Mel hadn't thought of that. She could work as a consultant, and her employer was off the hook for the payroll taxes. This probably had a downside, but it was not time to consider that just yet. So, she did have a competitive advantage after all.

"Listen," Lella said, "Umberto was supposed to join me for dinner, but he had to cancel. Would you like to join me? Just some pasta, nothing special."

"That's very nice of you," Mel smiled. She had planned to get some ravioli at the *pasta fresca* shop across the street, and boil some water on the cook top.

Lella seemed the perfect host. She generally kept to herself, knowing just when to poke her head in and be sociable. They had a lot to talk about at the dinner table. Lella had traveled all over the world in the five years since her husband Paolo died, and had plenty of stories. She was elegant, articulate, and aware of what was going on in the world.

"I used to have a cook, when Umberto and Amelia (my daughter) were home. But for me alone, it's not necessary. I love to cook."

Mel was enjoying the *orecchiette* with grated broccoli rabe and garlic, the most divine olive oil, and Parmesan cheese. "It's delicious," she said.

"Is it warm enough to go for a *gelato*?" she added, "I would like to treat."

"For *gelato*, always," Lella responded, "We can leave the dishes for Giovanna."

"I'll get my bag."

As Mel ducked behind the bookshelves to the secret staircase (she loved secret doors and staircases), a little woozy from the wine and the jet lag, she thought how very much she would like to become friends with Lella.

* * *

After they returned, Lella said goodnight and went to her room. She pulled off her sweater and put on her silk pajamas, took a sidelong glance at herself in the mirror, then straightened up. It was hard to maintain good posture when you were tired. She went closer to the mirror, ran her hands through her silver hair, and smiled. *I don't look half-bad for an old lady*, she thought. She looked around her bedroom and her eyes rested on the photo of her late husband Paolo at the helm of a sailboat, in a yellow windbreaker. He had been a real pain in the ass, she thought, but she missed him very much. Not that she wasn't capable of being on her own; she relished having complete control over her plans, her schedule, and her habits. But freedom can be a lonely place sometimes. Despite the loveliness of sleeping alone, she thought, as she pulled down her bed covers.

Lella had enjoyed her evening with Melinda, the American girl. She seemed confident and tentative at the same time. She remembered how she was herself in her late twenties, when she was working at Paolo's publishing company. She used to draw herself up every time she got up from her desk to walk around the office, pretending to be sure of herself. It made her laugh to think about it. Even when she became editor-in-chief of *Onda* magazine she would become paralyzed with fear when she was the only woman in the boardroom. She would look whoever was talking right in the eyes, in fear, until they looked down. This uncalculated reflex gave her a reputation for being discerning. How ironic the world is.

As Lella fluffed her pillows and grabbed her book, she thought that maybe she would like to keep an eye on Melinda, to see if she could make it any easier for her.

She read almost a whole page before she fell asleep.

Jonathan meets Pierpaolo

"*Madonna*, what is the matter with you people? Don't you know we have work to do here? Welcome to MI-LA-NO," shouted Pierpaolo Nervi, as he skipped across the polished concrete floor of his photo studio. "I want all of *this* stuff, over here, and all of *that* stuff over there! Where is Lucy with the coffee?"

"Right here, Pierpa'," Lucy called, walking in quick little steps, impeded by her heels and the tray of white ceramic cups and saucers with their sloshing liquid and foam.

Pierpaolo hated it when the coffee spilled onto the saucer. He always wore white shirts and couldn't stand getting them stained. He grabbed one of the little cups and knocked back his espresso like he was drinking a shot of whiskey.

"*Grazie*," he said, rubbing his hands together as he surveyed his scrambling assistants.

"That's better," he called. "Now come and get your coffee so we can clear the cobwebs out of your heads."

* * *

Pierpaolo Nervi's photo studio was located in a neighborhood northeast of the fashionable center of Milan, near a train station called Lambrate. It was an easy trip on the *Metropolitana* for someone who was used to the subways of New York City. There was a lot of activity outside of the station, but the sound was less intense than the thumping beat Jonathan felt at his starting point in the city center. Here he could hear trams moving on their rails, clanging their warnings, while the underground trains whooshed below. Buses lumbered through the piazza; pedestrians picked their way across it. There was a newsstand across the road, and behind that, the graffiti covered walls of buildings. Most of these had blocky proportions, with five to eight stories, depending on their age. The more austere architecture suggested

30

postwar vintage. They were not aging as gracefully as the ochre-stuccoed buildings with the travertine cladding on the ground floor, despite the polluting artwork. Balconies with French doors alternated with casement windows on the upper stories. The penthouses were set back, the greenery of their terrace gardens tumbling over the parapet. As he walked down the street, Jonathan could glimpse into broad courtyards around which these buildings wrapped like tall, rectangular doughnuts. The entries had large double doors, sometimes open to allow vehicles to enter, sometimes admitting only pedestrians through smaller cutout doors. Once you passed through the large doorway, the *portone*, you were in a vaulted space that gave you access to the stairs, the elevator (if fortunate), and the solicitous attention of the *portiere* who received mail, packages, news of the day, and favors, redispensing them to the inhabitants of the building. The dark of these tunnel-like spaces opened into the bright courtyards, ringed by the iron railings of the exterior passageways on each floor above.

After passing a few bar-cafés and the shops peppered in between, Jonathan arrived at the address Pierpaolo had given him. He found himself in one such covered passageway under the inspection of Signora Pia della Bocca, also known as Signora Pia, or *la Pia*.

Jonathan handed her a piece of paper with Pierpaolo's name and address, and she raised her arm and moved her hand up and down from the wrist to indicate the direction, while speaking words he only partially understood. He crossed the courtyard paved with cobbles and stone walkways just wide enough for a wheelbarrow or a hand truck. It reminded him of a blueberry pie with strips of pastry overlain. (He wondered if they had blueberry pies in Italy; he didn't think so.)

A short woman in heels and a Madonna T-shirt buzzed Jonathan into the studio. Her hair was in a ponytail with plenty of fringe hanging over her forehead and her right cheek. She indicated a well-worn sofa behind her workspace, a small peninsula that jutted out into the entry. She was chewing gum. Jonathan hated that.

He sat down and waited, in no hurry at all. He was jet-lagged, and traipsing around the city yesterday did not tire him out enough to get a good night's sleep. He surveyed the visible portion of the studio. It was a converted industrial space, with a series of saw-tooth windows in the ceiling of its large atrium. The concrete floor had been skim-coated, sealed, and polished since its manufacturing days. There were several rooms along the near wall that would have windows to the courtyard. Along the far wall, there were two open cubicles at each end and an iron and glass wall with a double door in the center. The cubicles, which were several steps below the main floor, had white walls and backdrop screens on rolls within. A small group of assistants was setting up a shoot in one of them. A woman with a clipboard was talking on her cellphone in the middle of the atrium, while another stood behind her with two large shopping bags.

A door opened, and Pierpaolo Nervi popped into view. He briskly walked over to the waiting area and held out his hand.

"*Jonatan*," he said, not quite able to get the "th" sound. "Did you have a good trip?"

"It was fine, thanks. I'm glad to be here."

"Well," said Pierpaolo, rubbing his hands together. "It's not such a bad day. Why don't we sit outside? Would you like some coffee? LUCY! Can you bring us some coffee outside please? And a couple of *brioches, grazie.*"

Jonathan had not had the time to answer, so he just nodded and smiled, following Pierpaolo to the glass wall with the small panes, out the door, down a few steps into an interior courtyard They sat at a small café table that was poised amid a jungle of potted plants. The paving stones were wet, and the leafy plants glistened. The sky was gauzy, but the sun was starting to peak through the haze.

"We just put the plants out over the weekend," Pierpaolo said.

Then he focused on Jonathan. "Now," he said, "I have some assistants here, as you can see, and I can't guarantee anybody steady work. These guys are okay, but nobody has any specific role. They are all equally well or ill-suited to their tasks, depending; but generally I would say they are usually motivated, somewhat insecure, and," he paused, "a little sloppy at times."

He paused, but Jonathan was quiet, waiting to hear more.

"So, based on the abilities that you told me about in your email, and after talking to Jenna about your work in her studio, I would like to try something." He leaned in toward Jonathan.

"I would like to have you stay here and observe for a couple of weeks, and then I would like to hear what you think we can do better. If this is a good conversation, then I would like you to manage production, if you want to do that. No guarantees." He raised his hands to underline the contingency of his offer.

Lucy carefully stepped down into the court, holding the door and the tray, balancing on her heels. She set the tray, with two tiny espresso cups, a little steel pitcher of foamed milk, and the *brioches*, on the table, and made her retreat.

Jonathan spoke. "That sounds great." He paused to take a sip of his espresso. Pierpaolo had already downed his.

"For this first week, would it be possible for me to have some sit-down time with you, maybe at lunch, or at the end of each day, to go over any questions I may have?"

"Of course. We'll see how it goes after that. Oh, and for now, I can offer you the little studio apartment across the main courtyard. After a month, we can talk about some money for you. Hopefully, you can make this place work better."

Jonathan suggested that he go back to Via Torino and get his bags, check out, and come back to start right after lunch.

"Okay, *Jonatan!*" Pierpaolo said, slapping both hands down on the little table and making the ceramic cups and metal spoons clink and jingle. "After lunch, we can meet the crew."

The "cousins" lunch

Lella, sitting at a table near the window, looked at her watch. Alberto was always late. She never liked sitting by herself at a restaurant; it made her feel conspicuous. Dining was never, in her book, a solitary activity. Eating, yes. Sometimes she *ate* by herself, but she didn't consider that a meal. That was just to stay alive. To dine was to live and share life with others, as a ritual of community.

A waiter brought a bottle of San Pelligrino and two glasses, and poured some for Lella. Alberto breezed in, smiling at her with a fetchingly roguish look. Lella shook her head at her own susceptibility as he bent over her and kissed her hair.

"Hello dear cousin, you look lovely today! Sorry I'm late. What looks good?"

"Well, I am thinking about the asparagus *risotto*. Would you like to join me? They won't make it for one."

"That would be perfect." Alberto lifted his finger and caught the waiter's eye.

He turned to Lella, "Are we having a glass of wine?"

"I guess one won't hurt. I don't have any obligations until later this afternoon."

"I have an editorial meeting at 2:30 myself, but I plan to sleep through it."

Alberto shook out his napkin and laid it on his lap.

"Nothing substantial ever gets done at those meetings," Lella said.

"True, but it is an excellent opportunity to appreciate the dynamics of the group, and to separate the leaders from the dead wood."

"And then there are the private phone calls afterward," Lella offered.

Alberto nodded, laughing. They each inquired about their respective children: Umberto and Amelia were fine; Alberto's elder son Leo was studying medicine, and his younger son Guido was preparing for his first year in architecture at the Politecnico.

"Speaking of young architects," said Alberto, "how is Melinda doing? Has she found a position?"

"I understand that she has had an offer, but it doesn't come with an immediate salary."

"That's inconvenient. How much do you think she needs to earn?"

"Well, she is paying me €2,500 for this month, and I know that's more than anyone will give her in this town. There are plenty of foreigners working under the table."

"She's not planning on staying with you, then."

"No, it's too much. I think she will need to find a roommate."

"Do you think I should introduce her to Giorgio? He has some foreign clients and his English is so-so."

"He is very demanding."

"Maybe we could arrange for them to meet socially? That way, he will have an idea what she is like, and possibly not treat her too badly. Now that you know her a little, do you think she is any good?"

"She showed me her portfolio, to make sure she was using the right terms in Italian. It looked solid to me. Creative (not like an Italian of course), but some good ideas, and well executed. *Better* than an Italian, in that regard. More detailed."

They finished their risotto and the Friulian white they were drinking, and agreed to have their espresso at the bar on their way out.

"How about dinner tomorrow night, then? See if Giorgio is free."

Alberto held the door for Lella.

They air kissed, touching their cheeks on both sides, and walked their separate ways.

Job hunting

Mel sat on a green bench in the *Giardini Pubblici* and lifted her heels out of her shoes so she could wiggle her toes, careful not to make contact with the bare soil underneath. She stretched her back and rolled her shoulders, thinking about her next move.

Every morning she woke up full of hope. She made a few calls while still in her bathrobe, from the armchair with the ottoman by the window in her room. Then she dressed and hit the streets.

Her second meeting had been with Cristina della Rovere. She was working on a showroom design, and had some drawings scattered on the table where she sat with Mel.

"I gave this detail to my assistant, Anna, to work on. She was supposed to make a drawing for a frieze to be made in plaster, and this is what she gave me," Cristina slid a sketch toward Mel. "Which as you can see is much too complicated."

Mel sat thinking for a moment. Cristina was waiting for her to say something.

"Look, I have some time before my next appointment. Maybe I could do a drawing for you? It would be a nice change from wandering the streets."

Mel quickly laid out a tile for the frieze, using a simple, abstract acanthus leaf pattern. Then she made a copy of the tile and butted it against the drawing to make sure the pattern flowed seamlessly. She adjusted the drawing, tweaked some small details, labeled it with dimensions, and looked at the clock. Two hours had gone by!

She sat down with Cristina again and showed her the pattern.

"This would be a 25 x 40 centimeter design that can be cast and tiled around the top of the walls. That would leave another 25 centimeters clear above the door molding."

"This is very simple, Melinda. And it works."

Mel felt very satisfied with herself, and hopeful. Hopeful of getting a job, and also hopeful that she didn't just do something stupid, giving her work away. Her impression was that this was expected.

"I must tell you," said Cristina, "that I don't have enough work for another assistant right now, but there is a project that may come in a month or two, and if it does, I would be happy to discuss this further with you."

Mel tried to hide her disappointment, but it had been a long shot, and Cristina *did* seem impressed. That was something, wasn't it?

"It would be difficult for me to let Anna go, as she does a lot of things I need. Things you wouldn't be interested in doing. In the meantime, I'd like to offer you lunch."

And so Cristina and Mel had lunch together, at a small, crowded place nearby, said goodbye, and promised to stay in touch. Mel crossed Corso Venezia and entered the park, where she sat mulling over the morning.

She slipped her feet all the way back into her shoes, checked her GPS for her next appointment, and summoned her determination once more.

* * *

Marino Contini thumbed through Mel's portfolio with one hand, tapping a mechanical pencil on his desk with the other. He glanced up at her webpage on the screen of his laptop, skimming her résumé. Then he rolled back in his chair and looked at her.

"The problem is not your qualifications, as I can see your technical skills and even your concept diagramming are quite good. I think, though, the kind of job you can have in a small studio may be too boring for you. Here, we have an atelier approach. People come in and start with very basic work. We have to trust them little by little until we are sure they can do things that follow the studio's brand. What do you think about that?"

"Well," Mel ventured, "I am here in Milan because I am trying to learn something. I would not expect to have a leading role, at least not initially."

She was faltering inside. Something about the way he said the word "brand" had gone against her grain. Indeed, the studio looked slick and polished, just like all of Marino's projects. She was, however, trying to be open-minded. Maybe Marino didn't notice the little twitch of her mouth.

It seemed like a form of violence to her nature, trying to get a job she didn't think she would like. To Mel, choosing was only Part Two. Getting chosen was Part One. She was always getting stuck there.

"Okay, Melinda," Marino said. "Why don't you keep exploring and maybe you can think about everything and call me in a couple of weeks." He wrote on a small piece of paper, and pushed it over to her.

"This is what I can offer to you."

The scribble on the paper read, *€400 per week.*

"Thank you, Marino," Mel replied, feeling herself blanch, "I will."

She headed out of the studio, down the stairs, through the *portone*, down the crooked street, onto Via Brera, and into the courtyard of the Accademia, finally releasing her breath among the refreshingly mute statues. She checked a nearby bollard for pigeon droppings before leaning on it. She looked up at the arches and columns surrounding the courtyard, and they seemed to throb as her eyes welled with tears. Mel bent her head so that nobody could see. Her heart and the columns in the courtyard were beating together, and she concentrated on trying to make them stop. She badly wanted to succeed in this venture, and was so afraid of failing. She began to understand that it was not about getting a position, but rather getting enough money. How would she survive? There were so many designers and most of the studios were small. You were basically the *Maestro* or the apprentice. And in a couple of weeks, her comfortable living situation would expire. *There must be a way*, she thought.

After a few minutes, the columns steadied, and Mel composed herself.

She decided what she needed right now was a *fior di latte* cone from the *Gelateria Edonica* across the street from Lella's place. Then, she would have a hot shower and return to the "helm," her armchair, in her robe, with her feet on the ottoman, and stare out the window at the bustling city around which she was orbiting, looking for a place to land.

She decided to get some gelato to bring to Lella, and rang at the upper floor. She had been getting off the elevator on the floor below, to avoid disturbing her host.

"Oh, good!" Lella smiled, opening the door. "How was the battle today?"

Mel smiled her half-smile, and said she would be happy to talk about it later, offering up the polystyrene container of gelato like a bird dog with a pigeon.

"I am going out to dinner," said Lella. "I will let you know when I come back, and we can have some of this."

"However," she added, "I would like to invite you tomorrow evening. We will have a special guest: Giorgio Monti. Alberto is bringing him."

"*The* Giorgio Monti?"

Lella smiled, "Yes!" Then she put on an admonishing face. "But it is not a job interview, strictly social. So don't worry."

Mel was still at the door, so she went back onto the landing and down the stairs to the fourth floor entrance, although she missed going down the secret stairs behind the massive bookshelves in Lella's living room. *Giorgio Monti!* She thought. He was a real celebrity among Italian architects. This

41

prospect would be dealt with in due time, but right now she needed to finish feeling lousy about her day.

Mel felt she deserved to sit in the armchair by the window, her feet on the ottoman. The shower felt good. She gazed at the sky, which was gray with clouds. The weather was changing, and it was starting to drizzle. Maybe she wouldn't even go out to buy dinner. She was still full from her cone. Anyway, she had some cheese and a head of radicchio in the refrigerator. But right now she didn't want to think of making an effort; she just wanted to sit and process things. Her mouth hurt from speaking Italian.

Mel remembered how she used to come home to Jonathan, and they would talk about work over a glass of wine or a beer. Jenna's studio was in walking distance, so he almost always stopped to buy food for dinner, sometimes at the market in Union Square. Mel arrived later, because she took the subway from Midtown, and it was often crowded and slow. When they lived together, she didn't feel so alone in New York. *Let's face it*, she thought, *you expected too much from him, too soon.* She wondered what he was doing these days. He had talked about coming to Milan himself, probably because he thought they'd be together, and he had been investigating possibilities. She thought about emailing him, but it seemed presumptuous. What if he was back there, just feeling awful? Anyway, there was no point to it. That relationship had been irreparably damaged by her impulsive and vindictive behavior.

Mel looked down from the window at the people on the street. There they were, everyone with a job, a home, and a place to go. They all fit into the puzzle. She rested her head on the back of the chair. Her hair was wet, she should go dry it; but she closed her eyes and fell asleep.

Mel awoke to Lella's gentle tapping on the wall along the staircase.

"Oh, sorry, Lella, I must have fallen alseep," she called from her room. She had left the door open and could see Lella peering from the steps. "I'll be up in five minutes."

Mel changed from her bathrobe to a flowered dress that she used when she needed to be dressed, but not *really*, and went up the stairs, emerging from behind the heavy wall of books.

"I don't think I can eat more *gelato*," she apologized. "That was the last thing in my stomach!"

"Then we'll have some brandy," suggested Lella. Mel settled into a corner of the sofa while Lella poured the beautiful golden liquid into her exquisite little glasses. They took a sip in silence. Lella waited for Mel to speak.

"So, today I had two meetings, with Cristina della Rovere, and Marino Contini."

"Ah, I know Cristina. She is the younger sister of a friend. Contini I have heard of, but have never met."

"Well," Mel continued, "from what I could tell, Cristina has a very traditional clientele, and works with a lot of rather classical décor. I even did a little drawing for one of her projects while I was there."

"Really!" Lella interjected, more like an observation than a question.

"Yes. I suggested it, thinking it would promote my cause. But there isn't an opening right now. We had lunch, though, and she was very pleasant."

"Maybe you can stop there before lunch everyday and work for your food, then."

Mel laughed. "Then I went to Marino's studio. There is a possibility there, the pay would be horrible, and...well, I don't really like his work, and I think he picked up on it. But he asked me to think about him and call back."

"How much did he offer you?"

"€400 per week."

Lella considered this. "You know, that is not enough to live on, but I am not sure you will get much more." She paused, and then added, "You may have to explore other sources of income, and also find a roommate to reduce your expenses."

"Yes, I was thinking of that myself today, I mean, of some other way to make money. I wonder if I could work a shorter day, earning that amount. I might be able to teach conversational English. What do you think?"

"That could work. And, perhaps you can find some other expats. They might be able to help with your living situation. There's a bar-café near the language school in Corso Magenta, and you will see they're hanging out there."

They had a little more brandy and discussed the ways that Mel could make it work.

Before Mel disappeared behind the bookshelves, Lella reminded her not to overdo it tomorrow so that she would be fresh for their dinner with Giorgio Monti. Mel needed to keep one hand on the wall going down. She felt a little dizzy when she got into bed, despite the three glasses of water she had drunk, leaning on the kitchenette, before she turned in.

Jonathan meets the crew

Jonathan set his large duffel bag and his camera cases on the floor of the apartment next to Pierpaolo's studio. Well, it was less like an apartment and more like a storage space. You accessed it off the main courtyard: rather than going straight ahead from the *portineria* to the studio, you went to the left, crossing the space diagonally. Outside the door were two sad clay pots with sadder plants in them. The large room inside had a counter running along the courtyard windows to the left, with a sink, a cooktop, and a small refrigerator underneath. This galley was separated from the rest of the room by a long, parallel counter, open on the "kitchen" side, with some disparate dishes and pots arranged on shelves. To the right, there was a short corridor leading to a bathroom. Beyond the bathroom was another space that had several metal clothing racks on wheels, and stacks of toilet paper. There was a door at the rear. Jonathan tried to open it, but it was locked. He tried with the key, and that worked. As he suspected, the door led to the back of the studio, beyond the line of enclosed offices. He walked back to the front room.

There was little furniture in the space. A mattress was placed on a platform in the corner, and unfinished, built-in shelves lined the opposite wall. There were sheets and towels. Jonathan made the bed so that the space would be more welcoming when he came back. He took a couple of towels and put them in the bathroom. The showerhead was attached to a flexible hose. Jonathan took it in his hand and turned the water on. The pressure seemed okay, but the water was coming out at weird angles. He unscrewed the head, took the gasket out and dumped the scale and sediment onto the little counter. He cleaned the pieces and reassembled them. Much better.

The refrigerator had been cleaned, and the door was open. It had one of those tiny freezer compartments with room for one ice tray. Jonathan closed the door and plugged it in. He typed a list on his phone: mineral water, dish soap and dishcloths; tomatoes, basil, coffee, bread, butter, honey, milk, and pasta. Wine. That would do for starters. It was one-thirty, so all the little shops were closed. He would go after five o'clock.

Jonathan was pleased. He was not getting paid, but this place was perfect. No frills, to be sure, but it was right next to the studio. He figured he had enough cash to last him six months, if he was careful. His *own* money.

He wondered where Mel was, and how she was doing, and then pushed the thought out of his mind. *First things first*, he thought. He went out, locked the door, and crossed the courtyard to the studio entrance.

At the far end of the atrium, there were some gray-painted plywood boxes that served as pedestals for the shoots. The assistants sometimes used them as tables or seating, and today they were arranged in tiers like bleachers. The full-timers and one of their free-lancers were sitting there chatting. Jonathan imagined they were expecting a performance.

One of the women spoke up as Jonathan approached.

"Pierpaolo said to start without him because he is running a little late."

Jonathan looked at them, and they looked back, expecting him to take the lead.

He felt a wave of signals coming from the group, at first one big push, and then a breaking, all of these little noises coming from each one, like the undertow, pulling away in nuanced currents. Distrust, judgment, expectation, physical assessment, curiosity. He would have liked more time to distinguish the signals better, to watch their expressions and movements, to draw them out on a fundamental and emotional level.

The tall, skinny one with the knit hat and the ruddy cheeks spoke first.

"I think we're supposed to get to know one another," he said, "I am Geert and I come from Utrecht."

The others laughed at the way Geert spoke, as if at a group therapy session.

"I went to Gerrit Reitveld Academie, and I worked in Amsterdam for two years before I came here. Enrico and I, we do most of the setup and lighting."

"And Enrico would be...?" Jonathan asked, looking at the other two guys.

"I am Enrico. I do location work and test shoots, lighting...a little bit of everything."

Enrico was obviously the Italian, and Jonathan felt a little foolish not to have caught that. The other guy, named Reiner, was clearly not. He had straight, longish blonde hair, tight black jeans and boots, and looked like he had just stepped out of an avant-garde Berlin club. Reiner was actually from Munich, and had lived in Milan for five years. He was very self-assured, maybe a little standoffish.

"I am maintaining all the camera equipment and doing the in-house post production," he offered, looking away and then at his hand.

One of the women looked around to see if it was clear for her to speak.

"I am Elena."

"She is the one that bosses us around," Geert interrupted.

They all laughed, and the wave came toward Jonathan again. He waited for the energy to separate, for the group to recede to a collection of distinct individuals once more.

"I handle the production schedule and the freelancers, like Leitizia here." She turned to a shy-looking, rather voluptuous woman to her right.

Leitizia said, "I'm a stylist. I have other clients, but I'm here a lot." She smiled, but obviously felt a little uncomfortable, not quite a full member of the group. Or maybe she was less certain about her English. She pushed back her long wavy black hair.

Reiner looked up at Jonathan.

"And what about you? Pierpaolo said you worked with Jenna McKenna, but not much else."

"Well," Jonathan started, looking around the group for some encouraging signs, "I've worked in New York since I left college seven years ago, and I felt it was time to get a different perspective."

Enrico asked, "What was the perspective of New York?" He was genuinely curious, given that, for them, New York was the paragon for photographers.

Jonathan smiled at Enrico's question, but at a loss for a short answer. He adjusted his glasses.

"It would be over-simplifying it to say *business* over *art*. But that might be a starting point."

"Some of us would like to work there very much," Geert added.

"Well, I am here to learn about the way you work, and, *maybe* I can share some things I have learned there."

"You mean you want to turn this into more of a business," Reiner suggested.

Jonathan was considering how to respond to Reiner's slightly smug tone just as Pierpaolo came in, skipping across the floor like a superhero. He set down his bag and took off his bomber jacket (made of the most *buttery* leather), tossing it onto the "bleachers."

"So," he said, "you have all met? Good. Then, this is how it's going to work: *Jonatan* is going to be following all of us around for the next couple of weeks. He is going to be asking questions and you are going to answer the questions. He's not here to slow you down, neither to help you. He's not trying to take away anybody's job, okay? That's all for now."

He nodded to Jonathan, and went to his office.

Elena came forward as the others scattered.

"That is going to be your office," she said, pointing. "Lucy has put some supplies on your desk. Let me know if you need anything, *Jonatan*," she said, mimicking Pierpaolo's pronunciation. By the end of the day, this would become his official name in the studio. *Fair enough*, he thought, it was a good way to ensure that he didn't take himself too seriously. *Jonatan*.

He went to the little office to check it out. It was in between Pierpaolo's office and the little corridor that led back to the apartment. There was a window looking out to the entry courtyard, facing north. There were some banged-up metal files along the wall. The desk was old, but it was made of wood, which Jonathan liked. There was a new desk chair, probably a perk from a furniture shoot, upholstered with red fabric. There was a stack of yellow lined note pads still wrapped in cellophane, and some mechanical pencils, fine-lined markers and a clipboard on the desk. Jonathan loved yellow note pads and clipboards. His started to put things into the desk drawers and made a list of some other items he might need. He looked up. A red and blue diagram was drawn on the whiteboard, a couple of chairs turned toward it. Jonathan erased the board and tested the dry markers that were in the tray.

Stop stalling, he thought, as he turned the chairs back toward the desk. He unwrapped the pads, took one out, and attached it to the clipboard. He wrote his first observation.

Misperception: Pp thinks they all do "everything," & they think they have "specialized" jobs. He wrote it on the second page and folded the first one in half as he always did to keep his notes private.

Then he went out into the studio.

49

Alberto at work

Alberto was dressed impeccably, as always. He was sitting at his desk, in his office. It was a beautiful room, elegant and understated. The furniture was vintage and meticulously restored, in hardwoods and tightly tucked upholstery. There were several early twentieth-century paintings, in black and blue and yellow and red.

He was going through a list of people to call, drawing a line through their names as he did. They were mostly courtesy calls of a social nature, but everything in Milan was tied to business somehow. The day was winding down, and the office was emptying. He occasionally stopped to put an event on his calendar.

How ironic, he thought, to have all this, and not be free to take off and go somewhere far away. Perhaps southern Chile, or New Zealand. Someplace fresh, and clean. But this legacy he was building was like a hungry baby needing constant attention. He thought of younger people like Melinda, trying to get on the merry-go-round. The push for career development, personal growth, and the avoidance of the dangers that could bring you down. He would never be able to show her what it looked like from his vantage point.

They had barely made it through the tech shake up. One of his editors had proposed the new Interactive Books Division, an experiment in adaptive digital stories. What an idea, to let the readers influence plot! That led to a whole new approach to presentation, and new, younger staff that was born to the digital world. And then there was an appreciable comeback of traditional print, so thank God they had kept that viable. The board meetings, despite their prosaic agendas, always evolved into discussions about what publishing *is*, and what publishing companies can offer writers, and readers. Then there was the new audio recording studio. That was Alberto's idea. It started out as an accessibility initiative, but then he convinced his athletic club to have a selection of audio books available on wifi for members working out. Together, they had set up Ripped Lit.

But the whole scene was a shifting target, and moving too fast for him at this stage of the game. Lella was on the board, and was very savvy about new ideas and their possibilities. She always said *yes*. Her son Umberto, who was learning to be a junior editor, was dragging his feet. Alberto thought that he had too much given to him, and none of the drive of a hungry, young person.

Amelia was the surprise. Once she had finished college, some travel, and graduate school, she threw herself into the business. Lella had trained her and moved quickly out of the way. Not because she wanted to stop working herself, but because she believed that the speed at which things were changing was better handled by the next generation.

"We will keep our eye on them," she had told Alberto. "But we have to give them a challenge."

Alberto had hesitated, considering whether he should be offended. Amelia was only seven years younger than he was. But Lella was right, as usual. Amelia was a handsome (rather than beautiful) woman whose stern nature surely hid her secret longings. She was rather cold toward Alberto and that made him edgy. At any rate, Amelia was being groomed to take his place. The company certainly needed a mix. Innovation was good, but one had to consider the finance and legal divisions. They had to rely on deep experience. The problem wasn't finding eager young people. It was finding experienced people who were staying on top of what was going on in the world. *Put the two together*, Alberto thought, and you have a winning solution.

There was still a lot to do. Alberto sighed, put his list in the drawer of his desk. He looked at his watch. He still had time to stop home and change, if he took the scooter. He went down to the courtyard where he kept his Vespa, and wove his way through the traffic, still preoccupied by his changing world.

51

Architects and old crushes

Mel was in her favorite spot by the window in her room, enjoying the low evening sun. Daylight savings time was such a boost to her morale. She still had plenty of time to get ready for dinner. She had made some calls in the morning, and then headed to the expats' bar-café (with the excuse of getting a sandwich) to check out the scene. There was a board with some hand-written notices about events and opportunities, so she took a couple of photos with her phone. Then she took the afternoon off. She wasn't expecting anything from this dinner (except perhaps that Giorgio Monti might be willing to see her at his studio sometime), but she didn't want her self-esteem to be polluted by another disappointing day.

She got up and went into the bathroom to dry her hair. She put on a pair of navy chinos and a blue and white oxford shirt. Then she thought it looked too butch. The women in Milan seemed pretty masculine in their dress. But she wasn't a Milanese woman, and didn't want to try too hard. She decided to wear a chambray shirt. Nothing says "American" like work clothes. She selected a handmade belt and some turquoise earrings. Lella came down the steps, tapping on the wall.

"Perfect," she said.

"It doesn't look too *Ralph Lauren*?"

Lella laughed, "No, not at all. It looks like you. Would you like to come up and help me prepare the *aperitivo*?"

Together, they went up the stairs and emerged from the wall of books.

* * *

"I'm always happy to see Lella," Giorgio Monti said to Alberto in the elevator.

"And she you," Alberto replied. "She has also invited her guest, a young American architect. I'm sure it will be a big deal for her to meet you."

52

"That's nice," said Giorgio politely, apparently not too interested. He saw plenty of American architects. They came to his studio to fawn over his work, especially during the *Salone del Mobile*, the Furniture Fair, in April, when many of them were in town. Lella, on the other hand, was someone he was always looking for opportunities to see. Ever since Paolo passed away he had been watching, waiting. He didn't want to approach too soon, nor wait too long. She was so self-sufficient and independent and, well, perfect. They had known each other for so long, being from the same "tribe," and now they were both free.

Alberto smiled and looked down at the elevator floor.

"I'm here to even things out at the table, you know," he said. He didn't want Giorgio to think this was a setup to meet Melinda, so he let him believe that this was an attempt of his to get Lella back into socializing with potential romantic partners. What harm was there in it? Giorgio was a successful, active, and passionate man. He didn't have a lot of baggage.

As the elevator approached the fifth floor, Lella was in the kitchen putting olives into a tiny bowl on a tray. She turned to Mel.

"Giorgio is a very nice man, you will see. My only concern is that he used to have a crush on me when we were both married. I didn't want to complicate my life. Paolo was never around, true...but then he got sick and, well, that was it. Giorgio is divorced now, and his wife is happy, but our history makes me feel a little guarded."

Mel looked troubled.

"I am so sorry if you are having him over for my sake, if you're not comfortable."

"No, no, I can handle it. You know, maybe we can use this to our advantage. For, you, I mean. By the way, I asked Amelia and Umberto to stop by for a drink before dinner, to make things more relaxed." She wiped her hands on a linen kitchen towel and went to answer the door.

Mel followed her, setting the tray on the coffee table, and hung back for a minute while everyone said hello at the door. They all knew each other so well, which made her feel awkward and conspicuous. Giorgio was tall and tan, his longish, curly hair graying at the temples. He had a beautiful, confident smile without that intense look that he wore for magazine photos. Alberto made his way over to Mel to say hello.

"And here is Melinda, Giorgio," he said. Giorgio came over and gave Mel his hand.

"It's lovely to meet you."

"It's an honor for me, *Architetto*," Mel replied.

"Just call me Giorgio, please."

Lella excused herself and went to get a bottle of spumante and some glasses. Giorgio followed behind her to help.

Alberto leaned over to Mel on the sofa and whispered, "We are playing at decoys, so just act naturally." He took two glasses from the tray Lella carried and handed one to Mel. They all raised their glasses and took a sip. Then they picked at the focaccia and olives on the table while making small talk.

Alberto was monopolizing Mel, offering to show her the view of Gio Ponti's building from the balcony. Mel's guard was down, and she was relieved to evade any inquiries from Giorgio Monti about what brought her here and anything else that would make her feel observed.

Amelia arrived and was greeted with enthusiasm by Giorgio. She asked him about his niece Gabriella, a good friend of hers whom she hadn't seen in ages. You know how busy it gets!

She glanced at Alberto and Mel out on the balcony laughing together, and took Lella aside.

"So Mami, what is this?" she subtly tilted her head toward the pair outside.

"Pfff! Nothing," Lella answered, dismissively.

Alberto caught Lella's eye and opened the door for Mel to return inside.

"Melinda, this is my daughter Amelia," Lella said proudly.

"It's so nice to meet you," Mel said.

"It's my pleasure. I'm sorry that my brother couldn't come. He had some date or something at the last minute." Amelia smiled apologetically, and kissed Alberto.

Lella and Amelia were skilled at keeping the conversation general, involving everyone. First they talked about how much they were enjoying the mild weather. Then they started to discuss the mayor's latest initiatives. Then Amelia turned to Mel and asked her about the political atmosphere in the States.

"Well, I'm not an expert in politics," she said shyly, "but things seemed to be increasingly skewed."

They waited for her to continue.

"I think it begins with the unfairness of our education. Poor children start out with such a disadvantage, and then they grow up without opportunities..."

"And we know how that turns out," offered Alberto.

"Yes," Mel agreed, "and the divide is not so much between the north and the south, but rather the cities and the rural areas." Having said this, she began to feel more confident.

"And, there is a fundamental defensiveness among many Americans that I can't reconcile with our place in the world."

Then Mel thought she had said too much, and looked down at her wineglass.

"Like the elephant afraid of mice," Lella suggested.

Giorgio nodded, "I think about the treatment of the African Americans, and the native tribes. How is that the basis for a democracy that prides itself on freedom?"

Mel allowed the others to take up the conversation, looking from one of them to the next as they each expressed their opinion.

"We all love America, you know," Alberto said. "It's in our nature to criticize, but we do it with affection." He touched her hand.

Lella stood up. "I'd better check the pasta."

"I have to go Mami," said Amelia. "It was good to meet you, Melinda. I'm sure we'll meet again soon."

Alberto walked Amelia to the door.

"So what's going on with the *americana*, Alberto?"

"Pfff! Nothing! I was just giving Giorgio an opening with your mother."

Amelia looked at him suspiciously.

"Okay cousin," she said, air-kissing him goodbye.

* * *

At the dinner table Giorgio was full of praise for Lella's cooking which, by any standard, was quite good. Lella continued to deflect this praise, and asked him about the work in his studio.

Giorgio described a few projects, some involving common acquaintances, and seemed happy to have an opportunity to mention his successes to Lella.

"Alberto," he said, turning his gaze to his friend, "do you know that Susanna is going to renovate her *rustico* on the lake?" He turned to Mel and added, "Alberto and I spent many weekends in this little stone house—now falling apart—in the hills above Lake Como."

56

"It's a charming place, with a beautiful, overgrown garden and an incredible view," Alberto added. Then, turning to Giorgio he said, "So what is she going to do, ruin her beautiful ruin?"

"Absolutely not! She wants to have more bedrooms, and larger bathrooms. You know, use it more often and hopefully attract her kids there..." He paused to take a sip of wine. "...While keeping the character intact."

"Do you remember, Alberto, how the entry drive just comes straight off the road at the back of the house?"

Alberto chuckled, "*Si, si*! I remember scraping the stucco with my car once, trying to park in that tiny space."

"Well, I had this idea to turn the drive to the right, and make it sweep around, so you descend more gradually and get a view of the lake when you arrive. Then, the house emerges in front of you." Giorgio held up his hands, framing the imaginary view.

"What about that magnificent group of Cedars? Will you be able to save those?"

"Of course. The drive will stay on the inside edge of the Cedars. The trees will conceal the view of the new structure from the lake. The cars will be below the terrace, so once they are parked, you won't see them anymore. Neither from the house nor the lake."

"It sounds lovely," Mel said. The wine was starting to embolden her. She felt like she had to say something, difficult though it was.

Alberto suggested, "Would it be possible to show it to Melinda some time?"

Mel wanted to slide under the table. Why was Alberto doing this? She didn't want Giorgio Monti to be put on the spot; it was too awkward.

Giorgio looked around the table, stalling.

Lella made a save: "I would like to go too! Perhaps we could have lunch at the *Trattoria Giuliana*. Is Susanna around?"

"No," Giorgio said. "She's in France for a week. But I have the keys. I was going to go on Saturday to meet a contractor, at ten o'clock."

"Perfect," Lella said. "We can drive together and look around while you talk with your contractor, and afterward we can have lunch."

Mel was very still, and felt her face warming, usually a sign of embarrassment. Only this time it was due to suppressed excitement.

Alberto poured Mel another glass of wine. Mel thought he seemed amused, probably because she felt so uncomfortable. It felt affectionate, but also a little condescending.

Lella turned to Giorgio, "Melinda has shown me one of her projects, very interesting. It's a little house outside of New York."

Alberto appeared interested, wanting to preempt Giorgio's possibly indifferent response. He thought Giorgio was a bit of a snob, despite all of his good qualities.

"Can you tell us about it?" Alberto asked.

"Well," Mel began, "it wasn't really mine. It was a project of the firm where I was employed."

They all waited for her to continue.

"What I showed Lella was a concept that I developed side-by-side with the lead architect's idea. My version was based on a conversation with our client about the way he wanted to experience his house. I did a few drawings and a sketch model. But it was never shown to the client, and we used the lead architect's plan."

Out of curiosity, Giorgio asked her, "Do you think the other architect's idea was more practical? Or what was the advantage of it?"

58

Mel considered how to answer. If she claimed that her idea was a better one, she might appear uppity and insubordinate. On the other hand, if she ceded her position, she might be seen as weak and ineffective. She didn't know how to play this, and then she scolded herself for trying to play it at all.

"Well," she ventured, "I like my solution, but we didn't develop it to the point where a fair comparison could be made. You'd have to see it, I guess."

Mel noticed that Alberto's expression relaxed at her response. He seemed pleased.

Why? She wondered. Did he feel responsible for making the introduction, even responsible for her behavior and personal qualities?

She realized that she didn't want to disappoint him, regardless of his motives.

That was her way, she mused. She always focused on the perception of others. If someone reacted negatively to her words or behavior, she would crumble. So much depended on people thinking well of her. After all, that's why her relationship with Jonathan failed. His mother thought her unworthy, and he hadn't defended her.

Stop thinking about that!

Lella suggested that they take a look at the drawings. She and Giorgio cleared the dishes and disappeared into the kitchen.

Mel looked at Alberto.

"I understand and appreciate that you have arranged this meeting," she said in her quietest voice, "but I don't want Giorgio to feel obliged."

"You'll be fine," Alberto said, with a downward gesture of his hand. "I'd like to see the drawings, too."

He walked over to the bookshelves and started to clear a reading table that ran parallel to the shelves.

"We can lay them here."

Mel started down the steps.

"If I'm not back in five minutes, please call the resuscitation squad."

Alberto was smiling. He liked the idea of having a protégé of sorts, and Melinda seemed so in need. That's the thing about Americans, he thought. So wet behind the ears in so many ways. Just the same, Melinda had some kind of spark, he could tell. After all, she had come here without any guarantees that she would succeed. It was curious how she lurched forward, and then made a hasty retreat. He wanted to understand this mechanism better.

Mel laid the drawings on the table. They included diagrams, plan sketches, and a rough cross-section. There were also several photos of a model she had made from corrugated cardboard.

"I prefer making models with my hands," she explained. "Computer modeling is okay for presenting but not so good for thinking."

"So," Mel began, "our client, Richard, expressed an interest in having an escape for the weekend. The site is small, and the house needed to be small, too. I wanted to avoid a miniature version of a standard house plan, with the entry and hall and everything in the expected location."

"A good instinct," Lella said, looking at the others.

Mel smiled, and took a breath.

"I asked Richard to describe his desired sequence of actions when arriving at his getaway. He wrote these notes."

Melinda read from a piece of paper:

On my drive I have started to shed some of the worries and thoughts of my day. When I arrive, I pull my car into a protected space, but it isn't a garage with its automatic door sealing me off from my neighbors or sucking me into a void. I get out, grab my things and enter into a clean and quiet space where I meet nobody, not a person, nor a pet. In this space, I undergo a transformation. I set down my things. I take off my jacket, my watch, and my shoes. There is a shower, and some freshly laundered jeans, T-shirts and socks. Before I enter the common space of the house, I am clean and fresh. I can see beautiful flowers in my garden. My daughter is picking basil, and I meet her before I enter the kitchen, giving her a kiss. My wife Marie waves to me from her office as she finishes a call. My son is in the next room, stretched out on the couch, reading. He gets up and joins us in the kitchen, where we work together to make dinner and talk about our day.

Melinda looked up at the others.

"This little story inspired me to create these sketches. The carport is parallel to the road, here, and has a plant-covered wall facing the road. There is a small, hidden garage beyond it that is used in the winter, which can be a workroom for the garden in the summer. It has windows facing the road. The neighborhood is dense, and the lots are small, so we are right at the setbacks all around. Alongside the garage, going into the house, is what I call the decompression chamber. It has shelves and cubbyholes with clothes and slippers, and a cushioned bench. Behind the wall on the left is the laundry—out of sight. Here is a hatch to toss the soiled clothes inside. Behind the wall to the right is a bathroom with a shower, small but adequate. These rooms each have a band of windows along the top of their walls—a clerestory—so the light and air can flow through while maintaining privacy."

"So," Alberto confirmed, "you walk in, take off your work clothes, and make them disappear to the left. Then you step in the shower to the right?"

"Yes," answered Mel. "And this block of three rooms is up several steps from the garage, so the upper windows clear the garage's flat roof, which is also a terrace." She moved her finger across the sketches and details to illustrate her story.

"Then," she continued, "there are two possibilities. You can exit the bath directly into this enclosed garden (which is also connected to the kitchen, here); or, you can exit from the middle chamber through a wide hallway with large bands of glass on both sides, and benches (here) along the walls under the windows. From this passage you can see the little kitchen garden to your right, and another garden space between the garage and Marie's office, to the left. You see here," she pointed, "you could also enter the house through this gate from the drive into the kitchen garden, as most guests would do. And the glass hallway is wide enough to set up the children's table between the benches when they have a large party."

"I see also that the kitchen is the central element of your first floor plan," Giorgio said. He paused. "It works well, *complimenti!*"

But Giorgio was now tired of looking at designs for the day. He turned to Lella.

"Now, unfortunately, I have to go. I have an early start tomorrow. But we will see you again on Saturday, no? I will discuss the details with Alberto on the way home."

In the elevator, Alberto chatted up Mel's work.

"I really liked the little cardboard model in the photos, too."

"Sure," Giorgio answered, looking at Alberto, trying to determine his motivation. Then he said, "Lella looks great. Is she going out much these days?"

But he was already weighing the advantage, with Lella, of showing some interest in Mel.

Alberto drove Giorgio home on his scooter, making his way through the crooked streets to Brera. When they arrived, Giorgio handed him his helmet, and opened the *portone.*

Alberto waved and took off, as the *portone* fell closed, and the latch caught with its characteristic sound.

Giorgio entered his apartment, and looked around at the studied perfection of it. The rich leather sofa; the vintage Modern coffee table; the deep, cozy armchairs, the brilliantly colored rug on the polished wood floor. He could just imagine Lella sitting in the peacock blue chair, her silver hair tied up, and a glass of wine in her hand. Or, walking up the five steps to the raised level where his library was kept, her hand elegantly poised on the mahogany railing.

He set his keys down, took off his coat and wandered into the kitchen to get some water. He saw the two of them there, making dinner together, laughing. He walked into the bedroom and looked at his luxurious, empty bed. How glorious it would be to walk in and see her there in her silk dressing gown, taking off her earrings, in a cloud of lavender sheets and down. He would walk slowly over the silver carpet, the happiest man in the world, sharing everyday life with Lella.

In the city outside, friends said good night, pulled out of their parking spaces, and drove home in their cars, circling their own blocks looking for another place to land. They, too, unlocked the street doors and heard them swing shut, and catch, as their footfalls echoed in the cobbled courtyards. Elevators were called, stairs were climbed, apartment doors were closed and locked behind the urban warriors now safely inside their places of refuge. Shoes were removed, jackets strewn, makeup removed, teeth brushed, and faces examined in mirrors. And there was the bed, such a welcome sight, and the book on the nightstand. Tomorrow is on its way here, and there will be much to do.

Jonathan digs in

Jonathan was pumped. It was Friday morning, initiation was over, and he had a full day in the studio to work. His fridge was stocked, and he had the whole weekend ahead. Last night he had arranged everything in the studio apartment, made a simple pasta with garlic, oil, and hot pepper. Then, unable to sleep, he had watched a movie from his laptop. He still missed Mel, wondered where she was, had forgiven her; blamed himself.

This morning he felt much better: he had work to do, despite the fact that his charge was actually standing around watching other people. He left, going into the studio through the courtyard rather than using the door from his back hall. He didn't want to seem like the resident troll.

Jonathan went into his office to get his notepad. Then he paused and thought that maybe that wasn't such a good idea. It looked too much like he was reporting on the crew and noting their "mistakes." He went into the studio space empty handed.

Reiner and Geert were setting up for a shoot in the cubicle closest to the reception area, which they called Cubi-1. Lucy set down a tray with espressos and cappuccinos, and was collecting money from them.

Reiner was pairing the equipment with their power sources, checking lenses, and going to the Cage next to Pierpaolo's office to get more gadgets. He had a set of keys hooked to a belt loop on the back of his black jeans, one of which was the coveted Cage key. Geert was playing around with fill cards and diffusers, putting them within reach for Enrico, who was running a little late.

"This *caffè americano* is for Enrico. He has been having stomach problems," said Lucy, as she turned to Jonathan. "I got you an *espresso*. I hope that's okay?"

"Sure, thanks, Lucy," answered Jonathan. He slowly selected some coins from a small pile in his hand, and gave them to her. Then he took a tiny sip from his espresso. He had just enough in his mouth to savor its flavor and power. It was deep and bitter and rich. He imagined the caffeine permeating the tissue in his mouth, going through his palette straight into his brain. Then he downed the rest of it.

While Reiner was at the Cage, Geert turned to Jonathan.

"We're trying to set this up for conflicting lighting requirements. Leitizia has laid out this table setting and is coming back with the food."

Jonathan looked over his shoulder, concerned about discussing the shoot in Reiner's hearing.

"Do you want to make the background stuff flatter?" Jonathan asked, helping Geert to see what he was thinking.

"Yeah, we want the food to pop. It will be a dish of pasta."

Reiner was making his way back across the atrium, alongside Enrico, who had just arrived. Jonathan sat back in a swivel chair he had wheeled across the atrium, concentrating on his new colleagues and closing off the peripheral stuff that was creating static. He wheeled himself back a few feet to get all three of them in the picture, and became quiet.

Reiner looks disappointed, Jonathan thought. Maybe he wants to be in charge and feels upstaged by Enrico. Geert is like a puppy: friendly and a little overactive. He seems aware of the tension between Reiner and Enrico, using humor to create a screen. Enrico came into Cubi-1 with an intense, critical look. He was embarrassed about being late, something he himself wouldn't tolerate in an assistant. Jonathan pondered this scene for a few moments, and then directed his gaze into Cubi-2, which was next to the inner court garden. The light coming through the window was soft and diffuse.

The three assistants started jockeying the tasks at hand. Reiner was mounting the camera lenses, and Geert was metering light and adjusting the fill cards.

"The food should be primarily lit from above, I think," said Enrico. His phone made a noise and he fired a text off as he walked away from the equipment to grab an espresso from the tray that Lucy held out to him. "Listen, *cara*, would you mind terribly ordering me a *broiche*?"

Jonathan held up a finger to second the request.

Enrico was now standing by Jonathan, and said hello, keeping his eyes on the setup on the pedestal in the cubicle.

"So, what do you think, *Jonatan*?" he said, nonchalantly.

"I'm only here to observe," Jonathan replied.

Enrico nodded, kept his eyes averted, but didn't go anywhere.

"But since you've asked," Jonathan continued discreetly, "I just happened to notice that there is some nice natural light in Cubi-2."

"Won't work for the food."

"No, but it would be perfect for the place setting. Maybe Reiner would be interested in doing a background photo and printing it."

Enrico looked up with eyebrows knit, thinking, then added, "He can shoot it with the the Hasselblad and the Zeiss 50, from above."

"Lucy!"

Lucy ended her call with the bar-café and came over with her quick high-heeled steps.

"Check the print paper supply for the Super Matte variety, please," Enrico said, and get Leitizia back here, now." Then he approached Reiner.

Jonathan watched with interest.

"Reiner, what do you think about doing the place setting in Cubi-2 with natural light? We can take a cool, flat background photo, and shoot the food on the print."

Reiner froze, considering.

"It's not a bad idea. How will we work the lighting in the second round?" He was looking into Cubi-1 thoughtfully.

Enrico looked at Jonathan, wanting to be sure that he was thinking along the same lines. Jonathan was mouthing something and making a shape with his hand, like a catcher's glove, where Reiner couldn't see it.

"Beauty dish," Enrico said, "and let's come at it from the opposite direction. If you get the camera set up, Geert and I can measure the light in Cubi-2 and complement it here."

"Do we have suitable paper?"

"Lucy is checking. Once you have the setup, maybe you could check the R2400, for the print."

Reiner looked pleased. He was going to be in charge of producing a *perfect* background that would have to be convincing in the second shoot, no reflections.

Enrico patted him on the back and walked over to Geert to explain how the shoot was going to work.

Enrico wasn't officially in charge of the shoot, but since he had been there the longest, everyone deferred to his judgement in absence of Pierpaolo. Elena was usually around to settle any differences, focusing on time expenditure (and she wouldn't like this; it was going to take longer) and "what the client wanted."

Jonathan felt awkward just sitting there, so he was relieved when Leitizia came, allowing him to help her with all the stuff she was carrying.

Pierpaolo came in with Elena. They had been at an agency meeting.

Since everyone was bustling in the cubicles, Jonathan explained what was going on, as he understood it.

Pierpaolo looked at Jonathan blankly. He was good at concealing his thoughts when he wanted to. Jonathan tried to read him. Was it doubt about the capability of his crew?

Pierpaolo turned to Reiner.

"How long before you're ready for me?"

"Another hour, at best," Reiner answered. He was standing in the light of the window, his long blonde hair concealing his cheek, as he bent over his work. It reminded Jonathan of a Vermeer painting. He pulled out his phone and took a couple of shots.

Pierpaolo nodded, and skipped across the atrium, trading Lucy his leather bomber for an espresso, and went into his office.

Elena helped Leitizia with the props.

"We need the place setting, ten minutes ago," said Reiner.

Leitizia looked at Elena and smiled.

Mel gets serious

On Friday morning, Lella called down the stairs to Mel.

"Melinda, come up and have coffee with me?"

Mel was just about to put the espresso in the *caffettiera* "down under" (Lella's name for the lower level). She put on her shoes and joined Lella in the kitchen upstairs. They sat at a small table in the corner by the window. The kitchen was furnished with beautiful, stainless steel appliances, and the countertops were in Carrara marble: white with veins of gray. The floor tiles were white, dark gray, and a blue the color of a robin's egg. The window trim was painted to match the robin's egg blue, and there were no curtains.

"I hate them," Lella had told Mel.

The table was set with hand-painted dishes, and a plate of soft croissants sat in the center. The *caffettiera* was still emitting its final gurgles, just removed from the burner. Lella filled a tiny pitcher with warm milk. Mel studied the little cherries decorating the saucers and cups. *Cherries are decidedly a happy fruit*, she thought. She remembered going to pick them at the farm near her childhood home. It really felt like summer had arrived when the cherries were ripe. She wondered where they grew cherries in Italy.

"So, what did you think about last night?" Lella asked.

"I thought Giorgio was very attentive to you," Mel responded.

Lella frowned, looking at Mel askance as she served herself.

Mel continued, "It was very kind of you to mention my work, but I was not prepared to show it, especially after a couple of glasses of wine! Every time I took a sip, Alberto poured more, so I have no idea how much I drank."

"Well, how do you feel today?"

"Fine."

"It was good wine." Lella laughed.

"These croissants are fabulous, Lella," Mel said. Their flaky softness melted like butter in her mouth.

"I asked the baker to get the ones in back, those that just came out of the oven."

"They're perfectly done. I hate it when they get hard and dry."

Mel poured some coffee into the cup with the little painted cherries, and then added some milk.

Lella returned to the subject of Giorgio.

"I think he was impressed with your little project."

"Well, it didn't actually get built." Mel wondered why she always came back to playing down her own work.

"But the design is what interests someone like Giorgio."

"You know, I wonder. Going around to the studios, it seems like they are one-person shows, with assistants doing the production work, greeting clients when they come in, and making coffee."

"There are many places like that, but you'll see. Giorgio has too many projects to be deeply involved with all of them. His studio is more diversified."

Mel looked up.

"He didn't mention anything about meeting at his studio."

"Did you ask him?"

"I don't have the courage to do that!" Mel laughed. "What do I have to offer him? He probably has a cadre of young Italian designers..."

Lella cut her off, a little disappointed.

"Then I guess you shouldn't ask him, if you have so little faith in yourself."

Mel felt ashamed. She didn't want Lella to think badly of her, and she desperately wanted to remain friends after she moved out at the end of the month.

"You know what I can do," she said, thinking aloud, "I can ask him if it would be possible to visit his studio to see what he's working on. I mean, if the atmosphere is right on Saturday."

"That is up to you, I suppose," said Lella. She got up and put her hand on Mel's shoulder.

"If they are roses, they will flower," she said in Italian, and left the room.

Mel took the last sip of her caffé-latte, and went down to get her things. She had a couple of appointments today. One was at a furniture showroom, not the greatest position, but she wanted to keep an open mind.

And then, she had an aperitivo with Lella and Amelia to look forward to at the end of the day.

* * *

Mel's first appointment was with *Architetti Associati*, a three-person partnership in a neighborhood called *Zona Solari*, north of the *Naviglio Grande*, one of Milan's remaining two canals. Mel took the metro to the Porta Genova stop and walked the rest of the way. She walked along a street with the usual bar-cafés, bakeries and the odd hardware or housewares stores. There was a mix of decrepit, semi-industrial, and newly renovated architecture. The neighborhood was changing. Many of the buildings were tinted in that ochre that was prevalent throughout the city. Lella had explained that the color was called *giallo Maria Teresa*, or Maria Teresa's yellow, after the Hapsburg archduchess who reigned over Milan when it was part of the Austrio-Hungarian Empire. According to the story (about which Lella was doubtful) their sovereign dictated the use of warm colors on the buildings to cheer the otherwise gray city.

The shops dwindled in number as Mel turned onto a side street. The buildings were attached as one continuous block, distinguished by changes in detail or color; sometimes only by their street number. The ground floors were finished in gray rusticated stone, with large openings for doorways, auto entrances, and the occasional restaurant window. Balconies with carved stone brackets and ornate railings cast shadows across the ochre facades, whose windows were framed by green shutters. The lower windows had iron bars on them. Across the street, a more austere building stood. It was made of poured concrete, with a smooth, putty-colored finish. Its doors and windows were metal, painted green, and on the ground floor, graffiti covered the available flat surfaces. A blue sky dotted with puffy clouds was reflected in the broad windows on the two upper stories. Alberto had told Mel about the air raids carried out by the English in World War II, and the destruction of buildings caused by explosive and incendiary bombs. After the war, there was a highly unregulated building boom, and that, he said, explained the heterogenous building patterns in some parts of the city.

This modern building was Mel's destination. She crossed the street, skirting the parked cars that were stacked tightly along both sides. There was no street life here, and the quiet was interrupted only by the *portone* latches closing as the doors fell to, or the occasional backup signal of a delivery truck.

The studio of *Architetti Associati* was a loft space, with a forest of square concrete columns, and a concrete floor painted a blue-gray. A metal grid with lighting fixtures hung over the workspace, creating a dropped ceiling effect. At one end, there was a long, worn wooden table. The three partners, Sylvia, Sergio, and Marco converged there to receive Mel.

"Would you like a coffee?" Sergio asked.

"Thank you," said Mel, smiling, after wondering whether saying yes would be a disturbance, or saying no would impede them from having one. "I would like that."

The three partners went through the usual routine of telling their respective stories, looking at Mel's work, and politely complimenting her. She had given up trying to understand whether they (or anyone she had seen) were sincere or not, because they invariably nodded approvingly. Mel wondered if Giorgio Monti would react the same way if he looked at all of her work, or if he would sniff and look distracted when–and if–she presented it to him.

The coffee came around and there was a moment of small talk. Mel looked around at the handful of designers working at their tables, some on computers, some laying out drawings or material samples.

Sylvia mentioned that their studio was a diverse collection of foreigners.

"They come and work for a while, then (because, as you know, the pay is not great), they leave to go elsewhere or home." We have a couple of more steady people like Midori, who is from Japan; and Mario, who is from Sicily.

"Which," added Sergio, "is somewhat of a foreign country."

Sylvia looked at him in mock disapproval.

"He is joking," she said.

Marco looked like he wanted to move on to his next activity, and made a move to conclude the meeting.

"Melinda, why don't you give us some time to discuss among ourselves. We do have people coming and going every few months or so. If we have your number, we can call you. Your work looks good. We just need to see an opening, and the right project opportunity. Is that agreeable?"

His eyes moved around the group, and everyone nodded.

Mel thanked them, left her card, and made her way down the dark stairs and out the metal door. It created a harsher sound than the heavy wooden doors in the old buildings when it closed. She decided to walk over to the canal and return home by a different route. It was cool, but the sun was out and she needed the exercise.

Mel went through the list of studios she had visited in her head, trying to remember all of the details. While she hadn't received any negative responses, there were no commitments either. She thought this might be due to the low "salaries." Marino Contini had given her a figure, and the others had simply mentioned that they couldn't offer much. She would be paid under the table, no way around it, until she became a resident.

So there was the question of a living situation to resolve. She had two weeks left at Lella's. If she could find a cheap place with some other expats, she might be able to make it work. She was stalling. Why? She fished in her pocket for the piece of paper with the phone number she had taken down from the board in the bar-café in Corso Magenta.

"Reiner H.," she read. Mel thought she would have lunch and call this guy. There was no harm in meeting him. Then she could make a list. Lists always helped her. She could write down all the pros and cons of the studios she had visited so far. She was going to have to make a decision about where she wanted to work, and then make her interest clear. She had a few more studios to visit, but she couldn't wait to try and close a deal. So, next week, she thought, she would mix first and second visits.

She found a little pizzeria near the head of the larger canal, the *Naviglio Grande*, and ducked inside. While she waited for her order, she called the guy named Reiner.

Wrapping up the shoot

Everyone in Pierpaolo Nervi's studio was happy about the food shoot. They were dismantling the equipment by 3PM, choosing to work through lunch because it was Friday and nobody wanted to risk working late.

Jonathan was helping Leitizia pack up the props and took the opportunity to get to know her better.

"So, where do you want to go, Leitizia?"

"You mean, tonight?"

Jonathan laughed. "No, I mean, where do you want to go with your work?"

Geert walked by with some gear and leaned into their space.

"She has a boyfriend."

Leitizia laughed, "Go away, Geert." Then she turned back to Jonathan.

"I love this work, and, well, I'm absorbing so much in this environment. I guess I haven't really thought much about the future. I mean, the present is a challenge."

"How many studios are you working with?"

"Let's see," she looked up, counting by nods of her head. "It varies, but I would say five regular clients. Maybe I do one or two shoots a week for each."

"How much time are you on the books each week?"

"What do you mean?"

"How many hours can you actually bill per week, would you say?"

"Well, that is a problem. I have to search for merch, and sometimes pick it up myself... Then I have to restore and return it."

"So, you don't charge for that time?"

"I usually charge a fee for the shoot."

"Do you only do food?"

"No, I do advertising in general, some fashion. I have a store display background. I did this shoot because Elena couldn't get the food stylist she usually uses, and she thought I would do a good job."

"Well," said Jonathan, "I had some of the pasta, and it was delicious."

"My job is to make it look good, but I am happy it tasted good, too."

"Let's get back to your income, if you don't mind. Can you estimate at least how many hours a week you're working without getting paid?"

"I would say that some weeks, I am working through Saturday. But I think I generally have about one day and a half to two days, out of six, without paid work. I employ that time, of course, meeting people, scouting props, and marketing."

"Good, thanks... So tell me about your boyfriend."

Leitizia, laughed, embarrassed.

"His name is Stefano, and he's an art director."

"That's convenient."

Jonathan and Leitizia exchanged a few more words as he walked her toward the door with the bags, and said goodbye.

He turned around to survey the studio. Pierpaolo was in his office, Jonathan could see through the glass, with his feet on the desk, talking on the phone. Geert was winding some extension cords. Elena was talking to Reiner as he dismantled lenses, wiped them, and carefully returned them to their place in the Cage. He approached them. Reiner was feeling pretty good about the perfect print he created for the background of the shoot.

"It was a letdown when Pierpaolo dumped the spaghetti on it."

They laughed.

Jonathan said, "It worked out nicely, *complimenti!*" Then he paused.

"I was wondering what you were doing after? Want to go for a drink?"

Jonathan's voice was a little shaky. He wasn't sure Reiner's day had gone so well that he was ready to consider being friends.

Reiner looked at his watch. "I have to go to an appointment at five with someone looking to share an apartment. I have a small room in mine that is available. But that will be done in less than an hour. If you want, we can all meet at *Bar Basso*. That's where I am meeting her." He shrugged his shoulders as if he could take it or leave it.

"Can you tell me how to get there?"

"Just take the *Metropolitana* to Piola. Then walk down to Via Plinio. You can't miss it. There is a neon sign in front."

Elena offered to enlist Enrico, and she crossed the atrium to Cubi-1, where he was dissembling the lights.

Jonathan was pleased that Reiner had softened a little, and maybe after a beer he would loosen up some more. Jonathan knew they all felt threatened by his *New York* experience. Whatever! He could tell that Reiner was a naturally precise and thorough person, and that was something that he valued. He needed to find a way to make him feel less defensive. Socializing was a way to do that; Reiner was clearly his superior there. He had a presence like a rock star.

"JONATAN!" Pierpaolo called from his office.

Jonathan smiled awkwardly at Reiner, and went to join Pierpaolo.

"So," Pierpaolo said, "was it a good day?"

"Sure," Jonathan replied, "I enjoyed seeing everyone at work. But it's frustrating not doing anything."

"Did you really not do anything? When I was giving Enrico my compliments, he mentioned something about your suggestion."

Jonathan was embarrassed. He tried to control it, but felt the tingling pink rising to his ears.

"It's just that we did a shoot like that once, and it seemed like Reiner wanted to be in charge of something."

"Well, good, and good," Pierpaolo said. "The instinct was correct. But don't be too worried about Reiner. He is a friendly porcupine. Be patient. And also we must be patient about you stepping into the jobs. Otherwise, you can't make a good assessment, no?"

"Absolutely, I get it," said Jonathan, rapidly coming down from his high about the day.

"Anything else?" Pierpaolo asked.

"I was wondering what is in the basement?"

Pierpaolo was happy to lead Jonathan down the dim stairs behind Cubi-1. The basement was quite large, and very dry. Light entered the space from two windows along the ground of the inner court garden. Through them, Jonathan could see the bottoms of the terra cotta pots outside. Pierpaolo flipped the light switch, filling the shadows with a more golden, artificial light. The space was an arrangement of tables and aisles, and looked like an archaeologist's workshop. There were props and broken things, pieces of wood and metal, boxes of hardware, and bolts of cloth. Rickety shelves sagging with their load lined the perimeter. A couple of pendant lamps with silver reflectors hung over each table.

"This is great!" Jonathan said.

Pierpaolo placed his hand on Jonathan's shoulder.

"I am glad that you are so easily pleased."

Bar Basso

Mel got off the *Metropolitana* at the Lima stop and then checked the location of Bar Basso on her phone when she surfaced. It was a straight shot down Via Plinio. She got there right about five o'clock. It was early for an aperitivo, but a few people were standing at the bar, chatting with the baristas, who were filling little dishes with savory treats and occasionally shaking a drink.

Mel walked in on this scene, immediately impressed by the atmosphere. She spotted a guy who didn't look at all Italian, and approached him.

"Reiner?"

"Hello," he said coolly. "You are Melinda?"

"Yes."

"I am having a beer. What would you like?"

Mel thought about for a minute. It seemed a pity to be in such a place and not order something that required a little skill to prepare. But then, she was meeting Lella and Amelia for a drink afterward and didn't want anything too strong.

The baristas were smooth and friendly, but they kept a respectful distance from their customers. One of them raised his eyebrows and leaned toward Mel expectantly. She explained her dilemma, and the barista offered to prepare just the right thing. A group of young artsy types came in the door.

"Those are students from the *Politecnico*," Reiner explained. "Architecture students."

"What do you do?" Mel asked.

"I work in a photo studio not far from here. But I studied philosophy in Germany." He shook his head, rolling his eyes.

"Oh," Mel said, distracted by the mention of photography. It made her think of Jonathan, a little regretfully, and of Cecil, very regretfully.

"I hung with photographers when I lived in New York."

No reaction.

Mel took a sip of the ruby colored drink that was handed to her.

"Oh, this is very nice," she said, smiling at the barista, "*Grazie.*"

Reiner was checking out the architecture students as he described the apartment's location and size, and the cost of the room he was looking to rent.

Mel explained that she was hoping to resolve her job search in another week or so, and wanted to be sure the commute wasn't inconvenient. Was he in a hurry to get a roommate? Her lips kept moving, to avoid embarrassment, but she was thinking, *this supercilious twit! I don't like him at all.*

Or was she reacting to the impression that he didn't like her?

Then his voice returned to her ears: "... and so I think if you want to wait a week, and then let me know if you want to see the place, that would be okay. But after next week, I'll want to get someone in there."

Mel turned to look straight at him. Objectively, he looked pretty hot with his long blonde hair and his black leather jacket with the lapels. She probably wasn't hip enough to warrant his attention.

"That's really nice of you. I'll be in touch before the end of next week."

She stepped outside where the architecture students were saying their goodbyes. She approached them to ask for directions, because she wanted to make contact with anyone who was friendly. Reiner had left a bad taste in her mouth. If her back hadn't been to the entrance, she might have seen Jonathan and Elena walking into the bar, chatting happily and remarking on the place.

"How was your meeting?" Jonathan asked Reiner.

"Fine," he shrugged. "An American. If you want to see her, she's outside talking to a group of students."

Jonathan craned his neck around the entry. The students were pulling away in their scooters, but Mel was already across the roundabout, obscured by a bright orange tram.

"Don't worry," Reiner said. "Plenty of Americans come here."

"I'm sure they do," said Jonathan, spearing a pearl onion with a toothpick.

"Elena, can I buy you a drink?"

Spumante with the ladies

Mel was feeling slightly altered by the bianco with a splash of Campari she had at Bar Basso. She got on the train and headed toward the Piazza del Duomo. She looked around at her fellow passengers. There were thirty-somethings in their jackets and ties, skirts and heels. Younger riders were on their phones making small gestures to swipe, enlarge, and text, sometimes sharing the screen with a friend. The older passengers were mostly Middle Eastern, African: immigrants weary of a day's work. They would ride into the center and out the other side of the city to reach the dingy housing for which they were grateful. But it wasn't home. Some of them had children, who went to school and learned Italian. They wriggled or pulled on their parents' coats like children everywhere, unaware of the struggle that awaited them. A father wore the determined face of one who will work himself to the bone to give his kid a better chance. He strokes his little girl's head and whispers to her. It was a definite dose of humanity, but nothing like the overly intimate urban-tattered jolting squeaking experience offered by New York's subway. But then, there was so much *more* humanity in New York.

Mel emerged from the *Metropolitana* and wandered down the crooked streets toward Via Brera and Bar Jamaica. As she approached the door, she saw Lella and Amelia taking a seat by the window.

"We may as well get a bottle," Lella said to Amelia as Mel approached.

"Is *spumante* okay for you, Melinda?"

"That would be lovely," Mel answered. She was a little flushed from her previous drink, and the walk, and her thoughts about Jonathan, and Cecil, and the little girl pulling her father's coat on the train.

"I hear you and Lella are going to see one of Giorgio Monti's projects on the Lake tomorrow," said Amelia.

"Yes," answered Mel, "I'm excited, although I'm a little nervous about it, too. Giorgio is somewhat intimidating."

"Alberto and I will be there to make you feel relaxed," said Lella.

"Alberto is going?" Amelia asked. She looked askance at Mel before turning to Lella, who nodded.

Mel looked down. For some reason, it seemed Amelia did not approve of of Alberto. There was something about her that intimidated Mel. She seemed strong, and a little defiant. Were Amelia's feelings about Alberto tied to competition at their publishing company?

"Just be careful of my cousin, Melinda," Amelia warned.

"Pfff!" Lella said, dismissively, "He is just trying to help her. You've probably taken so much work off his shoulders that he needs a little project."

Mel tried to change the subject, slightly.

"Did Giorgio and Alberto go to school together?"

"No," Lella answered, "Giorgio is older than Alberto. But years ago they went sailing together, and have been friendly ever since."

"That wouldn't have anything to do with Giorgio's interest in you, Mami?" Amelia suggested.

Mel listened to the teasing exchange between mother and daughter that continued, happy that the focus was on someone and something else. She was also not immune to the possible advantage of Giorgio's interest in Lella for her own prospects.

But what was she thinking? Was there any chance that she could get in to see Giorgio, one on one?

"What's the matter, Melinda?" asked Lella.

Mel recovered.

"Oh, nothing, I am just a little weary of the job hunt. It's hard on my ego, I guess. By the way, I met with someone today about an apartment share. He's a German photographer."

"Wasn't your boyfriend in New York a photographer?" Lella asked.

"Yes," Mel answered, "and I don't know if it's a good idea to live with someone who is going to remind me of him."

"But it's a world that you know, and that would give you some common ground," suggested Amelia.

"Well, that's true. But I also found him a little snobbish. You know, he is one of these avant-garde nihilist types in a motorcycle jacket. But he has given me a week to think about it."

A waiter came and topped off their glasses. Their conversation continued in a more general vein, and about people that Mel didn't know.

Amelia checked her phone, and said she had to leave. She leaned over to Mel and said, "Beware of the Italian male, and you will be fine."

Lella looked at Mel and said, "Let's go have dinner. I have some asparagus. We can make *risotto*."

Lago di Como

"Milano" comes from the Latin, *Mediolanum*, which means "in the middle of the plain." It is, in fact, like a city in a spouted skillet, the mountains gradually rising in every direction except the southeast, where the Po River valley carries water from the alpine regions to the Gulf of Venice, by way of the "spout."

This particular situation favors the settling of mist and fog in the morning hours in the cool season, as well as the accumulation of heat and humidity in the warm season. Nobody lives in Milan for the climate.

And yet Milan is the quintessential European, even global, Italian city. Its prominence in the world of design attracts visitors from all over the world. Collections of fashion and furniture are presented at regular intervals throughout the year, ensuring an influx of students, designers, and journalists. After a day of visiting showrooms, buyers from Bloomingdale's can be found combing the racks of the boutiques in Via della Spiga, discreetly, for their personal wardrobes. This wasn't New York, and they have to hide their urgency. At the end of that elegant, cobblestone street, a Japanese man and woman, dressed and groomed to perfection, exchange deep bows, and then part ways. The younger crowd, in search of opportunity and celebrity, take selfies backdropped by shop signs or shoes. The cafés and pastry shops are full, their customers jockeying for seats and a place to put their bags.

Mel thought of all these things as she sat in the back of Giorgio Monti's BMW, leaving the Design Capital for the first time since her arrival. As they wove through the Saturday morning traffic, breaking away to the north, her first perspective of Milan from the outside began to materialize.

She was sitting by Lella, who had declined Alberto's offer to sit in front. "This way I can show Melinda the sights."

The highway going north to Lake Como was less than scenic. It was sprinkled with manufacturer's showrooms and roadside billboards: furniture, fixtures, building materials. Prostitutes were sprinkled in the most unlikely places, tending to business travelers and truckers. Every big city has its "back room."

"We have to drive through hell to get to heaven," Alberto noted.

Then the landscape became greener, the mountains closer, and Mel caught a fleeting view down the long finger of the lake before they turned to the east and wound down into the city of Lecco. Eventually the lakefront reappeared; they turned north, ducking in and out of tunnels, experiencing a succession of light-dark-light-dark frames like an old time movie. Mel was adjusting to the speed, road widths, and curves, wondering if they would get to their destination without a scrape. Giorgio was talking animatedly, gesticulating. He didn't seem to be worried. They passed a small town, and then turned up the hillside. Giorgio eventually slowed down, and turned into the short drive that came up to the back of a small, two-story house in disrepair. There was a second, smaller structure (some sort of barn) upslope and beyond the house.

Most of the structures in the area were in masonry with roofs tiled in terracotta. They had functional shutters, often green, on all the windows. The settlements were arranged in dense clusters, like orange outcroppings in the green hills. The property was just beyond one of these. A little bit down the slope, a train passed.

Mel leaned against the car and took in the landscape. The lake was long and narrow, carved by the glacier that had long since retreated, winding through the rugged mountains that framed the view. These mountains were arranged in layers, like the wings on the set of a massive theater. Those nearer were green and richly textured, and the furthermost were two-dimensional silhouettes in blue-gray. Mel imagined the succession of unseen valleys, all leading north to the Alps. Behind her, the slope became steeper. They were on the east side of the lake, and the morning sun was just clear of the rock cliffs behind them. The faint hum of a scooter, hidden from view by trees with their first buds opening, announced spring. Mel felt a chill, and grabbed her sweater from the car.

Alberto was checking the wall of the house for evidence of his scrape of many years ago, as Giorgio greeted the contractor who had just arrived in his tiny Piaggio three-wheeled truck. Lella drew Mel toward the abandoned orchard alongside the house. They stopped to admire the lake.

"It's just beautiful," Mel said.

Lella smiled, enjoying Mel's awe of the landscape that she also loved.

"Yes, but I hope they don't alter this place too much. Did you notice those houses on the way up, so fixed-up and new looking? They have lost their character."

Below to the right Mel saw the stand of Cedars that Alberto had mentioned at dinner last week. They looked like hooded monks, confiding in one another, as they stood motionless on the hill. They allowed the view, but blocked the sight of the house from below. Oleander bushes continued the line across the slope. There was a small level area on the lake side of the house, partially paved with stone. Creeping groundcover filled the wide gaps in between. A rambling fig tree stood south of the house, before the orchard's gate.

Mel looked at Lella, shielding her eyes from the sun.

"The garden is perfect in this state of disarray. It has such a romantic atmosphere, as if we discovered it after many years."

"It's a witness to the passage of time, like a painting," Lella added.

"Or the dialogue between our actions and those of nature. And perhaps she should have the last word."

Alberto was hovering behind them, twirling a young leaf, and listening to them.

"The two of you are going to make me cry," he teased.

Giorgio, having bid farewell to the contractor, joined the group. He made them follow him along the path of the future driveway, which passed below the Cedars and curved back toward the back building between the Fig and the orchard. It would be a gravel road, he explained, like a country lane. Then they continued up toward the space between the two buildings.

"Now here, we are going to dig into the slope to create a room that connects the two structures. This won't give us much more square footage–the Town won't allow more. But we will have a connection to the barn through it, and so we can enclose everything, heat it, and portion the interior space. Technically, we are creating a 'root cellar,' although it will actually be the new kitchen. Some natural light will enter from the west, although most from a skylight. We are creating some underground storage in the hill, where we are also running a geothermal coil."

The group continued to meander around the property, splitting up, and then reuniting as their attention drew them here and there. At one point, Mel was upstairs in the main house with Giorgio. They were looking out of a lakeside window cut out of the thick, stuccoed wall.

"So, Melinda, I would like to ask you something."

Mel turned slowly, looking at Giorgio.

"I have had American assistants in the studio before. I found they were quite good at doing the technical drawings."

Mel's ears began to ring, something that happened when she was in a moment of guarded anticipation. She waited.

"But I am not sure," he continued, "that would be a good fit for you."

Mel tried to keep her composure.

"Well," she replied, "if I have to be honest, I find that work a bit tedious. But," she added, "I am very thorough and capable."

Now I am groveling, she thought.

"I am sure of it," Giorgio said, nodding, "although I have another project that I would like to talk with you about. It is not *exactly* architecture."

Alberto and Lella were coming up the stairs. Giorgio turned his attention to them. They all admired the view and discussed the merits of the small adjoining room and bath. Mel lifted the latch of the shutters on the uphill side, and swung them open, fastening them against the exterior wall. She thought about the decorative, "fake" ones used on the houses at home and sighed. These little gestures of opening and closing shutters, according to the light and temperature, were so graceful. She watched a little rabbit, frozen like a statue at the sound of her actions. She smiled at the similarity between them. The rabbit hopped off as she moved to release the fastener.

Giorgio held back as the others went down the stairs. His admiration of Lella's behind efficiently shifted to the practical means of acquiring access to it.

"So, Melinda, would you be available to meet me tomorrow at the studio? I know it's Sunday, but I'm booked the rest of the week."

"Of course, I would be happy to," she answered, feeling like the rabbit inside.

She followed him down the stairs hoping to hide the trembling of her legs. She stopped on the landing to get a grip. *This* was why she came to Italy, so that something like *this* would happen. She was having trouble adjusting to the actual possibility. It seemed too good to be true. Would she be able to convince him that she was good enough? Doubt began to overtake her.

Mel took a deep breath, trying to fend it off, and walked outside onto the gravel. There was a crunching under their feet as they made their way to the car. It pleasantly masked the sound of her heartbeat.

"I am getting hungry for fish," Alberto said, opening the door for Mel.

Jonathan explores Milano

On Sunday morning, Jonathan woke up, pulled on his jeans and a sweater, and headed to the bar-café across the street for a cappuccino and a soft, warm brioche. The day was drab, without fog. That meant it was going to be cloudy all day.

Jonathan loved shooting photos on gray days. Colors tended to pop without the sun washing them out. He decided that he would get some gear together and get lost in the center of the city.

There were some older men in the bar playing cards. It was the game called *Scopa.* Jonathan had learned it from his "Italian" grandfather. How ironic that his great-grandparents left Germany for Italy in the early 1930's, and that his grandad Josef was born in Ferrara. That was when they went by the name Guttmann. What if they had stayed there? Would he, Jonathan, be here today? He guessed they hadn't wanted to take any chances. They left Italy when Josef was a little boy—was it in 1938? He couldn't remember. Now *he* was here. Was he escaping something, or looking for something?

Jonathan could not drain all of the foam from his cappuccino, so he scooped it out with his spoon. Then he headed back across the street to his apartment and got properly dressed and equipped for his outing. He had a date to meet Reiner at noon.

* * *

Milan is encircled by two rings. The inner ring marks the location of an ancient canal system, now roads, connected to the *Castello Sforzesco,* the castle. The outer ring marks the location of the Roman walls and the gateways to the city. These days, they are both important public transportation routes. You ride around the city center on the ring roads, and then go in or out along the radials.

Jonathan took the *Metropolitana* a couple of stops, then walked to the outer ring. Here was a leafy boulevard with the tram running down the center. Soon the orange vehicle appeared, embellished with the crest of the City of Milan, clanging a warning as it approached a crosswalk. Jonathan climbed aboard and sat on the varnished wooden seat. He was going to the gateway called the Porta Ticinese, near a docking basin where the two remaining radial canals originated. The tram wasn't the fastest way to get there, but he wanted to see the city by traveling above ground.

The Porta Ticinese appeared as an imposing, arched structure in a rather confusing piazza. Once he got off the tram, Jonathan studied the sequence of crosswalks, and made his way through the traffic to the closest of the two canals. He stood before the headwall, and looked straight down the waterway. There were little pedestrian bridges, accessed by stairs on either side, at regular intervals.

The neighborhood was charming. The buildings were only a few stories high, stuccoed in warm tones, their roofs tiled in terra cotta. They were very old, although undergoing a steady renewal. The roads along each side of the canal were paved in stone, and the traffic was limited. People walked and rode bikes, moving to the side when a resident's car or a delivery vehicle needed to pass. There were small cafés and trattorias, but not much in the way of neighborhood shops. Jonathan imagined that rising rents had pushed those out to make room for the gentry, as evidenced by the occasional specialty shop or fashionable business. It's the same everywhere, as the Italians say: *tutto il mondo é paese.*

Arched entryways allowed a peek into courtyards paved in cobbles and lined with potted trees and shrubs. The apartments on the upper levels were reached by exterior passageways railed in wrought iron, from where you could look down and wave to your arriving friends after you had buzzed them in.

One of the buildings was hidden by scaffolding. Rolls of netting made a gauzy veil, hiding the façade like a bride's veil. Jonathan made his way to one of the little bridges, ascended the stairs, and leaned on the parapet, looking back toward the city. He photographed reflections, fixtures, and details. He saw an open-air laundry in an alley. Angled wash stones were embedded in the ground, and a tiled timber roof once shielded the women from the sun as they scrubbed. The narrow rectangular pool of water was dark and still, a window to the past.

Jonathan crossed the canal and started wandering through the labyrinth of back streets, still in transition from a poor to a wealthy quarter. He thought of how fascinating the layers of a city were: peeling off, adapting, resurfacing; evolving contagiously through unrelenting change. This was a hard city to read at first glance. It wasn't Florence, that three-dimensional museum of the Renaissance, with its perfectly proportioned solids and voids and consistent vocabulary of detail. It wasn't Rome, with it luscious curves and attenuated domes, all sensual statues and splashing fountains. It wasn't Venice either, with its deeply melancholy beauty gilded with decaying Byzantine richness. No, Milan was more reserved and businesslike, even in its ancient quarters.

He checked his phone. Time to meet Reiner. There was a really good pizzeria (he was told) near the head of the canal, and Reiner was happy to cross the city. It was a quiet day and he had nothing to do. (That's what he had said, probably so Jonathan wouldn't think he was overly enthusiastic about hanging out together.)

The place was small, and it was early by Italian standards, even more so because it was Sunday. They made small talk and drank beer until their pizza came. Then they took a walk before disappearing into an entrance of the *Metropolitana*, to return to their neighborhood.

During lunch, Reiner had invited Jonathan to see his apartment, which was walking distance from Pierpaolo's studio. They emerged from their local station, passing newsstands, bar-cafés, and the tobacconist with the official "T" sign that was lit at night. Men were in the doorway there, smoking and buying lottery tickets while their wives washed the dishes from their midday meal at home.

Reiner's place was a walkup close to the Lambrate station. The beer and lack of exercise for the past few days made the three flights challenging for Jonathan. Or maybe it was the pizza? Reiner was taking the steps two at a time, with a precise tempo.

The apartment was composed of three rooms. From the entrance, a short hallway passed alongside the bathroom on one side and a tiny kitchen on the other. The living room had a makeshift couch composed of a mattress and some pillows. A couple of bikes were leaning against the wall outside the kitchen. A young blonde woman wandered out of one of the bedrooms, her hair in a knot at the top of her head. She was wearing satin gym shorts and an oversize V-neck sweater that showed off a lacy bra strap.

"Do we have any weed, homie?" she said, yawning. "It is such a gray and lazy day. I just got up."

"Betta, this is Jonathan. He has arrived from America to work in the studio." Reiner looked at Jonathan, rolling his eyes.

"Nice to meet you, Jonathan," she said. Betta was focused on Reiner's movements as he rummaged through a small box on a shelf.

"Here you go," he said.

Betta rolled a joint, asking Jonathan the usual questions, and saying how much she would like to go to New York, where the action was. She lit up and passed it to Reiner.

"Betta is visiting from Germany," said Reiner, "That is her room that I am looking to rent." He tried to get the sentence out without exhaling.

Jonathan dragged off the joint disinterestedly, and passed it back to Betta, who had already assumed a lounging position on the improvised sofa.

"Let's have a look at the view," Reiner said, placing his hand on Jonathan's shoulder to help himself up.

Jonathan followed Reiner to the balcony, where they had a good view of the station, the piazza, the trams passing through, the newsstands, and the people milling around at their Sunday tempo.

"So, I don't know about this American girl who is possibly interested in the room."

"What was she like?" Jonathan asked.

"She was nice enough, kind of a proper, shy type. Her name is Melinda, and she is coming from New York, like you."

"She *comes* from New York," Jonathan corrected. Then he waved his hand in front of his mouth as if to take it back. He was feeling that hit of weed, for sure. *Melinda?*

"Wherever she is coming from," Reiner resumed, "I am not sure she will come here."

Jonathan was thinking it was possible that Reiner had met *his* Melinda.

"Is she an architect, by any chance?"

"Yeah."

"Shoulder length brown hair?"

"Like many girls."

"A funny half-smile? A few freckles on her nose?"

"She didn't smile at me. Freckles?"

"They are *Sommersprossen*," offered Betta from the living room.

95

"Oh, I didn't notice."

Jonathan worried that he had waited too long before calling Melinda. What if she moved in with Reiner? If he called now, how would that look? He couldn't pretend he didn't know about it, not to her.

"I'd better get going. I have some stuff to do at my place."

Jonathan walked past Betta, who was watching TV and texting.

He walked the few short blocks to his apartment quickly. Not because he was planning on taking any action, but because he wanted to be in a quiet place to think, right away. When he got back, he kicked off his shoes and threw himself on the bed. It was only three thirty, but he was high and had two beers in him.

He had been so busy starting his job and getting settled, that he had pushed the issue of letting Melinda know he was here to the back of his mind. Did she have a job herself? She must have arrived in Milan a few weeks earlier, maybe more. What if she needed help? Jonathan felt like he was trapped between two courses of action. As long as he did nothing, she would be free, doing her own thing without having to deal with him. On the other hand, if she found out he was here without saying anything, she would think he was stalking her. He lay on his bed, thinking, his head spinning every so slightly, until he fell asleep.

Mel receives a proposal

Giorgio Monti's studio was way up Via Solferino, a charming street that gradually, then not so gradually, transitioned from the older, residential buildings to mixed-use palazzi with storefronts on the ground floor. The shops were small and varied from the gastronomic bottega, unchanged for many years, to the new furniture showroom, all spit and polish. The trattorias appeared tolerant of the arrival of a sushi bar and an Indian restaurant. After all, Italians are cosmopolitan (although they will always come home to mamma). This mashup made Mel wonder what the right balance between diversity and cultural identity was. *I mean*, she thought to herself, *if every city in the world had every type of restaurant, would it lessen our desire to travel?* (It was another thing in melting pots like New York, or London, without a real cuisine of their own.) And what would happen to the cuisine of a country when the imported and local gastronomies started to leak into one another, offering a new spice or technique that appealed to the taste of the evolved foodie? And what, then, when all of these exotic cultural threads wove together a new tapestry? Would it just snuff everything out, everything that made the world rich with variety? Or would it become a seedbed for a newly local evolution?

"Spaghetti came from China, after all" Mel said aloud, shrugging, to nobody.

A scooter with two teenagers aboard buzzed by her.

This was a "limited traffic" street paved in warm-colored sandstone. There was parking on both sides, occupied by scooters and cars so small that they could park perpendicular to the curb. Short, rounded bollards that Italians call *panettoni* blocked some frontage, so that only bikes could park there. The arched entrances with their carved wooden *portoni*, the rusticated walls of the ground level with their iron-barred windows, and the awnings over the shop windows that protected shoppers from the sun and rain, were all familiar now to Mel.

She came up to the address, pushed the intercom, and was buzzed in.

"Through the courtyard and to the right, there's an elevator," Giorgio's voice said.

Mel found the studio to be simple and understated. It had worn parquet floors, white walls, tall ceilings, and modern furniture. At most, about a dozen people could work there.

"To expand, we would have to go further out of the *Centro*," Giorgio said, "and I like to walk to work."

Mel and Giorgio chatted about this and that, and the exchange was relaxed. Giorgio asked Mel what she thought of Milan, and that led to her musings about the diversity of the restaurants on the street below. Giorgio shook his head.

"It is an interesting problem. We make a lot of money on tourism, and people expect to find Italian restaurants. We need to keep this culture alive. But there are Japanese living here who are always at the sushi bar."

"It is also true," he continued, "that people coming from the outside have expectations about Italian restaurants, based on what they have experienced in their own country, such as in New York. It may end up that the true, high-level Italian restaurants will become an elite experience, with people driving to Modena, or Bra, or Liguria, and spending large amounts of money to get the best gastronomic quality. You need the quality of the ingredients."

After a pause, he added, "Do you like to cook, Melinda?"

"Very much. I am no expert, but my sister is a chef and she has taught me a little. She also gave me a list of restaurants that I *have* to visit and report on."

"Then you will need to make some money," Giorgio said. "Now, I have something to propose to you in that regard. It is a design rather than architecture assignment. But it is something that I have a hunch you could do (at least I am willing to give you a try), and I do not particularly want to spend time on myself right now."

Mel straightened up, and not knowing what to say, waited.

"A Japanese department store has asked me to produce a whole line of housewares. It is an unsigned collection, meaning it will carry their brand name. It will also be sold on line."

Giorgio waited, to gauge Mel's reaction.

"Tell me more," she said.

"Now, the Japanese love Italian design, but they think product lines like Alessi are too expensive and foreign for some segments of their market. So, if I asked you to come here tomorrow, and work on a concept for one week, what would you do?"

Mel leaned forward a little, considering.

"I think I would start by reviewing their catalogue and some data about their customers. Then I would like to visit some stores here and look at the items that I think have appeal, perhaps take some notes about their materials and prices, and... I guess it would be helpful to know what price range they want for the collection."

Mel paused, and then continued, "I would also look at some culinary trends in their market. You know, new behaviors relative to dining that could be evoked or supported by a collection. I guess that's how I might start."

Giorgio sat in thought, and then looked up at Mel.

"Then, on Friday, what would you show me?"

"Well, it would be too soon to have any concrete designs, but I think I could have a few themes to propose. Then, we could discuss and I could develop them if you think they're viable. I would need help with materials, as I don't know the economics of choosing, for example, polyester over bamboo."

Giorgio smiled. "You wouldn't have to worry about that. You would just need to describe the properties, performance, you know. They have a team that would work with us on developing the product. It would all be made in China, at least for now."

"Well, it sounds like a fascinating project. Of course I am interested. And after this week?"

"The week is a trial, just to see if you are a good fit. You will be providing me with good material to work from in any case. I will give you fifteen hundred Euros for the week, which must include a full report and some proposals. If it's good, we will talk about the project budget and what I can pay you. Now, the company is going to want to interface with me, but you will be introduced as my assistant for the project, which is good because they all prefer to speak English. They are coming for the *Salone* in April, which is in three weeks, so we would meet them at that time."

Giorgio took a breath and then added, "Every Monday here in the studio we have a meeting at 9:00, so I will introduce you to my team. Tomorrow. We are a small group. I will have a workstation for you. Come at 8:30?"

Giorgio looked up at her.

"Now, I have to get some work done. Thank you for coming."

Mel was in mild shock but thought she should leave quickly and try to make sense of this outside.

"*Grazie tanto*, Giorgio," she said, "I really appreciate this opportunity. I'll be delighted to come tomorrow."

Mel somehow made her way down the stairs, through the cobblestone courtyard and out the *portone*. She waited for the sound of the heavy wood door closing and the latch catching, then let out her breath. She looked around.

This street could become so familiar to her that she might be making jokes with the baker in the shop with the yellow awnings, and discussing the terrible weather with the owner of the wine shop with the hand-painted sign above the windows. She might stop at the pharmacy with the illuminated green cross that hung from the corner of the building, and she would definitely try an espresso anywhere, everywhere on the street.

Mel decided to walk all the way back to Lella's apartment, or at least until she got her wits back.

Lella considers Giorgio

Lella looked out the window at the leaden sky and let out a big sigh. She had spent the morning reading the newspaper, looking at the offerings of the movie theaters and art galleries, trying to keep her mind in a positive place. The end of winter usually made her feel exasperated. Her friends were usually on the their way to or from their March ski trips to Courmeyeur, Cortina, Madonna del Campiglio, or St. Moritz. She never much liked the scene on the slopes.

It was nice to have Melinda here during this time, and the thought made her smile. She had taken a risk, and it might have turned out much differently. In another week, Melinda would be gone, even though she had not settled on a place to rent yet. Lella knew she couldn't afford to stay with her any longer, and they weren't on such intimate terms that Lella could have her stay there without charging her. That seemed like a bad idea. Just the same, she hadn't yet accepted any requests to book the room for the following weeks.

She wondered how the meeting between Melinda and Giorgio was going. She shook her head, thinking about Giorgio's interest in *her*. It had always been there, in the background. She went to the kitchen to get something light to eat, and then pulled out an old photo album, opening it up as she sat on her bed. There was Giorgio with Paolo; here they all were with a group of friends. He always managed to be near her, regardless of whether he was single or attached at the time. Paolo was always oblivious, or so he appeared. He had his own occasional dalliances, and any expression of jealousy would have been hypocritical. Paolo had a lot of prickly character traits, but that wasn't one of them.

Lella thought she really needed to get some sun and fresh air. This time of year made her feel old and tired, and she generally fought it by taking some sort of trip. She considered her options. Visiting her friend Maura in

Paris was not a good idea; it was just as late-winter gloomy there. There was a lot to do in London, also gray and drizzly. Madrid was a sunnier possibility, but she knew nobody there. Maybe she would just take her chances on Rome, where her cousin Federico lived. Maybe Melinda would be able to join her. That is, if she succeeded in finding a job and could still afford the time to go away.

Lella's thoughts returned to the issue of Giorgio. Or, in a broader sense, to whether she had the confidence and the emotional stamina to get into a "situation," whatever that might be like. Her freedom was important to her. What if she gave it up, only to undergo more heartbreak and loss? She would have to start the process from which she had so brilliantly emerged all over again. More to the point, was she willing to have a physical relationship, with all of the initial embarrassment it entailed, at her age?

Italians have an expression, *gallina vecchia fa buon brodo*, old chickens make good broth. Lella laughed thinking about it. Her attorney (who was a good friend) had mentioned it last week after she had told him she wasn't seeing anyone. He had told her that was a regrettable waste. She admitted that Italian men did have a tendency to appreciate beauty in many forms. She had appreciated his encouragement as well as his humor.

Lella was roused from her musings by the key turning in the entry.

Melinda is back, she thought, and jumped from her bed to hear her news.

Jonathan discovers Elena

When he awoke on Monday, Jonathan's focus was back on work. Everything was quiet. He liked getting up early and enjoying a space of time before getting into high gear. He took a shower, put on a fresh pair of sweats and a T-shirt, and loaded some espresso into the *caffettiera*. He packed it lightly, by tapping it with the back of the spoon. When the *caffettiera* started to gurgle and hiss, Jonathan turned the flame down. He was heating some milk in a tiny saucepan, and toasting some multigrain bread from the bakery in the oven. Not the most efficient way to do it; he was going to have to buy a toaster.

The counter that was his kitchen ran along the wall facing the courtyard. The windows were barred, but there were no curtains. There was virtually no traffic through the courtyard at night, but Jonathan kept the lamps on the floor, or the nightstand, below the level of the windows. He would get some scrap foamboard from the studio, maybe, to use as shades.

He set up a place facing the courtyard, and sat on a stool, with all of his necessities in reach. Butter, honey, a knife, a napkin. The steaming caffè latte in an oversize cup. The New York Times on his tablet screen. Life was good. He watched a black cat saunter through the courtyard, jump onto the windowsill and peer at him. Jonathan yawned, and the cat jumped out of sight.

Looking out the window, he noted that the courtyard could use some new pots and plants. Maybe next weekend he could take a trip to Ikea and get the toaster, too. Did they have toasters at Ikea?

Jonathan finished the mini crossword puzzle in 3:23 minutes. Not his best time. Then he heard familiar voices outside and looked up. Pierpaolo and Elena were walking in together. There was an air of complicity between them that Jonathan had not noticed in the studio. He saw her glance over, but she wouldn't have been able to see him easily because of the dead plant in a pot on the sill. Pierpaolo turned the keys in the studio door, turned to her and gave her a kiss. Then they left whatever was between them behind and entered the studio.

This observation troubled Jonathan. If Elena had been acting as a *de facto* producer, and he was being groomed for that role, where did that leave her?

Elena was neither competitive nor insecure about her work; he could see that from the last week's interactions. Her job apparently was not at risk. Unless, of course, whatever she had going on with Pierpaolo fizzled and created tension in the studio. Jonathan thought that she probably needed some kind of safeguard. He might be able to devise a role for Elena that would be clearer than the one she had now. It would give her some independence, whether she thought she needed it or not. Her friendship with Leitizia wove its way into these thoughts.

And then there was Reiner. This led Jonathan's thoughts away from the studio. He needed to find out if he was going to be replacing his temporary roommate Betta with *his* ex-girlfriend Mel.

But first, business.

* * *

The next couple of days in the studio went smoothly and easily, with setups and knockdowns, and Pierpaolo waltzing onto the scene to comment on the final touches. Reiner had the cameras lined up like an arms trader proud of his wares. Enrico was endlessly tampering with the lights, Geert holding cards by his side.

Pierpaolo was out of the studio for part of the day on Tuesday, so Jonathan asked Elena to have lunch. They went to a little Thai restaurant a few blocks away.

"Is this my *interview*?" she asked Jonathan, smiling, after they had placed their order.

Jonathan laughed. "Not at all."

He was quiet, waiting for her to start the conversation. He found it was the best way to discover what is on a person's mind. Let them make the first move.

"I suppose you are wondering what I'm doing with my life?" she said, looking up at him with her head lowered.

"Not really," Jonathan answered. "You're just figuring things out like the rest of us, I suppose."

She smiled. *He's going to make me do all the work here*, she thought.

"Well, here's some recent history. I met Pierpaolo in Modena. He was doing a shoot on location, and I was helping on his client's end."

She took a sip of coconut water.

"We worked together closely all day. Then he asked me if I would consider coming to Milan to work in his studio. I think he liked my calm demeanor; you see how agitated he gets. Anyway, I came to try it out for a couple of weeks–this was last year. I stayed with a girlfriend of mine."

"One night, after a shoot that went into the evening, Pierpaolo invited me to dinner. (I am only telling you this because everyone in the studio knows about it.) After that, the guys in the studio assumed that there was a 'thing' between us. They changed their behavior toward me. It was a combination of caution and resentment at what they thought was my entitlement."

"The truth is that I wanted to have a relationship with Pierpaolo, but I promised myself that I wouldn't, not until I had gained the respect of the crew. Then I treated it like some sort of prize."

"And so did you? Have a relationship?"

"Well, yes and no. Back then we were together every night for a few weeks. Then it started to feel disruptive to me. We were always at his place. I always had to scramble in the evening or in the morning, to get my things, manage my clothing...you know, and it started to make me edgy. For him, everything was delivered to his door. It offended my sense of fairness, despite the more lavish lifestyle he offered."

"Were you in love with him?"

"In hindsight, I would say no. I think I was flattered by his attention, and I was lonely. I wanted to do something new, and he gave me the opportunity."

She looked up. "You're going to keep this between us, aren't you?"

"Of course!" Jonathan would never, in a million years, betray this kind of confidence.

"Well, I told Pierpaolo that I thought the situation would create a problem with my job. I needed more alone time, and I needed to sleep at my own place. I have a small studio near the *Politecnico*. The strange thing was, he was fine with it, as if he could take it or leave it."

"Every once in a while, we still enjoy a night together. I think it will just fizzle out, or one of us will find a more substantial relationship."

"Somehow I find that sad," Jonathan said.

"Well, I got myself into a difficult situation. But Pierpaolo has taught me a lot about this business, and he treats me professionally. But he does, as you might say, 'call the debt' occasionally. And don't get me wrong; it is pleasant being with him. I feel real affection."

"I should hope so," said Jonathan, leaning back so the server could set down their plates."

Elena's aura had gone from one of shining confidence to a weak throb. She looked embarrassed, defensive.

"What about you, Jonathan? Do you have someone in your heart? Some tragic story you left behind in New York?"

Fair enough, Jonathan thought.

"I lived with a woman in New York. I loved her very much. My mother didn't accept her. She's not Jewish, and that was an obstacle. I was trying to be patient with my mother, and give her time, but my girlfriend lost her patience. One time, I went home for the Jewish New Year, and she had an affair while I was gone."

Jonathan blew out some air, trying not to get emotional. Elena instinctively reached for his hand.

"I had seen it coming, but I tried to pretend it wasn't happening. Afterward, when I came back, she told me everything, and made plans to move out. I was furious, and said some things I wish I hadn't."

"After a few months, we spoke again. I apologized for the things I said, and asked her to reconsider. She told me that she had 'irretrievably polluted' the relationship. She couldn't live with being marked by an act of infidelity."

Elena poured Jonathan some tea.

"And is that the end of it?"

"Well, I still love her, and I understand better why everything happened the way it did. She is very insecure, and she wanted to feel loved and special. I should have stood up to my mother, but there is a long history there (of guilt, mostly), that I couldn't unravel fast enough."

"So you decided to come here?"

"Well, actually, she decided to come here. She is here now. So I decided I would come, too. It's a good experience for me, and maybe she and I will cross paths at some point."

"Wow!" Elena exclaimed. "That is a very romantic story! Does she know that you are in Milan?"

"Not exactly," said Jonathan, sipping some tea.

He laughed.

"I have to figure out how to let her know. She might be furious. She might think I am stalking her. I want to wait until she has had enough time to get settled into a job. If I appear on the scene and she is lost, she might grab onto me for the wrong reason."

"So you forgive her?"

"Completely. I am guilty, too, of a sort of betrayal."

"Maybe she is having a hard time forgiving herself."

"I think that might be the problem."

Jonathan asked for the check, and the two of them walked the few blocks back to the studio.

"On a more work-related topic," Jonathan started, "I was wondering when I could sit down and talk with you and Leitizia. I have an idea I want to discuss with you. That is, if you think you can keep it to yourselves for now."

"Leiti will be in the studio tomorrow afternoon. Would you like to go for a drink afterward?"

"As long as other people don't tag along."

"We will make it look like we are going alone together, a girls' drink. Then you can meet us."

"That works. And Elena...thank you for sharing your story with me."

"And you," she smiled. "This will remain between us."

After they entered the studio, they went their separate ways.

Jonathan was thoughtful, and disturbed.

Elena felt relieved, but somewhat diminished.

Elena searches her heart

Elena was going through a pile of mail on the counter shielding Lucy's desk. Geert was next to the cage, wiping down some equipment when Jonathan approached him.

"She is definitely off limits," Geert said to Jonathan.

Elena caught Geert's eye, as he looked sidelong in her direction. No emotion, she just froze him out. Geert flushed and looked away.

The addresses on the mail were starting to blur, so Elena took the pile and ducked into her tiny office, on the near side of Pierpaolo's. She suddenly felt as if Pierpaolo's office was like an ocean separating her from other possibilities, maybe even Jonathan. He was the first person (besides Leitizia, of course) in this place with whom she could talk. Enrico was friendly, though guarded, and the others were downright afraid of interacting with her because of Pierpaolo.

How did she manage to get into this situation? She had tried to be careful. Why was it that men (maybe it was just Italian men?) just pushed and pushed until they got you into bed? She never felt like they gave her enough time to understand her feelings, get comfortable. It was as if they were in a constant state of agitation, unable to begin a relationship until they uncovered the deepest secrets of a woman's body. It required so much trust on her part, and so little risk on theirs. And once they made their conquest, it was as if you became their property. They had the key to you, and you were powerless against them.

It was different for Lucy. Maybe the ten-year age difference meant a big change on the dating scene. She had told Elena stories of her "hook-ups" that made it sound like she was in complete control. Having a blast with casual sex. Elena didn't find it so easy to open up to strange men, and she didn't want to, either. She wondered if Lucy's ability to do so had anything to do with her unbridled drinking at parties and clubs.

Then Elena realized that this was not about Lucy, but rather about how she was feeling about herself since her conversation with Jonathan. It had made her feel weak and submissive. Sure, she had been able to back out of the regular sleepovers with Pierpaolo, but she was still on the spot whenever they had a late night in the studio, going over plans, eating pizza. He could be so charming, and she just had her laundry waiting for her at home. She felt there was no harm in it as long as she didn't have a better alternative.

But would she even be able to recognize an opportunity with someone else? Take Jonathan, for example. He was such a sweet, smart, caring guy; it was obvious. Of course, he was still romantically entangled. If he weren't, though, Pierpaolo and his ego would be a huge impediment. And what if things changed with Jonathan? Perhaps his New York girlfriend wouldn't want to see him. It was possible that he would then be available.

Elena tried to turn away from the tiny fantasy that was bubbling up in her mind. She remembered how friendly and kind Enrico was when she came to the studio. Then Geert and Reiner, whose antennae were longer than his, steered him away. He was still good to her, they were friends; it just wasn't easy because of the crew's perception of her as the boss's property.

Elena stumbled through the rest of the day, grateful that Pierpaolo was out. She went through her correspondence with her door closed. Reiner was at the workstation in an alcove of the atrium, editing in Photoshop. Enrico was setting up some lights in Cubi-2, as Geert metered and played around with cards, trying to get just the right effect. They were doing some catalogue work, nothing that required Pierpaolo to be present. Enrico could handle it. Jonathan was sitting on a rolling desk chair outside of Cubi-2, just shooting the breeze with Enrico and Geert. He occasionally looked over at Elena behind the glass partition of her office, and smiled.

She wished that she could talk to Jonathan again. Would he think she was needy? Wouldn't his unavailability give them the freedom to become friends?

Elena returned her focus to her work. She prepared folders for each of the shoots they were doing from Tuesday to Saturday, and placed them in a rack so that Pierpaolo, at any time, could pull them out and review progress, whether Elena was around or not. Her office was his office. Her body was his body.

Now she was just getting cynical!

She started to pack up her things around six o'clock when Pierpaolo came breezing in. He opened her door, stuck his head in.

"*Bouna sera, tesoro!*" he said, smiling, "how did everything go today?"

"Just fine," Elena answered. "The Modabella shoot is done, and Reiner is off to the agency with the proofs." She looked at her watch. "He should be done there by now."

"Well, I have some calls to return. How about some dinner afterward?"

"I'm a little tired," Elena said, looking him in the eye. But she couldn't hold his gaze. "I'm sorry."

"Absolutely no problem," he answered, a little standoffishly. Pierpaolo regularly employed guilt with her. *Look at me, I work so hard, and I need affection, too.*

Elena owed her presence in Milan to him, the beginning of a real career for her. But tonight, she wanted to do her laundry.

Mel and Lella gain time

Mel had made it through her first two days at Giorgio Monti's studio. She had stacks of print catalogues on her table, with brightly colored Post-It tabs marking the critical pages. Digital bookmarks populated her browser. On Tuesday she visited the showrooms that sold "Italian Design" to tourists as well as Italians shopping for last minute gifts in the city center. Lella had asked to join her, and suggested they have lunch afterward.

Together, they picked through charming household utensils, some of which had the look and personality of cartoon creatures: a scrub brush in colorful resin whose bristles formed a head of hair; a pencil sharpener shaped like a beaver. Others were elegant classic forms in stainless steel, created through minimalist cuts, bends, and welds. They held the objects in their hands, tried to feel their functionality, and passed their finds back and forth between them. They looked at the lineup of designer *caffettiere*, a standard for making espresso at home. Mel didn't want to take pictures like the Japanese scouts tended to fearlessly do; she discreetly took notes on a little pad. She could get the images online later.

Lella looked at her watch. "It's 12:30, she said, if we want to take a ten minute walk, we can eat at the *Vecchia Latteria* in Via dell'Unione. It's a tight space with one row of tables along the wall, but the food is good and the atmosphere is lively."

"That sounds great," Mel replied, and she followed Lella, who headed in the direction of Piazza del Duomo.

As they passed through the broad space, pigeons rose into the air like a ripple. Tourists stood in small groups, taking pictures or checking their map apps. Lella and Mel headed down Via Torino, which was flanked with crooked side streets whose gastronomy boutiques have been there forever. Mel wondered how they could hang on. Some of them had only a few tables; their charm appealed to traveling foodies and an occasional stockbroker emerging from the Exchange around the corner. They would stand at the counter, gobbling a sandwich of prosciutto on a ciabatta, washing it down with a glass of Pinot.

They made it to the *Latteria* just in time to snag a cramped table. Mel ordered eggs poached in tomato sauce, and Lella had a Tuscan bean soup.

"So, how do you like working for Giorgio so far?" Lella asked, once they had placed their order.

Mel laughed. "It's hard to say. I am enjoying it, but I haven't had much interaction with him. He rushes in and out, and just nods at me as he goes by."

"Well, this is your test. We will see how it goes when Friday comes along."

Mel looked thoughtful.

"You know, Lella, the timing this week is not so great for moving out of your place. I would really like to know how this goes before I make any other plans. Do you think we could work out a deal for another week or two?"

"What will you do if it doesn't work out with Giorgio?" Lella asked.

"Well, I have thought of that. I've calculated that I have enough to stay for a couple of months at the German guy's apartment."

"But you didn't really have a good feeling about him."

"I know, but I think he works a lot, and I would just make the rounds again, to the studios I have already visited. Cristina won't have anything until June at least, but Marino Contini said he was open. It wouldn't be much pay, but I might ask for a little more, and maybe pick up some English students on the side. One of the expats I met at the bar-café in Corso Magenta said that she makes a hundred Euros a week on lessons."

"And then when you get settled, you can look for a more stable living situation, no?"

"Yes. *If* I get settled. If not, I'll go to the *Salone del Mobile*, see the new furniture collections, and then I'll head back home. But I don't think it will come to that. I'm optimistic."

"Well, I would be disappointed if you went home, now that we are becoming friends. How about if I charge you half of the weekly rate for the next two weeks? And then, you can have the whole weekend after, to move out?"

Mel was surprised at Lella's generosity.

"That would be great, Lella. It will make things so much easier this week, not to have to worry about that. I don't know how to thank you!"

"Well, look at it this way: Now I don't have to look for your replacement, which is worth something."

"When are you leaving for Rome?"

"I thought I would go on Thursday, and come back on Monday. But I do expect you to call me on Friday evening to let me know how it went. You know, I wanted to ask you to join me, but it looks like the timing isn't right."

Lella paused, thinking. "Unless you want to take the *Frecciarossa* train on Friday evening! I'll be staying with my cousin, and there is room for you there. You'd just have to know by lunch on Friday, make your reservation, and go to the station right after work. I could pick you up at the station in Rome."

Mel looked uncertain.

"It's hard to think about that now. I would love to see Rome, but I think I have to get to Friday before I can even consider it. Is that okay?"

"Sure!" said Lella, "But I think it would be good to either celebrate—or commiserate. Now," she continued, as they received their change from the server, "let's make a quick stop at *San Satyro*, down the street. It is a rather obscure work of Bramante that you absolutely must see."

Mel develops a concept

By the end of Wednesday, Mel felt like she had made some progress on her project. She stayed late in the studio, organizing her material to bring back to Lella's apartment. She thought that with Lella gone on Thursday, she could spread everything out on the massive dining table and work there without any interruptions. By the time she made it back to the apartment, it was 9:30. Lella was packing for her trip, but she had saved a dish of pasta for Mel.

"You have to eat something," she said.

Mel ate alone in the kitchen, thinking about how she would organize her day's work tomorrow. She had the beginning of a slide presentation, and she really wanted to share it with Lella. She would be supportive, and discerning, while not directly involved.

After she cleaned up, Mel went into the living room. She set three boxes out on the long dining table near the windows and the balcony, and began arranging note cards in front of each box.

"All done!" Lella said, walking into the living room. She was the picture of elegance, even at home. She was wearing a soft gray wrap dress, and her bare feet showed off a perfect pedicure. Mel marveled at her simplicity and confidence.

"So," Lella asked, "what are these mysterious boxes? Are you going to show me what you've done?"

"Well, there is still some work to do tomorrow. I hope you don't mind if I work here."

"Not at all."

Mel went to the table and started up her laptop.

"I can show you the general idea, with a few slides."

The first image that appeared was a beautiful photo of a leaf, showing the articulation of its veins and droplets of water poised on it. This was followed by a slide with the word: "LEAF."

"This is the theme for a collection. Each item in the collection will share the properties of the leaf: strong, resistant, water repellent, and deciduous. It will be a disposable service, whose plates and cups can, however, be reused a number of times. The "leaves" can be folded like a tortilla, or shaped into a cup, but they all travel flat. Like origami. They can be used in emergency situations, as well as for parties. Like a leaf, they can be recycled. I'll write the description on this slide."

The next slide showed a smooth, round pebble in a stream, the water parting around it. The word: "PEBBLE" was on the following slide.

"This theme has to do with erosion and reconstitution. This collection will be made of a blend of recycled materials, as in the formation of a stone through sedimentation. I think the items in this line will be vessels, strong and earthy in their posture. But they will be visibly heterogeneous, with flecks of seemingly precious material embedded in their fabric."

Lella was nodding, but silent, as Mel continued. The third slide showed a campfire on a sandy beach, and the following slide displayed the word: "FIRE."

"This collection represents the heating of sand to make glass. The items will be made of recycled glass, and feature the incomplete mixing of color fragments on a transparent canvas. I see these as containers for hot or cold drinks, of the type that combines essences and spices into a magical cocktail. They will have transparency in the upper part of the glass, with the colored pieces 'mulling' near the bottom, as if they settled by gravity."

Mel paused, waiting for Lella to say something. Then she started to doubt herself.

"There is still some work to do on this, of course."

"No, I like them very much," Lella said thoughtfully. "I am just thinking of a couple of things..."

"Please tell me," Mel urged.

"Well," Lella began, "I like your slide that explains how the material is conceived, and what kind of appearance it has. But I think you need a slide in between that tells the story of the Leaf, or the Pebble, in an evocative way that gives the symbol more power."

Mel stood up. "You are absolutely right! I was thinking that my attachment to these symbols was merely personal, but I will write a little story about each, to make the association more meaningful."

"Yes," Lella said. "We're talking about Giorgio and the Japanese buying these ideas, and to them you have to speak the language of meaning."

"One more thing," Lella said, wincing. "I don't like the word 'Fire' for the third group. I think it is too removed from the final products, as you described them."

"Maybe," Mel started, talking while she was thinking, "it should have more to do with the combination of the bits of colored glass..."

"And the beach," Lella added.

"SEAGLASS!" Mel said, standing up again.

Lella laughed and put her hands together in a single clap.

"That's it," she said. "A magical though humble object found on the beach."

"It won't be too much like the 'Pebble' idea?"

"Um, no. The pebble is from the stream, and it's natural. The glass is man-made and so while it is a cousin to the pebble, it has a different provenance."

"I think I can make it work," Mel said, nodding.

She gave Lella a hug.

"Thank you so much."

Lella made a dismissive gesture.

"These are your ideas. Ideas always have to be shared and tested, and any other point of view will always make it better. You know, I don't believe in 'single authorship.' It doesn't exist in history."

"Now," Lella continued, "we both have a busy day tomorrow, so why don't we get some sleep?"

Lella felt good about Mel's prospects, and this made the idea of getting on a train to Rome tomorrow even more pleasant.

Mel walked across the spacious living room and disappeared behind the bookshelves. As she made her way down the stairs, the atmosphere around her became darker and deeper. *I wonder what Giorgio is going to think? He might not like it...*

She pushed the idea out of her head and flipped on the light at the bottom of the stairs.

Opportunities for Elena

Elena felt good on Thursday morning. She and Leitizia had met with Jonathan on Tuesday after work. It was a fun and productive meeting. He wanted Elena to set up an internal styling service that was also available to other studios. This would include a rotating props inventory to manage in the studio, freelance staffing, with Leitizia picking out the talent around town; and eventually, lower costs for Pierpaolo's own needs. Elena would still do some producing, but this would take up most of her time while Jonathan was starting up in that role. They made some calculations, and although Leiti would make a lower income than her best months, she would have a dependable salary. Jonathan also wanted to make it possible for Elena and Leitizia to have a small percentage of the profit from this business area. Leitizia thought she could get the younger stylists interested, because she could save them time looking for assignments. Sure, they would eventually leave and they would have to re-staff. But she would be able to train the new crop of stylists and raise the bar professionally. She liked it.

For Elena it was a way to get out from under Pierpaolo while doing something for him to better his business. If she succeeded in this, she might even be able to spin it off and build her own business. Jonathan said he would help anyway he could.

She smiled when she thought of Jonathan. He was so nice and thoughtful. He never acted inappropriately with any of the women around. She wondered if that was because his heart was engaged, or if it was just his way. In either case, it made him desirable.

When Elena entered the studio, Lucy directed her to Pierpaolo's office.

"I got you a *cappuccino* and a chocolate croissant," she said.

"Oh, *grazie!*" Elena responded. Lucy knew that Elena loved chocolate croissants, but the bar-café across the street rarely had any good ones by eight o'clock.

"Chocolate croissants are like tomatoes," Elena had told her once. "If they're not good, it's better not to have them."

Lucy wasn't sure if Elena was referring to something else regarding her specifically, or whether it was just a coincidence. She thought maybe she should stop sharing her exploits of the night before.

Elena waved to the guys setting up across the atrium, and ducked into Pierpaolo's office.

"You look sunny today," he said, looking at her. Then he quickly turned his attention to some papers on his desk. He was giving her the dejected routine.

Elena took a bite of the chocolate croissant, and then wiped her mouth with a napkin before taking a sip of the cappuccino.

"So, what's up?" she asked.

"You know the location work we need to do in Rome?"

"Yes, vaguely."

"Well, it has to get done before Monday. Are you going to have a problem with that?"

Elena was dreading the trip, because she knew that Pierpaolo might get a suite to share, and he might also expect her to be "available."

"The only problem is," he continued before she answered, "I won't be able to go."

Elena tried not to show any emotion, but this day was revealing itself to be auspicious: first the chocolate croissant, and now this news. She took another bite of the chocolate croissant, in order to delay her response.

"Okay," she said, after she finished chewing, or almost. She tried to sound neutral if not disappointed.

"Anyway, the hotel is booked, and I thought it might be good for you to go with Jonathan."

Elena was having trouble believing what she heard. She started to have that sensation she got when she was confused: everything seemed shrouded in a dull haze, and Pierpaolo's words seemed distant.

"It's a suite, that's the only problem, but there is a pull-out bed in the sofa. It's at the Martis. I thought Jonathan would enjoy hanging in Piazza Navona at night. You can take the train after work on Friday, get there around nine-thirty, and be ready to work on Saturday. You would return Sunday on the four o'clock train, so you can sleep in and maybe show him around if there is anything he wants to see."

The haze around Elena started to lift. This was really happening.

"Is Jonathan on board?"

"I wanted to make sure you could go first. He wouldn't be able to handle it on his own. His Italian, and the fact that he has never been to Rome, would slow things down. This way you can work on the train with him to map the places to check out. Here are five addresses, rooftop gardens with a view. Here are the phone numbers. Call them between tonight and tomorrow to schedule the go-see. Don't worry about plants; we will have them brought in. It's a little early in the season. Schedule the shoot for the best site, and make sure you get a rain date. Avoid Easter. It will be a mess."

"Now," he said, "I've got to get ready for the Borealis shoot." He picked up the papers on his desk and made a neat stack of them, a decisive gesture.

Elena got up to leave, picking up the uneaten half of chocolate croissant and the cappuccino.

"Oh, and one more thing," Pierpaolo said.

"I know we have been, you know, kind of fizzling, on the personal side of things. I wanted to say that it's okay. In fact, I have started seeing someone else, and I wanted you to know. Even if things are not well-defined between us."

Elena looked down, feeling oddly off balance. She thought this was her thing to end, and now he was doing it. She realized that their personal relationship had given her more of a sense of security, in a perverse way, than she had considered. She wasn't sure how she felt, or what to say.

"Well" she started, "I guess that is up to you. Thank you for telling me."

He smiled, confident, a little smug.

Yes, he was feeling some spite, Elena thought. She knew how vulnerable he was, underneath, though.

She smiled back. It was a weak smile, a little resigned and not entirely honest.

Mel's dinner date

Mel had a good grasp on her presentation by Thursday afternoon. She didn't want to spend the evening working, thinking it would be better to have a nice bath, sit in her armchair by the window, and enjoy the solitude. She took a break to make a train reservation for Rome. What the hell... No matter how it goes, a weekend in Rome would be good for her. She checked the weather forecast and packed a small bag for the weekend. Then she went back upstairs and loaded up the stuff on the dining room table: her laptop, her boxes of sample materials, and a folder with some hard copies of her research and analysis.

She went back downstairs to see what was in the fridge for dinner. Then her phone rang.

"*Ciao*, Melinda, I'm Alberto."

"Oh, *ciao*, Alberto, how are you?"

"Well, thank you. I wanted to know how your work is going."

"That's very nice of you. I think I am ready for tomorrow."

"*Molto bene*," replied Alberto. "In that case...would you like to join me for dinner?"

Mel was conflicted. This would interfere with her plan, but Alberto had been so helpful to her that it seemed ungracious to say no.

"Well, that's very kind of you. But I'm hoping to have an early night tonight. What time were you thinking?"

"We can have an early dinner. I think I can pick you up around...let's say, 6:45?"

"Okay," Mel said, trying to sound grateful and enthusiastic. "I'll expect you then. Thank you."

She walked into her room and threw her phone on the bed. She stripped down to her T-shirt and underpants and sat in her armchair. It was

124

drizzling outside. She could see the brightly colored fruit in the crates under the awning of the shop across the street. White cabs streaked across the gray, wet street.

She still had time for a bath, and she had to eat anyway. But she had never been alone with Alberto before, and she kept remembering Amelia's warning: *be careful of my cousin.*

Mel didn't need the stress of this encounter. She soaked in the tub and tried to dismiss her worries. *I am going, I can't change that, it will be fine, and I need to be confident.* Her self-coaching was ineffective, undermined by her memory of Cecil in New York. He had been charming and insistent, just like Alberto. She was in a weak moment then, just like she was now.

Why was she so strong in some ways and so submissive when it came to men? Instead of choosing, she let herself be chosen. She was no more decisive than driftwood floating among the waves, letting itself be carried this way and that until it landed on some beach, precariously, until it was pulled out to sea again.

Mel held her nose and submerged below the foamy surface of the bathwater.

Alberto was punctual, and advised her to grab her raincoat, through the intercom. He had come on his Vespa.

Once she was on the scooter behind him, he told her that he thought the best place for a quick dinner was at his place.

"Oh," said Mel, "I thought we were going out?"

"Well there would be one very disappointed *orata* who has sacrificed its life for us, in my oven right now. You don't have fish like this in America. They have a golden crescent between their eyes. The *fish of the gods.*"

Mel was resigned.

Alberto's place was beautiful, in a traditional way. The floors in his entry and kitchen were marble, and in the rest of the house, polished parquet. Bookshelves and books were everywhere, but nothing was in disorder. The dining room gave way to a small terrace, and a beautiful Murano chandelier hung over the mahogany table.

He was animated, as usual, as he moved around in the kitchen, preparing a salad, taking the fish out of the oven, skillfully liberating the white flesh from the bone. He scooped out some roasted potatoes, picking up a twig of rosemary and putting it in the garbage. They were drinking white wine.

Alberto and Mel sat at the table under the colorful sparkle of the chandelier. The terrace was gloomy. Its planters and pots held heavily pruned plants awaiting the sun. The chairs were tipped against the table to drain.

"It will be much nicer in Rome this weekend," Alberto said, "Federico has a beautiful place, very old, in *Trastevere*, with a rooftop terrace. It looks over the Tiber toward the center of Rome."

"So Lella told you? Well, I am very glad to be going there. It has been a challenging week."

They talked about her presentation, whether Giorgio might hire her (Alberto was confident that he would), and what she should see in Rome on her first visit.

"I recommend just walking, walking, and walking," Alberto said. "Just to get the feel of it. You can start at the Forum, or the *Campidoglio*, and go wherever your feet take you. If you start going to museums, you will find it too daunting. Rome is a Baroque city. It is all about movement. You need to feel the plasticity of the buildings, the elongation of the piazzas, the pushing and pulling of the space."

Mel laughed. "That sounds like good advice. The fish—the *orata*— is delicious, by the way."

126

"Good!" Alberto said, "I prepared it with Cecilia's own hands. (Cecilia takes care of the apartment for me.) But I did take it out of the oven."

Mel laughed. "So do you live here alone?"

"Yes, for the most part. My sons Leo and Guido are both in Milan. Leo has his own place and Guido stays at his mother's apartment. She is never there. She stays in a country house of her family in Umbria."

"Are you divorced?"

"Not exactly. It's complicated. Property that needs to be sold, everyone loses, Guido might need to move... We both live our lives, and it's okay like this."

"If it works for you," Mel offered.

They cleaned up, loaded the dishwasher together, and decided on one last glass of wine before getting Mel back to Lella's apartment.

Mel was looking at a print that was leaning against one of the bookshelves in the living room. Alberto came into the room after having put the bottle back in the fridge.

He put his hand on her shoulder, and felt her muscles tense.

"You are going to do fine tomorrow," he said.

Mel turned around to face him. His eyes were twinkling, and his smile was reassuring. She was scared. Not about her presentation, nor about money, nor about going to Rome alone tomorrow, nor about not knowing her future beyond Sunday.

Alberto gently moved her hair from her face and kissed her on the cheek.

Mel held her breath. She was surprised at her own physical response to him. She realized how starved for affection she had been during this difficult time. The heels of her hands were tightly pressed into the shelf behind her, but she felt herself starting to cede.

Then Alberto snapped out of it. "We'd better get you home," he said, his eyes widening. Big day tomorrow!"

The ride back on the Vespa was fun after a couple of glasses of wine. The drizzle had stopped, and the air was cool and moist. Mel got off, handed Alberto her helmet, and gave him a quick hug.

"Thank you for everything," she said.

"Good luck! Let me know how it goes. You can text me from the train."

Mel made her way back to the apartment. She got off the elevator on the lower floor that led directly to her room. The corridor was dark. She passed the empty rooms near the door, the counter with the fridge and the stovetop, the bathroom; and then entered her room. Clouds reflected the light of the city, creating a dull glow. She wanted to sit for a bit before going to bed. She poured herself a glass of water and changed into her silk nightshirt. She was feeling strangely aroused by Alberto's approach into her personal space. She felt as if she had done something wrong, though, something that violated an unspoken agreement with Lella. Her host was generous and helpful. Mel's role was to be grateful, and she couldn't ruin things by crossing the line. Amelia had warned her about Alberto. She didn't know how to interpret his kiss. It was innocent enough. Then why did it affect her this way? The silk felt so good against her bare skin. She started to massage her breasts, and closed her eyes. Then she got a text message. It was Alberto.

JUST WANTED TO SAY GOODNIGHT.

Mel turned off her phone.

All roads lead to Rome

Milan's train station, the *Stazione Centrale*, is a beautiful structure. The façade is technically in the French Beaux-Arts style, all top-heavy and imperial, its classical Italian details oversized. The scale of it is awe-inspiring to the mortal human.

Mel entered the cavernous interior, rode a tall escalator to the upper level, and passed through the turnstile to the tracks. The trains waited between the platforms like thoroughbreds at the gate. They were sheltered with a sweeping canopy of iron and glass, a contrast to the columns and winged beasts outside. The station was crowded, but she found the way to her train fifteen minutes before its scheduled departure at six-thirty.

The train was lined with compartments for six passengers on one side, and a narrow corridor where people squeezed past one another in search of a seat on the other. Once Mel found a spot, she put her bag on the rack above, her jacket on the seat. She had to call Lella and tell her that the presentation had gone well, and that Giorgio had offered her a job. She was still in shock, and this trip to Rome made her experience of it even more surreal. She stepped out into the corridor, spoke with Lella, who was not at all surprised (but delighted nonetheless), and confirmed that she was due to arrive at nine-thirty.

Mel was gazing mindlessly out onto the platform at the people, their bags, and their goodbyes, and thought she caught a glimpse of Jonathan. She did not trust her own senses, freezing as she tried to process this new information.

"Lella, I have to go. The train is about to leave."

Jonathan was walking with his typical lively step, talking to a good-looking woman with long dark brown hair at his side. Mel turned her head and leaned on the window to see where they were going. They hopped onto the same train, *her* train, but were obscured by the stragglers milling in the corridor. She quickly retreated to her seat, and closed the windowed compartment door.

Mel turned to smile at her fellow travelers, belying the violent commotion inside her. Her seat was by the door, facing forward in the train's direction. The woman with Jonathan looked into the compartment, and then passed by. Jonathan glanced in, and froze in his tracks. Mel was looking up at him, expressionless. He hesitated before he opened the door.

"Hi, Mel," he said sheepishly.

"Jonathan!" She answered, nonplussed. "What are you doing here? Are you vacationing?"

"I'll explain...Let me get settled, and we can talk once the train gets moving." He looked toward Elena, who was waiting for him. They needed to find seats.

Mel just nodded, and barely whispered, "Okay."

Jonathan found two seats a few compartments back in the same car. He didn't know how to explain the situation to Mel, or to Elena for that matter. Elena seemed so excited to be going to Rome to work with him, away from all the interfering influences that might pollute their budding friendship. Unfortunately, Jonathan had no intention of getting involved with Elena. Even if he wanted to, it would be way too sticky with Pierpaolo. Just the same, he felt that Mel's presence was Elena's loss. He had wanted to build her up, focus on her this weekend. Now there was this distraction.

He had also hoped that going to Rome would further delay the necessity of letting Mel know he was in Milan. Each day that passed made that task harder.

Mel had a magazine in her lap, which she pretended to look at, occasionally flipping a page. It was uncomfortable experiencing such a deeply emotional encounter while sitting among strangers. She thought about her meeting today. Giorgio liked her ideas (although he didn't think they were all equally feasible, or sufficiently distinct from one another). However, it had been "more than he expected," and he was "delighted." He had sent her off to grab a late lunch and asked her to return afterward to discuss a position in his studio.

Mel remembered going to the bar-café down the street and ordering a panino with prosciutto and arugola. She had a glass of beer while she waited. She was celebrating. Her eye caught the flickering neon cross that marked the pharmacy across the street. Well, it wasn't really *neon*, because it was green. What was the element, krypton? Then she felt a flicker inside her chest, and had to look away. Alberto came to mind. What *did* happen last night, anyway? God, she was glad she was going to Rome for the weekend. She really needed Lella's level-headedness and understanding to keep her on track. Not that she would tell her that she went to his place, was kissed (lightly) and had felt drawn to him. It was probably the weakness of the moment. Mel returned to the present, shook her head, looked at a Chanel ad. It seemed all of her mistakes with men happened in the *weakness of the moment*.

Crises are the seedbeds of change. Was her impulsiveness a fear response?

Once they pulled away from the city, Mel went out to the corridor to stretch her legs and look at the countryside. She heard a door slide and involuntarily looked toward the back of the car. Jonathan emerged from his compartment.

Mel turned her gaze to the countryside.

"So, I am guilty of being here without telling you about it," Jonathan started, speaking softly. He always took responsibility for everything, even when there was no blame.

"You're not required to tell me what you do," Mel responded. She paused, looking away. "It's just odd that you would come to Italy of all places."

"I'm not visiting, Mel. I got a job here." He took a deep breath, waiting for her reaction.

"When did this happen?"

"Well, I got a temporary offer while in New York, from an acquaintance of Jenna's. I've been here for two weeks. I don't know how it will turn out."

Mel continued to look outside. It was no use being angry with Jonathan. She felt so ashamed about what she had done in New York. She had communicated her insecurity to him in such a disloyal and immature way. Then, she couldn't lie about it. She had hurt him, and herself. There was no going back. She was trying not to cry, but a single tear gathered force at the corner of her eye.

Jonathan didn't know what to do. He wanted to touch her, but he was afraid she would recoil. She was having a hard time forgiving herself. He looked down, pretending he didn't see the teardrop, but then it hit the dirty linoleum floor. He continued to avert his gaze, handing her a tissue.

"So, have you had any luck finding a job?" he said, trying to be cheerful.

She nodded, and gathered herself.

"I just got one today. I'm starting on Monday."

At that moment, Mel realized how good it felt to be able to share the news with him. He knew her better than anybody. She left her emotional isolation for a moment.

Still, things were irreparably wrecked.

"Who is your traveling companion?" Mel asked him.

"Oh, that's Elena. She works at the studio. We are going to Rome to check out some locations."

They heard the sound of a compartment door opening, and Elena came out, looking for Jonathan.

"Excuse me," Mel said. She turned and went back into her compartment. She was not going to meet Jonathan's colleague, or flame, or whatever she was, in this state. She wanted to go back to being supremely happy about her new job. She saw Jonathan move out of her field of vision, preventing Elena from looking at her.

"So," Elena said to Jonathan, "are you going to tell me who that is? Is it your girlfriend from New York?"

"It *is* Melinda," he said, looking her in the eye. "But she is not my girlfriend. Not anymore."

The conductor was making his way down the car, so Jonathan and Elena went back to their seats to get their tickets ready.

* * *

The speed of the *Frecciarossa* train was something Mel had not previously experienced in overland travel.

"We are going at three-hundred kilometers per hour," said a businessman sitting across from her, in English. Then he gave his unwieldy newspaper a snap.

It felt good to be traveling so fast, although it was ironic that Jonathan was also moving fast, and parallel, to Mel. She wondered if that exchange in the corridor was the end of it. Jonathan was probably constrained by his travel companion, whatever their relationship.

After a little while, Mel got up to stretch her legs again.

Elena was halfway down the car, leaning against the window, texting. She looked up, and once they made eye contact, there was no avoiding an introduction. They walked toward one another, and said hello.

"So you're a photographer too?" Mel asked.

"Hardly!" Elena answered. "Of course, I'm an amateur, and have grown to love photography. But in the studio, I'm an assistant producer–for now."

She paused.

"It has been great working with Jonathan. He has so many good ideas. I hope he will be able to get through to Pierpaolo."

"He's our boss," Elena clarified.

Mel smiled. Elena was not only pretty; she was sophisticated. Her clothing was simple: jeans and a tailored jacket. She wore a beautiful pair of low boots, an expensive T-shirt, and a mixture of fine and bohemian jewelry. Mel was taking inventory of all the ways Elena was superior to her.

"So," Elena resumed, trying to get Mel to talk, "how do you like Milano?"

Mel laughed. "Well, it's been tense looking for a job, but I have met some interesting people."

She looked out the window. "The climate is quite gray. Maybe it's just the time of year. It suits my mood, though."

"Yes, the weather is an adjustment. I am not from Milano myself. Wait until the summer. It will be sunny and humid, and you will be praying for rain."

Mel checked her phone. "It looks like Rome will be sunny."

"It's the perfect time of year to visit Rome," Elena said. Before the Easter crowds. Will we see you down there?"

Mel shook her head, looking confused.

"No, I don't believe so. I am going to join my host, who is visiting her cousin. And I guess you and Jonathan have work to do."

Elena nodded.

Mel felt a little drained, and wanted to go back to her compartment, to the friendly businessman, the elegant woman with her five-year-old son, and the two twenty-somethings immersed in their devices.

134

"Well, it was nice to meet you, Elena."

Mel returned to her spot, closed her eyes and felt the rattling speed of the train. Exhausted, she nodded off briefly. Then her phone signaled the arrival of a text.

CAN WE TALK?

It was from Jonathan. Mel looked up. Jonathan was outside of the compartment. The businessman shuffled his newspaper and said, without looking up, "Your boyfriend is back."

Mel sighed and got up to crack the door.

"What?"

"Could you please come out?"

Mel stepped into the corridor and closed the door. The businessman quickly looked down at his paper.

"I just wanted to tell you that I am not here in Italy to stalk you. I had been investigating opportunities while we were still together. It was going to be a surprise. Then when I had the opportunity, I took it."

He paused.

"I was trying to figure out how to reach out to you without making you feel like you needed to see me, or address any issues you want to put aside."

"Honestly, Jon, it's okay. I can't ask you to stay away from Milan because I'm there. I am trying to work things out in my mind, that's all."

Mel looked at him, and saw how sincerely kindly he regarded her.

"Elena seems nice. She is very beautiful, too."

Jonathan shrugged. "She has been the boss's girlfriend for the last year."

"That's awkward."

"Well, nothing is going on between us, if that's what you think."

"Really? She seems interested in you."

135

"I think she just needs someone to talk to. She's going through some stuff."

Then Jonathan laughed, thinking of something else.

"I heard that you met my colleague Reiner." he said. "How crazy is that?"

"Really," Mel answered, making the connection. "I went to see his apartment. I still don't have a place to stay. Longer-term, I mean."

"Well, he's basically a good guy. Just a little bristly."

"I'll say. And arrogant."

"He's feeling a little threatened by me. He thinks I'm upsetting the power structure in the studio."

"Are you?"

"Of course." He smiled, feeling the conversation take on a more familiar tone.

"Anyway," Mel said, "now that I have a job, I'm going to try to look for something a bit closer. That neighborhood means a half-hour commute, at least. And to be honest, Jon, it wouldn't feel private, because of our history."

"I understand, you're right."

"Look," Mel said, "the snack cart is coming. We'd better clear the way."

Jonathan hesitated.

"Listen," he said. "I'd just like to say that what happened was unfortunate, and hurtful. But I should have stood up for you. You know the whole religion thing is meaningless to me."

Mel cut him off.

"Right now, Jonathan, going back there is too hard for me. I am still digesting it. You locked me out of the apartment."

"I was really angry." Now they were whispering.

"Rightfully so. But that didn't make it any easier for either of us."

136

"Okay," he said, realizing that the conversation was going to a place of rehashing, not where he wanted it to go.

"Maybe we can talk again sometime?"

"We'll see, ...sure, I guess," Mel answered.

When she closed the compartment door, the businessman rattled his paper again and raised his eyebrows. He wasn't taking sides.

Mel sat down and picked up her Italian fashion magazine. The ads contained some interesting idiomatic expressions. She repeated them silently to herself, trying to commit them to memory. She looked away from the page, and closed her eyes.

Why was she so wishy-washy? What would be the point in speaking to Jonathan again? Then she thought of Alberto. He had asked her to let him know how it went with Giorgio. And in fact, there were several texts from him asking just that.

Mel texted him back, THX. IT WENT WELL!! I GOT THE JOB :)

When they got to the station in Rome, Elena and Jonathan were already in the corridor, bags on their shoulders. Jonathan gave Mel a sidelong glance, and Elena made a small wave with her fingers.

The businessman caught this, looked at Mel, and shook his head. He folded up his newspaper and asked her if he could get her bag down from the rack?

"*Grazie*," Mel said.

* * *

Lella was the picture of happiness when she picked Mel up at the station. She was driving an old emerald-green Alfa Romeo spider with leather upholstery the color of caramel.

"It's Federico's," she said, laughing. "It is so crazy driving here, I don't know what I was thinking!"

"Lella," Mel said in a conspiratorial tone, "Jonathan was on the train!"

She saw him and Elena hailing a cab.

"There he is," she pointed, trying to be discreet.

Lella turned around to look. Jonathan was holding the door for Elena, who had already entered the cab.

"Not bad!" she said, tilting her head and nodding. "So, tell me about it! We have a lovely dinner waiting for us, and it's so mild, we're going to eat on the terrace. I am excited for you to be here. And congratulations on your job! Now, tell me about Jonathan on the way."

Lella pulled out and wove her way through the traffic. It was dark, and the lights of the city were cast dramatically on its treasures.

To Mel, it looked like a fantastical stage set. Rome!

All of her tension and worries disappeared.

When in Rome

Trastevere is an old, labyrinthine neighborhood across the Tiber River (called the *Tevere* in Italian) from the center of Rome. It was dark when they arrived, but Mel's first impression was of comfort in the age of everything. There were no new buildings around Federico's apartment, which Lella and Mel entered through an arched doorway. It was a three-story walk-up. Federico greeted them at the door, taking Mel's bag and talking animatedly as they ascended.

"Your room is here," he said, "across from Lella's." There was a short hallway flanked by two small rooms, with a bathroom at its end.

"Now, up one more flight," Federico said.

They walked back into the living area and up a spiral staircase.

At the top of the stairs, there was another small living area with a dining table, and a galley kitchen. Outside the kitchen, facing the Roman skyline, there was a terrace with a table set for dinner.

"Please, take a look around, while I throw in the pasta."

Lella showed Mel around the apartment. Federico's bedroom was above the two rooms and the hall below, and his bathroom was at the far end. He had sliding doors separating his bedroom from the living area, so that when he was alone (and his bed was made), they could be kept open.

"This was our grandmother's home," Lella explained. "Federico has done a great job renovating it. But none of us could afford to buy it today."

Mel peered down to the level below through a thick glass window cut out of the parquet floor near the wall.

"That is an architectural folly of mine, Federico said. I wanted more light below, and I thought the cutaway floor would resemble a ruin. Through it, you can see the old brick wall downstairs that was original to the building."

He handed Lella and Mel glasses of wine and gestured toward the terrace.

Mel stepped out onto the small space. There was room for a square table, planters around the edges, and a lounger. And there was the center of Rome, to the northeast. Its iconic architecture was illuminated, and the bridges were punctuated with rows of lights that made wiggly lines in the Tiber.

"Wow," Mel said, transfixed.

She felt as if she was in a dream. The setting was so dramatic. Thoughts whirled in her head like a merry-go-round. The morning with Giorgio and the job offer, a dream come true. Alberto, and his stirring little kiss. Jonathan, on the train. The beautiful Elena, who looked at him wistfully. And now this immersion in The Eternal City. Being in Rome was like walking onto a stage where anything could happen. Mel thought of how much *place* influenced our possibilities, how it inspired us. She wondered if it touched everyone equally. To her, it was inspirational and seductive.

The dinner was lovely, delicious pasta with Pecorino Romano cheese and cracked pepper, and a salad with tomatoes, anchovies and capers. Federico was charming and unaffected. They talked, ate, cleared the dishes, and went inside when the air became damp and cool.

"Our Italian mothers always told us to stay warm after having a meal," Federico joked.

Mel smiled. "You're so lucky to have this place," she said, still in awe of the quaintness of her surroundings.

"Well, in the summer I go away because it is impossibly warm and I cannot work. So, I rent the place to tourists for a couple of months. That helps me to pay taxes and fix up the place up—you have no idea how much work it needs! This building contains three condos, and we divide the cost of the work. You know, for the roof and the façade, and the plumbing..."

Mel was nodding off while she listened, then sat up straight.

"I think I may have to go to bed. I have had such a long day."

"Yes." Lella agreed. "And tomorrow we have a lot of exploring to do. We can make a plan over our *cappuccino*."

Mel turned down the covers and climbed into the bed with such gratefulness: for everything that happened today (apart from seeing Jonathan, which she wasn't sure about), for the generosity and friendliness of Lella's family (apart from Alberto's, which she wasn't sure about either), and for the cool sheets against her skin. She could hear Lella saying goodnight to Federico, and fell asleep to the buzzing of scooters outside her window.

* * *

Mel woke up, realized she was in Rome, and jumped out of bed. She wanted to have a look outside. First, she turned the handle on the casement windows and opened them inward. Then she unlatched the green shutters and fastened them to the exterior wall. The hum of traffic and the ubiquitous buzz of scooters were offset by the rustle of young leaves on the Plane Trees that lined the street. They looked like nature's urban warriors with their camouflage bark. The light of the sun seemed different here: instead of the pale, gauzy yellow of Milan, it had a more ardent, slightly yolky cast to it. She pulled on a pair of jeans and wandered out to the kitchen.

"*Buongiorno!*" Lella said. She was at the counter, dumping out the grounds from the espresso machine, tapping the *portafiltro* on the compost basket. "Federico went for a run, and he's stopping at the bakery. He should be back any minute."

Mel stepped out onto the terrace. The lights of Rome were gone. In their place were orange tile rooftops, leafy treetops, the domes with their cupolas, the hills in the distance, and the bright blue sky.

Federico arrived, and emptied a bag into a bowl.

141

Mel joined them in the kitchen.

"These," said Lella, "are *brutti ma buoni*."

Ugly but good, Mel translated in her head. They were knobby looking cookies of some sort.

"They're made with *nocciole*, how do you call them in English?" Lella asked.

"Hazelnuts," said Federico, "like in Nutella." He then took over the preparation of the cappuccinos.

"Right, hazelnuts, in a meringue." Lella explained.

They sat on the terrace and enjoyed the morning air, eating *brutti ma buoni*, and sipping their cappuccinos. Mel loved the fact that you could have dessert for breakfast in Italy.

"Ladies," said Federico, "I know you will want to do some traipsing around, and I do have some work to do today. I was thinking we could go to the market once you are ready. Then I could come back here and work. I will have lunch around one-thirty if you want to join me."

"Thank you Fede, we'll join you at the market, but I don't think we will be back for lunch," Lella said. "We can grab something while we are out."

The market was fun, and crowded, as markets tend to be on a beautiful spring day. On the fringes, African immigrants were selling bootleg items and some cheap beaded bracelets. They spoke a sort of Franco-Italian salesman speak.

Lella and Federico led Mel through the fray. They looked at the vegetables, and discussed the dinner menu. There were also articles of clothing and small housewares for sale. Mel listened to the distinctly different way of speaking, whether Italian, dialect, or a combination of the two. Mostly it was a change in manner, more expansive and emotional. It made Milan seem much less "Italian" somehow. She shared this thought with Lella, after Federico had left with the bags.

"You will find," said Lella, "that *Italian* is an elusive concept. When you step back, it looks so clear and homogeneous. And when you start to get close, you find a myriad of differences, things that change when you go to the other side of a hill. It's like a fine sauce made of subtle flavors that are distinct, yet blend to make the receipt."

Mel cocked her head. "I think you mean *recipe*."

Lella laughed. "Yes."

"Now, let's get a cab and go to the Colosseum. Then we can walk through the Roman Forum to the Capitoline Hill. From there, we can walk to the Pantheon and *Piazza Navona*."

"That sounds like a lot."

"Do you have good shoes for walking?"

Mel looked down at her feet. "I'm wearing my trainers, as a typical American would."

"Then we'll be fine. After, if we're not too tired, we can go to the *Passeggiata Gianicolo*, here in *Trastevere*, where we can enjoy a nice view when the light is low."

Lella paused, thinking.

"On second thought, we could wait until after dinner tonight to go to *Piazza Navona*. You really should see it at night. Or, we might want to hang out in Trastevere. There are a lot of young people here in the evening."

Mel was amused, letting Lella think aloud about their itinerary. She did not care where they went, or whether they got lost. Mel just wanted to absorb the richness of the city, to go where their feet took them.

The Roman ruins deeply moved her: the peculiarly ancient style of the column capitals, the audacious persistence of the arches, and even the provocative absence of parts. Also touching were the unkempt green spaces, the garbage, and the displaced men who hovered near the tourists. Would the trampling of the present, pure negligence, or the stress of humanity obliterate this precious heritage?

It was Mel who led Lella around and through the Pantheon, explaining its details, to Lella's great amusement. She described the materials and techniques the Romans used to lighten the massive dome. She told the story of Filippo Brunelleschi, who traveled here to study the Pantheon's structure, avidly taking notes and making drawings, in his quest to solve the problem of the dome of Florence Cathedral, twelve hundred years later. When they stepped back from the building in the piazza, Mel regarded it once more, in awe.

"I can't believe I'm actually here."

Lella decided they should walk north, toward the Spanish Steps, and look for a bar-café along the way for something to eat.

"We need to find a street of shops, away from the monuments and the tourists."

As the day progressed, Mel discovered another Rome: the Baroque city with twisting, dramatic forms, sparkling fountains, and oval spaces. The embodied movement seemed to push and pull you, even spin you around.

The layers of time and styles in Rome were like a tapestry with different colored threads emerging here, and there, creating a richness that was sometimes startling.

They had a panino with a glass of white wine, and sat at a table along the street for a rest. It was nearly three o'clock when they finished, so they decided to explore in the direction of home.

Back in Trastevere, Mel was glad to wander in the botanical gardens, and then walk the *Passeggiata Gianicolo*. While they were admiring the view of St. Peter's in the late afternoon light, She got a text signal.

The message was from Jonathan.

BEAUTIFUL HERE! CAN WE GET COFFEE IN THE AM?

"He wants to meet for coffee tomorrow morning."

"What do you want to do?" Lella asked.

An intimate conversation

Jonathan and Elena had a very productive day. They visited three locations in the morning, and two in the afternoon. They decided on the last one they scouted in the morning, and returned at the end of the day to check the light. The owner already had some great plants on the terrace, so it would take minimal effort to tweak the space to backdrop the furniture that was the subject of the shoot. The building had an elevator, too. Elena took down the contact information for the neighbors and discussed the fee with the owner.

Jonathan stepped away to text Mel. He couldn't pass up the chance to see her in this amazing place, even if for a few minutes.

She texted back that she and Lella were taking a ride into the countryside in the morning, and proposed they all meet for a drink after dinner instead, in Trastevere.

10:30 OK?

He checked with Elena and they agreed on a place suggested by Lella.

Back at the hotel, Jonathan put down his bag and flopped onto the pullout bed. Elena was arranged regally on the bed that had been meant for her and Pierpaolo to share. She took off her sweater and jeans, and went to pour herself a tall glass of water.

Jonathan had to admit she had an amazing body. He tried not to look at her, but she was making that very difficult.

"Are you okay with meeting Melinda and her friends after dinner tonight?" he said.

"Sure." Now she was thumbing through a magazine, sitting up against a stack of pillows. Her skin was golden and smooth. Jonathan wondered how it would feel to stroke her leg. Just out of curiosity.

"I thought we made a good team today," he said.

She smiled at him. "Of course. It was fun."

Jonathan felt the temptation pass, the tug of war pulling him back to friendliness. He put his hands behind his head and stretched out.

Elena asked, "Do you mind if I ask you what it is about Melinda that you like so well?"

Jonathan looked at her, divining her reason for the question.

"What I like about Mel is...both her creativity and her vulnerability. I mean, her strength of ideas is tempered by her insecurity. To me, that shows deep feeling."

"Do you find women usually sure of themselves?" asked Elena.

Jonathan looked at her, avoiding the generalization. "I guess you're insecure, too. It's hard to believe because you are such a beautiful woman."

Elena looked irritated.

Jonathan continued, "I didn't mean it like that. You know, I didn't mean that being a beautiful woman is the solution to all problems."

"You're right, it isn't. It is like being a well-wrapped gift, and everyone is so distracted by the paper and bows that they want it without concern about what is inside."

"Are you saying that Pierpaolo hasn't appreciated you?"

"He's a photographer. Sometimes at dinner he would move the candle a little to the side, and reach across the table to lift my chin with his finger."

"Are you kidding me?"

"No! And then would would say, *this is definitely your good side.*"

They both started laughing.

"One time," she continued, "after we made love, he got up and said, 'don't move, *amore.*' He took out his camera and starting taking pictures, twisting and squatting with his *pisello* hanging in the breeze."

Jonathan felt like this was more than he needed to hear, and though he was taken aback, the image of Pierpaolo got the better of him and he broke out laughing again.

Somehow Elena had managed to shift the conversation to herself, and the image of her naked in bed. He looked at her in her T-shirt and underpants, here, dressed (somewhat), trying to get it out of his head.

Jonathan jumped up and said, "How about going to *Piazza Navona* for an *aperitivo*?" He felt like he needed some air. "I'll take a quick shower while you get dressed."

* * *

They walked around the Piazza, went into Sant'Agnese church to see Bernini's sculpture, *Ecstasy of Saint Teresa*, marveling at its transcendent beauty. Then they re-emerged into the bright light and found a table at a nearby bar, obviously for tourists.

"It's a great place to people-watch, though," Elena said.

She returned to the topic of Mel.

"So, it seems that you find vulnerability to be an attractive trait. Do you find it is rare among women?"

That question again!

"I don't think it is rare among *people*," Jonathan replied. "Where we each differ is whether we recognize our own weakness, and how we communicate it to others. Mel is like a little animal that comes out of its hole, looks around, and then ducks back inside. But she always pops out again."

"It sounds like she appeals to your paternal instinct."

"It's not paternal," he responded, sitting up straight. "But she does make me want to move the obstacles out of her way. And she does (did) the same for me. I get in my own way, too. Mel has a way of surgically analyzing a situation. I am an emotional reader, so I see things differently."

148

"You seem to understand people well," Elena said. "Is that why you are not interested in making love to me?"

Jonathan looked around to make sure nobody was listening.

"Whoa!" he said.

Elena continued to hold his gaze.

Then he softened. "Elena, why would you use the wall between yourself and a real relationship as a lure?"

They leaned back while the server placed two glasses of spumante on the table. They decided to order some pizza.

"I don't know how else to behave."

"Stop acting sexy!"

"I'm not *trying* to act sexy," she said, taking a sip of her drink.

Then she continued, "I think that when I go out, I am afraid of receiving comments. So, I guess I have developed an attitude to deter men from approaching me."

Jonathan parked his chin in his left hand, elbow on the table, looking at her. "The unattainable woman. Which some find intriguing. But you're not like that with me."

"No, you make me feel comfortable. And in the studio, my relationship with Pierpaolo has protected me."

"But it has also imprisoned you."

"I don't know how to break the cycle. It's over with Pierpaolo, anyway."

"Well, why don't you start thinking about what *you* want instead of playing a defensive game? And don't waste your time on men who aren't available."

"Are there men who aren't available?'

"Now I am offended."

"Sorry."

149

"You are looking for a place to land right now. You need to think about taking off."

The pizza came.

Jonathan raised his glass.

"Here's to taking off," he said.

The clicked their glasses.

"To taking off," Elena answered, "okay."

* * *

Federico had prepared Sea Bass wrapped in parchment with potatoes and onions. The fish was tender and moist; the onions were buttery and sweet; and the potatoes were done to perfection. Mel and Lella cleared the plates while Federico scooped some homemade lime and basil sorbet into narrow parfait cups. The buzzer downstairs signaled the arrival of his boyfriend Massimo, who came in and immediately began picking at the leftover fish.

"Let me make you a plate, Massimo," Lella said.

"Thank you, *tesoro*, I am starved. I am sorry I couldn't join you earlier... And who is this, Melinda?" he asked, turning toward Mel. "Have you been enjoying Rome?"

"My eyes, yes, my feet not so much," Mel said, laughing.

"The place is a wreck!" Massimo said, embarrassed for the condition of his beloved city. He chewed on one of his fingernails until Federico pulled his hand away.

"Eat," Federico commanded.

The sun was gone, and the terrace twinkled with the tiny lights strung between two narrow poles and the building wall. The evening air was cool but none of them wanted to go inside. The lime and basil sorbet was tangy, aromatic, and bright.

"So," Massimo started, "tell me what is going on tonight. Is there a romantic intrigue? Fede, this *branzino* is fabulous."

Lella explained to Massimo that they were going to meet a certain Jonathan, Melinda's former boyfriend, who is traveling with his colleague Elena, who has a crush on him (according to Melinda), although *she* has been in some sort of relationship with their boss.

Mel was in no hurry to go out. She sipped her wine and flexed her feet. Putting her shoes back on would not be fun.

"Have you saved some room for *tiramisu*?" Massimo asked Mel.

"I might need to go around the block a few times."

"Well, there's no rush," Lella said. She and Mel left Federico and Massimo outside to catch up, and they went in to do the dishes.

When they got to *Caio & Gaio*, they found Jonathan and Elena standing in the narrow street, talking. Massimo went inside and secured a table among the few outside. It was too cool for the dinner clientele to be out there, but they were happy and comfortable in their jackets. Everyone was introduced. Massimo got the ball rolling by telling stories about his day, working on a corny commercial set in Ancient Rome at *Cinecittà* Studios. He was very entertaining, and provided a contrast to Federico's quiet, deliberate manner. Jonathan talked about New York, and his work in Milan, and then Mel told her story about the project she had worked on all week, and her new job. Elena was friendly, and seemed more relaxed than she had been on the train.

Before they separated (because everyone was very tired), Lella began conversing with Elena, while Federico and Massimo went inside to chat with the owners. Jonathan and Mel were standing apart from the others.

"I want you to know," Jonathan said, "that I am not going to pester you when we're back in Milan."

Mel gave him a weak smile.

151

"Would you let me know where you're living once you get settled, though? I mean, if you want to?"

"Sure," she said, "fair enough. I'm sure we'll run into to each other again anyway."

"Lella seems like a really nice woman."

"She's fantastic. I don't know what I would have done without her."

Mel turned at that point, just as Federico and Massimo came out. They started back down the narrow street; Jonathan and Elena went to the piazza to get a cab.

"Jonathan is very sweet," said Federico.

"True," added Massimo, "but he doesn't have much of an edge."

"Not everyone has to have an edge, Massimo."

"I guess not, but there should be an edge in every couple."

"He can have an edge," said Mel. "Once he pushed me out of our apartment and locked the door for two hours."

"What did you do?" said Massimo, scandalized.

Along the short way home, and up the stairs, Mel told them about the breach of faith between her and Jonathan.

It was easy for her to tell them about her mistakes. They didn't see things in black and white, or good and evil. They pointed to extenuating circumstances, made excuses for her. It was quite touching, actually. Lella was silent.

She was glad to get back and into bed, and she was about to turn off the light when Lella peeked in.

"What time do you think you can be ready for our road trip? Tivoli is about forty-five minutes away."

"How does nine o'clock sound?"

"Perfect. *Buona notte.*" Lella closed the door.

Mel could hear Federico and Massimo's footsteps on the stamped metal steps, and then the buzz of scooters on the street below.

* * *

Lella decided to return on the same train as Mel on Sunday, rather than going with the commuters on Monday morning. The trip back was uneventful; Jonathan and Elena had taken a different train. Lella confessed to having made a dinner date with Giorgio Monti that evening. Mel was happy for her, and decided to pick up a pizza and watch a movie. She was ready to be alone. Tomorrow was her first official day at work. The last seven days had been both rich and unsettling.

Leitizia love

Elena and Leitizia met for coffee at seven-thirty on Monday morning. They had to get a proposal written for Jonathan by Thursday so he could integrate it into his recommendations for the studio.

Their meeting with him last week had been productive. They had discussed their day-to-day activities and brainstormed about how to leverage their services. Jonathan proposed that Elena assume the role of Creative Director, and Leitizia, Creative Manager.

Elena looked at her notes.

"So, I'd like to start out my description as: *responsible for the understanding of the client's mission, social attitude, and policy, in order to ensure that advertising photography reflects that in every detail.*"

"That sounds great," Leitizia said. She tore off a piece of her chocolate brioche and used it to gesture, like a baton.

"And I should focus on execution of the vision through my understanding of social culture, fashion, consumer products and overall *zeitgeist.*"

Elena nodded. "*Zeitgeist.* I like that."

She paused, and then asked, "So, what is so special about our work that other studios would want to hire us?"

"Well, first of all, the small studios are not going to have the direction you can provide. In my experience, the client's rep often doesn't know how to put the company's culture into words. Or, they have the words but don't understand their meaning. At any rate, the stylist ends up doing what she agrees on with the photographer."

Elena wrote: *programming.*

"Next question: How do we avoid homogenizing everyone's work with our own stylistic prejudices?"

"Let's see," said Leitizia. "We might be able to handle that by diversifying the pool of stylists we use. If we can get an array of approaches, and figure out where *our* direction ends and *their* initiative begins, that would be great. No stylist is going to want to work with us over time if they don't have any creative freedom."

"I can see that. I suppose it would also be good, in the beginning, to sell our service to different types of clients, so the work will be inherently distinct."

"That I will leave to you. As far as props go, I think I'd like to focus on having some basic, timeless items that will save legwork, but the more trendy stuff should be rented, on loan, or returnable in ninety days. We have to give everything an expiration date. Other studios may use them after us, but they will be *copying*, and that is good for our leadership role."

They continued their discussion and note taking, and sipped on their cappuccinos. Leitizia promised to get her part written up and sent to Elena by Tuesday evening.

"So," she said, "may I ask how the weekend with Jonathan went?"

Elena laughed, shaking her head.

"It was nice, but nothing happened. We worked well together, and had a good talk. But," she added, "the most surprising part was that his former girlfriend, the one from New York..."

"The one that Reiner met?"

"Yes! She was there, too. We met at the *Stazione Centrale*, before the train even left."

"Oh, *Dio!*"

"Jonathan was a little moody on Friday evening, but he was fine when we got to work on Saturday. Then, when we returned to the hotel to relax, there was a moment, let's say, of possibility. However, he very skillfully turned it into an examination of my approach to my relationships."

"Which, arguably, sucks."

"Yes, you're right. He was actually very sweet, and I think we got close. So then, he made arrangements to meet Melinda and her friends. We went to Trastevere to see them on Saturday after dinner."

"It wasn't what you had hoped for, was it?"

"To be honest, no. But I think some progress was made on a deeper, personal level. You know, it's true that I just go straight to sex with guys. I feel like they are going to pester me until I give in, so I just want to get it out of the way to see if there is anything beyond that worth pursuing."

Leitizia was quiet, waiting.

"And often I find that there isn't. Now, that could be because there is not enough care on their part for the sex to be really good. Or, because I am too closed and submissive the first time. Maybe they think I am not enough of a challenge, and so I would never be faithful. Who the hell knows?"

They laughed.

"In any case, Jonathan thinks I am being too passive, that I should be deciding on my standards and looking for someone myself. You know, doing the choosing."

"Maybe you could write up your dating requirements while you are doing the proposal this week. I'd be happy to review it for you."

Elena smiled, "It's not a bad idea. I could keep a list with checkboxes."

She paused, reflecting then said, "I don't feel inclined to ever go on a date again."

They got up and embraced.

"I, for one, love you, Elena," Leitizia said.

A Cup of Tea

Mel had tea with Lella, who was in a good mood, when they returned from Rome. She was feeling cautiously optimistic about seeing Giorgio.

"He is just in such a damn hurry," she said.

"He seems to exude a sense of urgency, doesn't he?" Mel noted.

"It would be really nice to just hang out, go to a show, take a walk, have dinner. You know, let me get used to having a man in my life again. We often get caught up in the excitement of infatuation, and forget about the piece of our lives that we lose. It's not always a fair exchange."

"I would generally agree, although Jonathan was not like that. He was very focused on building the relationship. I guess I wasn't confident enough to weather the thing with his mother."

"It is as if he was an Italian man."

"Well, I think maternalism is part of it, although I wonder if that isn't just a screen."

"For your own desire for control?"

"You know, I guess I never considered that."

"You might."

Mel went down to her room to put her things—and these thoughts—away. She noted the comfort of her surroundings, thinking how difficult it was going to be to leave. Would Lella really still want to be her friend if she was living in a dumpy two-room flat on the city's periphery? She sighed, went back upstairs to say goodbye. Lella gave her a hug.

"Have a good time!" Mel said shooing Lella towards the door.

Lella exited, laughing softly.

Enrico emerges

Enrico was feeling a little off-balance in the studio on Monday. Jonathan and Elena had gone to scout locations in Rome, something he usually did. He was starting to wonder what his role was going to be in the new order. He saw that Elena was in her office and decided to approach her.

"So, how was Rome?"

"Productive," said Elena, writing something down. Then she looked up at Enrico. "You know that Pierpaolo planned to go down himself, with me."

"Why do you think he didn't ask me to join you in his place?"

Elena shrugged. "It could be that he wanted Jonathan to have the experience. It could be he was jealous, and didn't trust you."

Lucy popped her head in for orders.

"Just *espresso* for me," Enrico said.

"My usual," Elena added.

"Do you mind if I ask you something, Ele?"

"Go ahead."

"Are you and Pierpaolo still...," he trailed off, not knowing how to finish.

"Fucking?" she said, trying to help him out, irritated by the question, for a number of reasons. "No we are not, currently. It would appear that he is seeing someone, whatever that means."

"And so he delivered you to the hands of Jonathan."

"It wasn't like that. Jonathan is not available."

"But if he was," Enrico started.

"He isn't," Elena said, cutting him off. "Now, if you don't mind, I have stuff to do."

"Okay, okay. I guess I missed my window."

"Your window?" Elena said, unable to fathom his nerve. "Do you think that this is a game of gentleman's choice? The fact is: I am not available either."

Enrico studied her.

"Just be careful you are not running after another impossible love."

"Please leave."

Lucy was in the doorway with the tray. Enrico took his espresso and walked past her into the atrium. Jonathan was sitting on the pedestals stacked at the back of the space, talking with Geert. When he saw Enrico, he put his hand on Geert's back and thanked him, in dismissal.

Jonathan jumped up and asked Enrico if he had time to talk before the shoot. Enrico gave some directions to Geert and then sat down.

Jonathan dove right in: "I feel uncomfortable, having gone down to Rome in your place."

"It's okay, the situation is complicated," Enrico said, brushing it off.

Jonathan continued, "You know why I am here. I'm not in charge of anything or anybody. I'm just making some recommendations."

"What are you going to recommend for me?" He was mildly hostile.

"That's what I want to talk about. Elena and Leitizia are working on a creative direction proposal that I think can help the studio hire Leiti full time, and maybe cover the expense by providing the service to other studios. Reiner seems to be a natural for digital tech. You are more of a problem, because you know how to do everything. Locations, lighting, camerawork... So I guess I want to ask you what interests you most?"

"Being a photographer," Enrico said, without hesitation. Jonathan's recognition of his abilities had disarmed him.

"So, essentially, what Pierpaolo does?"

Enrico laughed, "I guess that's it. If I could come in to find everything set up and just get behind the camera, it would be a dream. When I am looking through the lens, I don't think about my problems, my frustrations, or my worries. I just think about what I see, and how this three-dimensional world, modeled by light in all its forms, will be transmitted into a two-dimensional message."

"So the production stuff, like location scouting, is something you could live without?"

"The only reason I like doing location work is so that I can understand the quality of the light, and the texture of the context. It gets me started thinking about the possibilities. I don't like the trains, the driving, the lugging of equipment... It's all a mindless waste of time."

"I guess the ideal solution for you would be if the studio had more work than Pierpaolo could handle, giving you more space?"

"Sure. Maybe I could move beyond the catalogue jobs."

Jonathan was quiet for a minute, saving the conversation to his memory, so that he could add it to his notes later.

"This has been helpful."

They talked for a few minutes about Geert. Jonathan wondered if he had any ambition, to which Enrico responded that he wanted to drink beer, meet girls, and be told what to do during the day.

"You need people like that, too," Enrico said. "He is good-natured, and can follow directions. If everyone in this place was trying to be a star, it would be untenable."

"True. But since I am not like Geert, I don't know how sustainable that is in the long run. Does ambition kick in at some point, and if so, what form does it take?"

"I take that as a rhetorical question?"

The conversation between Jonathan and Enrico continued along general lines. They understood one another, and this made their exchange unique in the studio. They were the grownups in the room.

"How did you like Rome?" Enrico asked as he stood up.

"It was great, we got some work done. And get this: I ran into my ex on the train."

"No kidding!"

Enrico was pleasantly surprised that there was a potential impediment between Jonathan and Elena.

"Yeah, and we all got together on Saturday night. It was good. I'm relieved that we finally made contact, and now she knows I'm here."

"So, what next?"

"I'm not sure, but I think, maybe, that time is on my side."

"Well, good luck." Enrico shook hands with Jonathan and went to find Geert.

Jonathan went to the reception desk.

"*Cara* Lucy, can I take you out to lunch today?"

Lucy looked up at him, surprised. Her hand went to her hair, as if to test whether she looked good enough to warrant such an invitation. Then she recovered and looked at her appointment calendar.

"Can we go to the Thai place?"

"Of course," Jonathan laughed.

At that moment, Pierpaolo breezed in, walking to the beat of the thumping club music Lucy was playing in the waiting area. He tossed his buttery leather jacket without losing a beat, like a fashion model on a runway.

"It is warming up out there," he said. "*Jonatan*, in my office. Let's catch up." Then to Lucy, "A double *espresso*, please. Urgent."

Jonathan smiled at Lucy, who grabbed Pierpaolo's jacket before it slid to the floor, and followed in Pierpaolo's wake.

Pierpaolo sat down, turned on his computer, and then turned to Jonathan.

"First," he said, next week is the *Salone del Mobile*, the International Furniture Fair. "Keep your calendar free. We are going to go, and there are a lot of cocktails and events. I have some clients who like to have photos of stylish people drooling over their furniture, in the context of the event. We also cultivate some new manufacturers. I am interested in the accessories for the home. Lots of new players, and they will need to see us around."

"Sounds like fun," Jonathan said.

"Now, I got your material from Rome, so let's talk about that."

They went through the whole process, and Jonathan took some notes to plan the shoot. He had already worked it out with Elena, but Pierpaolo wanted to be in the command role.

"So, how was your weekend?" Jonathan asked.

Pierpaolo leaned forward confidentially.

"I have met an amazing woman. She's blonde, Danish." He said it as if describing a selection at the pastry shop.

Lucy came in with a tray and left it on the desk.

"There's a package for you, Pierpaolo."

She retrieved a box from the reception desk and brought it to him.

Pierpaolo opened it up. "It's from Hanne," he said, "That's her name."

Then he rolled his eyes.

"What's in the box?"

Pierpaolo tipped the package toward Jonathan, showing the smooth, vanilla-colored cylinders of beeswax inside.

"Fucking candles. She had so many lit at her place I thought I would suffocate. She calls it *Hygge*, whatever the fuck that is."

He packed the box back up and put it on the floor behind him.

"But, she is gorgeous. Now, what's going on this week?"

Alberto is surprised

Alberto had heard about Mel's success with Giorgio through messages from her, and a phone call from Lella (who also mentioned their encounter with Jonathan in Rome). He was trying to digest the parenthetical information and to understand what effect it had on him emotionally. Was it jealousy, and if so, what did that mean? He was certainly attracted to Mel in a protective sort of way. She had the courage to come to Milan and take some chances (something that he didn't think he would be able to do), but at the same time, she struggled. It was as if Mel willed herself to do difficult things. It made him curious to discover the source of her determination.

To be honest, a part of him did want to make love to her. It was his way. Amelia and Lella didn't understand. It wasn't that he was a philanderer; he just needed to cross the threshold of intimacy to unlock a woman's secrets. Only then did he feel like he could drop his guard. Otherwise, the tension would always be there and it would distract him from being friends.

That was a problem for Marietta. She couldn't stand being in social situations without knowing who had slept with her husband before they were married. Or after, for that matter. Alberto never believed he was being unfaithful, as long as he didn't fall in love, and he never did. Sometimes his female acquaintances were looking for a romantic relationship. They would act like they were just having fun, like him, but then the possessiveness would kick in. That was a bit of poor judgement on his part, and dishonesty on theirs, to be fair.

He simply loved the complicity that sex enabled. The looks across the room, the raised eyebrows, the clandestine brushing against one another in the hallway. Maybe his life was too predictable and boring? Maybe he wanted more than one life.

Mel was young. He probably shouldn't pursue her. He was worried that Lella, and worse, Amelia, would find out. Mel was like an open book. And then there was this Jonathan. Lella said he was very *simpatico,* and seemed devoted to Mel. How could he get in the way of that?

His phone signalled a call. It was his elder son, Leo.

"*Ciao, Papá,*" he said.

"Leo, how nice to hear from you. How are your studies going?" Alberto was very proud of his son, and always introduced him as *the future Doctor Leo.*

"All good. Listen, I am calling you for a specific reason."

"Oh? Tell me."

"Um, have you talked to Mom lately?"

"Not for a while."

Leo paused, then charged forward.

"I think she's going to ask you for a divorce."

Alberto sat down; his first impulse was panic, related to money.

"Apparently, she is in a serious relationship. I met the guy over the weekend."

No reaction.

"Papá?"

"Sorry, Leo, I am just trying to digest this news. I don't know what to say."

"I'm sorry you had to hear it from me, but I thought you should be warned."

Alberto started flipping through his mail, the phone held by his shoulder.

"Well apparently she wasn't planning on making me wait long. Here's a letter from her attorney."

"That was fast. Well, I've got to go, let me know if you need anything, okay?"

"Okay. *Grazie, e ciao,*" Alberto said.

Why would Alberto be even remotely surprised? It's not as if he thought they would get back together. And she didn't need money. His main concern was Guido, who was living in their jointly owned apartment (which they referred to as *hers*) in *Città Studi,* the "collegetown" near the Politecnico. He didn't want *that* to end up on the chopping block.

He couldn't start thinking about these things until they had a meeting.

His mind wandered back to his previous thoughts. He realized, that once this was final, the protection afforded by his tenuous marriage would be gone completely. It was a scary thought.

Alberto and Marietta had married in France, in a little hill town above the Riviera. That would significantly shorten the time frame of a divorce if a friendly agreement was reached. He paced around the room and then called his attorney.

"Hello Tullio, it's Alberto."

Mel makes another friend

Mel was excited about the *Salone del Mobile*. It was a huge, international fair where all the new furniture, lighting, interior accessories, and design initiatives were exhibited. Giorgio had announced that the studio would close on Thursday so they could attend the *Salone,* and they should all plan on going to the cocktail at the Sofine furniture showroom in the evening, where Giorgio's new living room furniture designs would be displayed. During their meeting with Sofine to finalize the upholstery colors, Mel's suggestion of navy blue and red-violet won the day. Giorgio approved, with the addition of a lime-green ottoman, "Just to stir things up a bit."

On Wednesday, Giorgio's niece Gabriella stopped by for lunch. Giorgio invited Mel to join them, as Gabriella was nearer her age and looking for opportunities to speak English.

They had penne with asparagus.

"We have to get our fill while they are in season," he said.

Giorgio tolerated the conversation between Gabi and Mel. They seemed to have a lot to talk about. He checked his email.

"So, where are you living? Maybe we can get together sometime," said Gabriella.

"Well, right now I am a paying guest, but only for another week and a half."

"She's staying with Lella," Giorgio offered. "Amelia's mother."

"Oh," Gabriella said, thoughtfully. "So you're looking for a place?"

"Yes, I have been focusing on the job hunt, but now I really have to tackle that."

There was a moment of silence.

"Well, I have an idea." Gabriella looked at her uncle, who caught her drift and nodded in approval. Giorgio knew Gabi wanted a roommate. She

167

traveled for work, but didn't want the hassle of renting it by the week when she was gone. He also thought it would be better for *him* if Lella was living alone again. He certainly didn't want to be seeing Lella at her place with his new assistant wandering about.

Mel leaned forward, expectant.

"I have an apartment that is technically a one-bedroom. But there is an alcove off the living room that Giorgio is helping me to close off for a second, small bedroom. Would you be interested?"

"Certainly!" Mel answered. "Are you comfortable, though, considering that we've just met?"

"I have good instincts. But we can do a three-month trial, to see how much you mind fighting over the bathroom with me."

Giorgio went to pay the check, and left them to discuss expenses. It was workable for Mel. They decided to meet there after work for a glass of wine. The apartment was near Porta Garibaldi, within walking distance from Giorgio's studio.

Mel could not believe her good luck.

It's really true that if you take a chance, the world supports you. At least, that's what Mel believed.

The Salone

Mel met Giorgio and her new colleagues at the Porta Garibaldi station. It was a ten-minute trip to the fairgrounds. She sat next to Joji, Giorgio's Japanese intern, and across from Tatania and Ugo, who were both recent architecture graduates. Carlos–an industrial designer from Barcelona–sat across the aisle next to Giorgio. They were discussing a lamp design, a laptop straddling their knees. Carlos was inputting data, and together they looked at the resulting modification of the 3-D model on the screen.

"So, you find place to live?" Joji asked Mel politely.

"Yes!" Mel answered. "It's right near the station here. I have been very fortunate. Where do you live, Joji?"

"Near Metro stop Buonarroti, northwest of center city. I live with Japanese family I find on line."

"Is it a long commute to the studio?"

"No, it is easy with Metro." Then he smiled, "Much easier than Metro in Tokyo."

Tatania and Ugo were both on their phones, checking their messages and texting.

"Tati, save some juice for photos!" Ugo warned.

"I have my charger."

Mel sat back and closed her eyes. Gabriella's apartment was such an incredible godsend! Granted, the alcove-bedroom was small, but it was full of light. Giorgio had devised a partition wall that contained storage on both sides. It had a center section the length of a bed, and two wings that bent toward the main living area, creating two short corridors leading into the space. There was space for a desk facing the windows and a small chair. The wall-storage unit was being painted, and would be delivered in a week. Gabi had shown the drawings to Mel over a glass of wine.

169

Mel owed all of this to Lella, whom she met only a month ago. She shook her head, smiling to herself.

Then it was time to get off the train.

She had a small backpack with a water bottle, a couple of pears, a protein bar, and an extra pair of shoes. They were planning on being here all day, and Mel would return tomorrow. She wanted to have some time on her own to explore the things that particularly appealed to her.

The *Salone* was like a huge industrial park. The buildings were very dull on the outside, but once you entered, it was like the Disneyland of design. Displays the size of showrooms, pop up food stands and buffets, designers, architects, buyers, and journalists from all over the world made it hard to know where to look. The art direction was fabulous: once you were inside a "showroom" it seemed like the rest of the world fell away. You became enveloped in a carefully curated experience.

Giorgio led them first to the Sofine stand, where they were served cappuccinos and tiny croissants. He greeted some visitors who were nosing around his pieces, and was introduced to others by the owner.

"Well, I'm taking my flock around for a bit, but I'll be back later," he explained. Then he turned to us, "Let's have a look at *Euroluce*."

Mel was excited to see the lighting section of the *Salone*.

Carlos and Giorgio led the group, walking side by side like Plato and Aristotle, discussing their priorities.

Mel was fascinated both by the form of the lighting fixtures and the light they emitted. The technology and the sculptural character were beautifully dovetailed. And so much was about the quality of the light: patterns of light, colored shadows, pure magic. She tailed Giorgio and Carlos, hoping to learn something as they discussed the features of the most innovative models.

They spent a couple of hours looking at lamps, then moved on to see the work of young designers in the *SaloneSatellite* exhibition. There were many students milling about, hoping to meet industry reps. It was fun to peruse their experiments. Here Giorgio left his staff to go back to the Sofine display.

By three o'clock Mel was in a daze. She took a break to have a cool drink, upload images, and change her shoes. She felt so dehydrated walking around this place, but it was out of the question to stop. The rest of the day proceeded in the same vein, with Giorgio suggesting manufacturers to visit, sometimes escorting them like a tour guide.

"Mel," he said, "Our Japanese client is here. Let's go to the home accessories section so that I can introduce you."

Mel put her nice shoes back on, and popped into the ladies' room to fix her hair and makeup. She rolled up her jacket, a little worse for the wear, and put it into her backpack.

Giorgio mentioned that he would be meeting with them tomorrow morning, so could she be in the studio promptly at eight? Then she could return to the *Salone*. He briefed her on their client (what to say and what *not* to say), as she quickened her step to keep up.

"I put you across from Joji in the studio for a reason. You have to learn to understand the Japanese if we want to have a good business relationship with them."

When they reached their destination, Giorgio slowed down and composed himself. Introductions were made. Mel hung back slightly and made the faintest suggestion of a bow, almost stylized. She had seen a Japanese man and woman greeting each other that way earlier. She kept a low profile as she listened to the exchange. Afterward, Giorgio and Mel met the others to head back to town.

The day had seemed rushed, but once they were on the train looking back, it seemed like they had been there for a week. They cut out early enough to have an hour back in Milan before the Sofine cocktail, and Mel dreamed of a shower and five minutes in the armchair by the window back at Lella's.

* * *

After she had cleaned up, her feet soaked with cream and resting on a towel on the ottoman, Lella knocked on the wall of the stairs, and came down. She laughed when she saw Mel.

"A lot of walking today, no?"

"*Si*," answered Mel, smiling weakly.

"Well, you'll be happy to know you are traveling by cab to the cocktail. I'm going with you."

Cocktails at Sofine

Jonathan, Enrico, Reiner, and Geert got off the *Metropolitana* at Piazza San Babila and slowly made their way to the Sofine showroom. The sidewalks were full of foreign design groupies, professionals, and students. They were recognizable by their self-consciously stylish airs, in contrast to the more assured and understated Milanese.

Enrico was put off by the familiarity the foreigners claimed in their behavior, as if they belonged there. They ordered prosecco in forced accents at the sidewalk cafés. He checked himself, admitting his own quest for acceptance here. While at work, his Italian migrated toward the staccato cadence of his adoptive city, Milan; but when he settled in a chair for a conversation, the deliberate, scholastic language of the educated Neapolitan emerged. It was all about language in the end, wasn't it? Photography for him was a like a "green world," where all such trappings (except vision, and transmission of understanding) were left behind.

Reiner was busy trying not to look German, at least not the kind that didn't "get" Italy, especially Milan. His was in his usual black leather jacket, jeans and boots. Geert tagged along at his side, scanning the street for opportunity.

The bar-cafés lining the piazza and the adjoining streets had flung their doors open to the mild day. Their counters were stocked with bowls and plates with tiny pickles, pearl onions, bruschette, chips, and nuts. Baristas were agitating stainless shakers and straining cocktails, while exhibiting restrained politeness to their customers.

Jonathan walked along with the others, trying to gather himself. The pulsating emotions of everyone around him were unsettling. Their hopes, annoyances, triumphs, and exhaustion assailed him like waves of energy as he walked past. He involuntarily picked up their expressions, the tone of their voices. He was focused on getting to Sofine, and led the others through a small herd of taxis to the other side of the street.

Elena, Leitizia, and Lucy were near the entrance when they walked into the showroom.

"Your girlfriend is here," said Elena, tipping her head toward the interior.

Jonathan looked toward the buffet table, where Pierpaolo was speaking with a handsome, middle-aged man, Mel by his side.

"I guess everyone knows everyone else in this town," he said, shrugging his shoulders.

Elena exchanged glances with Leitizia, raising her eyebrows. Then she looked around. The room was fraught with dangers for her: Enrico to avoid, unless in company; Pierpaolo, who was expecting his Danish lady; and Jonathan, who still pulled at her heartstrings. A little.

Lucy and Geert made a beeline for the drinks table, and started their evening's work. Reiner approached Pierpaolo casually, looking for an opportunity to say hello to Mel without appearing eager. They had spoken last week at the appointed time, and Mel had declined the room offer, due to its distance from her new job. As they spoke now, she glanced over toward Jonathan and subtly waved her hand. He joined the group, and Pierpaolo introduced him to Giorgio Monti.

In an attempt to preempt further explanation, Mel said, "Jonathan and I are friends from New York."

Jonathan, with a barely perceptible look of disappointment on his face, smiled weakly in acknowledgement.

"No kidding!" said Pierpaolo. Then he turned, and seeing Hanne approach, extended his arm to greet her, squeezing her shoulders.

Hanne was wearing a minimalist outfit, with flowing pants and an oversize, loosely knit sweater. She was all soft and neutral, with a brightly colored, intricately patterned scarf draped casually around her neck. She was lean, with blunt blonde hair and a bright smile. She wore slender, silver jewelry.

Reiner, in his role of representing Northern Europe for the studio, came forward to meet her, followed by Lucy.

"Is she the candle one?" Lucy said.

Jonathan jumped in, "Lucy is referring to the beautiful candles you sent to the studio. Did you make them yourself?"

"Oh, no, I used to. Those are from my family's company," she smiled at Jonathan, calculating his worth.

Reiner gave Lucy a small kick in the ankle, and she turned away indignantly to get another glass of prosecco.

Mel picked up a glass of prosecco and took a sip. It was not exactly top quality, as one would imagine under these circumstances: there were a lot of people here. She knew she had to be careful about drinking it on an empty stomach.

Jonathan had walked away, and returned with a small assortment of cocktail food on a tiny plate.

"Are you interested in a snack?" he said, nonchalantly. He was well aware of Mel's vulnerability to alcohol.

"Thank you, Jon," she said.

"So I assume you were at the *Salone* today. Did you check out the lighting?"

Mel's eyes lit up. "Yes! It was awesome. I especially loved the lamps that make colored shadows. You saw those?"

"Yeah, brilliant use of such a simple principle, and much easier to do with LEDs."

"And I found that while the focus has shifted to the nature of the light itself, there were many pieces that were beautiful as sculptural objects alone."

Jonathan tried to keep a cool demeanor, but he felt happy that he and Mel were having a conversation *about* something, just like they used to have.

"Well, I'd better get back to Pierpaolo," he said, not wanting to push it. "He wants us to shoot some 'beautiful people' sitting on his sofa."

Enrico was surreptitiously rotating one of the red-violet sofas a few degrees to capture the right light. Reiner was metering and Geert was pretending to do something, a glass of wine in his hand.

Mel was overwhelmed by the swirling activity. So much had happened in such a short period of time. Lella was busy catching up with her many acquaintances, so Mel resorted to saying hello to a couple of the architects she had visited during her job search. Cristina della Rovere (who had designed this showroom) was there, and reminded Mel to keep in touch. Marino Contini congratulated Mel on her job, and said they must have lunch one day; his studio was close to Giorgio's.

Distracted by her discomfort, she unconsciously grabbed another glass of the warmish prosecco. Mel was an introvert who worked hard at being social. She was trying to focus on the people in the room, looking to see if there was anyone she could approach. But her head was flipping through a succession of images: her ride to Kennedy, Cecil's letter, and arriving at Lella's doorstep without knowing what it would be like. Then, the job-hunt, the trip to Lake Como, and Alberto's attentions. Only a week ago, she was struggling through her trial project for Giorgio, and now she was here after a day of stunning exposure to collection after collection of the latest furniture designs. Oh, yeah, and the Japanese! And what about the trip to Rome, and the encounter with

Jonathan? All of this had happened in one month. And now she was getting ready to move, to leave the womb-like environment that Lella had provided for her with so much kindness and generosity.

Mel wandered along the table, looking for some water. The pace she had been moving at was taking its toll. On top of that, everyone was expecting great things from her. It was too much. She looked for the bathroom, but there was a line. One of the showroom assistants she had met yesterday told her there was another toilet upstairs she could use and gave her directions.

Mel made her way into the courtyard, and crossed it diagonally. The cobbles were hurting her feet through her thin-soled shoes. She held onto the rail as she made her way up to the second floor, alone now in the dim light of the stairwell. She barely made it into the bathroom, was unable to take the time to close the door before she vomited into the toilet. Her eyes were watering. She started to panic about her responsibility to be downstairs, with Giorgio and Carlos and the others, but there was no way she could do it, not right now. What if they found out she was up here, puking? She held onto the toilet seat with both hands as more of the cocktail food came up, still quite close to its original form. She contemplated the chunky punch in the bowl.

She felt the door swing slightly open, and slammed it shut with her foot.

"It's me, Jonathan."

He opened the door and set a water bottle on the sink. He gathered her hair and pulled it back in his hands.

"Just get it all out," he said gently.

Mel did what she had to do: she stuck her finger down her throat and had another go. Afterward, she was quiet, still kneeling on the floor.

"Would you like to sit up now?" Jonathan asked.

She nodded.

Jonathan helped her up, put the seat cover down, and flushed the toilet.

Mel sat down and let him clean her face with some dampened tissues.

"I'm so embarrassed," she said, "but thank you."

It wouldn't have been practical to argue with Jonathan right now, although her mind starting throwing things at her, about Jonathan, his mother, Cecil...

"Stop!" she said.

"I'm not doing anything," Jonathan said.

"No, not you," Mel replied. She started to cry.

"I can't go back down there yet."

Jonathan was wiping Mel's blouse, "No need to do that. Let's see where the stairs lead. We don't want to get caught here if someone follows our trail."

Mel rinsed her face with icy cold water and ran her wet hands through her hair.

"My stomach feels fine now; I'm just a little shaky."

Together they made the ascent and found a door to the rooftop two flights up. They went outside and found the hidden side of the stairway bulkhead. They sat down and leaned back against it. The sun was low in the sky, and the clouds were tinged with an orange the color of sorbet. They didn't speak for a few minutes. Mel was taking small sips from the water bottle.

"Thank you Jonathan."

Mel thought she wanted to say something to him, to take care of unfinished business. Maybe he would see that it was pointless to keep caring about her.

"You know, I never would have converted to Judaism to marry you. I know we never got to that point, but I thought you should know."

"I figured as much."

"I just had too much religion growing up, and hated the way the priests tormented me. Like Father Connolly. He hated me because I spoke out in class."

"Yeah, I think you've told me about him. What a dick!"

"Did I ever tell you about the time he held a contest for our eighth-grade graduation? We had to write an essay about how great the school was, and our submission would be anonymous. I thought, *here's my big chance*. I was sure I could write the best essay, and then he would have to give me a cash prize in front of the whole parish. Well, I set to work, and laid on the syrup about how understanding the nuns were, and how we were held to the highest standards while always feeling their loving care. It was total bullshit."

"Did you get the prize?"

"Of course! I was snickering all the way up the aisle in church. It gave me a lot of satisfaction."

A voice came from the other side of the bulkhead.

"That's a good story." Reiner walked around as he dragged on a joint. He offered it to them; they waved him off.

"Do you mind if I join you? I have a story too. I used to go the youth group at our Lutheran church. One year, at Easter, we were asked to make a composition about what the death of Jesus meant to us."

He took another drag.

"So, I based mine on Nietzsche's famous quote, 'God is dead.' I said that we killed him, right here in Germany, exterminating millions of people," he nodded to Jonathan, "including six million Jews, under Nazi rule. And now we *must find away to live without God*. As you can imagine, that did not go over very well with our pastor. My parents were mortified."

He paused.

"But I never had to go back to church after that."

179

Mel looked at Reiner, contemplating. She looked down and saw that she had a text from Lella.

WHERE ARE YOU?

"I'd better get back down there, I think I am missed."

Reiner asked her if she had thrown up.

"How did you know?"

"I used the bathroom after you, to roll my joint."

Mel brushed her hair and put on some lipstick, then dug around in her bag.

"You will probably want some gum, too," she said to Reiner.

"Thanks."

Mel texted back to Lella.

I WAS ON THE ROOF WITH JONATHAN.

Lella would consider that a valid excuse, and Mel felt only slightly guilty for using Jonathan as a shield.

The three of them walked down the stairs, making comments about the pretentious people in the showroom and laughing.

Reiner slunk into the space and made his way to the food, looking for something fresh and cool to put in his mouth.

Mel walked over to Lella with Jonathan.

Lella said, "We have reservations for dinner. Giorgio, Pierpaolo, Hanne, and you two."

Jonathan looked at Mel.

"Is that okay with you?"

"Sure," she said. What choice did she have?

Dinner plans

Alberto finished trimming his beard and took a hard look in the mirror. He still looked pretty good. Dashing, in a mature sort of way. And just the slight hint of a gut, which in his view, showed that he was a lover of the good things in life: pasta, wine, gelato.

The mediation with Marietta had gone well. They decided to transfer the *Città Studi* apartment to a trust destined for Guido and Leo, giving Guido the right to live there expense-free until two years after he finished his studies. Until that time, Alberto and Marietta would share the taxes and condominium expenses. Then, the boys would split everything, and if Guido continued to live there, he would pay rent to the trust. Alberto owned his place before the marriage, so that was no issue. The country house in Umbria was Marietta's, although Alberto contributed the majority of the funds required for the renovation. He didn't want to squabble over that, since that property was going to the boys as well, but he leveraged it to keep the furnishings in his apartment, most of which were acquired during the marriage. The artwork was easy: he kept what he liked; she took what she liked. He didn't want reminders of those arguments around the place anyway. Alberto had been giving Guido money right and left, so they set up a jointly-funded allowance for him, beyond which he would have to find a way to make money on his own. Fair enough! (He knew he would end up giving Guido more money.)

So that was that! The lawyers were the winners, as usual, and they got to work preparing the documents, translating them into French, filing, and scheduling. And he had been so concerned about doing this. Maybe it was good that they waited. Marietta had a new love, and was no longer angry with him. At the meeting she had assumed a polite mien, with a touch of sarcasm. And yet, he was sad to see it end so definitively. Women were like jewels to him, and this was the loss of the most prized of his collection.

He made himself a cappuccio with the new Gaggia machine, and sat down on the green sofa facing the bookshelves. Actually, women were more like books. Jewels implied possession, and you never actually possess a book. Well, yes, the physical book, but not the content. But it does become a part of you, and together with everything else that you mentally and emotionally assimilate, makes you who you are. Maybe that's why books had such a prominent position in bourgeois Milanese homes. Your guests were free to peruse the shelves, nodding and emitting *Ahs*, raising eyebrows, pulling out unknown works for inspection, thinking of provocative things to say at dinner based on the host's collection.

What a joke!

At one time, Alberto had the idea of renting out libraries for such occasions. The client would answer a questionnaire about what kind of (false) impression he or she would like to give, and they could (maybe using a proprietary software program) generate a list of works based on the answers. They would specify how they wanted the books organized as well. You know, *Lolita* next to *Sense and Sensibility*, or Machiavelli next to Karl Marx, alphabetically. He would wager that a good number of people wouldn't even see it as a farce.

But back to women. He needed to reboot his approach. Some of his old flames were likely to resurface once the word of the divorce got out, and now that he had officially failed, he couldn't go back to his old ways. Besides, they would want to live together, get married, or otherwise *resolve* things. Alberto believed the appeal of someone like Mel wasn't the physical attributes of her age as much as her openness with respect to how life should be organized. After all, she had left her home environment and her assigned place in its social ecology. Here, she was a wild card: anything could happen without prejudice about where she went to school or who her father was. Although he had talked himself out of pursuing her sexually, Alberto wanted to stay close to her, to try to figure out what new models of coupledom were evolving.

He missed seeing Mel. She was in Rome last weekend and this week tied up with her new job and the *Salone*. He sighed, got up from the sofa, brushed his teeth and picked out a tie. Milan was crawling with designers, and Via Manzoni was going to be crammed with cabs. He grabbed his helmet and set off for the office.

It was a boring day, and Alberto felt like a snake whose skin was shedding, and all he could do was lie there and wait until he was free of it. He slogged through the correspondence and memos to write, and went home. He poured a glass of wine and stepped out on the small terrace off the dining room. The city was buzzing below him. He decided to call Lella.

"Hi Alberto. We're at the Sofine reception. We're going to dinner at the *Refettorio*...with Giorgio, and the photographer, Pierpaolo Nervi. You know him, don't you? And guess what? Jonathan (Melinda's Jonathan) works for Pierpaolo, and he is coming with us, too."

"So, are Melinda and Jonathan *together?*" Alberto asked. Things were moving too fast, in a way he couldn't control. Shit! He didn't want to lose access to her.

"No, I don't think so. But they were up on the roof together." She laughed.

The roof! That sealed the deal according to Alberto. You didn't go onto the old, sagging roof of the Sofine building unless you were in love.

"You're dining right around the corner from my place."

"Well, said Lella, why don't you join us? We can get them to squeeze another chair in."

Alberto shook his head, amused by his own situation.

"I am really feeling single today. I guess sitting at the corner of your table would be appropriate. How did you get a reservation there today, anyway?"

"Giorgio. He booked a table for eight, figuring he could fill it, weeks ago. So you won't be on the corner, and we can put a vase of flowers across from you, if you'd like."

Lella said goodbye and turned to Pierpaolo and Giorgio.

"I invited my cousin Alberto to join us. Shall we find another lady to fill out the table?"

"Elena," Pierpaolo said, nodding decisively.

Seating arrangements

Mel tried to be careful about where she sat when they got to Refettorio. There was, however, no avoiding logic: Pierpaolo across from Hanne, near the window; Giorgio next to Hanne, and across from Lella; Mel next to Giorgio and across from Jonathan, and Elena next to Jonathan. Pierpaolo wanted to be by the window because he liked being seen by the passers-by. Elena wanted to be as far from him and Hanne as possible, preferably with Jonathan in between as a buffer. And Alberto was the last to arrive, just as logically seated next to Mel and across from Elena.

So, after this incredible day, punctuated by puking in the Sofine building, Mel found herself sitting next to her new boss, with her new and ambiguously friendly male friend on the other side, and her ex across the table, next to his beautiful and admiring colleague. Their drink orders were taken.

"San Pellegrino for me, *per favore*," Mel said. There was no way she could drink wine. Her stomach was slightly on edge, and this situation was too surreal for her to alter her consciousness any further. Alberto made the rounds at the table, shaking hands with Pierpaolo, trying to recollect their last meeting years ago, and then Hanne. He kissed Lella, and enthusiastically shook hands with Jonathan.

"So nice to meet a friend of Melinda's," he said, not sure if that was true.

Jonathan then presented him to Elena, and Pierpaolo shot a glance down the table to see Alberto's reaction. But Alberto was neutral, conscious of the energy ricocheting around the table. He needed to assess the state of everyone's ties. For this reason, he only patted Mel on the back, congratulating her on her job again, and remarking on Giorgio's good luck to have her.

Elena, however, could sense Alberto's relief in being seated next to Mel, and she half smiled at her discovery. This new confirmation of Elena's interest in Jonathan was not lost on Mel. Furthermore, she was not happy about the possibility that Elena would share her speculation—because that was all it was—with Jonathan. Not that Mel "owned" Jonathan. She just didn't want him to think she was involved with Alberto, because she wasn't.

Jonathan smiled to himself when Hanne ordered another candle for the table.

Lella struck up a conversation with Hanne and Pierpaolo while Mel went over the day with Giorgio. Alberto engaged Jonathan and Elena while they nibbled on the antipasti. Then the conversations started to blend, across the table, diagonally, with each picking up threads and weaving them into a tapestry of dialogue. Mel was intrigued by this combination of individuals: she had feared a clash of personalities, but they had quickly evolved into a different, more resilient entity where the whole was much richer than the sum of its parts.

Jonathan felt this too, but for him it was a welcome reduction of emotional static, the kind that made it hard for him to be around people. The turbulence had subsided, and the group somehow absorbed each member's qualms. This must be what was meant by a *buona educazione*, the upbringing that focused on courteous social behavior. He was impressed.

Alberto had the perfect opportunity to turn over his new leaf, with Elena across from him. She was charming, with a naturally seductive air—she seemed interested in Jonathan and guarded with Mel. He noticed that Jonathan was measured with both women. He wished that he knew what was going on. But that didn't matter, he reconsidered, as he was trying to behave. Lella's eyes connected with his from time to time. So, he just relaxed and tried to be friendly with everyone.

Pierpaolo alternated between distraction by the passers-by, and worry that Hanne might not blend with his circle. Lella was masterful at bringing her in, and as the crowd on the sidewalk dwindled, he, too, was drawn into the conversation, and pleasantly surprised with Hanne's literacy in design trends as she chatted with Giorgio. His only concern was what was happening at the other end of the table. He wasn't sure enough about Hanne to give Elena up completely to somebody else.

Gelato, and a kiss

Alberto suggested they get an asparagus gelato (since the season was coming to an end) at a place a few blocks away. Lella and Pierpaolo passed, claiming they were too tired and full, so they left with Giorgio and Hanne. Alberto now felt conspicuously older than the remaining members of the group, and suggested leaving them to go on their own. Mel objected, saying it was his idea, hoping he wouldn't leave her alone with Jonathan and Elena.

So they walked along the street two by two, Mel and Alberto together.

"I'm glad I got to see you. You've been so busy!" Alberto said.

"Yes," Mel answered, "and thank you again for introducing me to Giorgio." She noticed that their conversation had attracted Jonathan's attention by the way he was not fully engaging with Elena. So as they approached the gelateria, she asked Elena if she was returning to Rome for the photo shoot they had planned last weekend.

"I believe so, I mean, either Jonathan or I will have to go with Pierpaolo. It will also depend on whether he takes Hanne. That would be a bit awkward."

Jonathan said, "I won't be able to go that weekend. I'll be writing up my recommendations for the studio. I'm meeting with Pierpaolo all afternoon the following Monday."

By this time Alberto had separated himself from the others to order the gelato, and didn't hear Elena's reference to her relationship with Pierpaolo. Elena was curious about Mel and Alberto. He was older, yes, but so charming and handsome. What was going on, and what influence did that have on Jonathan's romantic prognosis? Then she remembered Jonathan's advice, so she held back and tried to remain aloof, in case she might be giving off the wrong vibe.

Why was she even bothering with this nonsense? Wasn't it better to take a breather after Pierpaolo? She needed to center herself, and then focus on choosing a man that *she* wanted, not one that wanted her. But what if she thought she wanted someone because they were attracted to her (or to Mel)? How would she know what mechanism was at work? Would she ever be able to gain control over the process?

Alberto came back with the gelato, aided at the last minute by Jonathan.

Afterward, Alberto offered to take Mel home on the scooter, so Jonathan and Elena got an Uber. Jonathan kept looking back at them from what he thought was the corner of his eye.

In Alberto's courtyard, Mel put on her helmet and turned to him.

"About the other night at dinner," she said, "Do you think we were going someplace we really shouldn't have?"

"Perhaps," he said, "I have been wondering. Circumstances are not conducive. Maybe that's why the attraction persists."

"Let's go upstairs," Mel said simply.

Alberto slowly removed her helmet, and held her head between his hands. She was leaning against a column, and he kissed her, leaning into her. Mel felt like a flower whose petals were opening and falling off, one by one.

Then Alberto pulled away decisively.

"Not doing this," he said, straightening up. "But let's talk. Come on up."

In the apartment, Alberto poured out two tall glasses of San Pellegrino and placed them on his sparkly granite counter.

"Here's the thing," he started.

"First, I am not going to be your shield against Jonathan. Second, I am going to stop carrying on business as usual with women, and I want your help.

You know we are an impossible pair, if only because of your relationship with Lella; she would never approve, for your sake."

Alberto took a sip of water before he added, "Third, I am getting divorced!"

"Wow, really? When did this happen?"

"Just recently. My wife has a lover and he wants to marry her."

"Are you okay?"

"Oh, yes, my worries about the outcome have been dispelled. I think it will be an opportunity. In fact, it has hardened my resolve. So now that I am available, you are off limits."

He laughed at the irony.

"You know, Alberto, it's not like I wanted to get involved...it's just that I'm so..."

"Grateful?" he shook his head. "You will be my first experiment. A platonic, female friend."

"Won't Lella and Amelia think we are up to something else?"

"No, because we aren't going to go out alone together. I will be clear with Lella about this; she will understand. Amelia, not so much. She despises Italian men, especially in her own family. You know, when we do *men* things."

Alberto took a sip of water and said, "Now, do you think I could approach Elena? Is she too young?"

"She's no younger than I am."

"But aren't you too young, too?" Alberto chuckled.

"Elena seems to be in a weird place. She was seeing Pierpaolo, and now she seems to have transferred her interest to Jonathan."

Alberto quickly processed this. "Jonathan is like the knight in shining armour."

"He does appeal to women who are adrift."

190

"Isn't that all women?"

"You're kidding, right?"

"I mean in the sense that all people are adrift, in one way or another, once you drill down. His kindness is like a trap."

"I guess you lay traps, too, just of a different kind."

"*Touché.*"

"But back to Elena. You just met her."

"That is true, but we have had dinner together, and she seems intelligent, thoughtful and sweet."

"You forgot beautiful."

"Yes, okay, and beautiful."

"So, how do you want to proceed?"

"Well, I would like you to advise me as I go along. Things are different today. I am not sure how to behave. Could you help me find an opportunity to see her again, in company?"

"Hang on." Mel took out her phone and texted. After a few minutes, she got a response. Then another.

"Okay, I've arranged it. Tomorrow we'll meet at *Bar Basso*, near the *Politecnico.*"

"I know where *Bar Basso* is. It will be crammed because of the *Salone*"

"Somewhat. Let's be there at six o'clock and get a table outside if the weather holds up."

"I know the owner, I can arrange a table."

"One more thing: why did you kiss me like that down in the courtyard?"

"I couldn't resist, I'm sorry; it's a process." He shrugged apologetically. "It's like the last drag on your last cigarette. Now, let's get you home, before Lella suspects something."

* * *

Back at Lella's, Mel got off the elevator on the upper level, so that she could say goodnight. But the apartment was completely dark. It was eleven o'clock, too early for her to be asleep, and her bag and jacket weren't in their usual place. So Mel walked through the living room, lit only by the city lights reflected by the gathering clouds. She slipped behind the bookshelves that hovered like a shadow, and down the stairs. She didn't turn on the lights as she prepared for bed, enjoying the dark gray silence.

Lella and Giorgio

Giorgio Monti's success at the *Salone* was nothing compared to his triumph of having Lella come home with him. Lella, the woman of his dreams! It was just as he had imagined it: he had insisted she sit in the peacock-colored velvet chair that he had designed, which made her laugh. In a tiny crystal glass, he poured her a Mandarin liqueur, whose amber color she admired, holding it up to the light. He sat across from her, making sure that she was comfortable, and they conversed about their dinner companions.

"So Jonathan and Melinda lived together in New York? He seems like a nice guy."

"Yes," Lella agreed, hesitating. She wasn't going to share what she knew about the breakup. "Who knows what will happen, now that they're both here?"

"And you know that Melinda is going to live with Gabi?"

"Of course, what a good arrangement! Did you have anything to do with that?"

"No! Gabi showed up for lunch this week, and I thought she and Melinda would like to meet. When she suggested it, I did think it was a great idea. Now I have to get the work done in there, so Mel will have her own space. With the *Salone*, and the Japanese coming to the studio tomorrow, it has been crazy."

Lella realized she was keeping him up before his important meeting, and thought it better to leave.

"Oh, no, I am all ready for the meeting. Don't go...unless you must, of course. I am enjoying your company so much."

Lella smiled. "Will it ruin your aesthetic vision if I get out of this chair and come over there, next to you?"

Giorgio couldn't believe his ears, but tried to play it cool.

193

He savored that moment the next morning, when he was preparing their cappuccinos. She was so warm, and made the night seem so easy, almost unremarkable. But it was so very remarkable. Maybe it was because they had known each other for so long.

Giorgio prepared a tray with some toasted bread and preserves, and brought it into the bedroom. To see her there! Her hair and skin were so striking against the dark bedclothes. And the smile!

"Giorgio, what a spread!" she said. She reached for her sweater, in a heap on the floor, and pulled it over her head, sitting up in the bed. She resisted the urge to make excuses for herself: her age, her body, and her gray hair. But she wasn't going to prance around naked in the morning light, either.

She wondered what made her decide to come home with him? Maybe it was the energy at the table last night, with the other couples, the younger friends with all of their possibilities in front of them. She sincerely cared for Giorgio, although she wondered if their level of enthusiasm was the same. He went out of his way to please her when they made love last night. That was good, and decidedly different from Paolo's sexual behavior. *He* believed that being with *him* was enough, without going to any particular trouble. Sometimes it worked out, more often, it didn't. Now that Giorgio had made his conquest, how would he behave going forward? Was he going to place demands on her? Take away her freedom?

"What's on your mind?" he asked, bending over to kiss her on the forehead.

"Nothing, just my brain kicking into gear!"

"I was thinking," he said, "that we could see a film on Saturday afternoon. It's supposed to be rainy." He tossed the paper her way, open to the page with reviews. "See anything you like?"

"I'd like that," she said, thinking about setting the pace of this thing so it didn't get out of control. Saturday was tomorrow. "However, Federico and Massimo are coming from Rome this evening, to go to the *Salone* tomorrow. I will be having dinner with them afterward. We can still go to a matinee."

Giorgio looked slightly crestfallen, but of course he couldn't expect her to invite him to dine with her family after one night together.

She reached over and placed her hand over his. "Alberto will be there, with his kids, and mine of course; it's a cousins's get-together."

This made him feel a little better. He jumped up and showed Lella what he thought he might wear for his meeting, and she approved, laughing.

Then she got up and dressed, wanting to leave him to his preparations.

"Till tomorrow, then," she said.

Giorgio kissed her at the door, now distracted by the business at hand.

"The Japanese!"

He turned on the music in the bedroom and jumped into the shower.

Bar Basso

The atmosphere at Bar Basso was already lively at six o'clock. Foreign visitors and students alike were converging after a long day's immersion in the world of commercial design. True to his word, Alberto had secured a table, inside due to rain. He had picked Mel up by cab. Jonathan and Elena arrived from the *Metropolitana*, sharing an umbrella.

Jonathan was wondering about Mel's motivation for this meeting: did she want to see him, but not alone? Or was she trying to create an ensemble, where he was matched with Elena, she with Alberto? She did have the tendency to seek control. Mel clearly didn't understand how things were between Elena and him. Maybe that was because Elena appeared interested; but he couldn't help that.

Elena had nothing to lose by coming; she was always happy to be with Jonathan, and she found Mel's friend Alberto to be very charming.

"You aren't going to try to seduce Alberto, are you?" Jonathan asked her as they dodged the puddles on the street. Maybe, *just maybe*, he was selfishly trying to plant a seed in her imagination.

"Do you think he is available? It looked to me like he was interested in Melinda."

"I had that thought myself."

"Well, if you'd like, I can try to pry him loose."

"No," he laughed, regretting his suggestion. "Remember what we talked about. Slow and steady."

Elena laughed, "I'm joking." Then she became thoughtful. She wished that Jonathan wasn't chasing after what seemed to be an impossible reboot with Mel. She really did like him. But her infatuation was over. She valued him as a friend. That, however, didn't alter the fact that she would like someone *like* him.

They arrived at their destination. The windows of the bar were fogging up, and the *Bar Basso* sign in neon script stood out against the slick, prematurely dark surroundings. White taxis wheeled around the piazza, dropping people off, honking their horns. They wanted to get back to Stazione Garibaldi where the crowds were arriving from the fairgrounds: the demand was pressing, and the Americans tipped well.

Jonathan and Elena found Mel and Alberto, who were sitting down, waiting for them. Reiner was leaning against the wall, talking to Mel and shaking hands with Alberto. He was there with Geert, who was scanning the room, a beer in his hand. Mel couldn't help but notice how comfortable Alberto was with people of any age.

Mel had coached Alberto on their way over.

"Don't focus on her," she had said. "Let's keep the conversation of interest to everyone. That will keep both of you out of trouble until things get more comfortable."

Alberto offered to get the drinks, while Jonathan and Elena took off their raincoats and squeezed into the chairs.

"It's getting a bit crowded in here," Elena said.

After some scrambling at the bar, Alberto returned to the table with four glasses of spumante. Then he turned to Mel.

"So, Melinda, didn't you have a meeting with Giorgio's Japanese clients today? How did that go?"

Mel tested the spumante. It was good. Of course Alberto wouldn't get the low-grade stuff.

"It went well, thanks."

Elena and Jonathan remembered Mel's project from their conversation in Rome, so Mel skimmed the story of her LEAF, PEBBLE, and SEAGLASS concepts. Giorgio had thought they should start developing LEAF.

"So," she said, "the idea is that a leaf has incredible characteristics: it is strong, resilient and water repellent; but it is also deciduous. It renews itself in a cycle."

"If we look at some original native cultures, we see that leaves are used for many things, including serving food. The product line would be disposable dinnerware: plates, bowls, and cups all generated from the *leaf.*"

Jonathan moved forward, pulling his chair in.

"What are they made of?"

"Well, that's the thing. I needed to connect it to the Japanese culture more specifically, and I wanted the line to be low impact and easy to package. I also want it to be compostable. So I thought about origami papers, and started doing more research. Did you know there is a paper called Lokta that Nepalese women make from the bark of Daphne shrubs? It's very strong."

"How about Bamboo?" Elena added.

"Yes, well, we are looking at various materials. They have to have high 'fold durability.' You know, like origami paper: you can fold it and create stable three-dimensional forms."

"Does that mean," Alberto said smiling indulgently, "that if I have a party I'd have to build the plates one by one?"

Mel laughed. "As if *you* would use disposable dinnerware! The pieces would be packaged flat, but they would already have all the folds."

"Can you show us?" asked Elena. She rummaged in her large bag and pulled out some promo cards she had picked up.

"It needs to be roughly square, to start," said Mel, fingering the small pile. "Here, this one will work. And she began making some folds. Then, with her thumbs and forefingers, she pulled the flat object into a cup-like form."

"Very clever," said Alberto, "*Brava.*"

Jonathan contemplated the completed object.

"The cleverness lies in the fact that nothing new was invented. This is all stuff that is very familiar to them. I can see this for artsy types, or children. It would teach them about design while they are getting ready for their party."

Elena added, "I would think that, depending on cost, these products could be used for disaster relief, too."

"Indeed." Mel said. "The whole point of it is to uncover and celebrate the versatility of a humble material. Now, it needs to be water resistant, at least as much as a conventional paper cup. And, it needs to be compostable. We are looking at renewable pulp sources, including waste materials from other processes. I have even shown some secondary uses for the items, like these."

Mel scrolled through some images on her phone, showing a seedling in a soil-filled cup, and other uses for the plates and bowls.

"I can see the campaign already," Jonathan said. "Images of people in cultures that use leaves for serving food. Elemental, simple."

"And how about," Elena added, "showing children expanding the forms, and playing with them."

Alberto was chuckling, enjoying the energy at the table.

"So what did the Japanese say?" he asked, getting back to business.

"Well, as you may guess, they didn't jump up and down and 'high-five' it... They looked at one another, then at us, nodded, and said they would communicate with us soon. At that point, I excused myself, and left them with Giorgio."

"They'll work with you," Alberto said confidently, "they just need to discuss it among themselves before they give you feedback."

"That's what Giorgio said."

Mel felt like there was too much attention on her, so she tried changing the subject.

"Elena, I see you went to the *Salone* today. What did you think?"

Elena lifted her hair off of her back and released it again, in a simple, natural gesture. The others watched with undisguised admiration.

"I enjoyed it; of course there's so much visual stimulation. And at the end of the day, I felt a little depressed."

Alberto asked, "Why?"

"Well, despite all of the high tech, 'green' products, it still feels like an unrelenting consumerist parade. After all, do we really need all this stuff?"

"It's a lot to digest," Jonathan added. "I remember Mel telling me how much she wanted to be here in Milan because of the dumbfounding amount of beautiful design."

Alberto felt a little put off by Jonathan's proprietary knowledge of Mel; it felt territorial.

Mel said, "I can see how, over time, you might get too much of a good thing. I think that happens when you dive into something: sometimes you forget to come up for air."

"That's true for our work, too," said Jonathan. "Big cities tend to concentrate talent, competition, and output. The Internet has not changed that; people still want the critical mass, the physical interaction. Though it can be a bit much at times."

Alberto added, "I think that's why so many Milanese leave on the weekends, especially in good weather. We need to connect to air, mountains, the sea; and even the simple human interactions that take place in the country."

Jonathan asked, "Do you have a country place, Alberto?"

"I did. It belongs to my wife (my *ex*-wife; we are nearly divorced). But I have a family place by the sea, in Santa Margherita."

"How," asked Jonathan, "Is someone *nearly* divorced?"

Alberto took a sip of his drink. "Well, it has been an enduring separation–the embers have long since died. Just paperwork now."

To change the subject, Mel turned to Jonathan, and asked him about his job. The conversation continued easily, with Jonathan and Elena talking about their new ideas for the studio. They found their equilibrium, as their dinner group had the night before.

Mel thought about the idea of people sitting around a table, and the meaning of it: talking, dining, and sharing. Even working, or playing a game. The activities and rituals of every waking hour seemed centered around *tables*. She made a mental note to get some ideas down before she went to bed. That's how it happened with her. She would get some simple inspiration, and put it in her sketchbook. It was like a diary of her design evolution, and it had become heavily influenced by basic human exchange ever since she arrived here. Humanism was the root of Italian culture. *Social* had taken on a new meaning for Mel.

Her thoughts were interrupted by a text from Lella.

FEDE AND MAX ARE HERE.

"I have to go," she said. "Our hosts from Rome have arrived."

They said their goodbyes, and went back out into the dwindling rain.

In the cab, Alberto said, "I would use disposable dinnerware, you know, for the right occasion."

Studio trysts

Jonathan ordered an Uber because he was lightheaded from the spumante and didn't want to deal with the *Metropolitana*. Elena was relieved. She suggested they eat together; she really needed to get something into her stomach.

"Well, if it won't feel too much like you're going back to work, we can get a pizza and eat it at my place," Jonathan offered. Then he immediately thought maybe that wasn't such a great idea. Apart from the counter and stools, the only piece of comfortable furniture was the bed.

"That sounds good," Elena said, smiling.

Jonathan called ahead to the pizzeria near the studio and they had the cab drop them off there. The rain had stopped, and the air was mild.

When they reached the studio apartment, Jonathan got an idea.

"How do you feel about eating in the studio courtyard?" He said.

"Won't it be all wet?" Elena answered.

"We can wipe the table, and bring out folding chairs. Here's a sweater, just in case you're cold," Jonathan said, grabbing one from his closet.

"Ohh...Pierpaolo has some candles, a whole box, in his office!" Elena said.

They entered the studio from Jonathan's back room, set everything up outside, and lit a couple of the thick, vanilla-colored candles that Hanne had sent to Pierpaolo.

Jonathan poured some red wine, "Maybe just a little," he said.

"We wouldn't be out here if we weren't half drunk," Elena said.

As they were eating, they heard the main door alarm beep, then stop, followed by voices.

"*Merda!*" said Elena. "It's Pierpaolo."

Jonathan listened. "He's with Hanne," he whispered.

202

"What do we do?"

Jonathan wet his fingers and extinguished the candles, holding his finger in front of his lips. He was thinking they just came so that Pierpaolo could pick up something.

"So this is your studio," Hanne said, and she began dancing and twirling in the atrium, the sides of her raincoat floating in the air.

Pierpaolo joined her in the middle of the space. He held her hands in his and gave her a long, deep kiss.

Elena looked away, and took a sip of wine.

"Wait here," Pierpaolo said. He went to a closet and pulled out a white faux bearskin rug. He laid it down on the smooth, polished concrete floor.

Jonathan and Elena looked at one another, she with a terrified look on her face. He shrugged.

"Candles!" Hanne suggested.

Pierpaolo grudgingly went into his office and grabbed the box she had sent.

"That's odd. There are a couple of candles missing." Then he shrugged, "One of the girls probably took them. I can't leave anything around here."

Then he set three candles on each side of the rug, one at the head, and lit them. Hanne had flung her raincoat across the room, and took off her shoes. She was standing on the faux bearskin rug. Pierpaolo got a camera from the cage and set it on a trolley. He turned on some music. Then he approached Hanne and started to peel her clothes off, slowly.

"I am going to immortalize you," he said.

She giggled as he revealed her small breasts and smooth belly.

Elena leaned toward Jonathan, "She doesn't have any fucking tan lines!"

Pierpaolo slowly pulled Hanne's pants down, stopping to hold her butt cheeks in his hands while he kissed her neck.

Jonathan had his hand over his eyes, but raised and lowered it to check Pierpaolo's progress.

"I shouldn't be watching this," he whispered.

"If he finds us here..." Elena was shaking her head.

Hanne stretched out on the rug, and Pierpaolo was arranging her arms and legs like a star. By now, Elena and Jonathan could only hear their voices.

Pierpaolo grabbed his camera and started shooting, walking around her, then getting on his knees.

"Being exposed like this is making me so horny," Hanne said.

Jonathan and Elena both tried not to laugh.

"Maybe I can take care of that for you," Pierpaolo said. He started inching his way up between her legs, his camera in front of his face.

Jonathan and Elena could no longer see anything, and went back to eating their pizza quietly, as if nothing was going on.

"It feels cold," Hanne said, giggling.

Jonathan turned to Elena, "Excuse me, is he giving her a camera massage?"

"I can't give away any of Pierpoalo's secrets, but let's just say it's in the realm of possibility." Then, "Don't worry, he'll have the lens cap on."

Hanne's shriek made them both jump in their seats, and then they held their hands over their mouths to keep from laughing out loud.

Pierpaolo was standing up again, and offered Hanne his hand.

She stood up again, still naked, with her smooth, even skin and her blonde hair falling so straight, only grazing her shoulders when she bent her head.

She grabbed Pierpaolo's belt buckle. But he was focused on wiping down the camera.

"Ew! I've got to see which one that is," Jonathan whispered.

Pierpaolo smiled at Hanne, removing her hand. "Let's pick up at home where we can be more comfortable."

"Thank God!" Elena whispered, just before the music died.

Hanne and Pierpaolo headed for the door, then Pierpaolo came back, grabbed the rug and put it away.

Jonathan waited for a moment after the lock turned, then gave out a long exhale. Elena had a thoughtful expression.

"You know," she said, "seeing Pierpaolo (and I wish I hadn't) go through these motions with someone else really cheapens the experience I had with him."

Jonathan looked at her, his head tipped to one side, considering. There was a long moment of silence.

"Want to watch a movie on my laptop?"

They picked up everything and went back into Jonathan's apartment.

Jonathan set up the pillow and a bolster on the bed to make it seem more like a sofa, but before they were five minutes into the movie, Elena was fast asleep.

Saturday thinking

Everyone was busy on Saturday. It was raining again, but without the force of yesterday. Federico and Massimo set off early for the fairgrounds, where the *Salone del Mobile* was in its final days and now open to the general public.

"We're going to consume some design with the plebes," Massimo said to Lella, kissing her before he and Federico walked out the door.

The streets of Milan were full of comings and goings. White herds of cabs gathered at nodes near train stations and major stops of the *Metropolitana*. The brown paving stones of the streets in the city center were wet, and shone like brown patent leather. Umbrellas made the sidewalk treacherous: the Louis Vuittons battling with the Burberrys; the occasional sober black, and a rare pink or green one with an errant spoke at eye level.

Massimo pulled on Federico's rain jacket, pointing discreetly.

"Eight hundred Euros for that McQueen umbrella, can you believe it?"

"I suppose I should be glad we don't live here, where you would insist on having one," Federico answered.

They ducked down into the San Babila station and disappeared.

* * *

Mel was enjoying a lazy morning. The week had been crazy. Just like the last one, and the one before that. Maybe now things would settle down. She had underestimated the stress of being–*living*–in a foreign country. Speaking Italian all day even made her mouth sore. She was still struggling with it, mostly the vocabulary and the idioms; she had no problem uttering simple sentences. But listening required much more effort. So she was taking a linguistic break, relishing the New York Times on her iPad, with a nice large caffè latte and some *brutti ma buoni* that Federico had brought from Rome.

Today, she might have the place to herself. Federico and Massimo would be at the *Salone*, and Lella was going to see a film with Giorgio in the early afternoon. Lella was preparing dinner for her cousins and the kids, so that they could visit with Federico and Massimo. It was the perfect weekend to stay in her room and stare out the window. Mel had declined the invitation to dinner; they were all family. Lella seemed relieved that she would have an even table of eight.

Mel sat in her armchair, looking down at the city. The dense air muffled the street sounds, and the wheels of cars made a swishing noise as they spun the rainwater. The newsstand was draped with large flaps of clear plastic to protect the papers and magazines, and the greengrocer's crates were tucked close to the shop windows under the awnings.

Mel couldn't believe that she had done it. She was in Milan, she had a job with a noted architect, and now she had found a place to live. It seemed too good to be true. *I guess the hard part follows*, she thought. She had to assimilate into the day-to-day life and create a place for herself. She wondered what it was going to be like when she moved out. Would Lella, Alberto, and their circle become less accessible to her? They might then see her as a struggling bohemian, another of the many underpaid expats seeking the nectar of the Milanese design culture, whether in architecture, furniture, or fashion. The idea of hanging out with other expats, American or otherwise, did not appeal to Mel. She wanted to learn Italian, and *be* Italian while she was here.

Jonathan was another danger. He kept popping up, and while she did not seek him out, it was a relief, strangely, to see him. She wondered how long it would be before Elena won him over? Alberto seemed interested in Elena, but Mel wasn't sure whether he was sincere about it or not. He had enlisted Mel's help, but was that just a guise and and means to stay close to her? Alberto couldn't just decide he wanted to try a "real" relationship, and then pursue the first (good-looking) woman who crossed his path. Still, Mel believed that the exercise of getting to know a woman slowly would be good for him. She needed to find out more about Elena, and understand where *her* interest lay. She couldn't ask Jonathan; it would look like she was jealous, and this would get his hopes up. She had to tackle Elena head on.

Signora Pia sweeps

Across the city, Jonathan was standing at the counter, packing the espresso into the *caffettiera*. Then he pushed down the lever on the toaster, startling Elena, who sat up abruptly in the bed. He turned his head and looked at her, laughing lightly.

"Oh, Jonathan, I am so sorry! I must have fallen asleep during the movie."

"At the beginning of the movie is more like it. Are you ready for some coffee?"

He carefully set up two places at the counter, looking out at the courtyard. Signora Pia was out there, sweeping the cobbles and surreptitiously looking around, trying to catch a glimpse of any human activity in her quest to know all. The back of the building where Pierpaolo's studio was located had no floors above it, while the front and side wings went up four stories. She glanced up as someone opened their window, and scuttled back to her station when someone came down the stairs. Jonathan had bought some plants for the inside window ledge, and arranged them densely where their places were set, improvising a screen.

"Last night seems like a dream," Elena said, "with the crowd at *Bar Basso*, the rain, then our pizza outside...and," she looked at Jonathan and they both broke out laughing.

"I may never be able to look at Pierpaolo with a straight face again," Jonathan said.

"Jonathan," Elena started, "about me sleeping here..."

"Pff, don't worry about it." Jonathan went to sit on the bed and took her hand. "You and I are friends. We talked about this already. That is not going to change. So it's no big deal, okay? I am more worried about Signora Pia seeing us together and gossiping about it. It wouldn't be good if it got back to Pierpaolo. And we'd never hear the end of it from Geert."

She still looked troubled.

Jonathan continued in his most gentle voice, "Tell me, Elena, are you still hoping something will happen between us?"

"I am trying not to. If you weren't so nice it would be easier."

"Well, I think you just have this pent-up bundle of emotional energy, and you don't know what to do with it. Maybe you feel incomplete without a lover. But you aren't. In fact, you need to puff up your chest like a rooster and dig your heels into your life. You're getting stronger every day."

"You think I am on the *rebound*."

Jonathan laughed. "Where did you learn that expression? And yes, possibly."

"You know, he continued, "I think relationships are the icing on the cake, but they are not the cake. You have to be strong and complete, on your own, before you have something to offer someone else."

"Then the 'someone else' must also be a whole cake?"

Jonathan laughed, the *caffettiera* started gurgling, and the toast popped up.

They went over to the counter.

Elena asked, "Do you think that Melinda is strong and complete, for a relationship?"

"Well, that is a very good question. She has wanted to prove herself as long as I've known her, and I think this time in Milan is what she needs to develop her confidence. When we were in New York, she was overwhelmed. Milan makes more sense for her."

"Why is that?"

"I'm not sure, but there are a couple of possible reasons: one, the design community is more concentrated, so she doesn't have to deal with the sheer mass of 'other' people populating New York; and secondly, the culture appeals to her so much that it may distract her from the difficulty of the whole competitive, urban environment."

"What did you think of Alberto?" Elena said.

"He's nice. Very elegant and cultured. He seems to like Mel a lot."

"Maybe they are just friends, like you and me."

"Maybe... Are you thinking about him?"

"I don't know. Like you said, I need to focus on myself for now. That doesn't mean I can't *look*, no?"

Jonathan spread honey on the toast. "Elena, you can do whatever you want. Just don't underestimate your worth, and don't settle for anyone who doesn't appreciate you."

Signora Pia was back in the courtyard, sweeping, and the sound of the broom on the ground, still damp, kept a steady rhythm. *Swish, swish, swish.*

"What will you do today?" Elena asked.

"Laundry, I guess. I was hoping the sun would come out." He checked his weather app. "It looks like there is some hope for the early afternoon."

"I thought it was supposed to keep raining."

"I guess things have changed," Jonathan said.

Elena and Mel

Mel heard Lella arrive with her groceries, so she went upstairs to help her carry things into the kitchen and unpack.

"Is there anything I can do to help while you're at the movies?"

"No, thank you, Melinda. Federico said they'll be back by four o'clock, so I am going to text him some directions... I should be here myself shortly afterward, and dinner is at eight. I'm going to wash everything now."

Mel stayed and helped, and they chatted about everything except the fact that Lella hadn't returned home Thursday night (Mel pretended she didn't notice) and that she was a little bit excited, a little bit nervous, about going to the movies with Giorgio.

"Should we put these in the refrigerator?" Mel asked, pulling out a carton of eggs that Lella had just placed in the cupboard.

"I must be distracted," said Lella, grabbing it and making a face at Mel.

Then she turned to go to her room.

"By the way, Melinda, please make yourself at home up here. You can watch something on the large television. Nobody will be around. Invite someone over if you like."

"What a great idea, thanks! If only I had friends."

But then she had an idea. Maybe she should go out, too. She texted Jonathan.

CAN YOU GIVE ME ELENA'S #?

Jonathan was loading his clothes into the washer in his back room when he heard the text ding. Elena was waiting for Signora Pia to make her way up the stairwell before leaving.

"Is it okay if I give Mel your number?"

Elena cocked her head, trying to understand.

"I guess so."

Soon she was out on the street, the heavy door closing behind her, listening for the catch of the latch. She had evaded Signora Pia. She was close enough to walk home, but the bus was arriving on Via Porpora, so she decided to hop on. She was on her way upstairs to her second floor apartment, her mail under her arm, when her phone signalled a text.

HI, THIS IS MELINDA

CIAO, MELINDA, WHAT'S UP?

DO YOU WANT TO COME INTO CENTER (*Woop*)

TO SHOP ON CORSO VITTORIO EMANUELE?

Elena thought it odd that Mel would reach out to her, but she remembered what it was like when she was a newcomer in Milan. The idea of a shopping expedition today appealed to her. The Corso had covered walkways, and if Jonathan's app was correct, it was going to clear up anyway.

HAVE TO SHOWER AND DRESS (*Woop*)

IN AN HOUR AND A HALF? (*Woop*)

MEET @ CAFFE PASCUCCI, C.SO EUROPA

OKAY, SEE YOU THERE!

Mel was unsure of how this would play out. Did Elena consider her a rival? She took out her little sketchbook and drew four boxes, arranged top, bottom, left, and right on the page. Inside each box she wrote a name in her neat block letters: *Elena, Jonathan, Mel, Alberto.* This would help her think. She started drawing arrows between the boxes, testing the direction of each person's affection. She squinted at her result for a minute, tore out the page and crumpled it in her hand.

It had stopped raining completely by the time Mel and Elena met. They each had a panino with prosciutto, and then started wandering through the streets, stopping in at an occasional store. Elena steered Mel into her favorite places, sometimes just to look at shoes. Mel was enjoying herself, despite her original intention of staying at home in the quiet apartment. Then she remembered that Elena had met Federico and Massimo in Rome, and suggested they get some gelato and go back to Lella's.

It was three-thirty when they entered the downstairs level of the apartment. Mel brought the gelato to the upstairs freezer after showing Elena her room, the bathroom, the writing alcove, and the other bedroom, which was a mess.

"This is where Federico and Massimo are staying," Mel said.

Elena followed her upstairs into the open living area, then the kitchen.

"This is a lovely place," she said.

"I know. I was very lucky."

Mel told Elena about how she found Lella on line, their conversations, how she connected to Giorgio through Alberto, and that she would leave in a week to live with Giorgio's niece Gabriella.

"So, how did *you* end up in Milan?" Mel asked Elena.

"Well, I am from Emilia Romagna. Pierpaolo was doing a shoot there, and I was his local contact. He enjoyed working with me, and invited me to come to Milan. I thought it would be an excellent opportunity. After a short time, we became lovers, although that has recently died down." Elena involuntarily thought of the scene she and Jonathan had witnessed the night before and broke out laughing.

"What's so funny?"

"Oh, nothing, I just remembered something ridiculous. It's a little personal."

"What flavors do you want?" Mel asked with the scoop in her hand.

They heard the lock on the entry door, followed by Massimo's animated voice. Mel was somewhat disappointed about the interruption.

"The boys are back," she said, then in a louder voice, "We're in here, having *gelato*, do you guys want some?"

Federico and Massimo came into the kitchen.

"It's the beautiful Elena, from Rome!" Massimo exclaimed.

Mel served everyone, and they went to sit at the dining room table.

"The two of you make an interesting combination," Federico noted.

"Yes," Massimo added. "But then, where is Jonathan?"

Elena and Mel both colored at this.

"Don't be an oaf, Max," Federico said.

"How was the *Salone*?" Mel asked.

"It was great, although the place was a bit dog-eared after the pillaging by so many visitors. And we are so parched, this *gelato* is perfect," said Massimo.

They compared notes about the *Salone,* reminisced about Trastevere, and debated the differences between Romans and Milanese.

Elena got up, and said she needed to get home.

Federico stood up and gave her a hug.

"If you come down to Rome again, please stay with us."

Elena laughed, "Well, I may be down there soon. We have to do the shoot we were scouting when we were there last."

Massimo air-kissed her. "Then we will expect you."

After she left, Mel cleared the dishes and helped to set the table for dinner, explaining that she wouldn't be joining them. Federico starting chopping vegetables, according to Lella's directions. Massimo and Mel sat at the little breakfast table, keeping him company.

"So, what's going on with this Jonathan thing?" Massimo asked Mel.

"Nothing!" Mel answered. "I just keep running into him. I think Elena had a crush on him, but she has lately had a new distraction."

215

"I'm waiting," said Massimo.

"Alberto," Mel said.

"Interesting! Is this something you are trying to engineer? To keep her away from Jonathan?"

"Not really," she said, pausing, "although I wonder. I think Alberto really wants to try to have a real relationship with someone."

"I wouldn't count on that," Federico said.

"People can change," Massimo insisted.

Federico lowered his head and raised his eyes, fixing Massimo.

"Has Alberto made any moves with you?"

Mel looked down.

"I think we felt a fleeting attraction, but decided against it, for obvious reasons. That was before he started the divorce proceedings."

"How do you feel now?"

"He's very attractive, but in the grand picture, I don't want anything to ruin my new friendship with Lella."

"That's wise," Federico said.

"You won't say anything?" Mel asked.

"Of course not," said Massimo."

"Anyway, I think he has shifted his interest to Elena."

"What should we do, then?"

"I'm not sure," said Mel. "Let's think about it."

Enrico

Enrico was in the studio by himself. He had planned to spend what he thought would be a rainy day indoors, but now that the sun was starting to come out he was conflicted. He unpacked the camera bags from yesterday's location work, logged all the equipment, cleaned it and put it in the cage. He walked into Elena's office to look at the schedule for next week. She kept the schedules pinned to a corkboard, for everyone to annotate. He looked around the small space. It was neat and tidy. Elena had placed a beautiful lamp on her desk, and several plants on the deep windowsill, to protect her from Signora Pia's invasive peering. She had also attached a half curtain, like the kind you see in cafés, made of little translucent disks strung like beads. There were colorful pillows on the two chairs that barely fit before her desk, and her own was draped with a fuschia colored shawl. It felt much warmer and more *domestic* than the rest of the studio.

Enrico filled in the column designating which cubicles would be used for concurrent shoots, so that Geert would know what to put where. Then he went to Reiner's post-production station and composed an email to Geert and Reiner, so they could get a sense of the upcoming work. They would most likely read it at midnight on Sunday.

He chuckled to himself. He he was having his "Milan" experience, and his colleagues (besides Jonathan) were German and Dutch. He guessed that was why people said that Milan was a Middle-European more than an "Italian" city. As a Neapolitan, he felt conspicuously "Italian" here. He had dark hair and dark eyes. Fortunately, he wasn't short, at least not by most standards (he was only an inch shorter than Jonathan). The way he spoke was flowery compared to the way the Milanese did. They seemed to struggle with the past tenses, while he navigated them with grammatical precision. Funny how the past became more articulated as one moved further south.

Milan was easier to work in than Naples, no doubt about that. The crooked stuff was less in your way, and the people were less emotional. Naples, however, was much more beautiful: it was situated on a sweeping bay embraced by the islands of Procida, Ischia, Capri, and the peninsula of Sorrento. The shore was lined with palm trees and backed by mountains, including the dramatic Vesuvius. What a terrible, terrible pity that it was an unsustainable place to live and work. Enrico had left—with a heavy heart—at his first opportunity.

Enrico's mother had a lovely house on the island of Procida, where she was born. Its stuccoed exterior was tinted pink, like the sunrise. It was rented from June through October, which enabled them to keep the place up and pay the taxes. Except for August. Then, it was for the family and their friends, so that they could celebrate *Ferragosto* together.

Enrico was stirred from his reverie by Jonathan's entrance from the back door of the studio. He was carrying a folding drying rack for clothing.

"Oh, hi Enrico," he said, "I thought with the sun coming out, I might hang my stuff outside."

"Please, go ahead," Enrico said, "I am finishing up."

Jonathan set up the *stendipanni* in the inner courtyard, and went back for his basket of wet clothes. He and Enrico opened both sets of French doors to let some air into the studio.

It was not Naples, Enrico thought, but today was proving to be better than the gray rainy days they had been experiencing lately. He went out to keep Jonathan company while he carefully arranged his wet socks and T-shirts. He walked around, inspecting the plants.

"You know, at our house on *Isola Procida*, off the coast of Naples, we have Prickly Pears and Palms."

"It must be beautiful," Jonathan said. He noticed that Hanne's candles were still sitting in his saucers, and waited for Enrico to turn his back before quietly placing them in his basket, under his laundry.

Enrico turned to Jonathan, "Do you run?"

"I do, but I haven't in weeks."

"Would you like to go to the *Castello* and have a run in the park?"

"I would love that," Jonathan said.

"Okay, I'll go back to my apartment and change."

Enrico gave Jonathan his address, a few blocks away. They would go in his car, since he would not ride public transportation in his workout clothes. Then he left, optimistic that he would make the most of his time in Milan, and even seek out a slice of nature wherever he could find it.

Saturday evening

Mel sat in her armchair, watching the city streets empty before the dinner hour. She was sorry she didn't have any plans for the evening. The sun was low and the air was clear and mild. She was going to have some cheese and crackers and fruit for dinner. It would be nice to have a walk after, but with whom?

Elena texted her.

ARE YOU FREE LATER?

WHAT FOR?

JONATHAN, REINER, ENRICO & I ARE @ NAVIGLIO

Mel had been to the neighborhood surrounding the canals during her job search, and the idea of going there in the evening appealed to her. She guessed, that at least for now, it was going to be hard to avoid Jonathan. She hadn't made friends with anyone in Giorgio's studio yet, although they were all very nice. She liked Elena despite everything, and Jonathan's colleagues were cool. Why not?

Mel texted back.

OK. WHERE?

GINGER COCKTAIL LAB @ 9:30

KK

Mel clicked the link and found the bar. It was on the *Naviglio Pavese*, the canal she hadn't yet explored. It seemed forever since the last time she was there, when she had found the little pizzeria on the *Naviglio Grande*. She went to the fridge to get her food, and brought it on a tray into her room.

Massimo came down stairs and called to her.

"You look so forlorn, eating here by yourself," he said, standing in her doorway.

"I'm fine Massimo. I am actually meeting up with some friends later, on the *Naviglio Pavese*."

"Maybe we could meet up with you once this family thing is over."

"That would be great. I think we're just hanging out, wandering around, maybe looking for music."

Alberto had arrived, and given that Massimo was downstairs, felt he could come down, too.

"Look at you, eating alone!" he said, putting his hands together to make a chopping gesture, a sort of reprimand.

Mel laughed, "I'm fine. Go up and see your family. We'll talk soon."

Massimo grabbed Alberto's arm and they went back upstairs.

"She going out with her friends, so don't worry."

* * *

Mel knew the way on the *Metropolitana*. Then she walked up Via Vigevano to the head of the canals. Some of the bars and restaurants had their tables out to take advantage of the fine night. She found the others, they ordered drinks, and chatted about the day. Jonathan described running in *Parco Sempione* with Enrico, and was now sharing everything he had discovered about the *Castello*.

They decided to go outside, and started walking outward along the *Naviglio*. They climbed the stairs of the first bridge and leaned on the parapet, looking back towards the activity, the lights, and their reflection on the still water. In the summertime, these narrow streets would become impassable.

To Mel, it felt like a stage set. Here she was, in Europe, in Italy, in Milan. Anything could happen! And yet, here was Jonathan, somehow. No, she wasn't going to go there. That was in the past. She approached Enrico, who was leaning on his elbows, looking down on the water.

"You look pensive," she said.

"From my summer house, I can see Vesuvius," he said.

"How dramatic! You must miss it very much."

"I miss the view, the sea. But I can be more productive here." He sighed, "I'll go there in the summer."

"This must look like a puddle to you," Mel said, laughing.

"It has its charm," Enrico said, shrugging, not wanting to be negative. "You know, Milan is near to many nice places. If you go a couple of hours in any direction, you can find beautiful mountains; the Riviera; even Venice is an easy train ride. You should take advantage of it."

"Speaking of travel," Mel said, "Elena mentioned that you might be going to Rome soon to do the shoot that she and Jonathan scouted."

"Yes, maybe. It depends on Pierpaolo."

"What is it like to work for him?"

"He's a photographer...basically a narcissist," he said, laughing. "Perhaps all photographers believe everyone should see things through their eyes."

He turned to look at Mel. "Pierpaolo is talented, but I don't know how far I can advance in that place. You know, your friend Jonathan has been asked to reorganize everything. So, we'll wait and see."

Mel got a text from Massimo, and responded to let him know where they were. She sighted him walking with Federico and Umberto toward the bridge. Mel and Elena walked down the steps to meet them, and the others followed. They found another place to have a drink, but Jonathan, who was a bit antsy, suggested they explore the side streets a little.

Umberto took charge, leading them with Reiner by his side.

Mel was walking next to Federico.

Massimo walked alongside Jonathan, telling him how much he liked Mel, as Jonathan nodded, laughing softly. As if he needed to to be convinced!

"I mean, she has this discipline to her personality, but then she turns sideways, so to speak, and she is full of chinks!"

"The chinks are the part I like best," Jonathan said.

Massimo observed, "I guess you're the type who likes Emmental cheese for the holes."

Enrico, walking alongside Elena, took the opportunity of apologizing to her.

"I'm sorry I said that thing about missing my window with you."

She waved her hand, dismissing the thought.

"Don't worry about it."

"Well, it was presumptuous, and doesn't represent how I feel. I was jealous when I learned that you were with Pierpaolo, and then, when Jonathan came along, it seemed like he grabbed your attention so easily. It just made me feel unnoticed."

"Enrico, I have a great deal of esteem for you, and you've taught me so much." She put her arm around him.

"I have been frustrated myself, and yes, I was drawn to Jonathan. But that is not going to happen. In fact, we have become good friends, and he has been very supportive, nothing more."

"He's a nice guy. I spent some time with him today. At first, he seemed like, you know, Mickey Mouse. The one who does everything right while all the comic characters around him get into trouble, only to be saved by his prudent watchfulness."

"And afterward? Your impression, I mean."

"Well, he has been very hurt by Melinda. He told me about it. We were in *Parco Sempione*, and we sat down on a bench after our run, to have a *limonata*. He was violent, he told me, when she confessed her infidelity. Then he realized that was not who he wanted to be."

223

Elena looked at him.

"So he is running toward her to cancel out his bad deeds, and she is running from him to cancel hers. They may be going in circles for some time."

"We should catch up with them," Enrico said. "I mean, the others." He pointed ahead.

Umberto had discovered a green space in Via Magolfa, and proposed a game of flashlight tag. Federico claimed he was too old for that, but Massimo convinced him to join in. Umberto delineated the limits of the field, and pulled out his PenTorch.

"Okay, now I have to point my PenTorch and try to hit each of you, one at a time. Any one of you can try to touch me from behind, and then I am out."

They all ran around, taunting him by making noises, then moving into the shadows. But Umberto was a pro and hit five of them. Then, when he called, "Massimo, you're hit!" Federico came up behind him and tapped his shoulder.

They had another round with Federico, who easily got everyone because he had the emotional detachment of someone who was not into the game.

"I've had enough," he said. "As champion, I call a truce. I think I'm ready to go home. Massimo, is that okay with you?"

"It's more fun if everyone has a torch," Umberto said, so you can free people after they have been hit."

They made their way back to the canal, and followed it up to the piazza.

Umberto offered Reiner a ride on his scooter, as they both wanted to go to a club. Enrico had his car and offered to give Elena and Jonathan a ride; Mel returned with Federico and Massimo to Lella's place by Uber.

When they got back, Alberto and Lella were sitting in the living room. Federico and Massimo went down to bed. Lella offered Mel an herbal tea, and prepared one for herself. Alberto stuck to his wine.

Mel sat in a chair across from them. She thought about how awkward it would have been to play flashlight tag with Alberto there.

"We were discussing Giorgio," Lella said.

"And?"

"Lella wants to see him but doesn't want to get too involved." Alberto said, looking Mel in the eyes.

"His enthusiasm," Lella said, "makes me cautious."

"I can understand that," Mel said.

Looking at Lella, Alberto asked, "Do you think that it is inevitable that he will lose interest once he has gained his prize?"

"I don't intend to move in with him, if that's what you are calling his 'prize.' We have already had sex," she added, nonchalantly.

Then she continued, "He seemed disappointed that I was having a family dinner tonight and didn't ask him to come. He is already closing in on me."

"Hmmm," Alberto mused. "Small doses would be in order."

Lella stood up.

"Well, I am going to bed. Please stay as long as you like, Alberto."

Lella headed off down the hallway to her room and closed the door.

Alberto suggested they get some air on the balcony.

Mel enjoyed being alone with Alberto. There was a sense of care to his presence, with a thread of tension. They leaned their elbows on the rail close to one another. He laced his arm through hers, and took her hand. Neither said anything, they just looked straight ahead.

After a bit he said, "Well, I'd better go."

Back to work

The following week was uneventful, yet life moved forward for everyone. Lella was doing some editing for Alberto, happy to sit at her dining table with the French doors to the balcony open. The sounds of the city were all the company she desired. People generally made her tired after a short while. She was grateful for Federico and Massimo's visit, but glad to have some quiet again. The words on the pages before her described people and relayed what they said, though she was able to keep a respectful distance.

Jonathan was advancing his understanding of the studio's operations, and spent some time with Pierpaolo, flushing out all of his concerns. He had put Lucy to work making folders for a handful of representative projects, selected by Pierpaolo. Her task was simply to put all of the invoices in one pocket, and all of the expenses in the other, including every receipt from the bar and the taxis. He wanted to make sure that Pierpaolo knew where and how much profit he was making. He couldn't go on forever by simply keeping the cash rolling in seamlessly. Jonathan was beginning to wonder if there was any hope for Pierpaolo as a businessman, and what that meant for him.

Elena and Enrico were planning their trip to Rome. Enrico learned that Elena had never been to Naples, and convinced her to accompany him there after the shoot. Something about her had changed. She seemed more rested, grounded. They would return to Milan one day later, on Monday. Federico was happy to have both of them stay with him on Friday night. Enrico was relieved to have things smoothed out between him and Elena, as well as for the opportunity of paying a short visit to his mother. It had taken him some effort to convince her that the woman he was bringing down was not his girlfriend, just a colleague. *Please don't embarrass me!*

Mel was busy at Giorgio's studio. He decided to involve her in the renovation of Susanna's property on Lake Como, since she was the only one in the studio who had actually been to the site. She familiarized herself with the drawings for the addition, and got to work on the color palette and selection of things like fixtures and hardware. Giorgio gave her a shortlist of products and companies that he had in mind. Mel was excited about working on Susanna's house, and she hoped she could contribute to maintaining something of its primitive and quiet character, as Lella had suggested during their visit.

On Saturday, Mel would be moving her stuff to Gabriella's house. Lella offered to drive her with her things in the morning, and after she got settled they would have dinner together.

Giorgio's excitement about having spent a night with Lella was tempered by her evasiveness afterward. He wasn't sure what the problem was. The sex was enjoyable, as far as he could tell. This was a long time coming. From his point of view, at their age, they should just dive in full throttle and have the relationship they should have initiated years ago. Now they were just wasting time. He was pleased that Mel was moving out on the weekend; that would give him wider berth. Maybe Lella just wanted to be in her own place, where she had her stuff.

Pierpaolo was relaxed as much as Pierpaolo could be that week. The *Salone* was over, the backlog of work was solid, but not pressing; and he enjoyed talking about the organization of the studio and their projects with Jonathan. Hanne was keeping him amused, although she had her quirks. It was challenging to be with someone who wasn't Italian. There were some things she just didn't get about Italian men. She couldn't cook either–not that he was looking for a wife–but that was always nice. And then there was her obsession with herself. Her hair, the golden skin she cultivated in the tanning bed, even her pubic hair, which was trimmed perfectly (and severely). He sometimes felt like he was dating a teenager. All things considered, though, the situation with Hanne was much less volatile than that with Elena.

Bella Napoli

The shoot in Rome on Saturday went well. Elena and Enrico had arrived early Friday evening to get the location staged and set up for an early start on Saturday. They worked well together, and were done by one o'clock. Federico told them they must have lunch before getting the train to Naples, and he usually ate around one-thirty on Saturdays, having slept in and done the shopping. He insisted on taking them to the station, because of the equipment and their bags.

On the train, Enrico told Elena that they would be going to Procida, not the city center where his mother's principal residence was located. Now that May had arrived, she was getting the place ready for the first tenants of the season.

"It's not known as an island for tourists," he explained, "like Ischia or Capri. Anyway, we didn't choose it; it chose us. The view to Naples is gorgeous, and sometimes I prefer to enjoy the city at a distance. We keep a sailboat in the marina in a place with the impossible name of Chiaiolella. In the summer, we sail around the nooks and crannies of Ischia."

Elena appreciated Enrico's excitement about going home. She missed her father.

He pulled up a satellite image of Procida, and pointed out the bays formed by the broadly curved arcs, remnants of volcanic craters. Then he zoomed out to include the hills around Naples, including Vesuvius.

"So, I'd like you to consider the Neapolitan landscape as defined by the craters and their rims, evidence of the volcanoes. Many people overlook this aspect of my city, because the experience on the street is so intense. To me, it is deeply significant that this place has experienced such a letting off of steam: the eruptions, the violence of nature. The culture also expresses this volatility and explosiveness. They say that a population is formed by the landscape that gives it life."

Elena looked at Enrico thoughtfully. She had never heard him speak like this before. He seemed repressed in Milan, and now, as he approached his home turf, his assuredness, engagement, and pride were emerging.

Enrico pointed to Vesuvius as a reference, then scrolled through the hills showing her that this crater was a park, that one a lake, then over to the twin arcs that formed the southeast-facing bays of Procida, and finally a third arc formed by the small island of Vivara and its causeway.

"This is a nature reserve," Enrico said. "We take the boat there to go swimming. The coastline is steep all round the island, but the far side is particularly rocky. In a way, that has saved the island."

Elena sat back and rested her head on the seat.

"Are you looking forward to seeing your mother?"

Enrico assumed a concerned tone.

"Oh, yes, poor dear, she can barely get around these days, so please forgive me if I have to run some errands for her. And, by the way, her Italian is so-so, so if you have trouble understanding her, don't let on. She may get offended."

Elena smiled halfway, not sure how to take this, so she remained silent.

"Sure." *It's only for a day*, she thought. Well, two nights and a day.

When they got to the Naples station, Enrico looked at her with determination.

"Are you ready?" He took her hand and wove skillfully to the taxi stand, then maneuvered around and poked his head in one window, then another.

"Here," he said.

"We need to get to Pozzuoli quickly, he said to the driver," showing him a ten Euro note. "There's another one if we get to the Flavian Amphitheater before it closes."

Then he turned to Elena, "Hang on!"

The driver began a series of roadway gymnastics such as she had never seen, and Elena found herself drawing in toward the center of the vehicle. He wove in and out of dialect as he did of the traffic, and he often turned around while speaking to Enrico. He slipped under red lights to the sound of horns, saying, "I had already passed through that one, in my mind. People are so impatient."

After they got onto the expressway, the *tangenziale*, there were no more traffic lights. Now Elena had to adjust to high-speed tailgating.

"This isn't the scenic route, but time is tight," Enrico apologized.

The taxi eventually stopped on a nondescript street with the usual condominiums and stores on one side and a large open space on the other, surrounded by a rusted iron fence set on a stone wall. Through the trees on the inside of the enclosure, Elena could see the crumbled brick walls of ruins, the Flavian Amphitheater.

The man at the gate said, "We're closing in ten minutes."

Enrico gave him some money, and they went in. The attendant closed the gate and decided to give them a tour. They walked underneath the great structure, a maze of barrel vaults and arches, with pieces of large fluted columns and detached capitals lying on the ground like dismembered gladiators.

"Thanks to volcanic ash from the Solfatara Volcano, much of this has been well preserved," Enrico said. "You know, there are about forty volcanoes around Naples. Not active. Only Vesuvius is active."

They passed under light wells (now covered with grates for safety), that punctuated the dark corridors. They went out into the arena where the attendant stopped for his spiel.

"This is where San Gennaro, our patron saint, was martyred in the year 305. They set the wild beasts on him. But he blessed the beasts, and they kneeled to him. So the Romans took him to the *Solfatara* and beheaded him."

Elena looked at Enrico, suppressing a smile.

Enrico said, to her, "It's true that San Gennaro was not killed by the beasts, and had to be taken away for the beheading. The kneeling part may be a bit of an exaggeration."

They continued their walk into the stands, then made their way back to the exit.

"We'd better get going, we have to catch the ferry," Enrico said, looking at his watch.

When they got out, their taxi driver was still there, talking on his phone. They got him to take them to the ferry for Procida, which they made in plenty of time. They would get to Procida Porto by six-thirty.

On their way across the water, Elena turned to Enrico.

"Thank you so much for what you've shared with me."

"You know," she continued, "I had only been to Rome once before last month, and never further south. You've opened my eyes to a whole new piece of Italian culture."

"People up north don't really understand Naples. Have you ever heard the joke about the Milanese who comes down here, to Capri, and scolds a Neapolitan guy on the beach? The Milanese says: *I work hard all year to be able to bring my family here for a vacation. What do you do?* And the Neapolitan says: *As you see, I am already here.*"

Elena chuckled.

231

"How do we get from the port to your house?"

"My mother is picking us up."

"I thought she was infirm?" Elena said, getting up and following Enrico to the gangplank.

Enrico's mother was standing under a canopy at the end of the pier. She was an elegant, gray-haired woman, taller than Enrico in her heels.

Elena had been expecting a short, plump woman tearfully carrying sweets to them in her apron; Enrico had played her.

"Elena, so nice to meet you. Please call me Dida. Enrico, what a charming houseguest you have brought us!"

They got into an impossibly small car, and drove out of Procida Porto. The roads were barely fifteen feet wide, if that, and the buildings and garden walls came right to the edge of the pavement.

"How do people walk around here?" Elena asked.

"With their rosaries," Dida answered.

After a small string of shops in a locality called Olmo, Dida took a left fork and soon slowed down as a solid, green metal gate began to slide. She waited for a scooter to pass (the island was swarming with them), then pulled in.

As the gate opened, it revealed a beautiful view toward Naples. The sun was low, creating a *chiaroscuro* effect: golden light and deep shadow. The stucco of the house was glowing pink. The windows were framed with green shutters, their flower boxes already filled with Geraniums. The small garden was arranged on two terraces, and was bordered by Oleanders and Maritime Pines, their branches curling upwards to catch the last golden embers of the sun.

* * *

Enrico's brother Michele arrived shortly after they did, carrying a net bag full of mussels. Angelina, whom they all called Lina, was preparing dinner.

She scolded, "Signor Michele, you're dripping all over my floor! Give me that," she said. She took the bag and brought it to the sink.

Michele put his arm around her and said, "It was not I, Lina, but the mussels that were dripping. Let me take care of them for you."

He rinsed the mussels with a cold-water spray, and left them in a shallow soak with some ice and coarse salt. Then he washed his hands and dried them on a towel as Enrico came in to introduce him to Elena.

"This is my brother Michi."

"I am in the guest house," Michele said to Enrico, "Mother has put Elena in the Tower." He smiled and bowed to Elena, swinging the towel with a flourish.

Enrico gave Elena a tour of the house on the way to her room. The floor below them was a walkout to the garden. It contained a workroom, a laundry, some storage for food and wine, and a room and bath for Lina.

"She has been with us since we were kids, Enrico said. My mother has always worked, so we're very close to Lina."

They walked outside and back up the stairs, through the kitchen to the living room. The wall facing the sea opened through four pairs of French doors, with the dining table set nearby. The next floor up had three bedrooms, two baths, and an alcove area on the landing that was set up like an office. One more flight led to the Tower, which was a smaller story made of one large room, a bath, and a generous terrace with a stone balustrade, facing the sea.

"I feel like a princess," Elena said.

Enrico laughed. But he didn't say, you *are* a princess. In fact, he seemed to have unwittingly assumed something similar to an upper hand. His love for the place was filling his heart right now.

"I will leave you, so you can get ready for dinner. Towels are in the bathroom."

Elena kicked off her shoes, laid out a simple dress she had packed, and jumped into the shower. Then she stretched out for five minutes before getting dressed. She chose a pair of jade earrings that Pierpaolo had given her; they matched her dress. Then she went down to join the others.

The brothers held the chairs for Elena and Dida, and they all sat down. The breeze was coming in, lifting the sheer curtains and then receding, letting them fall, mimicking the push and pull of the sea.

"We weren't sure what your tastes were, Elena, so we decided to have steamed mussels and *bruschette* as appetizers, rather than putting seafood in the pasta. Lina has made a *puttanesca*, with capers we picked from our garden last year."

Michi opened a bottle of white wine and poured out the glasses.

Enrico turned to Elena and said, "It's hard to believe we were working on that shoot this morning, isn't it?"

"Seems like a long time ago. Umm. What kind of wine is this, Michele?"

"It's called *Greco di tufo*. It is a grape of Greek origin, grown in our soils fortified with volcanic ash. If you prefer, I can get you some Pinot."

"Oh, no, thank you. Not after the initiation Enrico has given me about the volcanoes. I would like to engage with the *spirit of place*."

Enrico asked, "When did you get here, Mick?"

"I came with Mother on Thursday. I'm working on a contract, so I set up my office in the guesthouse. In the afternoons, I have been cleaning the boat. I thought we might take Elena out for our pre-season sail."

Dida added, "We can have Lina prepare a little lunch for you to take." Then she turned to Elena.

"Enrico tells me that you are from Emilia Romagna. Do you have family there?"

"Yes, my father and my paternal grandmother. We have a farm between Modena and Bologna. My mother passed away almost six years ago."

"I am sorry to hear that."

"She was a professor of Agricultural and Resource Economics at the University of Bologna."

"Fascinating. Especially for a woman."

"That's how she and my father met. He distributes agricultural products. She had the theory and he, the practice. We don't operate our farm ourselves. It's part of a collective."

There was a pause. Elena thought she should change the subject.

"Sailing sounds like fun, where will we go?"

"Not very far," Michele said, "Just between the marina and Vivara."

Enrico added, "We just check to see if we remembered to do everything before the season starts. Have you done any sailing, Elena?"

"I went once to the Dalmatian coast in the Adriatic, with my parents, when I was sixteen." She laughed, "I wasn't very useful."

"It must be beautiful there," Michele said.

Enrico said, "Well, our boat doesn't require much crew. Michi and I will suffice. You'll perform the role of passenger only."

* * *

In the morning they had the most delicious *pastiera* made with fresh ricotta and zest from Amalfi lemons. Elena wrapped her hands around her caffè latte. Lina poured espresso for Enrico and Michele.

"The *Signorina* wanted milk in hers," she said to them apologetically.

Once on the boat, Enrico and Michele were impressive; they worked harmoniously, communicating without words.

235

"We look good because the wind is easy." Michele said.

"So Michele," Elena said, "You stayed in Naples. I take it you work with your mother?"

"Yes, we are both attorneys, as was my grandfather. He wanted my mother to study jurisprudence very much. It was an established practice, so it seemed like the logical thing for me to do."

"We need to turn, watch your head," Enrico said.

Michele ducked and continued, "Enrico didn't want to get his hands dirty."

"Do you have to get your hands dirty?" Elena asked.

"Let's put it this way," Michele said, as he turned the winch. "Down here, you have to choose your clients very carefully. And even then, there may be surprises. My position is that lazy people break the law; those with skill *interpret* it."

They got to one of their favorite spots and dropped anchor.

Enrico felt the need to defend his own career choice.

"My family's law practice is honorable. I just don't have the talent for it."

"No," Michele added, smiling. "Some families have a son who go into the priesthood; we have an artist."

Mel moves in

Lella approved of the work Giorgio had done on Gabriella's apartment. She thought of the days when Gabriella came to hang out with Amelia during college, and now they were both thirty-five! It seemed impossible. She sat down on the sofa while Gabriella made some coffee and wondered, *what do we do with our lives?* There are the big events, to be sure, but the majority of our time is spent in between things: walking to work, sending emails, planning our activities. This is our consciousness. And so is this moment of moving in, opening suitcases, and making up the bed. The coffee was a celebratory, communal act of recognition.

"I'm very happy to be here with the two of you right now," she said, accepting a mug from Gabriella.

Gabriella said, "I am leaving for Paris at four, so Melinda will be spending her first night here alone. I have a meeting Monday, so I thought I would get there, rest up, and prepare on Sunday."

"Then I suppose I can't take you to lunch," Lella said.

"No, but thank you so much."

Mel added, "I am going to have to get unpacked and arrange things, then I'd like take a walk around the neighborhood."

"Well, then I think I will go do the shopping for our dinner before the shops close," Lella said, looking at her watch. She embraced Mel, then Gabriella.

"Buon viaggio, Gabi," she said as she left.

"See you at seven, Mel?"

Gabriella cleared a small writing table for Mel's laptop and notebooks, and went to prepare for her trip. By one o'clock, Mel had received instructions on the washing machine, the oven's quirks, and the locks. Now she was alone in her new home.

The apartment was on the second floor (which was really the third floor, when you counted the ground floor of shops). Mel and Gabriella each had a balcony, with two large windows in the living space between. The windows all faced west, overlooking the newly renovated piazza below. It was a perfect location, halfway between the Stazione Garibaldi and Giorgio's studio, and right by a stop of the *Metropolitana*. Gabi (or rather, her father) had bought the apartment before the neighborhood underwent its revitalization. It had meant picking her way through a construction site for a while, but it was well worth it.

After a short nap, Mel went out to explore her surroundings. The piazza had some nice sized trees, Horsechestnuts, she thought, which in Italian were *Ippocastagni*. Scooters lined the curb all around it, and people were sitting on benches, wandering into cafés, or just standing around talking to their friends. She bought a bottle of wine to bring to dinner. She also bought a beautiful lavender chiffon scarf for Lella, as a parting gift.

The idea of a goodbye dinner made her a little sad.

* * *

That evening, Lella and Mel had a lovely dinner of pasta primavera, salad, and a selection of cheeses. They talked about everything that had happened in the past few weeks, and agreed it had been a remarkable time.

"I don't know whether it is a good thing or not—yet—but I don't think I would have started to see Giorgio if you hadn't been here," Lella said.

Her phone signaled a call. "It's Alberto, shall I take it?"

"Please, do."

Alberto knew they were having their farewell dinner, but he wondered if it wouldn't be appropriate to bring them some gelato and spumante? Mel shrugged and nodded.

"Maybe I should see if Giorgio wants to join us?"

Mel thought that was a good idea. Even if it made them seem like two couples, it would dilute the situation a bit, and keep the conversation general. Giorgio just happened to be free; he had been watching a documentary about his work to get his mind off the slight he felt, not being with Lella for the second Saturday night in a row. He told Lella that he had to "work himself free of something," but that he would be there soon.

He turned off the TV and went to his wardrobe to get a clean shirt and some nicer shoes. He looked at himself in the mirror; brushed his teeth. He called a cab and grabbed a bottle of French champagne from his refrigerator.

"So how do you feel, going out on your own, Melinda?" Alberto asked when they were all sitting in the living room.

"Well, it's exciting. I love Gabi's neighborhood. I am sorry to leave here, though Lella has promised we'll still be in close touch."

"We're all connected now," Giorgio said, trying to catch Lella's eye.

After they had a glass of champagne, Mel admitted to being very tired from all the emotion. Alberto offered to give her a ride home, which she accepted.

Once they had left, Giorgio stood up and said that he should go, too, but Lella asked him to stay.

"I would like that very much," Giorgio said, stroking Lella's arm. He tried to hide his excitement.

Alberto drove his scooter like a maniac, at least from Mel's vantage point sitting behind him. But he skillfully skimmed the meager space that separated them from every obstacle. When they got to Mel's new home, he asked if he could come up and get an impression.

"So when I imagine you making breakfast, or drawing, or sleeping, I can have the context right."

Mel said okay, and up they went.

They sat down on the couch with two glasses of sparkling water.

"Why do you Americans drink so much water?" Alberto said, looking at the bubbles rising to the surface, wishing it was spumante.

"To counteract the wine."

"Why would you want to do that?"

Mel sat up straight to change the tone and asked, "So, how is your personal rehabilitation plan going?"

"Well, if you mean Elena, I can't very well see her without your help. And if you are wondering what else I have *not* been up to, well, he paused, I haven't been to bed with you, which is what I would have liked most of all."

He saw Mel's expression fall, and continued, "But we have decided against that. Now, I understand that we are just friends. Why ruin it? But then, you don't live with Lella anymore, so how would she even know?"

"We're not having this conversation, Alberto. Sex always changes things, even if you don't believe it. You told me yourself that some women react in unexpected ways afterward."

"You wouldn't."

"That's not true. I think you would feel more ownership over me. That would make me feel confined."

"I can't believe we are having an intellectual discussion about something that is natural and emotional."

"Well, I have made one big mistake, and I am not about to make another." Mel looked at the time on her phone. "I'd better go to bed."

Alberto left, obviously put off. Mel felt like their friendship had now become tenuous because he didn't get his way. She remembered how skillful Cecil had been, in New York. He just kept showing up, biding his time, waiting for a moment of weakness. She was angry with Alberto. He had taken away some of her joy about being in her new apartment. She got cleaned up and went to her sleeping alcove. The sheets were fresh and cool. She grabbed her book, hoping to clear her head, but soon fell asleep.

Sunday awakening

The next morning at Lella's was like Sunday morning every week: fresh baked goods, foamy cappuccino, beautiful, hand-painted china, and pressed linen napkins. Giorgio sat at the dining table near the balcony, where the sun was slightly veiled by the morning haze. As the day progressed, this would lift and reveal a lovely, unseasonably warm day. For now, the haze was nice, familiar: like Lella who drifted in from the kitchen in her silvery blue translucent robe.

They sat together for a while, pulling off the corners of croissants and dipping them in their foam. Giorgio hulled a few strawberries, placing them on a tiny dish for Lella. Then he squeezed a few drops from a lemon, and sprinkled them with some sugar.

Lella laughed, a little embarrassed by the attention, making Giorgio turn serious.

"You're holding back, Lella. Why?"

Lella put her hand on Giorgio's.

"I'm being myself, Giorgio. If you think that's cautious, perhaps you should look at your own behavior."

"My behavior? I am here in adoration of you!"

"That's just it. It is a bit much for me to process."

Giorgio calmed down.

"Okay, I get it." Then he went quiet, instinctively giving her an opportunity to backpedal.

Lella said, "Giorgio, you know I care about you very much. I am enjoying our time together. But it feels like you are trying to steer this someplace."

"And you are an unwilling passenger?"

"Unknowing would be a better word. What do *you* want, Giorgio? Do you even know?"

He sighed deeply before beginning.

"Lella, I have always been in love with you, throughout your marriage, throughout mine... Now we are both free. I don't understand why we just can't be together."

"We *are* together!"

"Lella, I want to be with you every day. I want to live with you."

Lella looked down, genuinely sorry.

"That's not what I want."

A panicked expression crossed Giorgio's face.

"I will marry you, if that's what your concern is."

"Giorgio, do you really think I care about what people think at this stage of my life?"

He was silent, brooding.

She continued, "I spent many years tending to Paolo, bending to his moods and inclinations. I raised two children and started a career for myself. I don't regret any of it; I don't think there are perfect marriages. But now I feel free for the first time in my life. I want to expand my work as an editor, and I especially want to help young women who are starting out. It is as important to me as your work is to you."

"You can do that. You know how busy I am with the studio. I am out nine or ten hours a day."

Lella shook her head, realizing that he didn't get it.

"Giorgio, I need my space here. I need to be able to come here and close the door on the world. People give you energy; they tire me out. When people look at you, it makes you feel admired; I feel picked apart."

She took the last sip of her cappuccino.

"I recharge when I am alone. I like being alone. It balances me."

"Then why do you have people, like Melinda, stay with you? You don't need the money."

"The money is helpful, Giorgio. I am using it to fund a small scholarship program. More importantly, I need to make sure I don't isolate myself too much. Mel was the perfect guest. And I believe I gave her some support, beyond a place to stay, while she found work."

"Mel is a good worker," Giorgio conceded.

"I am grateful that she is working with you. You will teach her so much."

"Now you're trying to bolster me, after your refusal."

"I haven't refused you! Isn't a relationship made of a road traveled together? You can't just go down a path of your choosing and drag me along. We have to take one step at a time, together, no?"

"We aren't going to live forever."

Then he laughed, involuntarily. "What if I can't get it up in two years? Can you see me taking drugs to have sex?"

"We are getting older, but I am trying to focus on what I have to offer, not any deficiencies we may develop."

Giorgio returned to hulling strawberries, doing it roughly now, and popping them into his mouth.

Lella carefully stacked the dishes on a tray and carried them into the kitchen. When she came out, Giorgio was getting his jacket out of the entry closet.

"You're leaving." Lella said.

"Yes, I have so much to do today. And I need some time alone, too."

She tried to embrace him, but he pecked her on the cheek and left.

244

Lella closed the door, let out a big sigh and then returned to her room to make the bed. She opened the windows and turned the sheets down. She fluffed the pillows and set them at the foot of the bed. Then she smoothed out the imprint of Giorgio's body, tucking the sheet to remove every wrinkle.

* * *

The haze lifted and the day did prove to be warm and sunny. Mel was reading the Times at an outdoor table in the piazza below the apartment, wondering what she should do. Gabi was away; Elena was in Naples; Jonathan was busy preparing some write-up; Alberto was angry with her. It seemed weak to call Lella so soon to get together, so she resigned herself to spending her Sunday alone.

Jonathan was indeed working on his write up. He had gone for a run, passing Signora Pia, who looked at his scantily clad body, scandalized. When he returned to his apartment, he opened the windows, rearranged the plants on the sill, and made an espresso. While it was coming up, steaming and gurgling, he spread honey over a thick piece of whole grain toast and heated some milk.

He went through the back room, found an extension cord, and then entered the studio with his laptop and notepad. He would set up out in the courtyard, and finish his draft. Then he would have a nice shower and change before one o'clock. Leitizia had invited him to lunch to meet her boyfriend Stefano. Afterward, he would come back and do the fine-tuning. Maybe see if Reiner wanted to grab a beer later. He wondered what Mel was doing.

Pierpaolo hadn't spent the night with Hanne, because her best friend from Copenhagen was in town, and she was out club hopping with some Danes. He slept in and then got up to pack the large *caffettiera* for his double espresso. He didn't know how much longer his stomach could take it: three or four glasses of wine at night, then a heavy dose of coffee every morning. So what? One look in the mirror told him that he looked pretty fucking good. He foraged in the cupboard for some breakfast cookies to soak up the coffee. He was on his own today, and he had to go over something that Jonathan was sending him around dinnertime, so he would have to spend the evening alone again. Two in a row! Well, if he got through it early enough, maybe he would call Hanne. Although she was one of those "pay to play" types: she wanted to be taken out to dinner. He didn't think she would respond well to a booty call, but then again, he hadn't yet tried.

Was he in love? No, not really. He was in love with physical beauty, though, and she had that going for her. So if he loved beauty, and she was beautiful, did that mean he loved her? He scrunched his brow, and was saved from further deliberation by the gurgling and hissing of the *caffettiera*.

Giorgio's vendetta

Giorgio decided to walk home from Lella's to cool down. He was pissed off. What was her problem? There were plenty of women who would give anything to be with a man like him. He was successful, creative, and (he thought) fun; he was invited everywhere. But there weren't other women like Lella. Just the same, he had to do something to even things out between them. She had the upper hand; there was no doubt about it. He had been too open about his feelings.

He fumed through the morning, stopping in the studio to see what was on everyone's table. He checked his correspondence. He couldn't focus, so he went for another walk. He picked up some take out and went home to eat lunch. *This is ridiculous,* he thought, *I should be having lunch with Lella.*

After he ate, he looked for some mindless activity, and found some project photos to go through and file. He opened the windows and turned on some music.

Later in the afternoon, he thought he would go to Bar Jamaica for a drink. He could sit at a table outside, in Via Brera. It was a beautiful day, and he needed to be around people. Being in the house by himself was making him feel depressed.

Giorgio did find a good table, which he immediately adjusted so that it wouldn't wobble on the paving stones of the street. He was a little uncomfortable being there by himself, so he brought a notebook and one of his favorite fine-tipped drawing pens. He decided to order a Negroni. That would take a while to drink, so he wouldn't feel as if he had to move on.

He gave his order to the waiter.

"We have some *focaccia* from Liguria if you'd like a little, *Architetto*," he said, addressing Giorgio, a known customer, with the usual deferential title.

"*Molto bene, grazie,* Franco."

Giorgio sat back in his chair, his elbows on the armrests, legs extended, taking in the sun. He couldn't wait to go to the seaside, to have some lasagne with pesto in Portofino, to go sailing with friends in Santa Margherita, or host an aperitivo at his place in Camogli.

"*Ciao*!! It's Giorgio, isn't it?"

Giorgio opened one eye. Standing before him was the blonde Danish girlfriend of Pierpaolo Nervi. He stood up and air kissed her.

"Hello, Hannah?" he said.

"It's Han*ne*," she giggled. "This is my best friend, Liva, from Copenhagen. She's going home today."

Giorgio shielded his eyes and looked from Hanne to Liva, and from Liva to Hanne again. It was a smorgasbord of smiling blonde beauty. Liva's hair was long and tipped with a silvery purple color, just like his chair upholstered in velvet, for Lella. Hanne wore a sawed-off, close fitting white T-shirt that showed off her salon tan nicely.

He introduced himself to her friend.

"*The* Giorgio Monti?" Liva asked, her eyes wide.

Giorgio stood even taller, puffing his chest up ever so slightly.

Hanne explained, "Liva is also an architect. She was here for the *Salone*, and a little vacation."

"Is it too late to offer you ladies a drink?"

The girls spoke to each other in Danish, Liva looking at her watch and nodding. Giorgio could not fucking believe his good luck. He was going to be sitting at Bar Jamaica on the first warm, sunny day of the spring, flanked by two gorgeous Danish women. He felt his energy surge. The morning's conversation with Lella seemed so insignificant now. Rather than being a roadblock, it now seemed like a twig on the path that he could pick up with two fingers.

They decided that Liva could spare a half hour, get an Uber to the Garibaldi train station, and take the Malpensa Express to the airport.

"I'm having a *Negroni*," he said.

They wanted one, too.

Once their drinks and the focaccia–which Franco had cut into bite-size pieces–arrived, Hanne and Liva swirled their drinks, admiring the deep ruby red and the little piece of orange peel dodging the ice cubes.

"It's delicious," Liva said.

"I *told* you," said Hanne. "Besides, it always helps to drink before you travel. It takes the edge off."

Giorgio sat back, enjoying the conversation. They talked a little about the *Salone*, but mostly about their impressions of Milan. Liva talked about an urban design project that she was involved in at home, and the designers she worked with there. Giorgio gave her his card to *please use the next time she was in town*, and she handed him hers, in case he ever came to Copenhagen. Her ride eventually arrived, and after tearful hugs with Hanne, she disappeared down a side street.

Hanne looked at Giorgio as if to say, now what?

Giorgio cleared his throat. "Shall we have another?"

Hanne laughed and said yes, her silver earrings sparkling against her neck.

"So where's Pierpaolo today?"

Hanne shrugged. "He's working on something." She didn't want to talk about Pierpaolo when she had a bigger fish in front of her.

When their second round arrived, Giorgio pursued a less sensitive line of questioning.

"So, Hanne, I don't think I caught what you do, and why you're here in Milan."

"I am a wellness trainer. I work with alternative emotional healing techniques."

"I can see where you'd be good at that."

"Anyway, we are opening a center here. It will also have a home furnishing section, because the things you surround yourself in your home are very important to your well being. And we're going to create a Danish-Italian home accessories exchange to trade between the two countries."

"That is a good idea."

"You must have a beautiful home, being an architect and a furniture designer."

"I like it, modestly speaking," he said.

Hanne had finished her second Negroni, which in Giorgio's book meant she must be pretty close to drunk. She drained her glass with her head back, and began chewing on ice cubes.

"I'm kind of hungry," she said, between chomps.

Giorgio studied her for a moment, thinking. It wouldn't be good to take her to a restaurant, though she was clearly hinting at that. Someone in his circle (meaning Lella's) might see them, and then there would be awkward explaining to do. There was also the issue of Pierpaolo, although Hanne didn't seem to have any qualms about that. Anyway, it was just dinner! They were acquaintances, not strangers.

"Well, since you mentioned an interest in home furnishings, I wonder if you would be satisfied with a simple pasta at my house. He pointed down the street. I live right there, around the corner."

Hanne turned her head, feeling slightly dizzy. She had probably had one more than she needed. The apartment, so close, looked like the path of least resistance. Giorgio paid up, and they started down the street.

"You know," Hanne said, "Pierpaolo is a big baby."

"Everyone likes babies better when they are little, don't they?" Giorgio answered.

Hanne burst out laughing. "You are so cute!"

"Don't say *that*," he protested, "I'm not a baby."

He opened the *portone* and held the door for Hanne.

"Watch your step," he said.

Giorgio walked in front of Hanne to lead the way on the stairs. She was out of his field of vision, allowing Lella and this morning to return to his mind. He felt entirely justified in having Hanne over for dinner–it was just dinner– and his resentment at Lella's lack of, well, gratitude, suppressed his feelings of guilt.

Hanne absolutely loved Giorgio's place, the deep colors, the modern furniture, and the polished wood.

"It feels very restful," she said.

Giorgio prepared an aglio, olio and peperoncino pasta–a panacea in his book–and they drank San Pellegrino. When they finished eating, he carried the dishes out to the kitchen and left them on the counter, not sure how to conclude the evening. Should he get a cab, and go with her to make sure gets home safely? Wherever that was?

He went back to the table.

"Would you like an *espresso*?"

Hanne was rolling a joint. "Is this okay?" she asked.

Giorgio shrugged. "I guess so."

After she lit it, she passed it to him. He thought, *what the hell*, and took a drag. It felt good.

"You really should," she said, trying not to exhale, then coughing, "... get some candles in here," she finished.

Then she put out the joint, and stored it in a little tin.

"I don't want to get stoned," she said, "just wanted to take the edge off."

Giorgio wondered what sort of edge she needed to take off at this point.

She stood up and walked up the mahogany stairs to the bookshelves. The lower bookshelves were deeper, creating a ledge at about desk height. She looked at the books, stroking the smooth wood with her hands. She started moving her hips side to side, too. Giorgio had never seen such a perfectly formed butt. He thought he should go up to where she was, perhaps to suggest that he call a cab? When he came close she turned around to face him, and put her hands on his hips.

It was the most natural thing in the world for Giorgio to kiss her on the mouth. Whatever!

"I should get you home, no?" he reconsidered.

She unfastened Giorgio's belt, then unbuttoned his pants.

"Not with your pants down," she answered.

"I guess we need a level playing field here," he said. He pulled her pants down and lifted her to sit onto the ledge, pressing her against his leather bound series on Italian history.

Pierpaolo smells a rat

After Jonathan packed up his papers and laptop on Monday morning, he put on a freshly pressed shirt (his mother taught him how to iron: "Make sure you don't let the shirt dry," she had told him). He smiled at the memory. His missed his mother, but she was going to need some straightening out about his life. But that was for later. He went into the bathroom and wiped the steam off the mirror. He fixed his collar. Then he went out of his apartment the official way, through the courtyard, saying hello to Signora Pia (who was pretending not to notice him) on his way.

Pierpaolo was expected at nine o'clock, precisely fifteen minutes after their scheduled appointment, so Lucy did what she always did in that fifteen-minute period. She went into his office, cracked the window, drew the shades halfway, and ordered the coffee. Jonathan tried to look busy as he hovered.

Pierpaolo breezed in.

"*Jonatan*," he called, "let's go, in my office."

Lucy arrived almost instantly with the tray, and then backed out of the room.

"No calls, Lucy, thank you."

"So," he said, turning to Jonathan, "I read your report last night. Very good. Why don't we run through it? I can ask you questions as we go. I have them marked on my copy."

Jonathan began with the organic structure of the studio staff, and how to migrate to a more resilient model.

While he spoke, Pierpaolo was tapping the edge of his desk with his Pilot Precise V5 pen incessantly. Jonathan was distracted by it.

"Excuse me, Pierpaolo, is something wrong?"

"Close the door, please."

Pierpaolo raised his eyes to him once Jonathan had resettled in his chair.

"It's not about this. Can I trust your discretion?"

"Of course."

"I just have to get this out of my system." He took a gulp of his espresso.

"Hanne was with her friend from Copenhagen this weekend, or so I thought. She said her friend's flight was at eight in the evening. So, I didn't expect we would have dinner together. Well, I called her at nine o'clock, after I finished reading this. Then ten, then eleven. I drove to her apartment, no lights, and no answer on the intercom. Okay, I thought, she went out with other friends. There is a little bar across the street. I thought I would wait. After a while, a taxi pulls up, and she gets out. But there is a guy in the cab! So by now I am furious, as you can imagine." He paused, and then helped himself to Jonathan's espresso.

"Ugh! You put milk in it!"

Jonathan tried not to smile.

"I can imagine that must have upset you," he said.

"I couldn't see who the guy was."

What Pierpaolo didn't know is that Giorgio, in the cab, had taken Hanne's hand in his, looked her straight in the eye and said, "No-one must ever know what happened tonight." Hanne nodded, disappointed. The cab driver glanced into the rearview mirror.

Pierpaolo continued, "After I figured she must have reached her apartment, I texted her."

WANTED TO SAY GOODNIGHT

And she answered, after a couple of minutes,

: (I MISSED YOU. FELL ASLEEP EARLY

"Then, nothing!"

Jonathan shook his head, not knowing what to say.

"I'm sorry."

"That bitch was with someone else. It's unbelievable. I am not going to get thrown over by a twenty-something aromatheraphy guru!"

"Isn't she a wellness consultant? Maybe she was just out with a friend."

"Oh, no. She is like this little beautiful butterfly, who flits from one flower to the next, looking for the best opportunity. And she doesn't even own a place to drop dead."

"What are you going to do?"

"Nothing. Wait until she shows her slutty face and hear what she has to say. You know the Italian expression, *Chiodo schiaccia chiodo*?"

"No, how would I?"

"It means one nail drives another in. That is what I intend to do. I am going to consider myself single again."

"That sounds reasonable, under the circumstances."

There was a moment of silence.

"I know you will be discreet about this, *Jonatan*," Pierpaolo said. "I feel better, having got that off my chest. Let's get you another coffee." He got up and opened his door, too impatient to use the phone.

"LUCY! Two more, and some almond croissants; no, get *Jonatan* a *cappuccio*."

He sat back down and rubbed his hands together, indicating he was ready to dig in.

Jonathan went over his plan, which was simple and organized. He combed through roles and responsibilities, equipment deficiencies, the impact of uncontrolled expenses on profit margins, opportunities for new revenue. For

Jonathan, the elephant in the room was Pierpaolo's detrimental impact on the success of the studio. He clearly considered it a cash cow for his own use.

Pierpaolo leaned back and put his hands behind his head.

"According to this...*plan* of yours, well, it seems I am not necessary in the operations of the studio."

Jonathan smiled. "That's not an accurate interpretation, Pierpaolo. If you want this studio to grow, then your role has to change. That means you solidify your business development role, which you have always done and know how to do well. And you spend more time with the accountant, P.R. people, and others who support the business of the studio."

"I don't need a P.R. firm."

"Then spend more time going to events. People need to see that you're plugged in."

"And I have a good accountant."

"Lucy found some mistakes. She's quite good with numbers, you know."

"Really?"

"Yes, and I think she should have more responsibility. If we get the stylist service going, I think we can afford to have someone come in part time to cover reception, so Lucy can go over the accounts. Then she can interface with the accountant's office."

"Okay, *Jonatan*, I get it, you have done a good job. I agree that I need more time to be out on the scene, developing the image of our studio. But it's not necessary that the outside world knows that I am not *always* behind the camera, right?"

"Absolutely not."

"So who is going to decide where I should go and what I should do?"

"I thought we could have a weekly meeting, let's say on Wednesdays, with Leitizia and Lucy. They are very tuned in. Once you get going, the invitations will just come and Lucy can schedule you."

"I suppose a lot of this stuff will be in the evening."

"True. But that means you can sleep in. Come to the studio later, check in, go to lunch with someone."

Pierpaolo nodded, considering.

"There's one more thing," Jonathan said. "Regarding me. Do I have a job?"

"Well, it's your fucking plan, of course you have a job. Since you know what we can afford, why don't you write a proposal and give it to me in a couple of days. You can include the use of the apartment, for an initial period, if you wish. At least until we need the space for something else."

They shook hands and Jonathan left.

He passed by Lucy and said, "I'm going for a quick walk."

Jonathan needed to get some air. He had done it! It was amazing how just a minimal amount of analysis and common sense could leverage a business. His recommendations were mostly things that were no-brainers in New York. Here, there was a more organic, fluid, and obscure approach. Information in general was not usually on the surface. Tracks were covered, confusion considered an advantage. The trick was implementing a transparent, efficient system in this jungle of Baroque procedures. Well, this was a step. And he had a job! He didn't have the patience to text, so he called Elena. She was on the train back, with Enrico.

"Elena, congratulations on your new position. Yes, he did...and tell Enrico that Pierpaolo is going to be stepping back from the shoots... Well, it may be a gradual process, but there is hope! See you later."

He went around the block one more time before returning to work.

Pierpaolo gets greedy

There was a somber air at Giorgio Monti's studio, although none of the assistants knew why: Giorgio was racked with misgivings and guilt about his retaliatory sex with Hanne on the weekend. Who knew that it would provide so little satisfaction? Well, apart from the moment itself. If he had to keep it secret, how would it punish Lella for her ingratitude toward him? If he told her, it would ruin everything. And then there was the issue of Hanne's trustworthiness. She might want to brag about it, and word would get around... Maybe he needed to keep an eye on her, take her out a couple of times to normalize things.

Fuck!

Whatever was bothering Giorgio made everyone keep his or her head down, stick to the work at hand, and avoid interacting with him.

The atmosphere at Pierpaolo's studio, on the other hand, was upbeat. Pierpaolo was upset in his own way, but a temporary (as he saw it) setback in his romantic affairs was not enough to affect his engagement with work. Once he had got it off his chest with Jonathan, he started putting the nails in the imaginary coffin, with Hanne inside, still breathing, and fantasizing about his expanded role as social ambassador for the studio.

Enrico humored Pierpaolo completely, setting things up, asking for his advice on the finer details, and standing aside while Pierpaolo made tiny adjustments for the sake of being needed. After a few repetitions, Pierpaolo's desire to control was surpassed by his desire to be admired by the world. He spent more time talking on the phone and looking at his social calendar with Lucy.

Elena was his only distraction. Why had she set him up to rush into things with Hanne? If only she had been more amenable, this whole thing could have been avoided. He watched her move through the studio with a

258

natural grace, his admiration mixed with anger. She talked and laughed with Jonathan and Enrico, who treated her with respect, like a colleague. Pierpaolo was puzzled by their complicity. But they were working to make his studio great! And they were a good team. Still, things would be better if Elena's first loyalty was to him.

Pierpaolo called Lucy on his phone. "Could you please tell Elena to come to my office?"

Lucy was farther from Elena than Pierpaolo, and he usually stood up and shouted his orders; this confused Lucy. She got up from her post anyway, and went to Elena.

"Pierpao' wants to see you in his office." She shrugged.

Elena set her clipboard down on the trolley and went to Pierpaolo.

He was silent as she sat down across from him.

"So," he started, "how is this new situation working out for you?"

Elena laughed. "Well, we haven't done much yet, but I am meeting with Leitizia this afternoon to get a few things started."

"I would like to get briefed on that meeting afterward."

"We aren't meeting until four o'clock, and we'll probably need a couple of hours."

Pierpaolo scrunched his brow and flipped through his calendar.

"What's today, Wednesday? Hmmm, I am booked solid after today. Why don't you come to my place at six thirty?"

Elena held her breath.

"I am only asking you to come there because I will be out beforehand, and prefer not to come back to the studio. It's closer to your place, anyway, isn't it?"

"Yes. Okay, I can do that."

Elena went back to work with Jonathan and Enrico, who were preparing a shoot that would start in the late afternoon. They would be there until dinnertime, maybe later.

"I was going to stick around for the shoot, but I have to meet with Pierpaolo."

"He's not going to be here in the studio is he?" Enrico asked.

"No," Elena answered. "We're meeting elsewhere." She was too embarrassed to tell them the Pierpaolo asked her to come to his place. She could handle this. Anyway, he was going out with Hanne, so everything would be fine.

Jonathan had promised not to say anything about Pierpaolo's situation with Hanne, and had his own concerns, anyway, about not appearing too custodial toward Elena.

Elena's meeting with Leitizia went well, and they were both excited about working together with more autonomy. Elena gathered her notes and bag, and headed toward the *Metropolitana*.

When she got to Pierpaolo's apartment, she found everything neat and tidy, as usual. There was a bottle of white wine and two glasses on the table. Pierpaolo acted very cool, almost standoffish, as he listened to Elena going through the outline she had prepared. She and Leitizia already had two outside styling jobs for the following week, and they were able to purchase some useful props and still come out ahead.

"We will be able to cover Leitizia's salary here in about three months, and then we will work on making a small profit. I would say a couple thousand Euros a month in six months or so."

"Some of which *Jonatan* will want to use for the part-timer to help Lucy. It seems like *Jonatan* has everything all worked out."

"It's not that complicated, Pierpaolo. It's just that we have all been so busy, we haven't taken the time to review things."

"Right," Pierpaolo said, pouring the wine. "Here you go."

He waited a moment before turning to her again.

"Do you mind me asking if there is something going on between you and *Jonatan*?"

Elena laughed dismissively.

"No, there is not. But with respect, Pierpaolo, I don't know that it is your business to ask me about my personal life—anymore."

He raised his eyebrows.

"I guess we must find a new balance now that you are in a managerial position." He got up and walked behind her as if to put the bottle in the refrigerator. Then he set it down on the table and put his hands on her shoulders.

"I am quite proud of you, you know."

Elena froze, hoping this was just a friendly gesture.

"I know you like nobody else does."

He gathered her hair in his hands and kissed her neck.

Elena tried to pull away.

"You're hurting me, Pierpaolo."

"I certainly don't want to do that."

He let her hair drop and slid his right hand well under her blouse, squeezing her breast.

"Pierpaolo!" Elena shouted, standing up, knocking over the stool and her wine glass, which broke on the smooth, dark granite.

Pierpaolo backed off, his hands in the air as if under arrest.

"Okay, relax!" he said, laughing. "It was just for old times' sake. I thought you would be on board."

Elena started packing up her notes, her hands shaking, as Pierpaolo wiped the bar with a cloth, collecting the broken glass.

Elena's lips started to tremble. She saw the dream of building her career crumble, and she hated Pierpaolo for it. *So, this is what I am.*

"Listen," he said. "It's no big deal. Let's pretend it didn't happen."

Elena just wanted to get out of there. She couldn't think. But she had to be careful. He was her boss, and a lot was at stake.

She simply said, "I have to go."

He held the door for her, "See you tomorrow."

Out on the street, Elena couldn't assess her surroundings. Her adrenalin was surging, and she walked aimlessly, bumping into someone on the sidewalk who grabbed her arm, asking if she was okay.

Elena tore her arm free, her face fearful.

"*Una roba da matti,*" she heard the man say, as she kept walking.

She put one foot into the street and was greeted by the horn of a taxi. It was free, so she got in, and gave the address of the studio. Maybe Enrico and Jonathan were still there; maybe she should grab her things and clear out of there. She was trying not to cry in front of the driver.

"Did your boyfriend break up with you, *Signorina*?" he asked.

"Please... no," she said, shaking her head.

"Alright, have it your way." He drove on in silence.

The shoot had ended, and Enrico had left, just rounding the corner out of sight as Elena pulled up.

She went in with her sunglasses on, even though daylight was fading. She walked quickly past Signora Pia, who was at her small kitchen table eating her dinner, facing the window.

Elena entered the studio. It was as quiet as a church. Then she heard footsteps in the atrium. Jonathan was coming toward the entrance to see who was there.

"Oh, I though Enrico forgot something," he said, then seeing her expression, set down the extension cord he had in his hand.

"What's wrong, Ellie?"

She came to him and he put his arms around her. She was now sobbing freely.

"Whoa, let's sit down here on the couch. Let me get you some water."

She explained what had happen, how her new career was ruined, how poor Leitizia was now going to be high and dry because she was going to have to leave, and how much she despised Pierpaolo, especially because he said *it was no big deal.*

Jonathan was furious, but kept it to himself. He waited till Elena had calmed down a bit.

"Let's get out of here, out the back way, into my place."

He walked her back with his arm around her, and got her settled by propping some pillows on his mattress, so it was less ambiguous, less like a bed.

"Now," he said, with his hands in prayer position against his chin, "I am going to make you some *penne all'arrabiata,* because we are pissed as hell."

Elena emitted a short laugh.

"Thank you, Jonathan. Is it okay if I go wash my face?"

She went into the bathroom, which although rough in construction, had a shelf with fresh white towels on it. *That is so like Jonathan,* she thought. She took off her shirt, and her bra, brushed her hair and tied it back. Then she soaped up a washcloth and rubbed her face, her neck and her left breast where his hand had been. She rubbed her skin until it was pink, then rinsed the cloth with cool water and wiped the soap away. Then she dried herself, and called out to Jonathan.

"Do you have a sweatshirt I can borrow?"

Jonathan rummaged around and then passed her one.

"I've only worn it once," he said.

Elena pulled it over her head. It smelled pleasantly of Jonathan.

Then she rolled up her clothing and stuffed it into her bag.

"That's better," she said.

She went back to the improvised sofa, and sat with her legs crossed.

Jonathan put on some music, put the pasta in the boiling water, and set two places at the counter. He went through his usual ritual, moving his potted plants closer together to make a screen from the courtyard.

"You should get some curtains."

"I hate curtains. Furthermore, I am not nesting here."

"You have bought some nice towels."

"Yeah, well, I have my weaknesses."

Jonathan served the pasta, and they sat down to eat.

"I made it extra hot."

"Wow, I guess so!"

After a few forkfuls, Elena turned to Jonathan.

"So, what do you think I should do?"

Jonathan exhaled heavily.

"To answer that, I have to ask *you* something."

"Go ahead."

"How determined are you about your work?"

"Very."

"How patient are you?"

"Nobody's really patient, are they?"

They laughed.

"Okay, then, how strong are you?"

"I can be strong. My anger will help me to be strong."

"Good. So this is what I think you should do: go to work tomorrow. Don't avoid Pierpaolo. In fact, ask to speak with him. Once you are in his office, he is bound to apologize. Give him the space to do it. Then, thank him for his apology, and reassure him that you would like things to remain professional between the two of you, and shake his hand."

"Am I just supposed to swallow this?"

Jonathan shook his head.

"How do you think he will react to that?

"I think he will be so fucking grateful that you will disarm him completely."

"Then what happens?"

"*Ghe pensi mi,*" Jonathan said, using a Milanese expression for, *let me worry about that.*

"Where did you learn that?" Elena laughed.

"Signora Pia, of course."

Jonathan poured a glass of wine for both of them and raised his glass. He had a fleeting vision of breaking it into Pierpaolo's face.

"To forging ahead, and screw those who would impede us!"

Elena called an Uber after they had cleaned up together, promising to call Jonathan if she got upset during the night. On her way, she phoned her father.

"Papá," she said. "I'd like to come home this weekend. Will you be around?"

Once Jonathan was alone, he also got on the phone, to Enrico.

"Hey, *Jonatan.*"

265

"Enrico, listen. Now that our plan is in place, how about we start thinking about the next steps?"

"Already?"

"Yes, I think circumstances warrant it."

"Okay. It's a bit late to get together tonight. How about tomorrow?"

Thursday evening was fine for Jonathan. Then he called New York.

"Hello, Jenna! This is Jonathan... Of course I'm calling you from Milan!"

Elena goes home

Jonathan was right about Pierpaolo apologizing. He came in early on Thursday hoping to talk to Elena before the studio was full of activity. He was somewhat afraid that she wouldn't be there, so he was pleased when he saw her canvas jacket hanging up in the entry way (unaware that it had been there for several days).

He walked by her office, then turned around and thought it better to meet her on her own ground. It would seem more contrite. More importantly, he would have his back to the studio, so no one could see his face.

Elena was unable to make it through the short conversation without shedding a tear, a single one that collected at the corner of her left eye. She tried to call it back with her will, but it balled up and rolled down her cheek anyway. She quickly wiped it away with the back of her hand. It was because she hadn't slept much.

After they had shaken hands (the strangest and worst part for Pierpaolo), Elena told him that she was going home on the weekend, and would like to leave after lunch on Friday.

"We've all been under a lot of stress. Maybe I'll close the studio tomorrow afternoon, and transfer the calls to my phone."

This seemed out of character for Pierpaolo, to Elena, and she considered it an act of penance. (It was also true that nobody called on Friday afternoons.)

Pierpaolo checked in with everyone else briefly, and then made himself scarce. He had a hard time dealing with female emotions. That was one thing he liked about Hanne. She was in it for the fun, and simply demanded material compensation, whether dinner, or gifts. Elena was a train wreck when it came to emotions. It was like she had her period every fucking day. So unpredictable!

Everyone was in a good mood because of the Friday afternoon holiday, and the studio work went quickly and well. Elena mentioned her plans to go home on the weekend, and asked Jonathan and Enrico if they would like to come.

"That's great that you're going to see your father," Jonathan said, "but there's something I have to do this weekend here in Milan."

Elena didn't press him for details, and looked at Enrico.

Enrico started to answer, looking down.

"I'd be happy to come with you," he said, raising his eyes at the end of his sentence. "If it isn't any trouble."

"My father loves company. And if I have a guest, he won't feel badly about immersing himself in his newspapers, or working for a couple of hours on Saturday."

They decided that Enrico would pick Elena up in his car tomorrow, and they'd drive to work together with their bags. Jonathan could take them to the station in time for the three-thirty train, and keep Enrico's car for the weekend.

Jonathan was hoping to finally see Mel without other people around, and wasn't sure how to arrange it. Now that he had a car, he could propose a trip outside of the city. He texted her to ask if she was free to talk.

"Hey Jonathan, how are you?"

"Doing well, you? I was just calling to see what you were up this weekend. Do you have any plans?"

"Well, I am supposed to go to a project site on Lake Como to see how the work is progressing. But Giorgio has been weird all week and I don't know how to get there without him driving me."

"Well, I just happen to have a car for the weekend. I was calling to see if you wanted to visit anywhere outside of the city. Would it be awkard if I took you there? I mean, is your client going to be around? I could take some photos for you."

Mel was happy to take him up on his offer.

"Maybe we could have dinner afterward?"

"Sure." Mel was relieved to be able to make the trip without having to deal with Giorgio's mood. Seeing Jonathan made her feel remorse about New York, but she was going to have to accept that as a fact of life.

* * *

Elena and Enrico were comfortable together on the train, veterans of the Naples trip. Elena's family's farm was between Modena and Bologna, so they would get off in Modena where Elena's father, Giancarlo, would pick them up.

They were leaning on a couple of bollards, their bags on the ground, when Giancarlo pulled up in his red Alfa Romeo Giulia. He hopped out of the car and walked briskly to Elena, giving her a powerful hug.

"*Tesoro*, I am so happy to see you! And who is your friend?"

"Papá, this is my colleague, Enrico."

They shook hands.

"Colleague? That sounds so serious," Giancarlo said.

"Well, he is also a friend, of course."

"I apologize for not picking you up in the Ferrari, but alas, we wouldn't fit comfortably."

"Do you really have a Ferrari?" Enrico asked.

Elena and Giancarlo laughed.

"Yes, but it's an old one," he winked at Elena. "I only keep it because Ferraro, (he's our farm mechanic) loves to tinker with it. In the summer, we rent it for weddings, and that is how we support our expensive habit."

Elena said, "His name is not Ferraro, it's Piero, but my father has rechristened him."

"Shall we get an *aperitivo* here before we go?" Giancarlo asked.

"Papá, it's only four-thirty!"

"But it's Friday."

They got into the car and parked it somewhat closer to where they were headed. Then they walked into the Centro. Modena was all of a piece, Enrico thought. Red tiled roofs, brick, and warm colored stucco. The Centro was was tightly knit, with few structures, like bell towers, peeking over the others.

"Enrico has never been here," Elena said.

"You're from Naples, I take it?" Giancarlo said.

"Yes, I confess," Enrico answered. "And the atmosphere here is quite different from that of my city."

They strolled under a covered walkway, its arches and columns edging the granite cobbles of the street, closed to vehicles. They entered a bar and had a glass of spumante. Elena told her father about their trip to Procida, and the kindness and hospitality of Enrico's family.

On their twenty-minute drive to the farm, Enrico admired the broad expanse of farmland they drove through (quite speedily, he thought).

Giancarlo turned off the main road, and drove a little further along a gravel lane. They came to a gateway between a pair of brick pillars. Elena got out and opened the gate. Inside, the compound was composed of several blocky structures: a partially open structure that contained farm equipment on the left, near the road; a small residential structure a little further down, on the right; and the main house, further down the drive.

They passed through a small orchard in bloom. The more cultivated gardens near the house were full of perennial plants on the verge of flowering.

There was a small courtyard with a geometric design that was planted with spinach, arugola, and herbs.

The central hall of the house was dark and cool with a polished floor. The rooms were arranged around it like a doughnut. The kitchen was on the left and also opened onto the herb garden. Two women were working there, cutting rolled pasta dough on a large table with a well-worn white marble surface.

"*Nonna!*" cried Elena and ran to her grandmother, who was wiping her hands on her apron.

"*Elenuccia*! And look, you have brought such a nice young man with you!"

Enrico offered his hand to Elena's Nonna, but she gave him a hug instead. "Let's not stand on ceremony," she said. "We'll all be food for the crops soon!" She laughed, and presented Anna, who lived in the little house and helped her with the big house. Anna's husband, Luca, ran the farm, which, she explained, was part of the Cooperativa.

"*Nonna*, we'll let you get back to work. What's for dinner?"

"We are making *tortellini* with ricotta, dressed with bacon and leeks."

"Yum!"

Elena's nonna then took on a tone of complaint. "Your father says he wants to take you out to dinner tomorrow. But shouldn't we have my *tagliatelle* with ragù, if your friend hasn't been here before? Fresh, *fatti in casa?*"

"We will talk to him about that, *Nonna*! Now, please let me get Enrico settled."

"Go, go." She shooed them out of the kitchen with her hands.

Elena led Enrico to the far side of the hall, which opened to a room they called the Giardinetto, or little garden. It stretched the entire width of the house, and was populated with dark green vintage wicker furniture upholstered with floral fabric. There was a table for cards; a sofa and armchairs around a low table, and a pair of chaises that looked outward through the small-paned windows that wrapped all around the room above the wainscoting. Potted plants filled every leftover space.

"*Che bella*," said Enrico, "I could die here!"

"Well, this is where we generally live," said Giancarlo, rustling his papers from one of the chaises.

Outside, fields stretched in every direction, interrupted only by other farm compounds and the hedgerows that partially obscured them.

"You know, this landscape is kind of like the sea. It is so open and there is so much sky." Enrico was pleasantly surprised. He had seen farms along the train routes, but never this broad expanse, so flat and manicured.

"It's really true that Italy is the most beautiful country in the world," he said, like a prayer.

Giancarlo looked up at Enrico above his reading glasses.

"Do you play ping-pong, Enrico? Elena, why don't you get him settled in his room and then I'll have a game with him before dinner."

And so the evening progressed in this friendly, lively manner. Giancarlo beat Enrico, and Elena beat Giancarlo. They had a lovely dinner and a small dish of rhubarb gelato with coconut cream, served in the Giardinetto.

On Saturday Elena and Enrico went for a bike ride while Giancarlo took care of some business. Then Elena visited with her nonna while Giancarlo took Enrico out in his vintage Ferrari. The roads were straight and empty, and Giancarlo knew where he could get away with opening it up a little.

Nonna did get her way. They stayed home and had the tagliatelle with ragù, and a simple scoop of gelato with espresso poured over it for dessert. Giancarlo brought a tray with beautiful crystal bottles of grappa infused with various plants. Enrico tried one or two, but Elena decided it was better not to risk the Deadly Grappa Headache and had some herbal tea instead.

In the morning, Elena was up before Enrico, and she and her father had a caffè latte together.

"So, are things over with your boss?" Giancarlo asked.

"Yes, Papá," Elena said, looking down. "I'd rather not discuss it."

"I like Enrico," said Giancarlo.

"He's just a friend."

"From my point of view, he seems to regard you differently." He opened his newspaper. "But I could be wrong. Anyway, are you feeling better?"

"Yes, I am." She smiled at him. "You always know when I am a little down."

"That's because you came home for Nonna's *tortellini*."

Elena thought about what he said, and she said, about Enrico.

Lake Como with Jonathan

How strange it was for Mel to be getting into the little Fiat with Jonathan at the wheel, going to a job site on Lake Como! Giorgio was relieved that Mel had found another way to get there, reviewing all the things she needed to discuss with the contractor as well as check with "her own two eyes." He repeated this several times, as if he was distracted.

Jonathan was enchanted with the site. The contractor was there, waiting, so he walked around by himself while Mel attended to her work. After the little flatbed *Ape* left, buzzing like bee, Mel gave Jonathan a tour.

The connecting corridor between the house and the "root cellar" consisted of a stone retaining wall embedded in the slope, and a freestanding wall running parallel, eight feet away. Into these walls, about waist high, a greenhouse structure was set: stone on the bottom, glass and iron on the top.

"The 'root cellar' is really going to be a kitchen," Mel explained as she led the way.

Jonathan admired the cave-like space, whose openings seemed as if they occurred naturally: the slice of light on the hill side, the skylight above, and two small, deep windows glowing on the west wall.

"I like the idea that in this space, your view to the lake is restricted," he said. "It makes it that much more special."

Jonathan took progress photos for Mel, and then some for himself. They went out into the garden. The plants had leafed out fully, making it even lusher than at Mel's last visit. Jonathan climbed the Fig tree and took a few more photos from his perch.

"It's a shame the grass is too wet for a picnic," he said.

"And that we don't have any food," Mel added.

"I brought some."

Mel smiled to herself, and looked at the barn structure.

"There is an open-air space in the barn loft. It is going to be a little terrace with a view up the lake. It's just bare concrete now."

"That'll work." Jonathan went to the car and pulled a backpack out of the trunk. Then he rolled a large piece of canvas and carried it under his arm. In the barn, there were some knocked-down corrugated cardboard boxes against one wall. Jonathan passed them up to Mel, who had already climbed the ladder to survey the space. They spread the canvas over the flattened cardboard, which made a comfortable sitting surface. They faced an openwork brick wall, used in barns for ventilation, which was partially ruined. Its ragged, stepped edge framed a beautiful view.

"This is going to be the master suite up here," Mel said. "The barn will be like a separate apartment for Susanna. Her guests will stay in the main house, and everyone can meet in the middle, in the kitchen."

Jonathan was focused on the food.

"Okay, here's what we've got: some crackers full of seeds; some cheese; peanut butter (which I got at the International Store); and a few apples. Oh, and...a bottle of wine. Except for that, I guess it's kind of American."

"Well, there's no fried chicken. Really, it's perfect, Jonathan."

"It'll do the job."

"It was really nice of you to bring me here."

"I guess I'm hoping that nice guys don't finish last," he said.

Mel focused on spreading some peanut butter on a cracker, at a loss for words. Jonathan changed the subject.

"You said Giorgio was in a bad mood this week? Well, so was Pierpaolo. It just happens that I know why."

"You know why Giorgio was?" Mel said.

"I believe so."

"Well, are you going to tell me?" Mel asked, laughing.

275

Jonathan took a bite of an apple, chewed and swallowed, leaving Mel in suspense.

"It is a truly Italian tale," he started.

"Last weekend, Pierpaolo's girlfriend (if you want to call her that), Hanne, was tied up with a friend visiting from Denmark. So Pierpaolo was on ice all weekend. As you know, I've been working on this plan to reorganize the studio for him, and sent him a draft on Sunday to read before our Monday meeting."

"Then I decided to go to *Bar Brera*, where I had stopped on my very first day in Milan. I was going to get a drink and something to eat because I had been holed up most of the weekend."

"The next day when I met with Pierpaolo, he was foaming at the mouth about Hanne. He had tried to put in a booty call Sunday night, but she wasn't answering her phone. He decided to go to her house, thinking her phone was dead. No answer there. So he waits in the bar across the street until he sees her pull up in a cab, with a guy in it."

"Did they both get out of the cab?"

"No. The guy apparently dropped her off, but it was around midnight."

Jonathan stopped to pour another glass of wine for both.

"Well, that explains Pierpaolo, but how does Giorgio fit in?"

"That's the thing. When I was at *Bar Brera*, I saw Hanne and another woman walking up Via Brera. She didn't see me, so I didn't try to get her attention. After a while, I started walking down *Via Fiori Oscuri* (I love the name of that street!) and then realized I wanted to go in the other direction to get the Metro. So I turned around, and there is Giorgio turning into *Via Fiori Chiari*, with Hanne. I was twenty paces behind them the whole way. Then they stopped, I guess at Giorgio's apartment?"

"Yeah, he lives on that street," Mel said, nodding.

"She was clearly drunk. He had to help her over the threshold. Then, he looked around as if he was checking to see if anyone saw them."

"He didn't notice you?"

"Well, I had this knee-jerk reaction of turning away, so I was looking into a shop window when he looked my way."

"Wow. I don't get it. I thought he was head-over-heels for Lella. Something must have happened..." Then Mel realized where she was going and stopped herself. It was too similar to her situation. Was she like Giorgio? Looking at it from the outside, it seemed so foolish, reckless even. Gratuitous infidelity, to communicate nothing to nobody, only hurting, eventually.

"Jonathan, I..."

"Don't say it Mel."

"I was such a jerk to you! I honestly don't know how I could have done that!"

Jonathan took a sip of wine. "You know, at the time of my bar mitzvah, Rabbi Rabowitz told me something I'll never forget."

He said, "Jonathan, your humanity is going to cause you to hurt other people, and to be hurt by them. And, it is that same humanity that will enable you to forgive yourself, as well as others."

"Humanity." Mel repeated. "Is that his real name? I mean, the rabbi?"

"No," Jonathan said, laughing.

"Is that a true story?"

"No, I made it up just now."

Jonathan took Mel's hand. "You are going to have to forgive yourself at some point. I have forgiven you. In fact, I take responsibility for the whole thing. My mother was against you, and I didn't stand up to her. I couldn't hurt her after all she's done for me."

Mel shook her head, "And nothing has changed there."

"Actually, that is not true. I have changed. I have been talking to her, every week. She has admitted to liking you after all." He laughed.

"But," he continued, "she has dug her heels in on the religion thing."

"I care about you very much, Jonathan, but I've already told you that I wouldn't convert. I have no faith. I look around the world, and through history. I see so much death and destruction in the name of religion, and in the absence of any real morality. Being 'signed up' as a Catholic, or a Jew, wouldn't change the way I live one bit. If there *was* a judgment, I believe it would be of our deeds, not how hard we beat our breasts or how much money we put in the till."

Jonathan smiled.

"I agree with you," he said.

"We should get back," said Mel. Her legs were a little shaky as she stood up. She shook out the canvas and folded it to hide her unease.

They climbed down the ladder and saw there were two women in the kitchen. They looked just as startled.

"Melinda!" said Amelia. She turned to the other woman. "Susanna, this is Melinda, she works for Giorgio."

"Susanna, it's nice to meet you. I'm sorry for this intrusion. I came to look at the work. My friend, Jonathan, was kind enough to drive me here, and we were having something to eat in the loft. It was too wet on the grass for our picnic."

"Oh, don't worry," Susanna laughed. "It looks like everything is coming along nicely. At first I thought you were a couple of lovers taking refuge."

Mel was embarrassed, but tried to overcome it, and asked Susanna if she could show her a few things. The two of them walked around together.

Amelia turned to Jonathan.

"So, you are the famous Jonathan?"

278

"I didn't know I was famous."

"Well, let's just say your name has circulated in my family with regard to Melinda, and now I finally meet you."

Jonathan said nothing.

"You know, this house has a lot of memories, some good, some bad."

Something about Jonathan made her feel like opening up, something she didn't do much, except with Lella. He was foreign, outside of the gossipy Milanese circles. And being here with Susanna uncovered a box of buried emotions.

"My cousin Alberto and I—you've met Alberto?"

Jonathan nodded.

"Well, we had an unfortunate conflict here years ago, and it has left a wound that has never completely healed."

"I'm sorry for you."

Amelia looked off, remembering.

"Yes, we were both in love with the same person."

Secrets revealed

The sun was strong and bright on Sunday morning, and Mel could feel the heat through the windows. Gabi was up. Mel could hear the *caffettiera* gurgling in the kitchen. She pulled on her sweatpants and wandered out to say good morning.

"I got some croissants across the street," Gabriella said.

They say down together and had breakfast.

"I ran into Amelia when I was on the lake yesterday," Mel started. "She was with the owner, Susanna."

"Really!" Gabriella answered. Then she smiled a little smile.

"May I ask you something?"

"Sure," said Gabriella.

"Do you know anything about the rift between Amelia and Alberto? I mean, Alberto and I have been friendly, and she seems to bare her teeth at the very thought of a woman falling into his hands. Then yesterday she mentioned, to Jonathan, that she and Alberto were in love with the same person once."

"Is there something going on between you and Alberto?"

"No. I mean, he has been very helpful to me, and introduced me to Giorgio. Perhaps there was a moment of flirtation, but it has passed. He is very appealing, no doubt about it!"

"What about Jonathan?"

"Jonathan is a question mark, and the reason I lose sleep at night. I am not sure whether he is an obstacle to my adventure or complicit in it."

Gabriella looked at the ceiling, twirling her hair.

"I had a big crush on Alberto for the longest time."

Mel was surprised.

"I used to hang out with Amelia a lot in college, when she lived with Lella, and sometimes he would be there."

Gabriella took a sip of her caffè latte.

"Then," she continued, "we went to Susanna's house one weekend. I was with Uncle Giorgio, and Amelia came with Alberto. Susanna was like a queen, presiding over her tiny house like it was a palace. Amelia was in awe of Susanna. She had such beauty, strength, and grace."

"That night, Susanna, Giorgio, and Alberto slept upstairs, where the bedrooms were, and Amelia and I slept in the living room. Something changed that weekend. After we returned to Milano, Amelia wouldn't speak of Alberto, and whenever he came to Lella's after that, we had to stay in her room. Of course, my attempts to cross paths with him were stifled, and I couldn't mention him anymore. We didn't hang around much after that, because she had grown a little cold toward me, by association."

"I had known for a while that Amelia was gay, however discreet she was about it. Her father, Paolo, was still alive, and he was such a classic Italian male that she was afraid to tell him. But that weekend never made sense to me until you told me that you saw her with Susanna, and what she said. Amelia and I have lost touch, so I don't know what, if anything, is going on."

"I saw her next at her father's funeral, and after that we became friends again. Although it was not like it was before. She had become harder somehow."

Mel and Gabriella sat in silence as they finished their croissants, then cleaned up.

"What are you doing today, Melinda?"

"I am overdue for at visit to Lella. She's expecting me at four o'clock. How about you?"

"I'm getting ready for another meeting in Paris, on Tuesday. I will fly out tomorrow and back probably on Wednesday morning."

* * *

Later that day, Mel and Lella were having tea in Lella's living room. It felt strange being there, to Mel. She felt at home, and yet a visitor.

Mel got right to the point.

"So, may I ask you what's going on with Giorgio, Lella?"

Lella raised her eyes and shook her head.

"I believe his is undergoing some injury to his ego, that I inadvertently inflicted upon him. He was here last weekend, on Saturday, if you remember. Well, he spent the night. It was very nice." Lella wasn't one to talk about her sex life in anything other than general terms.

"The morning," she continued, "began with a lovely breakfast. And then he started making demands on me. After two nights together, he wants us to *live* together! It's crazy. He has so much urgency about him."

"That he does," Mel agreed.

"I tried to talk to him, but he was so adamant, it was useless. He left angry, and I haven't heard from him all week. I've considered reaching out to him, but then I thought it was better to give him some time to understand his feelings: does he want to be with *me*, or does he want to have a woman at his disposal, with all the benefits in bed, in the kitchen, and at social events?"

"How are you doing?"

"By now," Lella said, "I am made of steel."

"You know," Mel added, "Giorgio's behavior reminds me painfully of my own."

"Melinda, what you did in New York was wrong, but it is not exactly the same. Jonathan wronged you, by his weakness. You should have moved out. We agree on that. But how did I wrong Giorgio? I was happy to have a relationship, a consensual one."

Mel was wondering whether she should tell Lella what she knew about Giorgio and Hanne. She decided to ask her something first.

"May I ask how you feel about Giorgio, and what you want?"

"Melinda, you will discover one day that your feelings become more a result of your judgment of a person's qualities than of hormones. Yes, I was attracted to Giorgio and care for him, but his behavior last week has given me pause. I don't want to be with a man who is looking for a caregiver."

"Well, let me ask you something else. If I knew something about Giorgio's trustworthiness, would you want me to share it with you?"

"You've baited me, now you must tell me whatever you know."

Lella listened quietly, while Mel told her Pierpaolo's story, relayed by Jonathan, and Jonathan's own account of what he witnessed on the street in Brera.

"This is the man who says that he has loved me his whole life and offered to marry me!"

Lella didn't cry, but she was obviously seething with anger. She excused herself and went to the bathroom. Mel put the cups on the tray and carried them into the kitchen.

Lella came out composed.

Mel said, "I am so sorry that my story has made you upset."

"It's funny, because I was happy to spend time with him, to see where it might lead. But now that's impossible."

Then she hugged Mel.

"I have mourned him for ten minutes too many. Shall we go out to dinner? My treat."

At the restaurant, they both ordered risotto with strawberries. Spring was well advanced, and the beautiful red fruit was proof. Lella ordered spumante.

"Lella," Mel said, "I'm concerned about working for Giorgio now, given the situation."

Lella waved her hand dismissively.

"If people in this country stopped doing business with one another because of their sexual dalliances, there would be no economy."

She poured the spumante into their glasses.

"I was not fully into the relationship, although he may have been way ahead of me. That's how people get hurt."

"Do you think there will be repercussions at the studio because of our friendship?"

"Because of what *he* did? I should think not...but who knows?"

"Are you going to speak with him?"

"That, my dear Melinda, is inevitable. I will handle it the best I can. I promise I won't throw plates or resort to kitchen knives."

Mel changed the subject.

"So have you seen Alberto? How is he doing?"

"I haven't. He has been tied up with a new project."

"Lella, may I ask you something about Alberto and Amelia?"

"Certainly."

"Gabi told me about a rift in her relationship with Amelia when they were in college. It had something to do with Alberto, and I wondered if you knew anything about it?"

"Yes, I do know about it." She paused. "Do you know that Amelia is gay?"

"Yes, I do."

"After her father's funeral, she came to me, in tears, and told me. She had been afraid of telling Paolo, and felt such remorse when he died, for not having been honest. I asked her if she had had any relationships, and she told me about her infatuation with Susanna. Apparently, Susanna had encouraged her, or so Amelia believed. Then, one weekend, Alberto, Giorgio, Amelia and Gabriella were at Susanna's house."

"I have heard about that weekend from Gabi," Mel said.

"Well, Gabi doesn't know the whole story. According to Amelia, she was sleeping with Gabi in the living room. Once everyone had fallen asleep, Amelia had the idea of going to Susanna's room. She believed that Susanna would welcome her. But when she got to the room, and carefully opened the door, she saw Alberto most decidedly making love with her."

"Wasn't Alberto married at the time?"

"So what? That never stopped Alberto from his escapades."

An elegant woman approached their table, interrupting their conversation.

"Hello Ladies." It was Cristina della Rovere. She turned to Mel.

"Melinda, I didn't know that you knew Lella."

Lella got up and air kissed Cristina.

"You look wonderful Cristina. You obviously survived the *Salone*?"

"Just barely. I had so much work leading up to it, that I was in a daze. Now I have been approached by a couple of American furniture companies to do their exhibits next year, as well as some showroom work in the States."

Then Cristina addressed Mel.

"And you have obviously found a job, or you would not be sitting here eating *risotto alle fragole* and drinking *Ferrari spumante*?"

"I am working at Giorgio Monti's studio."

Cristina looked at Lella and back at Mel.

"Well, that is a good place to land. Does that mean you aren't interested in returning to see me in June? I am going to take a trip next week, but once I get settled after that, I would love to meet with you again."

Lella looked at Mel, urging her with her eyes.

"Of course I'll come, I'd love to visit your studio again."

They shook hands and Cristina returned to her table.

"*Brava*," said Lella. "Never be complacent. It's just a conversation."

But Mel was mildly troubled. She thought she would come to Milan, get one great job, work for a couple of years at most, and then turn around and go back to the States. Little did she know what kind of a ride she had embarked on, and how many changes might lie in the path ahead. It was both exciting and scary.

"Now, what do you think about the Perch in lemon sauce?"

* * *

When Lella returned home, she took off her shoes and earrings, and washed her face. She changed into her long robe and stretched out on her bed. She flipped through the channels on her TV, found nothing of interest, and decided to order a movie. Then she got a text message.

CAN YOU TALK?

It was from Giorgio.

SURE

The phone rang.

"Hello Giorgio. I was wondering when I would hear from you." Lella's voice was cool.

"Frankly, I have had a lot of thinking to do." Giorgio's voice was unsteady.

"And have you done it, the thinking?"

"Yes, I believe so. But I wanted to speak with you in person."

"I'm already in bed, Giorgio."

"Well, alright, I guess we can talk about it over the phone."

"Good. We need to clear the air."

"I've thought about what you said, and I think you have the right to have the life you want."

"That is good of you."

"I then I thought, what does that mean for *my* right to have the life that *I* want? And I got stuck there."

"Well," said Lella," I can't help you with that; you have to find your own answer."

"If you aren't willing to live with me, or even stay together every night, would that mean that we are free to spend time with other people?"

"Giorgio, let me explain something to you. We have made love twice. That is what is between us. If the feelings that you have for me are an impediment to 'spending time with other people,' then you should follow your instincts."

"Well, would *you* spend time with other men?"

"Not if I was in love with you. Loyalty is very important to me, especially after what I went through with Paolo."

"If you were in love with me? I suppose that means that you aren't."

"Giorgio, it sounds to me like you are dancing around something. Is there anything that you would like to say to me?"

There was a pause.

"Do you think we can start on a clean slate?"

Lella waited for more.

"I want to tell you about how I reacted, stupidly, to our talk last Sunday..."

Lella interrupted him, "Are you going to make a confession?"

"Yes."

"Then find a priest. Now, I have a movie queued, so I have to go."

Lella ended the call, and turned off her phone.

Dinner at Gabi's

Now that Mel knew the reason behind Giorgio's behavior the previous week, she was cautious about showing any sign of understanding or disapproval. To her surprise, Giorgio was extremely professional, and went out of his way to be kind. Mel suspected this might be calculated on his part, but was relieved just the same. In their morning meeting, she asked for some of Carlos and Joji's time to work on the LEAF collection.

By Tuesday, Carlos had mastered the material challenges, and Joji was working on the second version of the conceptual presentation. Mel gave them each an outline of the copy that would explain the product to users. Carlos didn't understand Mel's lack of jealousy regarding her project—she risked getting pushed out—but Joji appreciated the value of sacrificing individualism for the good of the studio. Mel headed out to get something for lunch, confident that she had some backup if needed.

After she had walked for five minutes without any particular destination, she ran into Alberto.

"Mel." He said. "It's good to see you."

"Hi Alberto."

"Have you had lunch?"

"I was just going to grab a panino and sit on a bench."

"Do you mind if I join you?"

"No, please do." Mel figured they needed to talk after their last meeting ended on a sour note.

"I have honestly been too tied up to find the time, but I have really wanted to apologize for my behavior at your apartment."

"Thank you, Alberto. I would also like to apologize for being ambiguous. I let my emotional vulnerability get the better of me."

"Mel, your emotional vulnerability is one of the most beautiful things about you. Please don't apologize for that."

After they got their panini, they found a sunny bench and sat down.

"Do you think we can be friends?" Alberto asked.

"Of course," Mel answered.

After a pause to take a bite, Mel turned to him.

"Alberto, do you mind if I ask you about your relationship with Susanna?"

"Whew! That was a while ago. Why?"

"I saw her at her lake house, with Amelia. That's why I am asking. It's hard for me to navigate these relationships from a position of ignorance."

"Well, I am assuming I can trust your discretion. It started one weekend up at the lake. Giorgio and I took Amelia and Gabi there, to take a break from their studies. I had been married for five or six years, and working at LibriVeri, our publishing business. Marietta was tied up and stayed in Milan."

"I was very attracted to Susanna. She was—and is—as bright as the sun, unencumbered by convention or the judgment of society. I wanted to have some of that magic of hers. I know you disapprove of my unbridled sexual curiosity, but since you've asked, I ventured into her room during the night, when everyone was asleep. We made love, and it was beautiful. None of the politics and 'what ifs,' just pure enjoyment. I was constrained by my marriage, and she by her sexuality. She generally preferred women."

"The next day, I sensed that Amelia had picked up on what had happened. I had suspected that Amelia was gay, but had no confirmation. I assumed she was in a relationship with Gabi."

Mel broke in, "Gabi isn't gay, Alberto."

Alberto stopped his story to consider this new piece of news. Gabi and Amelia had stopped seeing each other afterward, and he had been sorry. He had always greatly enjoyed Gabi's spirit. He assumed that it was a romantic breakup. So it was his fault? History began rewriting itself in his head.

Then he resumed his story.

"Once we got back to Milan, Amelia went out of her way to show her disapproval of my behavior. Susanna and I got together a few more times; it was an infatuation that passed. Much later, word got back to Marietta, who was furious, as you can imagine. That was when our relationship started to crumble. I had not been with another woman before that. Marietta wouldn't be with me anymore, so I began to look elsewhere. Oddly, once we actually separated, I didn't get involved with anyone. It didn't mean anything anymore. I threw myself into my work."

"Do you think," Mel asked, "that Susanna and Amelia are together now?"

"Well, that would explain her behavior at work this week. She has been more friendly and relaxed. I thought she might be laying a trap for me."

"Do you think you should straighten things out with her?"

Alberto considered whether it was better to leave things alone, or to have a talk with Amelia. He could tell her about his misunderstanding of her situation on that weekend; of the mechanism of his attraction, which she must understand if she loved Susanna herself; and how much he wanted her to be happy as well as for them to get along again.

"Alberto?"

"Yes, I think I should. We have a meeting at two-thirty. I think I will give it a try, since this is my Day of Reparations." He laughed.

"Well, we'd both better get back, then," Mel said.

290

As they walked down the street together, Mel invited Alberto to come to dinner.

"Gabi is away till tomorrow, so we can catch up some more. We have a lot to talk about. And I would love to hear about your conversation with Amelia."

"So you're just hungry for some gossip?"

"For some confidence, yes. It isn't gossip unless we tell other people."

They parted ways, and Mel went up to the studio with a lighter heart.

After work, Mel picked up some groceries and wine, and headed home. She took a shower, and set the table. Then she dressed and went into the kitchen to start cooking. Alberto arrived at seven, just as Mel received a text from Gabriella, saying that she was coming this evening and would be home at eight o'clock. As Alberto set down the bottle of wine he brought, Mel considered the situation. She knew that Gabi really liked Alberto, and Mel didn't want her to come home and find her with him (regardless of how things stood)...unless Alberto was there to even things out for Gabi's benefit. *Yes!* Mel thought.

"Alberto, Gabi is coming in time to join us. Do you mind if I invite a fourth?"

"For example?"

"I was thinking Jonathan, if he is available. We'll still have some time to talk before they arrive."

And so Mel contacted Jonathan, who was delighted to come see Mel's new apartment. He put away the food he had been preparing and got ready to leave.

In the meantime, Mel and Alberto had some olives and a glass of wine as they told their stories. Mel briefed Alberto about Giorgio and Lella, which he was sorry to hear, although equally relieved that Lella had dodged a bullet. He swore not to tell. Alberto reported his conversation with Amelia, which had ended in her recognition of her own jealousy and spite, and there were hugs and congratulations on her relationship with Susanna. Amelia was cautiously optimistic about her future; Alberto was cautiously optimistic about his relationship with Amelia. It might, to a certain degree, depend upon the happiness that was bestowed on her by others. He didn't think she could generate it on her own.

Mel swore not to tell.

"And what about Jonathan?" Alberto asked.

"I still don't know," Mel answered. "It is so easy for me to be with Jonathan here, away from the influence of his family. Although isn't this a false reality? I don't trust it, and I can't bear the thought of another failure with him."

"Well, if you focus on failure, it's bound to happen. You know, Melinda, my feelings for you have been sincere, in whatever form they have taken. But I am not in love with you; he is."

He sliced a piece of bread and handed it to her.

"You will always be a stone that is unturned to me, but I will have to live with that like I live with a crooked tooth or a mole."

"I don't know how to take that!" said Mel, laughing.

"By the way," Alberto said, "your life here is real. Milano is just as real as New York. Don't treat it like a parenthesis."

The buzzer sounded, and Mel was relieved that Jonathan had arrived before Gabi. He came in, giving Mel a hug, and shaking hands with Alberto. Jonathan still felt somewhat threatened by Alberto. He was so charming and *Italian*. Alberto did his best to dispel Jonathan's unease in his engaging way, talking to him about photography in an effort to disarm him. He made a point of asking about Elena, whom he had found so bright and charming, although she had dwindled to a minor distraction in his mind.

Gabi arrived, and was pleasantly surprised to finally meet Jonathan, and overjoyed to see Alberto. She excused herself to change from her travel clothes, and put on her favorite blouse.

The four of them sat down to dinner together as if they had done so every day. Gabriella told them about her work as a merchandising consultant (which was boring, she said) and about Paris (which was fascinating).

"It's such a sprawling city, a bit overwhelming, like New York," she said. "The streets are filled with wariness, a feeling of impending conflict like a low hum. The immigrants are conspicuous in their suffering, and the Parisians staunch in their haughtiness."

"Yeah," Jonathan said, "You can see a lot of contrast in New York, too, except that New Yorkers are unfazed by diversity. People have been flowing into that city since we ripped it off from the Natives. I think we may be more jaded than tolerant."

Gabriella turned to Alberto.

"So what's going on in the world of publishing these days?"

"Well," said Alberto, "we are working on a new project. It's a software program for eBooks. I don't want to bore you with it."

"No, please, tell us."

"Well, it allows the reader to give feedback at the end of each chapter. There are two propositions available to click. Based on the selection, one of two possible sequences is delivered. Then after the next chapter, there are two choices again, making four pathways, and so on."

"It sounds like that would be very complex to write," Jonathan said. "The story, I mean."

"Not so much. First, you have to limit the number of chapters. Then, you start offering the choices more toward the middle of the story, once the reader knows the characters. Finally, the changes need to be subtle rather than revolutionary to the story."

Gabriella joined in, "It is an interesting philosophical problem. What if, no matter what you choose, the story ends the same way? No matter the obstacles, what if the conclusion is like a form of destiny for the characters?"

"Well," said Alberto, smiling, "that's the thing. Not all of the alternative choices have to be influential to the outcome."

"To consider a parallel," Jonathan said, "in American films it is always so disappointing when a character you love becomes ill, loses a great deal of money, or is shot. Even though you suffer, however, you know they will somehow be vindicated. It's the same formula, over and over. They deliver what the viewer wants."

Alberto and Gabriella looked at each other, laughing.

"That's what we call an *americanata*," Alberto said, "The ending that resolves everything in a positive way, despite any losses."

"The *happy* ending," added Gabriella.

"It's still an unavoidable outcome," said Jonathan.

"Isn't your project also about the control the reader believes they have over the result?" Mel asked.

"And then they realize, at the end of the story, that maybe they don't have so much control," said Gabriella.

"At any rate," said Alberto, "we have been having fun doing a mock up of a very simple story to try it out. It's not a new concept, but one that we have to adapt. Now, may I take some more pasta?"

Afterward, Alberto helped Gabriella in the kitchen.

"Americans are so charmingly naïve, aren't they?" Alberto said.

Gabriella laughed. It was great to be around Alberto; he had such a sparkle in his eye. How did he do it, with all he's been through? She turned to him.

"You know, Alberto, when you got married, I cried for three days. Maybe four."

"How old were you, sixteen?"

"No, I was almost eighteen!"

Alberto felt his heart swell with nostalgia for the old days. They all used to hang out at the house in Santa Margherita in the summertime, for weeks. They would play billiards or cards on rainy days, and hike, swim, and sail when it was sunny. Gabriella was always there with Amelia, her strong spirit ready for anything. And yet, she also had this cynical edge that made her more credible, and her humor more delightfully sarcastic.

"I'm very touched by that, you know," Alberto said.

Gabriella turned to leave the room. Alberto stood still in the kitchen, absorbing the significance of what she said.

"Aren't you coming?" Gabriella asked.

"Oh, yes," Alberto replied, collecting himself.

They went back into the living room, and Alberto announced that he had an idea.

"I would like to organize a weekend at Santa Margherita, at my villa," he said. "Let's decide whom to invite. There are the four of us, and Lella, of course. How about Elena? Would she like to come?"

They checked their calendars and decided that it should be the weekend of the summer solstice. The twentieth of June would fall on a Saturday.

Jonathan texted Elena, who replied that Enrico had invited her to go sailing that weekend.

"Have I met this Enrico?" asked Alberto. "Tell her to bring him, we can get them into a boat."

The time in between

It rained in Milan off and on for the rest of May. Mel's shoes were all lined up next to the door, in order of dryness. Wearing rain boots was out of the question in the fashion capital, and she feared ridicule if she defied that stoic dictate.

Things proceeded normally at the studio. Giorgio was still cordial to her, praising her work, albeit somewhat detached. His expression suggested he had eaten a bad mushroom that would compromise his digestive tract forever.

Pierpaolo was back in the swing of things, his memory being short and his ego large. When Jonathan confessed to having taken a couple of the candles that Hanne had sent, Pierpaolo immediately handed him the box.

"Please," he said, "take them all."

With Jonathan producing the shoots, and Enrico at the camera, Elena was generally able to avoid Pierpaolo. Jonathan arranged full staff meetings, in the interest of saving Pierpaolo time, while eliminating the need for one-on-one confrontations in the boss's office. Pierpaolo was out a lot, drinking coffee until it was time to start drinking wine, and showing up either wired or sedate to go over the books with Lucy.

Enrico was biding his time with Elena. He supported her work, but tried to include Jonathan in their coffee breaks and lunches. He was not certain of her feelings beyond a warm friendliness, and knew how much she hated it when men became demanding. He didn't want to ruin the team dynamics, either.

Jonathan and Mel spoke on the phone a couple of times a week, but neither of them had much time to get together. Jonathan was working on some project with Enrico, and Mel was juggling the work on Susanna's house with the LEAF line of disposable, reusable, recyclable, compostable party ware.

Elena and Mel went out together on the weekends, to shop, visit museums, and have lunch. Gabriella would join them when she was home and not too busy. One Saturday in early June, they decided to meet for a drink at Bar Basso. It was there that they saw Hanne hanging out with Reiner and Geert: drinking beer, laughing, and speaking in English.

"She gets around," Mel said.

"You Americans are such Puritans," said Gabriella. "They are young kids having fun."

Elena told her about Hanne dating Pierpaolo, but refrained from the story of their studio encounter. She thought it would appear, to Mel, as a moment of intimacy between her and Jonathan.

Mel certainly wasn't going to tell Gabriella about her Uncle Giorgio's incident, not so much to protect him (who was her boss, after all) as Lella.

Reiner eventually spotted them, excused himself and came outside to their table. He sat on his heels on the sidewalk, next to Elena. They exchanged the usual pleasantries, after which Reiner lingered.

"I have a question," he said, turning to Elena. "How weird would it be if Hanne rented my extra room?"

Elena turned to him, "You mean, move in with you?"

"She would have her own room," he insisted, rolling his eyes.

"Well, I just would make sure Pierpaolo doesn't find out. Can you do that? More importantly, can *she* do that?"

He got up and said, "Let's hope so. Nice to see you, Melinda."

Gabriella was clueless, but Mel turned to Elena.

"I guess she is planning a break from her gold-digging activities?"

"Not exactly," Elena answered. "Reiner owns his apartment, so I doubt she will be paying 'rent' exactly. And Reiner's father is a big banker or something, so he is loaded. You know that black leather jacket he wears all the time? He has three or four of them."

"She is a very attractive woman," Gabriella noted, trying to be involved in the conversation. She was a little older than Mel and Elena, and had learned to be more tolerant of the ways that other, less gifted, women survived in this man's world. Everyone works with the tools they have at their disposal, she allowed.

* * *

Lella was very busy with the editing assignments she was getting from Alberto. The September deadlines made for a busy early summer, given that in August many people would disappear for their vacations. What would she do in August? She had considered suggesting a trip to Amelia, but was dissuaded by recent news of Amelia's love story with Susanna (about which she was nonetheless pleased). Susanna was solid, familiar, and settled in life. Amelia was still looking for a place to land. She seemed happy now. Lella only hoped Susanna wouldn't decide on being with a man again, down the road. That would kill Amelia. Lella didn't trust bisexuality, didn't understand it. Although Susanna did have a quality that transcended her sex, that was certain. Even Lella had felt her magnetism.

She hadn't spoken to Giorgio since their phone call. He was too proud to take the initiative, though Lella knew that they would meet socially, sooner or later, and that things between them could be civil again. It might even be in Santa Margherita, on the Midsummer weekend that Alberto had planned. Giorgio would be down there on his boat, if the weather was nice.

Lella was looking forward to that weekend. She loved the spacious villa that their grandfather had built on the hill terraced with gardens overlooking the sea. The only downside was that Federico and Massimo were coming to Milan at that time, and she would miss them.

Despite his workload, Alberto found the time to arrange a lunch with Gabriella and Amelia for old time's sake. They went to the Japanese restaurant Suntory, around the corner from the opera house *La Scala*. Over their two-hour meal, they got a little tipsy from the sake–the waiters kept replenishing the small, warm carafes on the table until it looked like a bowling alley–and Gabi and Amelia had many laughs about their college days. Gabriella then said goodbye, and Alberto and Amelia headed back to their office. Next to them, *La Scala* seemed to sway back and forth, as if in a mirage.

"I've always enjoyed Gabi," said Amelia.

"So have I," said Alberto. He looked back to see her walking away and smiled to himself.

"Now," said Alberto, taking Amelia's arm, "I feel like I can review the new set of endings for our whatever-ending story."

"What are you talking about, the uStory?"

"Is that what we're calling it?"

"It's just a working title."

The pigeon perched on Leonardo daVinci's beret watched them proceed along Via Manzoni, moving its head forward and back.

Santa Margherita

The day to leave for their weekend finally came, as did long days that stretched well into the evening. The group discovered that there would be a full moon on Saturday night, so Alberto made reservations to have dinner in the hills above Santa Margherita overlooking the sea.

Gabriella had planned to ride down with Lella, Alberto, and Mel after lunch on Friday, but decided in the end to take the train the prior evening. Giorgio was down on his boat, and she thought she would go for a sail with her uncle before joining the others.

"So Giorgio is going to be in Santa Margherita," Alberto said, on their way down. Lella turned to look out the window.

"I think I would like to run into him as soon as possible, to get the discomfort over with."

"Do you want to invite him to dinner?"

"Absolutely not."

Mel was in the back seat, thumbing through a fashion magazine.

"Why don't you pick Gabi up after their sail? I can go with you if you'd like."

"That's a good idea," said Lella. "Maybe you could get Gabi to go to the bar at the pier to get a drink, and that way I can exchange a few words with Giorgio."

Alberto asked, "When are the others arriving, Mel?"

"Jonathan said that they were leaving the studio by three-o'clock. Enrico is driving."

"I hope they miss the rush."

The traffic was moving along pretty well so far, and once they passed Genoa–and all the tunnels that wound through the mountains–the sea was their near constant companion as they continued along the autostrada. The train traveled parallel below them, stopping at the coastal towns; above, the hillside was dotted with villas and condominiums tinted in pastels. The window shutters were invariably green, and the roof tiles, terracotta. An occasional garden came into view, perched above the sea, dotted with Palms and Maritime Pines. The branches of the Pines were turned up in a sweeping gesture that made them look like women lifting their tresses to the sun.

"So this is Liguria," said Mel. "It is so beautiful!"

"Now you can understand why people leave Milan on the weekend," said Alberto.

They got off the autostrada at Rapallo. Alberto drove past the harbor, and along the narrow, winding road that nearly brushed the iron gates of more colorful villas and lush gardens both above and below the road. Scooters were everywhere, and came zipping around the curves, barely warning drivers with their buzzing. Birds were chirping in the background, and the air had a sweet scent to it. Alberto didn't like air conditioning, so Mel had lowered her window, her head tipped outward.

The landscape was dense with buildings and plants. People were everywhere. Boats bobbed in the harbor as tanned men in shorts and top-siders stood talking and waving their arms on the piers. Girls walked hand in hand, or in small groups, in summer dresses and sandals. The little shops along the road were overflowing with beach gear, the latest toys and inflatables as well as the traditional brightly colored buckets.

Once they entered Santa Margherita, the road flattened out, but never stopped curving, around the little park with the statue of Christopher Columbus, and along sidewalks filled with tables where waiters served late lunches and early drinks. The road then followed the façade of the majestic Hotel Miramare, bright white with its sky blue shutters. On the sea side of the road, the beach was obscured by red and white striped cabanas hung with potted geraniums. Then, the view to the water opened up again.

At one of the the corners cluttered with stacked directional signs pointing to every hospitality venue in the area, Alberto turned right and started climbing the hill. He turned again, and then stopped before a large, green iron gate. He got out of the car and went to the intercom.

"Paola, we're here... *Grazie*." Then a buzz, and the gates slowly swung open. Alberto got back in the car.

"You're kidding, right?" Mel said.

Alberto laughed. "This is it."

The car moved slowly, making a crunching sound on the fine light-colored gravel of the driveway. The villa loomed above them, three stories of pink-stuccoed walls, balustraded terraces, and flowers cascading from pots. They drove around to the back of the villa, where a man who was cutting flowers came to meet them. No flat space here, beyond the driveway; the garden rose in a series of narrow terraces flanked by steps, each level populated with a combination of flowers and vegetables. There were small groves of Lemons and Olives. The air smelled of Rosemary and Lavender.

"Hello, Beppe," said Alberto, as they all got out of the car. Paola was at the back door of the kitchen, wiping her hands on a kitchen cloth. Alberto introduced them to Mel, and they were very happy to see the Signora Lella after so long.

"What a lovely wind has carried you here, *Signora Lella*!" Paola said, "I'm making pesto." She made an apologetic gesture indicating her apron.

Then she conferred with Alberto about room assignments as Beppe moved the car into the garage. Steps ascending along the side of the garage led to a tiny apartment above it. It was just beyond the massive villa, with an unobstructed view to the sea.

"I think we will have Melinda and Gabriella up top," Alberto said, and Signora Lella in the master suite. I will take the room next to that. Then we have two young men and a young woman arriving before dinner, so we can put one of the guys in the *garçonniere*, and the other two in the front rooms on the second floor."

"What's a *garçonniere*?" asked Mel.

"It's a bachelor's apartment. That's what we call it," Alberto answered, pointing to the garage. "Although it was mostly used by my father, to get away from the family and keep his own hours."

When the others arrived, Enrico volunteered to stay there. Elena and Jonathan took the two front rooms. When they set their bags down, they each opened the French doors to the front terrace. The two of them laughed when they stepped outside and found each other there.

"This is so incredibly beautiful!" Elena said.

Mel called from above.

"Hello down there."

They looked up, and she was standing on the smaller, third floor terrace.

"I've been having a nap," she continued. "Why don't you come up and take a look?"

The stairway to the top floor was more discreet than the wide main stairs that led down to the hall. Halfway up, on the landing, was a door leading to a precious little room, almost hidden, with a bath. The family called it the *sgabuzzino*, the closet.

Mel was looking down from the top of the stairs.

"Alberto said that's where they put anyone who is naughty."

The top floor was much smaller, with a broad landing where a couch and TV were snugly arranged. There were two rooms and a bath. Mel's room

304

had access to the small terrace that wrapped around the bedroom on the south and east, where it faced the sea. A few sailboats were motoring into the harbor, wrapping their lowered sails as they put in.

Jonathan wished that he was staying on this floor with Mel, but he understood that Gabi didn't know Elena as well. He didn't want to be above the garage, either, although he believed that Enrico stepped forward because of his good manners. Oh, well.

"Melinda," Lella called from the bottom of the stairs, "We should go retrieve Gabriella."

Jonathan and Elena followed Lella and Mel outside because they wanted to check out Enrico's pad. They walked up the steps, knocked, and entered.

Jonathan said, "So this is a *garçonniere!*"

"Enrico must be the *garçon*," Elena added.

Enrico walked about the room with an air of regal possessiveness, his arms extended. "*C'est moi!*"

Jonathan looked through a telescope that was pointed out the broad window. Elena checked out the bath, and the armoires, even the mattress.

"Very luxe," she said, "you could be happy just staying here by yourself for the weekend."

Jonathan decided he needed to check out the garden, and left.

"By oneself," Enrico said to Elena, "is not the best and highest use of a bachelor's pad." Then he turned to unpack his bag.

Elena started to leave, then turned and kissed Enrico on the cheek.

"I'm glad you're here," she said.

"Come and visit any time," he replied.

* * *

Lella was meticulously dressed, as always, in a linen shift, espadrilles, and large sunglasses. She and Mel drove down to the center of Santa Margherita, spending a good while looking for a place to park. They eventually found a spot along the road, and started to walk toward the place where Giorgio docked his boat. There was a large building stuccoed in a peachy red, with yellow and white trim. Some of the windows were painted—in *trompe d'oeil*—to complete the façade composition. They were hard to distinguish from the real windows, if not for their shutters, which remained permanently closed.

"That," said Lella, "is because there was once a window tax."

They walked down a bit, and spotted Gabriella and Giorgio putting things in order on the boat. They all said hello, then Mel asked Gabriella if she wanted to get a drink, pointing with her head to urge her away.

"We'll be at Skipper," Gabriella said.

Giorgio was coiling some rope, squatting and looking up at Lella. She thought he looked very handsome after a day out on the water: tanned with tousled hair. He straightened up.

"It's good to see you, Lella."

Lella smiled politely. They air kissed.

"We belong to the same tribe, Giorgio; we can't be at odds with one another. Did you have a nice sail?"

"It was lovely. Gabi is such good company."

He paused, and took a deep breath.

"Lella, I'm sorry I let you down. And I know you well enough to realize that I won't have a second chance."

Lella rested against a bollard.

"Giorgio, I know that fidelity is just a vocabulary word in this country. But you, more than most, know what I went through with Paolo. It's a question of feeling valued."

306

"I understand. Well, we can be friends, can't we?"

Lella could tell that Giorgio said these words with a great deal of difficulty and she felt a wave of compassion she couldn't control. She stood up and gave him a hug.

"I do value you," he said into her shoulder.

"Then maybe you don't value yourself."

Because he was silent, she said, "Shall we join Gabi and Mel for a drink?"

Lella offered him her arm, wondering if she could ever forgive him, and thinking that she could not. Giving him up made her sad, just the same.

* * *

When they got back to the villa, everyone was sitting in the large hall, on a sofa and chairs arranged around a large, low table. Gabriella headed up the stairs to get cleaned up, and then joined the others.

The dinner was delicious. Everyone praised Paola's pesto. A roasted chicken prepared with lemons and rosemary from the garden followed.

"Tomorrow night," Alberto announced, "to celebrate the Midsummer and the full moon, we are going to dine at *La Stalla dei Frati*, in Nozarego. It is up in the hills. I have already made reservations."

"It has a beautiful view!" Lella added, delighted at the news.

After dinner, they returned to sit together, enjoying the gentle breeze and the view of terracotta rooftops and gardens tumbling down to the water. The color of the sea was changing to a deeper blue as the light lowered; they sipped limoncello.

* * *

The next morning found Alberto and Lella sitting at a small table in a windowed alcove in the dining room, having caffè latte with toast and jam.

Alberto got a text.

IS THERE ROOM FOR US?

"Oh *Dio!*" said Alberto. It's Federico. They want to stop here today, and stay the night. Where will we put them?"

OF COURSE, he responded.

Alberto moved the table accessories around, trying to visualize an arrangement. Gabriella came down and looked over his shoulder as he explained whom the sugar bowl and the butter dish represented.

"Easy," she said. "Put Mel in my room with me."

"We can't put Federico and Massimo up there with you two, with just the one bathroom."

Lella suggested, "Put Enrico up there, and they can go in the *garçonniere*."

Alberto certainly couldn't stay on the third floor with Gabriella and Mel himself. That would be too weird.

"No good, Massimo will feel excluded. I'll go there, and they can have the large room next to yours, where I was."

Gabriella was hoping Alberto would come up to their floor, rather than Enrico, but she remained silent.

"That works," Lella said.

Mel ran into Jonathan on the second floor and they went down to breakfast together. Jonathan was a little disappointed when he learned of the new arrangement, which made Mel even less accessible to him. But he was glad that he would see Federico and Massimo again. Who was he kidding, anyway? This was probably not the best place to reunite with her...even though there was a magic about it that made him wish for it.

Sailing

Enrico had been promised a sail, so after breakfast he asked who was coming along besides Elena. Jonathan and Mel joined. Alberto gave Jonathan the keys to the scooter so that he and Elena could stop at the bakery for some focaccia. He drove Enrico and Mel down to the boat. Gabriella decided to go to the market with Lella, who wanted to avoid the port.

Enrico assisted Alberto with the preparations, threading sails, running the sheets through the winches, showing Mel how to tie a cleat hitch. Once the others arrived, Alberto showed Jonathan how to feed the sail into the boom and put Enrico at the tiller. Elena and Mel pulled up the fenders once they were clear of the docks.

Enrico started the motor and slowly chugged out of the crowded port until it was safe to raise the mainsail. Elena had learned a little when she was in Procida, and shared what she knew with Mel.

Alberto was instructing Jonathan on how to pull the mainsail sheet in using the winch; Enrico was getting a feel for the wind.

After tacking along the coast, they eventually arrived at a secluded spot near a cove and decided to stop for a swim. The water was the color of sapphires, changing to shades of turquoise and jade, depending on its depth and surroundings. Large rocks emerged from the water closer to the stony shore.

They had an invigorating swim that included a near encounter with a jellyfish that Mel had mistaken for a plastic bag. Alberto called her away in time, and she scrambled onto the boat to everyone's laughter.

Elena rummaged for her Swiss Army knife, and began to cut the focaccia while Alberto opened the cooler he had stocked with white wine and sparkling water. They sat rocking in the sun for a while, remarking on the beauty of the sea, and the coastline, and the day. It was the longest one of the year. Alberto studied the interactions of Jonathan with both Elena and Mel. He seemed more comfortable with Elena, while his behavior toward Mel was guarded. Enrico was in his own world, and Alberto considered what a unifying element a love of the sea could be. Then he thought of the lives the sea had recently claimed, of desperate people trying to find refuge.

"You seem pensive, Alberto," Mel said.

"Just meditating. The sea brings out the philosopher in me." He put away the wine. Jonathan pulled the anchor and they started moving outward to catch the wind.

"The Mediterranean Sea," remarked Jonathan, "is more beautiful than I had imagined."

"It's a strong and harsh beauty," Enrico said, "and hides so many secrets. Now, everybody get ready, we're going to come about."

* * *

When they got back into port, it was three o'clock, and they spent another half hour tying up, packing up the sails and cleaning the deck. Mel was wearing a wide-brimmed hat and a gauzy tunic; she had had too much sun, and was sent to sit in the shade, on the cooler. When the others joined her, they all got some lemon soda, then made their way to the car. Elena drove Mel up on the Vespa.

Massimo and Federico were there when they got back to the villa. They were chatting with Gabriella, whom Massimo had just met and Federico hadn't seen for years. Lella had gone to take a nap.

This was the time of day when weekend sojourners go off on their own, to shower off the salt or sand, read, rest, and prepare for the evening. They would reunite before six, cleaned, brushed, and dressed for dinner, their skin glowing from their day in the sun. It was a routine, a ritual even, followed on every holiday.

Enrico went to retrieve some of his things from the garçonniere, where Alberto was settling in.

"Thanks again for the sail," Enrico said. "I feel lost when I'm away from the sea for too long."

"I understand the feeling," Alberto said, "and you're very welcome."

Alberto hesitated, and then said, "Do you mind if I ask you something that is none of my business? Is there some kind of love triangle going on between you, Jonathan, and Elena?"

Enrico sighed and shook his head.

"We are all friends. We work together. Elena has had some tough times with men. Jonathan and I are supporting her. Jonathan, as far as I know, is still interested in reviving things with Mel."

"Who is mildly confused."

"I don't know her well yet."

"I have only known her for a few months myself. But she seems to be good at depriving herself of what she needs."

"I like her," said Enrico, shrugging, "but she does seem to be a little uptight. It must be hard, worrying about making a false step, when you're in a foreign country. I know myself, coming from Naples to Milano," he laughed.

Enrico shook hands with Alberto, grabbed his bag, and left.

Alberto thought about what Enrico had said about Mel. He had recognized her uncertainty, but had not attributed it to being on foreign soil. He wondered what she would be like in her natural habitat. Maybe she was evading Jonathan not because she was punishing herself, but rather so that she could become stronger without using him as a crutch. She was certainly single-minded.

* * *

311

Mel and Gabriella were stretched out on their beds in terry cloth robes when Enrico got to the top of the stairs. He said hello, remarked that 'this place feels like a spa,' and then went to his room for a nap.

"Great idea, Gabi, let's do a mask," said Mel. She jumped up and grabbed some Cretan Clay from her bag, brandishing it.

Jonathan was in his room with his laptop open when Massimo knocked on his door.

"So who is in the next room?" he asked.

"Elena," said Jonathan, not raising his gaze.

"You know these rooms have a common terrace," he continued.

"Yes."

"It's too bad Melinda is not in that room."

Jonathan looked up.

"Yes, I guess it is."

"Well, I'll let you get back to whatever you're doing," Massimo said, and left.

Massimo never napped in the afternoon himself; he found it boring. Lella was resting, and so was Federico. He decided to go out into the garden. Elena was there, walking along one of the terraces, inspecting the plants.

"I thought you were asleep, like everyone else," he said.

"No, I'm not sleepy right now. I'm enjoying the air. Milan can be so confining. It's gray and there's so little nature."

"It's all *culture*," Massimo said, "all human artifice. That's its strength, though, isn't it?"

Elena laughed softly.

"I suppose you're right."

"Did you enjoy sailing?"

"Oh, yes. It has reminded me where I belong. Away from what you call *human artifice*."

"I'm sorry I didn't get to spend much time with you when you were in Rome last."

"It was a quick trip."

"I heard you went to Naples?"

"Yes, with Enrico."

"Enrico is an interesting type. Very elegantly Italian, in a traditional sort of way."

Elena didn't say anything.

"So," he insisted, "is there anything going on between you two?"

"No!" Elena said, looking at Massimo and laughing. "You're the matchmaker type, aren't you?"

"I'm just saying, *cara mia*, that he seems like a valuable catch. And he obviously has more character than Jonathan."

"If you mean that he is more passionate, perhaps you're right. But Jonathan's character is impeccable."

"You're hopeless," Massimo said, throwing up his hands.

The Midsummer's night

Later in the afternoon, the guests trickled downstairs. They convened on the lower terrace outside of the entry, the sun now behind the villa. Still, there was little shade. They gazed over the balustrade at all of the activity below. Boats were coming in, and although the trees and villas scattered on the hill obscured the roads below them, they could hear friends calling out to friends, and the surging buzz of scooters as they passed along the *lungomare*.

Alberto and Lella came out with glasses and prosecco. Lella dribbled a little bit of Campari into each glass before Alberto poured the sparkling wine. Then she added a tiny piece of orange peel before passing the glasses around. They all toasted to the full moon, the solstice, friendship, and to Italy.

Mel noted how elegant Alberto was in his navy pants and white linen shirt. His skin tanned almost instantly after their day on the water, while her general color was pink, especially on her forearms and her nose. Mel and Gabriella both chatted with their host, admiring his look and teasing him. Jonathan and Lella were standing apart, engaged in a conversation about light and the color of the sea. Federico and Massimo were discussing film and photography with Enrico and Elena.

The reservation was for eight o'clock, so they went out back to divide up the cars. Alberto took Gabriella and Mel. Jonathan joined them at the last minute. Lella was with Massimo and Federico, so Enrico and Elena needed to take the flatbed, three-wheeled *Ape*.

"It will be downhill on the way back," Enrico said.

Alberto led the way to Nozarego, up the winding roads. The sea and the sky came into view as they turned around the curves, and then disappeared again. Alberto was playing some incredibly beautiful music; he explained that it was Jessye Norman singing Richard Strauss's *Ver letzte Lieder*, or Four Last Songs. Though she knew nothing of lyric opera, Mel was overwhelmed by the combination of the soprano voice, the bittersweet music, and the mysterious landscape that was deepening around them.

Gabriella leaned over and kissed Alberto on the cheek.

"It's beautiful," she said.

"I should play this more often," Alberto said, smiling.

* * *

The restaurant had an awesome view of the coastline and the *Golfo del Tigullio*. A large table was set for them outside under an awning, so that their prospect was framed like a picture. Jonathan's head was still swimming with the music and the low light cast on the landscape. He went to the railing beyond the table and looked out over the space that tumbled down the hill below him, all the way to the sea. The sun would soon sink behind the hills, though in this moment he felt a peace that he had never felt before. Mel approached him and put her hand lightly on his shoulder. Massimo elbowed Federico, and pointed toward them with his head. Federico tried to stifle him.

Alberto placed Lella at the head of the table, and then asked Gabriella to sit next to her, across from him.

"I am going to have trenette with pesto, then some grilled shrimp. Anyone else?"

The server came, and Alberto ordered some antipasti, and selected a wine after consulting the others. The conversation during dinner was relaxed, almost quiet. Everyone felt the velvety atmosphere that was gradually enveloping the table.

During their meal, the moon had risen, and tiny lights slowly appeared on the distant shoreline of the bay. Fishing boats bobbed in the water, recognizable only by their lanterns. It was not yet dark beyond their canopy, but they remained in the shadows, lulled by candlelight and the rhythm of crickets.

"I hope we'll be alert enough to drive back," Enrico said, pouring wine into Elena's glass.

"We'll have gravity on our side," said Alberto.

"Let's have some *espresso*," said Massimo, "I don't think anyone is in a hurry to go to sleep tonight."

After dinner and an espresso, they stayed and talked for a while, enjoying the evening view of the distant hills, whose myriad lights lit like a deep green sky full of stars above the bay. They agreed to drive down to the beach before returning to the villa. After following the ridgeline, they descended Via Fortunato Costa, which made its way through a series of switchbacks down to the shoreline. They parked, walked along the sidewalk to a stone terrace with benches, and sat down to enjoy the air rolling in from the sea.

Alberto was animated. He pointed to landmarks, discussed boats with Enrico, and teased Gabriella. He felt strangely happy. He was unattached, and it didn't bother him at all. In fact, it made him feel like he could finally become *really* attached. He felt the irresistible optimism of good weather, as he had every summer he spent here when he was younger. It was so easy! Leaning on the rail, he told stories about the ferociousness of his grandfather, how his mother dreaded coming here because of it. Then, after his—and Lella's—grandfather died, everything changed. There was an air of congeniality between the families who shared the place. Lella took her younger cousin Alberto to the beach (Alberto pointed to the spot), and later he taught Lella's daughter Amelia how to swim.

Lella stood up.

"I," she announced, "think I am ready to go to bed now."

Back at the villa, everyone said their goodnights and made their way to their rooms. Alberto lingered, making sure all the doors were closed and the lights out, before he went out through the kitchen to the back garden. He made a crunching sound as he walked on the gravel to the stairs that led to the *garçonniere*. He stopped at a tiny moonlight garden on the terrace next to the landing, halfway up. There were white Hydrangeas, Peonies, and Roses; a Carrara marble bench sat among them, the ground covered with crushed limestone. This was the night for which this little spot was created. Alberto took off his shoes and lay on the smooth bench with his knees bent. It was cool under his back and his feet. He looked at the lights in the windows. Lella's was lit still, as were the two above.

***

In the hall on the second floor, Massimo was pacing. He looked at Jonathan's door, then Elena's. Federico was in the bathroom, so he went to Lella's room. She was reading in bed, enjoying her time alone.

"Is it okay if I come in?" Massimo asked.

"Certainly."

Massimo sat on the edge of Lella's bed and asked her about her book. He was agitated, and didn't much like being alone. Lella had such a soothing voice.

Upstairs, Mel and Gabriella were sitting up in bed in T-shirts and running shorts, talking and laughing quietly.

They heard a sound like a small stone hitting the window. Gabriella opened the window and looked down. Nothing. Then, a small piece of gravel flew in, landing on the floor between them. Gabriella took a better look, and saw Alberto standing below.

"It's beautiful down here," he said in a near whisper. "Why don't you come out?"

Gabriella turned to Mel.

"I'll be too conspicuous if I go down the stairs. Everyone will know."

"I take it that means you plan to join him?"

"Are you kidding?"

Gabrielle inspected the outside wall. There were climbing plants, and a small tree, slightly out of reach.

"You're not thinking of climbing down the wall, are you?"

"This is nothing. I used to go rock climbing. Now, help me secure this sheet to the bedpost so I can get down as far as the ledge. Then I can easily reach the the vines, then the tree, if I edge along sideways."

Mel looked at the proposed route, and it looked doable. However, the first part was scary. She was sworn to secrecy, and given the charge of making sure the knot held fast.

"Should I leave the sheet out?" Mel asked. Gabriella put her finger in front of her lips.

* * *

On the floor below, Massimo and Lella heard some noise outside the garden window.

"It's the branches scraping the wall in the breeze," Lella said. "I've told Alberto to get that tree pruned."

"She's climbing down some plant," said Massimo, who had peeked out behind the shutters. "It's Gabi."

"I hope it's not the Bougainvillea, she'll hurt herself." Lella said dispassionately.

Massimo was silent, holding his hands in a gesture of prayer, then, clapping noiselessly.

"She did it!" he whispered.

A twig snapped, and they heard soft giggling.

"It must be the full moon," Lella said, "keeping everyone up."

"Well," said Massimo, "I have to go, I have something to do."

"So soon?" Lella said, picking up her book.

***

Back out in the hall, Massimo took stock of his options. Then he quietly knocked on Elena's door. She cracked the door to see who was there.

"Parma!" he said, noting the team colors on her football jersey.

"That's the password," she said, opening the door.

Elena waved him toward two wicker chairs at a small table.

"Listen, Elena, I wonder if I can ask a favor of you. It's not for me, it's for Jonathan."

"Oh? What is it?" she asked, smiling.

"Well, I was wondering if you could ask Melinda to switch rooms with you."

"But Gabi is with her."

"Not anymore," he said, lowering his voice.

Then he continued, "But, there is a caveat: you have to tell her it's because you want to be upstairs with Enrico."

Elena colored at this.

"Just so she won't be suspicious," he added.

"What is Enrico going to think?"

Massimo waved his hand. "He's probably asleep by now, don't you think?"

"Well, okay."

Elena straightened her bed and gathered a few things from her night table, and then exited the room with Massimo. She walked carefully up the steps to the third floor. Enrico, who had taken possession of the bathroom in the *sgabuzzino* on the landing, cracked the door, toothbrush in mouth, to see who had passed. It was Elena! What was she doing? He quickly closed the door until he was sure Elena had reached Mel's room. She obviously didn't want to be seen. Now he was going to have to stay here until she came back down. What a pain!

After a few minutes, he heard someone on the steps again. With the lights out, he poked his head around the door to make sure she was downstairs.

This wasn't Elena! It was Melinda! What did this mean? His heart started pounding, but he had to go back upstairs. He waited a little longer and then made his way up, ducking quietly into his room. He left the door ajar, and a small light on, just in case.

* * *

Federico was telling Massimo to come to bed, but Massimo waved his hand at him to be quiet. He went out into the hall and then into the passageway to the bathroom. Here he would remain concealed while having a clear view to the door of the unoccupied bedroom. When he saw Mel enter the room and close the door, he walked softly, barefoot, to Jonathan's room.

"*Jonathan*," he whispered, barely tapping the door.

Jonathan came to the door and cracked it open.

"What's going on?"

Massimo scratched his head.

"Well," he whispered, "I just saw the strangest thing. Elena has left her room to sleep upstairs, and Melinda is now in that room," he emphasized by pointing to the left.

"Oh!" said Jonathan, digesting this news. "Do you think we need to be concerned?"

"Jonathan, really! You are exasperating." Massimo made a dismissive gesture and left.

Once he had closed the door, Jonathan could barely refrain from dancing. He sat on the edge of the bed, thinking. He pulled the mattress off and set it against the bedframe. Then he took a deep breath, and opened the

French doors to the terrace. The night was beautiful and quiet. You could hear the sea brushing over the stony shore, faintly, like breathing.

He knocked on the French doors of the next room. Mel turned the handle, surprised to see Jonathan.

"Hi," she said with a questioning face.

"Um," said Jonathan, "what happened to Elena?"

"Were you looking for Elena?"

"Oh, no! It's not what you think," he said, realizing how it looked. "I just wanted a favor."

Mel looked at him distrustfully, waiting.

"It such a beautiful night. I wanted to pull my mattress out here, but it's too clumsy for me to do alone."

Mel followed him into his room where, in fact, she saw the mattress against the bed.

"It takes two to get it through the door, you see?"

The two of them got the mattress out, and butted it against the wall between the rooms, facing the sea like a sofa. Then Jonathan arranged a few pillows. Mel turned to go back inside.

"Um," Jonathan started, "wouldn't you like to sit out here for a bit?"

She laughed. "Well, sure, I'm not sleepy yet." She grabbed a light bedspread from her room and came back out, taking her place next to Jonathan.

* * *

Gabriella and Alberto sat in the moonlit garden, reminiscing about the summers they had spent here, Gabi as Amelia's guest. They had played all sorts of pranks on Paola, Beppe, and even Lella, together. They had hiked, and sailed, and rode around on the scooter.

"You took me for my first ride on that red Vespa," she said.

They were silent for a few minutes.

"Gabi, how would you like to play another game?" Alberto asked in his most playful voice.

"What game?" she asked innocently.

"I'll show you," he said. He picked her up in his arms, reached the door of the *garçonniere*, managed to turn the knob, and carried Gabriella over the threshold. He pushed the door shut with one foot and then gently placed her on the bed.

"Is this game okay?" he asked.

She only nodded.

* * *

Elena couldn't sleep, thinking she should act, but not sure how. Enrico was in the next room, but she didn't know if she wanted to mess things up by doing something stupid. Then she remembered what Jonathan had told her in Rome: *You must be the one to choose.*

He was probably asleep, anyway. Elena decided to go to the bathroom. She noticed his door was ajar, and there was a light on. She looked inside, and saw that he was asleep, a book open, pages down, on his chest. She tiptoed in to turn off the light, and reached for the book.

Enrico opened one eye, saw her, and smiled. He took hold of her arm and pulled her down onto the bed.

"Thank you," Enrico said, "for getting the light for me."

* * *

Jonathan and Mel talked for a while out on the terrace, until Mel assumed the dreamy voice she had when she was falling asleep. Jonathan put his hand behind her head to lay her down on the mattress. Her face looked so warm, and her lips so soft. She reached up and pulled his face down to kiss him.

322

Daybreak

Gabriella woke up to the sound of Alberto snoring. She bent over to kiss him, hoping that would make him stop. He opened his eyes.

"Is it morning?"

"Yes."

He sat up, taking stock of the situation, and his surroundings.

"You know, one advantage of staying here above the garage is that we have our own kitchenette. How about a nice *caffè latte*?"

"Not quite as good as sleeping in some more, but thank you." Then she added, "Do you think I need to get back to my room before the others get up?"

"Paola is already in the kitchen, and you are not climbing back up. The sheet is gone. You are marooned with me. Your best strategy now is to wait it out."

They sat on the bed eating toast and honey and drinking coffee. Then Alberto took on a serious tone.

"You know, Gabi, we don't need to hide this from anyone."

"Stop," said Gabriella, "you are making me giddy. It's early, and besides, I'm still absorbing the situation."

"It's okay; you can feel happy. I do," Alberto said.

* * *

Enrico was sitting up in bed, with Elena leaning against his chest, his arms wrapped around her.

"What next?" he asked.

She considered his question for a moment.

"You mean, for us?"

Enrico nodded.

"Well, my dream would be to get out of Pierpaolo's studio."

"Well," Enrico said, "I am happy to tell you that Jonathan and I are starting our own studio. And you are part of the plan."

"You mean all three of us would leave Pierpaolo?"

"And Reiner. Apparently he wants to go to New York with Hanne, and Jonathan got him a gig."

"This will kill Pierpaolo." (*Why did she care?*)

"No it won't. He has Lucy, and Geert, who will be happy to become more important. Leitizia can still work for him, through us or on her own. He'll be fine."

"*Bello!*" said Elena joyfully, jumping up with her arms in the air.

"I can't believe it. Now I want my breakfast."

* * *

Mel woke up in Jonathan's arms, feeling the warmth of the morning sun. It was the most comfort and peace she had ever experienced. She could hear Beppe cutting plants in the entry garden below. Her view through the balustrade was only sea and sky. The birds were chirping, and she smelled that fragrance of Liguria, so sweet.

She had to go to the bathroom, and scurried through the hall in her nightshirt. She ran into Massimo. He wore a knowing smile.

"Don't even say a word," she warned him.

When she got back to the terrace, she and Jonathan returned the mattress and the pillows. She rinsed her face in the little sink he had in his room, and drank some water from her cupped hands. The water had the same wonderful sweetness as the air.

Jonathan took her hands and asked her if she was okay.

"This is all so perfect," she answered, "I don't even want to think about the obstacles right now."

"The only obstacles are in your head," he said, smiling.

"What do you mean?"

"I mean that I want to marry you, and I am not asking anyone permission to do so."

Mel sat down on the bed, her mouth open as if she wanted to speak but didn't know what to say.

"Look," Jonathan said, "If we go to the *Comune* this week, they will post the banns on line and we'll have our license within a couple of weeks. Then we can get married.

"Will you?" he asked.

She looked at him.

"Marry me?" he continued.

Then Mel stood up and started pacing. "What will you do about your mother?"

"Well, I have thought this through. We can visit the States around Chanukkah/Christmas. Chanukkah is a light-hearted holiday (by Jewish standards!). If they want us there, we will go. It will be their choice. In any case, we'll visit your family for Christmas. That's it."

"What does this mean, Jon? Do you plan to stay in Italy?"

"I think, for the foreseeable future. We can be together here so much more easily. We both love it. Oh! And I found out that I am eligible for citizenship through my grandfather, Josef Guttmann. He was born here!"

Mel sat down on the edge of the bed, trying to process this information, and Jonathan's request.

"Well, I should tell you that I am thinking about leaving my job at Giorgio's studio. It's out of solidarity to Lella, but I am waiting a bit so that isn't conspicuous. I am doing it for her."

"Wow. Do you have any other possibilities?"

"I do. I met with an architect named Cristina della Rovere when I did my first round of studio visits, and we had dinner last week. I am meeting her again on Tuesday."

"Well, I am changing jobs myself. Rather, I am starting a studio with Enrico. Hopefully, Elena will join us."

"What are you going to do for a place to live? And a studio?"

"It may be rough for a while. But it will work. The three of us share the same work ethic, and we'll figure it out. Leitizia and her fiancé have offered to promote us. They know a lot of people."

Mel smiled. "This feels like an adventure."

"Only now?" Jonathan shook his head, laughing.

"Jonathan?"

"What?"

"*Yes.*"

"Want to go down and get some breakfast?"

* * *

Usually, family and guests would trickle down in twos and fours for coffee, but on this Sunday, there was not enough room at the breakfast table in the dining room alcove. Paola shooed them into the sitting area in the hall, and carried out the coffee, the steamed milk, the toast, the butter, the homemade grapefruit marmalade, and the honey, with everyone's help. Alberto and Gabriella had gone on a focaccia expedition, and the buzz of the scooter in the driveway announced their return.

Federico was enjoying Massimo's pacific mood, uncritical of its origin. He was sitting next to Lella, pouring her coffee, and picking out the prettiest of the hand-painted dishes to serve her some toast.

Once Alberto and Gabriella sat down it was obvious that something was different. Lella noticed that all of the tension in the air yesterday had somehow dissipated. She had run into Alberto in the kitchen before he left on the Vespa.

"I hope you're going to be careful with Gabi, Alberto," she had said.

"Lella, I am telling you, Gabi is wonderful, she always has been, and this is not a fling, I promise. I am not hiding behind my wife anymore. It feels different. I don't know why it took me so long."

"Maybe you needed to be ready. She was too close to you for you to be cavalier about it."

"Maybe. Or simply the fact that I thought she had been involved with Amelia." He laughed.

Alberto started the Vespa, seeing Gabriella arrive with her helmet.

"Be careful, you two," Lella said.

Now, sitting on the walnut sofa with the red upholstery, she felt like she was officiating at some ceremony. She felt conspicuous, the only person not leaning on someone else's shoulder, not holding a hand, not exchanging a glance. She needed to escape this feeling, and assume a confident stance.

Lella said, "It would appear that the full moon had some effect on this household last night. You all seem covered with fairy dust. I'm glad that everyone's uncertainties have been worked out, and that you have all found a way to flourish."

Mel blurted out, "Jonathan and I are getting married. Next month, in Milan."

Massimo's eyes widened. "Jonathan, I guess you aren't as hopeless as I thought! Hugs all around!" He gestured *come here* with his hands.

"Well, Melinda," said Lella, "this is what was meant to happen. How could you expect Jonathan to follow you here and receive no assistance from this beautiful place in winning you back?"

Then she felt everyone's eyes on her, and continued, "Don't feel bad about me; I have made my own conquest. I have won my dignity and my freedom. Somebody around here has to take an uncompromising position, and I am happy to play that part."

"*Brava*," Federico said, and the others followed his lead.

* * *

Later, when everyone was leaving, Lella leaned into the back window of Enrico's car, where Mel was sitting next to Jonathan.

"Melinda, I wonder if you'd like to come over for dinner on Thursday? I have a new house guest arriving and I'd like you to meet her."

THE END

(Fine)

Glossary

Accademia– Academy, in this case the art academy of Brera in Milan

Alessi– renowned brand of designer housewares

americano(a)– American

americanata– a somewhat derogatory term, used for films, etc. that have a predictably happy, or "American," ending; also extravagant

amore– love

Ape– a small three-wheeled, flatbed truck made by Piaggio and whose motor sounds like a buzzing bee, means "bee"

aperitivo– a cocktail before a meal, usually served with appetizers

Architetto– title used to address an architect

arrivederci– until we meet again

arugola– (rucola) peppery salad greens, also called rocket

autostrada– highway

Bar Basso– a trendy bar in the northeast quadrant of Milan

Bar Brera– A cafe in the Brera neighborhood of Milan

bar-café– the term used in Italy for a coffee shop that is also a cocktail bar

barista– bartender, also one who prepares coffee

Bel Paese– "Il Bel Paese" Italy; literally The Beautiful Country

Bella Napoli– beautiful Naples

bello(a)– beautiful

bianco– white wine

branzino - Sea Bass

brava– or bravo, (if male), great job, used especially with applause

Brera– formerly bohemian, now gentrified, neighborhood of Milan

briosche(s)– (French) pastry made of enriched bread, term used in Italy

bruschetta(e)–grilled bread rubbed with oil, tomato, garlic and hot pepper

brutti ma buoni– knobby hazelnut and meringue biscuits (cookies), means "ugly but good"

buona educazione– good upbringing

buona notte– goodnight.

bouna sera, tesoro– good evening, darling

buongiorno– good morning

caffè americano– espresso diluted with hot water

caffè latte– a "latte," or espresso with an abundance of milk

caffettiera– (*pr. caf-fe-ti-**er**-a*) stovetop coffee (espresso) maker

Caio & Gaio– the name of a café in Rome

Campidoglio– the Capitoline Hill in Rome

cappuccino– espresso with a "little hood," or *cappuccio*, of foamed milk

cappuccio– another way to say *cappuccino*, means hood

caro(a)– dear

cara mia– my dear (*caro mio* if male)

Castello Sforzesco– Milan's castle, built by the Sforza family

Centro– term used for center-city, for any city.

c'est moi– (French) it is I

che bello(a)– how beautiful

chiaroscuro– high contrast lighting, literally "light-dark"

330

chiodo schiaccia chiodo– one nail drives another, meaning an act (or a relationship) can be obliterated with another

ciabatta– name for a relatively flat loaf of bread, literally, "slipper"

ciao– hi and bye

Cinecittà– the "Hollywood" of Italy, a film production center outside of Rome

Città Studi– college town

complimenti– my compliments! well done!

contributi– payroll taxes

Corso (Europa)– A wide avenue, called Corso rather than Via (road); Europa means Europe

Corso (Venezia)– see above; Venezia is Italian for Venice

Corso (Vittorio Emanuele)– see above; a wide avenue of shops in Milan, named after a king of Italy

C.so– abbreviation for Corso

Dio– God

doccia telefono– hand-held shower head with a flexible hose, like a "telephone"

Elenuccia– diminutive form of Elena

Euroluce– Exhibit of lighting fixtures at the International Furniture Fair

espresso– strong Italian coffee made by forcing boiling water upwards through dark-roast coffee

fatti in casa– homemade

Ferragosto– A national holiday on the 15th of August, coincident with the Catholic Feast of the Assumption

Ferrari– A make of automobile, also a brand of Italian sparkling wine (spumante)

fior di latte– a simple flavor of gelato, made from pure cream, literally "milk flower"

Fiori Chiari– light flowers (street name)

Fiori Oscuri– dark flowers (street name)

focaccia– Italian flatbread similar to pizza, sprinkled with herbs or containing a soft, sour cheese called stracchino

Frecciarossa– Red Arrow, the name of the super-rapid train from Milan to Rome

garçonniere– French term, also used in Italy, a bachelor's apartment

gelateria– Italian ice cream shop

Gelateria Edonica– Hedonic Gelateria (fictitious name of an ice cream shop)

gelato– Italian style ice cream

ghe pensi mi– a Milanese (dialect) expression meaning, "let me worry about that"

giallo Maria Teresa– a yellow or ochre color used on many stuccoed buildings in Milan, after the Hapsburg Archduchess Maria Teresa

giardinetto– little garden

Giardini Pubblici– the public gardens, a park in Milan

Golfo del Tigullio– the gulf, or bay, where Santa Margherita is located.

grazie– thank you

grazie tanto– thank you very much.

Isola (Procida)– Island of Procida

Lago di Como– Lake Como

La Scala– renowned opera house in Milan

La Stalla dei Frati– a restaurant, literally, "The Monks' Stables"

La (Vecchia) Latteria– a small eatery in the center of Milan

latteria– literally, milk bar, usually informal eatery similar to a deli

limonata– lemonade

limoncello– an alcoholic drink made with lemons, sometimes homemade, served after dinner

lungomare– auto or pedestrian way along the coast, also boardwalk

Madonna– an interjection, invoking the Mother of God

maestro– master, of a craft, also title of respect

merda– shit

Metropolitana– Milan's underground transit system or subway

molto bene– very well, that is good

Naviglio Grande– the Grand Canal, the larger of Milan's two remaining canals

Naviglio Pavese– the canal in Milan that once led to the city of Pavia

Negroni– a cocktail made with gin, campari and red vermouth, with a twist of orange peel

nocciole–hazelnuts

nonna– grandmother

orata– a type of Mediterranean fish

panettoni– bollards used to block vehicle access, named after the dome-shaped Easter cakes of the same shape

panificio– bread bakery

panino(i)– sandwich

palazzo(i)– blocky urban residential building, originally single family "palaces"

Parco Sempione– The park surrounding the Castello Sforzesco (castle) in Milan.

Passeggiata Gianicolo– An elevated promenade in Trastevere (Rome) with a view to the center of Rome

pasta primavera– a pasta recipe using seasonally available (springtime) vegetables

pastiera– a pie-like pastry

penne– pasta shaped like diagonally cut tubes, like simple "pens"

penne all'arrabiata– penne with a spicy tomato sauce.

piazza– city square or place

Piazza del Duomo– the main square of Milan, where the Duomo, or cathedral, is located

Piazza Navona– a large, oval open space in Rome, popular at nighttime, in Ancient Rome flooded for staged naval battles

pisello– means "pea" but also used as a kid-friendly nickname for penis

Politecnico– Milan's polytechnic institute, which includes the school of architecture

portafiltro– The filter holder on an espresso machine, with a handle for screwing it in and dumping the grounds

Porta Ticinese– a gateway in Milan featuring a large archway, in the direction of the Ticino River

portineria– entry to a building, where the custodian resides

portone– large double door at the entrance of residential buildings, allowing for automobile passage into the courtyard

portiere– doorman or woman (portiera)

prosciutto– ham, crudo (cured) or cotto (boiled) if not specified, usually means crudo

Procida Porto– the port of the island of Procida, off the coast of Naples

prosecco– semi-dry, sparkling white wine

puttanesca– a pasta sauce made with onions, garlic, tomatoes, hot pepper, olives, capers and anchovies (or variations thereof)

radicchio– Italian chicory with white-veined red leaves

Refettorio– the name of a restaurant, means "refectory"

risotto– rice cooked in a skillet over a sauté, a typical dish of the northern plains of Italy where Milan is located

risotto alle fragole– risotto with strawberries

rustico– small agrarian dwelling

Salone del Mobile (also called the Salone)– the International Furniture Fair held in Milan every April

SaloneSatellite– an exhibit of student work at the International Furniture Fair in Milan

San Satyro– A church in Milan, part of which was designed by Renaissance architect Donato Bramante

scopa– means broom, but also refers to a popular Italian card game

sgabuzzino– closet, like a broom closet

Sofine– fictitious name of a furniture company or showroom

Signora– madame

Signorina– Miss

simpatico– nice, easy to connect with

Solfatara– the site of the Solfatara Volcano, which emits sulfurous steam, in Naples

spumante– Italian sparkling wine, produced similarly to champagne

Stazione Centrale– central train station in Milan

stendipanni– a clothesline or rack for hanging clothes to dry

tagliatelle– long ribbon-shaped pasta

tangenziale– high speed loop road that links to important points of a city

tesoro– darling, means "treasure"

tiramisu– a rich dessert made with Mascarpone cheese, egg yolks, marsala, heavy cream and espresso powder, layered on ladyfingers and chilled, means "pick me up"

tortellini– stuffed pasta similar to ravioli, with a form like a tied headscarf

Trastevere– a Bohemian-chic neighborhood of Rome, means "across the Tiber"

trattoria– an informal, generally economical restaurant

trompe d'oeil– (French) trick of the eye, used for mural painting meant to create an illusion, also used in Italian

tutto il mondo é paese– literally, "the world is a town" (things are the same everywhere)

una roba da matti– that's crazy

Vespa– Piaggio scooter name, means "wasp"

Via– street (St.) precedes the street name, e.g., Via Brera

Via Monte Napoleone– an exclusive street of boutiques in Milan